Berkley Sensation Books by Veronica Wolff

MASTER OF THE HIGHLANDS
SWORD OF THE HIGHLANDS
WARRIOR OF THE HIGHLANDS
LORD OF THE HIGHLANDS
DEVIL'S HIGHLANDER

DEVIL'S HIGHLANDER

Veronica Wolff

BERKLEY SENSATION, NEW YORK

THE BERKLEY PUBLISHING GROUP
Published by the Penguin Group
Penguin Group (USA) Inc.
375 Hudson Street, New York, New York 10014, USA
Penguin Group (Canada), 90 Eglinton Avenue East, Suite 700, Toronto, Ontario M4P 2Y3, Canada
(a division of Pearson Penguin Canada Inc.)
Penguin Books Ltd., 80 Strand, London WC2R 0RL, England
Penguin Group Ireland, 25 St. Stephen's Green, Dublin 2, Ireland (a division of Penguin Books Ltd.)
Penguin Group (Australia), 250 Camberwell Road, Camberwell, Victoria 3124, Australia
(a division of Pearson Australia Group Pty. Ltd.)
Penguin Books India Pvt. Ltd., 11 Community Centre, Panchsheel Park, New Delhi—110 017, India
Penguin Group (NZ), 67 Apollo Drive, Rosedale, North Shore 0632, New Zealand
(a division of Pearson New Zealand Ltd.)
Penguin Books (South Africa) (Pty.) Ltd., 24 Sturdee Avenue, Rosebank, Johannesburg 2196,
South Africa

Penguin Books Ltd., Registered Offices: 80 Strand, London WC2R 0RL, England

This is a work of fiction. Names, characters, places, and incidents either are the product of the author's imagination or are used fictitiously, and any resemblance to actual persons, living or dead, business establishments, events, or locales is entirely coincidental. The publisher does not have any control over and does not assume any responsibility for author or third-party websites or their content.

DEVIL'S HIGHLANDER

A Berkley Sensation Book / published by arrangement with the author

PRINTING HISTORY
Berkley Sensation mass-market edition / August 2010

Copyright © 2010 by Veronica Wolff.
Excerpt from *Devil's Own* copyright © by Veronica Wolff.
Cover art by Phil Heffernan.
Cover design by George Long.
Interior text design by Laura K. Corless.

ISBN: 978-0-425-23627-7

BERKLEY® SENSATION
Berkley Sensation Books are published by The Berkley Publishing Group,
a division of Penguin Group (USA) Inc.,
375 Hudson Street, New York, New York 10014.
BERKLEY® SENSATION and the "B" design are trademarks of Penguin Group (USA) Inc.

PRINTED IN THE UNITED STATES OF AMERICA

10 9 8 7 6 5 4 3 2 1

For Cindy Hwang, whom I trust and admire.
I've handed her time-traveling women, a hero with a cane,
vampires, one anguished pirate, and now this.
I can't seem to make her blink, and for that I am grateful.

Acknowledgments

As always, there are many to whom I owe a heartfelt thank-you:

Cindy Hwang, and all the wonderful people at Berkley, with a special shout-out to Leis Pederson. I can't thank them, or my lucky stars, enough.

Stephanie Kip Rostan, agent extraordinaire, for her unflagging enthusiasm and support.

Kate Perry, for being a critique partner and so much more than a critique partner. I'd want her by my side in any lifeboat.

My trusted friend Monica McCarty, even though she made me wait to go to Aberdeen.

Jami Alden, Bella Andre, Barbara Freethy, Carol Grace, Tracy Grant, Anne Mallory, and Penelope Williamson, for their uncommon support—both when times are tough and when they're not.

I'm also grateful to Catherine Coulter for her kind words, a gentle nudge, and for inspiring me long before I even met her.

Special thanks to Jim and Lisa for "Camp Aunt Lisa," which, I fear, showed my kids a better time than *I* generally do. A standing thank-you to my parents, too, with a salute to the Captain, my go-to guy for all nautical matters.

And finally, as always, my thanks to Adam. The man manages to be thoughtful and brilliant in everything he approaches, up to and including our marriage.

His shirtless back was to her, his *breacan feile* slapping at his legs in the wind. He was hauling in his nets. A fisherman now, as his sister had said. Hand over hand, the flex of muscle in his arms and back was visible even from a distance.

Gasping, Marjorie stumbled back a step, leaning into the rocks for support. She'd told herself she came because he could help her. But she knew in that instant the real reason she'd come. The only place for her in this treacherous world stood just there, down the beach: *Cormac*.

She hadn't moved, hadn't spoken, but he turned, as though he'd felt her there. Her hand went to her chest, reminding her heart to beat, her lungs to draw breath . . .

continued . . .

Sword of the Highlands

"Entrancing, luminous, and powerful . . . heroes you never want to let go."
                              —National bestselling author Monica McCarty

"A passionate tale . . . Very entertaining."
                              —*Night Owl Romance*

"A delightful time travel . . . refreshing and intriguing."
                              —*The Romance Readers Connection*

Master of the Highlands

"Powerful, riveting, and vibrant. A must-read page-turner destined to be a keeper."
                              —*USA Today* bestselling author Sue-Ellen Welfonder

"A clever time travel that . . . adds a charming freshness, thanks to intelligent characters and [an] appealing backdrop."
                              —*Romantic Times*

"A beautiful and poignant story."   —*Night Owl Romance*

The estates give hereby power to any of his majesty's subjects to take and apprehend such idle and sturdy beggars and employ them or to dispose of them to others to be employed in work for their meat and clothes only.

—ACT CONCERNING THE POOR, JANUARY 4, 1649,
EDINBURGH, PARLIAMENT

Prologue

Aberdeen, Spring 1647

"Not the fire again," Aidan whined.

"Aye, the fire." Cormac stared defiantly at his twin, linking arms with the girl by his side. Their mothers were out, wanting to experience as much as possible during their weekend visit to the city. It had left the three of them with the run of the house, and they were taking full advantage. "Marjorie wants to."

"But we always play the Ogilvy fire."

"I'll have your head," Cormac shouted, ignoring his brother. He waved his wooden sword with a dramatic flourish. "I will claim my revenge!"

Aidan narrowed his eyes fiercely. "Why do I have to be Campbell again?"

Marjorie stepped forward to peer at his face. "Because your nose is bigger than Cormac's."

"But we're twins!"

Cormac quickly shrugged. "It's not my fault we don't look alike."

"I always play the cursed Campbell." Aidan wiped

his nose on his sleeve, a boyish gesture that robbed the menace from his words.

"Revenge shall be mine, I say!" Cormac spun, grabbing Marjorie's hand. A quick jerk of his head loosed his dark brown hair from where it had tangled in his lashes. "Fear not, Lady Ogilvy, I shall save you from the blaze!"

Aidan threw his wooden sword to the ground. "Why do *you* always get to save Marjorie?"

Cormac's gaze met Marjorie's, and his chest swelled. He always got to save Marjorie because Marjorie was *his*.

Marjorie scooped up Aidan's sword, thrusting it back to him hilt-first. "That's just how we play it, Aidan."

A flush of color brightened her face, and Cormac stared. The twins had known her since birth, and in their ten years, only recently had he noticed the pretty blushes that sometimes reddened her cheeks. The phenomenon confused and mesmerized him both.

Shooting Cormac a glance, Marjorie paced to the window, and he wondered if maybe she'd noticed him noticing.

He paused only a moment before following at her heels. Leaning against the windowsill, he let his shoulder graze hers, making as though to study the street below. He inhaled deeply. Lately Marjorie even *smelled* different. Nice, and sweet, like a *lady*.

"You boys should climb the chimney," she said suddenly, "like the sweeps." They both watched as a handful of chimney boys straggled out from a cart on the street below. The oldest couldn't have been a day over eight, the others seemed closer to five or six, and their brooms and metal tools were almost as large as they were. "My castle is afire, and you'll need to *climb* to save me."

"You mean up *in* the chimney?" Aidan scowled. "I'm not climbing your uncle's stinking chimney."

Cormac swung around, leveling his pretend sword at his twin's chest. "You'll not speak so to the lady."

"Those boys do it," she said, pointing out the window.

"*You* climb the chimney," Aidan told her in disbelief.

"I'll do no such thing." She set her shoulders and

continued to stare intently out the window. "I shall wait here for my rescue."

"Aidan," Cormac warned, "Mum will be back soon. And soon we'll be gone from Aberdeen, and then it's back to home. Don't be so contrary—"

"She's afraid." Aidan went to the window to study the ragtag boys covered in soot and tar as they disappeared into the neighboring town house. "I should've known a lass would be afraid."

"I am not afraid."

"Och, she's not afraid, Aidan. As I recall, she climbed higher than you last time."

"That was a tree, not up into some stinkin' chimney." Aidan crossed his arms defiantly. "And I could've gone higher if I'd wanted."

"It's just that I tore my dress last time."

"Your family has enough money to buy you twenty new dresses," Aidan said. "Your mum is with our mum right now, buying you even more."

"Leave it." Cormac tried desperately to keep his eyes from said dress. The delicate lace along her neck and sleeves fascinated him. When had she started wearing such ladylike clothes? "Her family has money, but not so much that she can go about mussing her gowns."

"All right, then." Marjorie turned, giving them a regal sweep of her eyes. "We shall *all* climb the stinking chimney."

"You don't need to, Ree," Cormac told her quietly, using his private nickname for her. "We'll play something else. Come on, Aidan," he said more loudly, "let's play at something else."

"I dare you." Marjorie set her hands on her hips. "Whoever climbs fastest, wins. Unless it's you *boys* who are afraid."

Cormac bristled at once. "I'm not afraid." He stormed to the fireplace and knelt down to peer up the flue. The boys working as sweeps were small, most no older than eight. But her uncle Humphrey's chimney struck him as overlarge—wide enough to accommodate their bigger bodies. The hearthstones were charred from the years, but the grate was cold, still blanketed with ashes from the previous night's fire.

Not that it mattered. Cormac would climb the tightest of tunnels with a full blaze beneath his feet if it would prove his worth above Aidan's. His eyes darted back to Marjorie. Her full attention was on him, pinning him with an unreadable look. It made him feel like a conquering hero. "I fear nothing," he repeated, standing tall.

Curling his lip, Aidan waved at the fireplace. "*You* climb it then, if you're so keen to."

With a decisive nod, Cormac stepped onto the grate, his head and shoulders disappearing into the darkness.

"Cormac," Marjorie gasped. "You're truly going to climb it?"

"*I'm* not climbing it," Aidan said to nobody in particular.

Marjorie craned her neck to look back out the window. "Hurry now. We've not much time before the sweeps come to Uncle's house."

The inside of the chimney was cool. Staccato gusts of wind whistled in, hitting him with surprisingly fresh bursts of air. Cormac put his hands on the stones. The passage was narrower than it'd looked, and he tried not to think how high it went. Despite the air blowing in, he was unable to see any light shining in from the top.

"What's it like in there?" Marjorie's voice echoed loudly in the cramped space.

Cormac skidded his hands up along the stones, groping for seams that could be used as climbing holds. Soot clung thickly in the mortar and was unexpectedly gummy under his fingertips and nails. "It's sticky!"

His fingers found a deep groove between stones. "Here goes," he muttered, and jumped, pulling himself up hard. His feet scrabbled wildly in the air. He heard an explosion of hysterical laughter and grunted, "Shut your trap, Aid!"

Cormac began to slip, and he brought his knees up hard to brace himself in the narrow passageway. A sharp ridge cut into his calf, and he hissed with the pain of it. But he was up off the ground now and spared a quick laugh at his success.

He worked silently for a time, his elbows and legs splayed out, slowly maneuvering higher, pushing from his feet and pulling with his hands.

The light from below dimmed, and the sound of breathing echoed up the chamber. "You still in there?" his brother called.

"Move it, stink breath." Cormac scuffed his toe along the stones, sending old mortar crumbling onto his twin below. "I can't see."

Aidan chuckled. "When the climbing boys stop their climbing, the master sweep lights a fire to get them going again."

Marjorie's voice carried up, hollow and distant. "You'll do no such thing!"

"Ow!" Aidan screeched. "Criminy, Marj, I was only joking."

"It's *Marjorie*, you beast."

"That's the way, Ree," Cormac said. "Now, stop breathing my air," he growled to his brother. "I think it's getting smaller up here."

"You getting scared?" Aidan taunted.

"No, I'm not getting—oh!" Cormac's foot slipped, and his elbows scraped hard along the chimney walls as he began to slide down.

Marjorie shrieked.

Slamming his knees out, he braced himself along the passageway to stop his fall.

"That's enough, Cormac," she cried. "You win! Now just come back down."

He smiled in the darkness. "I best get a good prize for this, Ree." He flushed as he said it, wondering what exactly he'd meant by the words.

He redoubled his efforts, climbing up at a rapid clip,

trying to ignore the way the flue narrowed the higher he went. *Hands slide up, fingers hold tight, knees brace the wall . . . and ups-a-daisy.* "I'm getting the way of it now. Like a wee monkey I am." Laughing, he grew careless, and his shirtsleeve snagged on the sharp edge of a stone. "Och, hell."

"Och, hell, *what*?" Marjorie sounded nervous.

For once Cormac ignored her. He tried to jiggle his sleeve free, but that only pulled it taut. He was stuck. Unexpected fear struck like lightning, splicing his chest.

"You answer me right now, Cormac MacAlpin," Marjorie said sternly. *"Och, hell, what?"*

He shimmied his arm up to free it, but only grew more tightly wedged into the passage. His heart kicked hard in his chest. "I . . . I think I'm stuck."

Aidan laughed. "You've ate too many pasties from the Aberdeen baker!"

"It's not funny," Marjorie snapped.

Though their chatter carried to him, it didn't fully pierce his thoughts. He was trapped, and that fact alone filled his head.

"I'm stuck," he said, and though his voice was brave, he knew his twin would understand the truth of it.

"Aye, I hear you." There was a clatter from below as Aidan propped the grate onto its side, like an impromptu ladder. "Och, Marj*orie*, could your uncle no' sweep the bloody hearth?" Aidan was silent then, trying to find his balance. He fell once, then carefully clambered back up to teeter on the top edge of the grate. It plunged Cormac into total blackness. "You get to save Marjorie, but it seems you need me to save *you*." His tone was light, but Cormac heard the seriousness underneath. Aidan would help him. They always got each other out of jams.

"Thanks, Aid." Cormac's breathing reverberated loudly in the tight chamber. He closed his eyes, forcing himself to calm. He stretched his toes down as far as they'd reach.

"Eh, don't fash yourself over it. Though it does mean you lose the dare." Chuckling, Aidan jumped, and Cormac felt a hand swipe at his foot. There was a loud clanging, and a cloud of ash exploded as he landed.

"Mind the grate!" Marjorie shouted.

"Thanks," Aidan said dryly, "I hadn't considered that." He coughed. "Losh, Cor, how'd you get up that high?" He slapped at his clothes. "My breeches are a wreck. Mum will have my hide."

Aidan repeated his jump, and then again. His fingertips grazed Cormac's feet each time, but he didn't manage to get purchase.

"Aye, Marjorie," Aidan said, his voice booming up along the chimney stones, "what say we bring one of your uncle's chairs to—"

There was a whoosh of air from below, and Cormac's twin was suddenly gone from beneath him.

Cormac waited a moment, and panic prickled in his chest. "Aid! Don't you dare leave me here."

Marjorie cried out.

What were they doing? Had Aidan gotten bored trying to help? It was strange and confusing and a little scary.

"Aidan," Cormac yelled, "what are you playing at?"

"No!" His twin was shouting, and there was real fear in his voice.

Had their mothers returned home? Marjorie's uncle? Were they in trouble?

Dread shot up Cormac's spine. "What is it?" he shouted lamely.

His question was met with muffled cries, and his heartbeat surged with renewed force. Something was wrong. He began to wriggle and jerk his body roughly, desperate to free himself.

Aidan shouted again. "Take your hands—"

There was the sound of scuffling, and his brother's cries grew silent.

Marjorie began to shriek, and it chilled Cormac to

the bone. She shrieked until her voice grew ragged and she seemed barely able to catch her breath. And then, unimaginably worse, the shrieking was cut short.

"Ree!" Cormac screamed, writhing madly now. The movement wedged him more snugly into the stones. The chimney was a tomb, sealing him in. "Aidan!"

There was one last yelp from his twin, a terrible faraway sound, and then silence.

"Where are you?" Panic shrilled in Cormac's brain and exploded in his chest. *Trapped.* The chimney stack seemed to shrink around him, and he panted, desperate to catch his breath. His pulse thundered, and he wondered if it were possible for hearts simply to burst.

Think. He had to think. Fear could kill. But he had a job to do. Something had happened to Aidan and Marjorie. He had to help them. He'd gotten himself into the chimney, and he'd get himself back out.

Relax. Fear nothing.

He needed to shift his arms over his head. *Slowly.* Exhaling as much as he could, he gently snaked an elbow up along his belly. One arm slipped free, and then the other.

His fingers roved blindly overhead, looking for anchorage. *There.* He found a thick seam between mortar and stone.

Flexing his wrists, Cormac fisted his hands and ground them onto the chimney walls, just beneath the protruding stone. Mortar crumbled, falling into his eyes. The old masonry scored his knuckles, and wet warmth trickled along his arms. He ignored the pain, focusing only on what he had to do.

He exhaled again, making his body as compact as possible. Then he pushed.

His body crept an inch at a time, and then jolted suddenly, as though sprung from a trap, and Cormac plummeted down the chimney, falling hard to the bottom. He landed on the metal grate; it smashed just below his ribs, momentarily stealing his breath. Still, he rolled off, jumping at once to his feet. "Aidan? Marjorie?"

He spotted Marjorie's feet, splayed on the floor, poking from behind a small divan.

"Ree?" Cormac ran to her, his heart in his throat. He tenderly gathered her head in his hands, shuddering at the large lump on the back of her skull.

She'd been hit. Someone had *hit* his Marjorie. Rage boiled hot and sour in his gut.

He gently threaded his fingers through her hair, and breathed a sigh of relief when they came back dry. No blood was good, and a lump was better, or so he'd been told, since it meant she'd not be bleeding inside her skull.

"Ree?" At the sound of his voice, Marjorie's eyes fluttered open. "Ree, lass? What happened? Where's Aidan?"

"Aidan . . ." Clutching at Cormac's sleeves, she looked around frantically. Tears spilled down her cheeks.

"Did Aidan hit you?" His eyes swept the room, taking in an overturned chair, a displaced rug. "I'll kill him."

"No," she said quickly. "A man. Two men. They took him. They took Aidan."

As though on cue, a burly workman sauntered into the room, sizing up the two children twined on the floor. "What's this, then?"

Cormac sprang to his feet, his hand going instinctively to his side, where a grown man might sheath his sword. "Who are you?" he asked in a booming voice, standing as tall as his ten years would allow.

The man narrowed his eyes, assessing Cormac. After a moment, he said, "I'm the master sweep. You two run along, then." A handful of chimney boys drifted in behind him, their eyes dazed and cheeks blackened with soot. "We've work to do here."

"Was it you?" Cormac demanded. "Did you take him?"

Marjorie grabbed Cormac's arm, shaking her head. "That's not the one," she whispered hoarsely.

"Took *who*?" The man glanced from Cormac to the

spill of ash on the hearthstones. A look dawned on his face. "Oh, good Christ help us, 'twas the bloody yeoman. To the carts," he shouted to the boys.

Terror quickly infused their blank eyes, and the sweeps scrambled at once from the room.

"Who?" Marjorie cried.

"Who's the yeoman?" Cormac demanded.

The master sweep went to peer out the window. "Sometimes the men come; they gather the sweeps."

"Gather them?" Marjorie said slowly, as though repeating foreign speech.

Cormac pulled Marjorie to her feet, setting his hand at her back. "Where'd they take Aidan?"

"They take the boys to Barbados." Distracted, the man hurried to the door. "Or the Americas. Wherever their plantation is."

"Plantation?"

At Cormac's question, the man paused in the doorway. "You wee fool," he said in a voice thick with disdain. "What do you think happens to lads too poor to be claimed? To lads who need to beg for their supper? The boggies come and snatch you away."

"But . . ." Cormac stammered, "we're not poor. Our mother's just gone to the shops. Aidan's not a beggar."

"Then this'll learn him he shouldn't have played at one. Because the lad, he's surely a beggar now." The man turned and walked out.

Chapter 1

Stonehaven, Aberdeenshire, 1660

Marjorie skittered down the steep path, purposely descending too quickly to think. The specter of Dunnottar Castle felt heavy over her shoulder, looming in near ruin high atop Dunnottar Rock, a massive stone plinth that punched free of Scotland's northeastern coast like a gargantuan fist. Waves roiled and licked at its base far below. Chilled, she clambered even faster, skidding and galloping downhill, unsure whether she was fleeing closer to or farther from that grim mountain of rubble the MacAlpins called home.

She shook her head. She'd sworn not to think on it.

She'd done entirely too much thinking already. Much to her uncle's consternation, she'd chosen her gray mare, not his carriage, for her ride from Aberdeen. She'd realized too late that the daylong ride offered her altogether too much time to brood over what felt like a lifetime of missteps. And she hoped she wasn't about to make the grandest, most humiliating one of all.

She was going to see Cormac.

Whenever she'd thought of it—and she'd thought of

little else on her interminable ride—she'd turn her horse
around and head straight back to home. But then those
same thoughts of him would have her spinning that mare
right around again, until her horse tossed its head, surly
from the constant tugging and turning.

She reached the bottom of the hill, where the knotted grass turned rocky, its greens and browns giving way
to the reds and grays of the pebbled shore. The beach
curved like a thin scimitar around the bay, its far side
concealed from view by the ragged hillocks and blades of
rock that limned the shore as if the land only reluctantly
surrendered to the sea.

Marjorie slid the leather slippers from her feet and
set them carefully down. She wriggled her toes, leaning
against the swell of land by her side. The pebbles blanketing the shore were large and rounded, and looked warmed
by the late afternoon sun. She stepped forward, moving
slowly now. The water between the stones was cold, but
their smooth tops were not, and they sounded a soothing
clack with each step.

She was close. She could feel it.

Cormac. *He* was close. Amid the gentle slapping of
the waves and the sultry brine in the air, she sensed him.

She'd not needed to stop in at Dunnottar to ask his siblings where to find him. She and Cormac had known each
other since birth, and Marjorie had spent every one of her
twenty-three years feeling as though she were tied to him in
some mysterious and inextricable way. Though they hadn't
spoken in what felt like a lifetime, she'd spared not a penny
nor her pride to glean word of him, writing to his sisters for
news, aching for rare glimpses of him through the years.

She'd offered up the prayers of a wretched soul when
he'd gone off to war, and then prayers of thanks when he
returned home whole. And, God help her, the relief she
felt knowing he'd never married. She couldn't have borne
the thought of another woman in Cormac's arms.

No, Marjorie knew. Alone by the sea was exactly where
she'd find him.

She screwed her face, shutting her eyes tight. There were many things she knew.

She knew that Cormac blamed her. To this day, he blamed her, just as she blamed herself for the foolish, girlish dare that had ripped Aidan from their lives. Because of her silliness, the MacAlpin family had lost a son and brother that day. And Marjorie had lost more still than that. She'd also lost Cormac.

She froze again. What was she thinking? She couldn't do this. She couldn't bear to see him.

But she couldn't bear not to.

The draw was too powerful to resist. Her feet stepped inexorably forward before her mind had a chance to stop them. She told herself she had no other choice. Events in her life had led her just there. She needed help, and Cormac was the only man with skills enough to come to her aid.

The hillock at her side dropped away, revealing the far edge of the beach, revealing Cormac.

His shirtless back was to her, his *breacan feile* slapping at his legs in the wind. He was hauling in his nets. A fisherman now, as his sister had said. Hand over hand, the flex of muscle in his arms and back was visible even from a distance.

Gasping, Marjorie stumbled back a step, leaning into the rocks for support. She'd told herself she came because he could help her. But she knew in that instant the real reason she'd come. The only place for her in this treacherous world stood just there, down the beach: *Cormac*.

She'd willingly suffer his blame, suffer his indifference, yet still, like the embers from a long-banked fire, she knew Cormac would give her solace, despite himself.

She hadn't moved, hadn't spoken, but he turned, as though he'd felt her there. Her hand went to her chest, reminding her heart to beat, her lungs to draw breath.

He turned away abruptly, and tears stung her eyes. Would he spurn her?

But she saw he merely bent to gather his nets, dragging

them farther up the shore where he carefully spread them out.

Relief flooded her. She scrubbed at her face, gathering herself, and tucked errant wisps of hair behind her ears. She knew it was purely a nervous gesture; the strong sea wind would only whip her curls free again.

She tempered herself. This meeting would not go well if she were this vulnerable from the start. But of course she was this vulnerable, she thought with a heavy heart, considering all that had recently come to pass.

She took a deep breath. He'd seen her. She couldn't go back now. She *wouldn't* go back—Cormac was the only one who could help her.

Marjorie picked her way toward him. He stood still as granite, waiting for her, watching her. His dark hair blew in the wind, and his brow was furrowed. Was he upset to see her? Simply thoughtful?

Suddenly, she regretted the absence of her slippers. She loved the sensation of the smooth rocks beneath her feet, but now she felt somehow naked without her every stitch of clothing. She fisted her hands in her skirts. She imagined she'd always been a sort of naked before Cormac, and there was nothing that could ever truly conceal her. He was the only one who'd ever been able to read her soul laid bare in her eyes.

He was silent and still. What would he see in her eyes now?

She felt as though she'd forgotten how to walk. She made herself stand tall, focused on placing one foot in front of the other, but she felt awkward and ungainly, unbearably self-aware as she made her way to him. *Lift the foot, place it down, lift and down.*

He was not ten paces away. He was tall, but with a man's body now, broad with muscles carved from hauling nets, from firing guns. That last gave her pause. She spotted the fine sheen of scars on his forearm, a sliver of a scar on his brow. He'd been long at war. What kind of a man had he become?

Inhaling deeply, she let her eyes linger over his face. She was close enough to see the color of his eyes. Blue-gray, like the sea. Her heart sped. She forced herself to step closer.

She'd been unable to summon an exact picture of him in her thoughts, but now that he stood before her, his face was as familiar to her as her own. There was Cormac's strong, square jaw, the long fringe of dark lashes. But he was somehow foreign, too. The boy had become a man. A vague crook had appeared in his nose, and she wondered what long-ago break had put it there. Where had *she* been the moment it happened, what had *she* been doing while he'd been living his life?

She stopped an arm's length from him. Intensity radiated from him like the sun's glare off the sea.

Her throat clenched. She couldn't do it. What had she been thinking?

He blamed her still. He didn't want to speak to her. He didn't welcome the sight of her.

The silence was shrill between them. She swallowed hard, wondering how best to get herself out of there, how to gracefully back out, never, *ever* to see him again.

For Davie. She had to do this for Davie. That thought alone kept her anchored in place.

Cormac opened his mouth to speak, and she held her breath.

"Ree," he whispered, in the voice of a man. "Aw, Ree, lass."

Her every muscle slackened. Her fear, her disquiet stripped away, leaving Marjorie raw before him. Hot tears came quickly, blurring her vision.

"Cormac," she gasped. "It's happened again."

Chapter 2

Cormac heard the hollow clack of rocks shifting behind him. Years of savage training had attuned his senses, sensitized them, rendering him as acute as any predator. The merest rustle could sound at his back, and pure instinct flared, making him ready to fight or to kill.

He'd spun, but it was her: *Marjorie.* The sight of her was a punch in the sternum.

She was his guilty pleasure. Through the years, he'd hold himself off, until he could bear it no longer, then he'd allow himself to ask after her, or more delicious still, find an excuse to travel to Aberdeen and the promise of a chance glimpse or two. To his family he feigned casual disinterest, but Cormac felt certain the world saw through his mask to the anguish beneath.

He should've saved Aidan that day. If he'd been stronger, less clumsy and inept, he could've fought to save him. But like a fool he'd gotten himself stuck in a damned chimney flue. He'd borne the shame of it every day since. His stupidity had lost him his twin, and his grieving mother hadn't survived the year. Two losses on his head, all before his eleventh birthday.

The third loss, though, the crushing blow, was this woman who approached him now. This fine and beautiful creature whom he'd never deserve.

He suspected Marjorie saw more in him than his shame, but he could not. He was beyond feeling love or joy, and he'd sealed that fate when he'd gone off to war, craving battles like a parched man water, baptizing himself in blood. But rather than washing his soul clean, the blood of others had only stained it blacker.

Marjorie grew closer, gliding across the rocky beach as though it were a ballroom. She held her head high, and long strands of her golden brown curls whipped in the wind. The ache in his chest turned sharp, from the punch of a fist to the twist of a knife.

Rarely did he truly *see* anyone anymore. All faces looked the same to Cormac. All, except for hers. She emerged from the world's meaningless bustle as a goddess would a frieze.

Marjorie was close enough now that he could see her eyes. He'd been seeing them in his dreams for years. He'd convinced himself it was merely a last remaining boyish fancy that had embellished his memories, but he knew now he'd been wrong. Her eyes were as brilliant as he'd remembered. They were wide, a rare blue that had always reminded him of the petals of *barraisd*. Her eyes, like the flower, impossibly vivid and bright.

"Ree," he heard himself whisper. And with that, a veil cleared from before those startling eyes, and he saw her pain; it sliced through his armor as easily as a blade between ribs. "Aw, Ree, lass."

"Cormac, it's happened again."

He understood at once and fought the urge to reach for her. "Tell me."

"I live with Uncle now, in the old town house." She paused, the memory of that house and that day hanging between them. "I've been helping tend the children at the Saint Machar poorhouse."

He nodded, even though he already knew where she lived and how she'd been spending her time. She'd been battling her own demons, just as he had.

He wanted to give her some reassurance, but instead he felt his eyes narrow.

He damned himself. Perhaps he'd never remember how regular folk acted, how they comforted, how they smiled.

"I was with Davie—" Her voice caught.

Jealousy spiked his veins with acid. Had Marjorie come to him to discuss another man? Rage overcame him, then disbelief. He waited for Marjorie's explanation in pained silence.

"I was with a boy named Davie," she began again, "down by the docks. He's a wee lad, just five, and clings to my skirts like a limpet, he does."

Cormac's chest eased, and he realized he'd been holding his breath.

Marjorie peered at him for a moment, a curious look in her eyes. "I had business in Castlegate," she continued, "and so gave him a bawbee for some food. The baker had a pan of rowies hot from the oven . . ." Her voice drifted off.

Dread lanced him, and for a moment, Cormac knew what it was to be a feeling man again, instead of the brittle husk he'd become. He hardened his stance. "And?" His voice came out harsher than he'd intended, his battle to remain remote making his voice sound a snarl.

Marjorie looked down. "And he never came back to me," she finished quietly.

He forced a casual shrug. "Maybe he ran off. He's just a boy after all." But even as he said it, Cormac knew. No boy in his right mind would tear himself from the skirts of the fine Marjorie Keith.

"No," she said simply. She collected herself, inhaling

deeply. "I know him. He'd not run off. And . . . there have been rumors . . ."

Cormac regretted it, but there was nothing for it. Marjorie deserved to hear the truth. "Not rumors, Ree. Fact. Parliament decreed long ago that able-bodied poor found idling be gathered and claimed as property."

"Like Aidan?" Her voice was barely a murmur.

He set his jaw. "Aye. Precisely like that."

She swiped a tear from her cheek, and Cormac fisted his hands at his sides. He would not—*could* not—comfort her. "'Tis a cruel world, Ree. There are even some who say the poor lads are the better for it, breathing the fresh air of the Indies, or the Americas, rather than—"

"Rather than climbing chimneys?" she asked coldly, putting a fine point on both their pain. At his nod, she blanched and then darted her eyes down to stare at her foot as she toed a rock. "It's horrible. How can men do that, and to children?"

"Aye, man is horrible." He'd seen it firsthand. *He'd* done horrible things.

As if she'd read his thoughts, she reached for him. The touch of Marjorie's hand on his arm was light, but it was as though lightning cracked, splitting his heart wide open. Her touch shattered him, exposing the pale, bleak creature hidden at his core.

In that instant, he was vulnerable. Alone, and aching with yearning.

He looked at her fingers wrapped around his forearm, and a lifetime of want burst to the fore. His eyes rose to find her gaze on him. He'd loved her so. The sight of her reminded him of all he'd lost. Of all he was missing.

Cormac stiffened. He let his mind rove to a dangerous place, one where he eased Marjorie down to take her along the rocks, running his hands over her body, through her hair. She'd let him; he saw it in her eyes. He could bury himself in her, forget it all. She'd absolve him of his pain.

His eyes clenched shut as he let that pain roil through him. He couldn't touch her. He wasn't the man she needed. He could never be good enough for one like Ree.

Cormac pulled away, turning to heave a basket of fish higher up the shore. "Forget the boy, Marjorie."

He set his haul down with force, his eyes shut in a grimace. He'd never used such a tone with her. He hadn't called her by her full name in he knew not how long. But he couldn't help that the world was a cruel place.

"Marjorie!" his youngest sister shouted from up the beach. He told himself he was grateful for the interruption, that the pang in his chest was relief.

Cormac busied himself with his nets. He heard a rustling as Bridget enthusiastically embraced her.

"Marjorie," Bridget exclaimed, breathless. "It *is* you! I never thought we'd ever see *you* come calling. I sent you a letter just yesterday, planning my next visit to Aberdeen, but . . . Losh! Here you are. Are you well?" She added with feigned innocence, "Cormac was asking after you just last week."

He scowled, untangling and smoothing the twine webbing, even though the nets were already in impeccable shape. If he could, he'd tan his sister's meddlesome hide.

Bridget trilled merrily on. Cormac could hear from the laughter in her voice that she knew she'd gotten under his skin. "Truly, Marjorie, it distresses me that it's taken you so long to visit. We've lived here nine years! Imagine that. I do love the times I've gotten to see you in Aberdeen, but, *och*, what a stranger you've become. You'll stay for a time with us, of course."

Cormac winced. "She'll not want to bed down in our pile of rubble," he said, not looking up from his work.

"Cormac MacAlpin!" Bridget leaned down to swat his shoulder. "It's not so grim as all that. Come"—she linked arms with Marjorie—"and be welcome at Dunnottar Castle."

He rose slowly, meeting Marjorie's gaze. They locked eyes and, for a blessed instant, the rest of his world fell away. He lost himself, the past, his pain, drowned in vivid blue.

She blinked, and something shifted in her gaze. Cormac swore he felt it shimmer like electricity across his skin. Marjorie narrowed her eyes, assuming a look, *her* look, the one she used to get before issuing one of her infamous dares. That glint aimed straight for him, and Cormac braced.

Marjorie patted his sister's hand, her gaze never leaving his. "Thank you, Bridget. I look forward to my stay."

Chapter 3

"This was all from the wars?" Marjorie ogled a patch of severely damaged masonry. "Aren't you afraid the walls will tumble about your ears?"

Bridget laughed. "It's not as though we were here when it happened. 'Twas a Covenanter siege that left the castle in a wee bit of disrepair."

"*Wee* bit?" she muttered, then shuffled to catch up to Bridget, who was leading her on a brisk tour of Dunnottar. "And you wonder why folk call you the Devil's Own!"

Marjorie came to a breathless halt in the doorway of the dining hall. The sight of Cormac seated at the table scuttled her merriment. Intent on a mug of ale and some bread, he didn't look up. Why had she thought he'd help find Davie, when he couldn't even bring himself to look at her?

"Och, the villagers." Bridget strode in and squatted before the hearth to stoke the fire to life. "Since Father died, they claim we've been a pack of devils."

"It's Dunn's Devils," Cormac muttered. "For Dunnottar. That's what they say."

Marjorie watched as he studiously dunked a heel of

bread in his ale, just like he used to do when he was a boy. She fought a sudden smile and marveled at the foreign sensation. Since Davie'd been taken, her pleasures had been rare. But Cormac, he'd always made her smile. He used to tease them from her relentlessly, until she couldn't hold back.

But that had been in the time before.

The warmth that had been spreading through her chest clenched, leaving Marjorie sadder than ever.

"Oh aye." Bridget laughed. "A pack of Highland demons we are, for want of living parents."

Cormac remained focused on his bread. "Demons, just here in our wee slice of hell."

His sister shot him a hard look. "Dunnottar's been perfectly suitable since we patched the roof."

"It's as drafty as a boat on the open sea."

Marjorie felt his presence like a stitch in her side; she couldn't seem to breathe easily. She pulled her shoulders back to stand taller. "It certainly is . . . *massive*." She looked around, taking in the gargantuan dining hall.

"Aye, 'tis a great big sprawl of a place. There are stables, cellars for wine and beer, even barracks and a chapel . . ." Bridget's voice grew distracted as she stabbed angrily at the stubborn embers. "It's housed armies, kings." She straightened and hung the poker back in its spot by the fireplace. "Och, this cursed fire."

"And all these years, folk have simply let you . . . stay here? Nobody's tried to make you leave?"

"I challenge anyone to try," Bridget proclaimed. "In any case, it's been nigh on nine years now. They're not going to drag us out now."

Cormac slowly leaned back in his chair, and for the first time since they'd stood together on the beach, he met Marjorie's eyes.

The force of his gaze was a physical thing. She'd had something she was about to say, but it froze on her tongue. She tried desperately but couldn't seem to make her mind produce words.

"It *was* abandoned, after all." Bridget's tone was breezy, and if she'd noticed anything pass between Marjorie and her brother, she didn't let it show.

Cormac cut his eyes down, the spell broken. "Abandoned? It's barely livable."

"Och, 'tis a fine place." Bridget clapped the ash from her hands. "Folk know we've no other home, and so they let us stay."

Cormac sneered. "Or they're afraid of us."

"Aye." Bridget giggled. "That, too." She turned to Marjorie, explaining only half-jokingly, "My brothers make a fearsome trio. You should've seen them when we lost our cottage."

Marjorie pasted a smile on her face. *Trio. Because the fourth went missing thirteen years ago.* The thought didn't seem to occur to Bridget. So pretty and carefree, she'd been only two years old when Aidan was taken.

"You mean when you lost your tenancy?"

"Aye, when Father was killed in battle." Bridget sauntered to Cormac's chair, and Marjorie sensed him bristle. "Oh Marj," she said, patting her brother's shoulder, "these lads were glorious. And so young, too—Gregor was sixteen at the time, and Declan only ten! But they looked out for me even then. I worried the laird would resort to burning our old, wee cottage down in his attempts to remove my brothers from it."

"I'd always just assumed . . ." She'd always thought the MacAlpin siblings had simply made the odd choice to live there. It'd never struck her that they had no other recourse but to squat in an abandoned castle. "Have you no place to go then, no other family? Nowhere in all Scotland?"

Bridget shrugged. "Gregor made inquiries, after Father's death. But no distant relatives popped from the heather to deed us any sort of ancestral home."

"Is Gregor here?" Marjorie brightened. Gregor was the eldest MacAlpin son, and he was a hard man not to like.

"Why would he not be?" Bridget asked.

"Oh, I suppose . . ." Marjorie furrowed her brow. "I just assumed he was living in Aberdeen now."

"Gregor doesn't live in Aberdeen," Bridget said, as though Marjorie had just asserted that the sky was green. "Well, sometimes he *travels* to Aberdeen, but he certainly doesn't *live* there."

"Oh, I'm mistaken, of course." Though she would've sworn she'd heard rumors that Gregor kept a home near Broadgate.

"Aye, and Declan's about, too." Bridget shot one last look of disgust at the fire and strode toward the door. "Come, we'll finish our tour, and perhaps we'll run into them."

Marjorie stole a glance at Cormac. He was staring into his empty ale mug, his face blank. A dull ache crept across her chest, until breathing became a conscious effort. She nodded a mute good-bye, which he didn't acknowledge.

How would she ever get him to help her? She was as alone as she'd ever been. Was she deluding herself to think he'd ever come to her aid? She'd written her fate, a silly fool of a girl, with a dare thirteen years ago.

Marjorie left the room with a heavy heart but quickly came back to herself when she realized she'd lost sight of Bridget. Looking left and right, she spotted her down the hall, already bustling up a spiral staircase. Marjorie jogged after her, struggling to catch up while keeping a careful eye on her feet so as not to slip on the treacherously narrow stone steps.

"It's for the better, you know," Bridget said when Marjorie reached her. "Dunnottar *is* more spacious. Though I know as well as any that it's a mite threadbare . . ."

Her voice trailed off, and Marjorie followed the girl's line of sight. A window that'd been destroyed by cannon fire had caught her eye.

She felt a pang of sympathy, wondering what Bridget's life was like, just seventeen and shut away in this dreary castle, probably never knowing when her brothers would breeze in or out. Bridget had only been three when her mother died and seven when her sister Anya was married off, leaving no other women about. And that had been before they'd even moved into the castle—aside from kitchen help, Bridget had always been the *only* female at Dunnottar.

With Bridget's outgoing manner, Marjorie was certain she had friends. But still, did the girl have true intimates with whom she could share her innermost secrets? At seventeen, she'd be interested in men. Who would guide her? Certainly not her brothers, who'd probably sooner kill a man as see him woo their youngest sister.

When they reached the top of the stairs, she stopped Bridget with a hand on her shoulder. "Soon you'll be wanting to find yourself a husband."

Bridget gaped, and Marjorie wasn't sure if she'd offended or simply surprised the girl. But she thought of surly Cormac, staring into his mug as though willing life to pass, and her confidence redoubled.

Despite Bridget's cheerful assertions, Dunnottar was a dismal place. Especially when compared to Marjorie's life in Aberdeen. But if the MacAlpins had no known family, Bridget had no place else to go.

"You know you're always welcome to stay with Uncle and me in Aberdeen," she said impulsively. "Learned men come the world over to study at the university. There's polite society, and gentlemen galore—"

"Bridge has no need for city life."

Marjorie startled. Placing a hand on her heart, she turned. Cormac stood right behind her, silent as a wraith. He'd followed them.

"I think I'm able to speak for myself." Bridget rolled her eyes, transformed to her old self again. "I'm loathe to admit it, Marj, but—"

"*Marjorie*," Marjorie murmured apologetically.

"*Mar*jorie," Bridget continued with an easy smile, "but I fear my brother has the right of it. I'm not ready for a husband just yet. And I don't wish to leave Dunnottar. If the crash of waves doesn't wake me, it's the sound of the lads' sparring that does, and I'm afraid I'd be lost without either one."

Marjorie canted her head, considering. Surely the villagers wouldn't let the MacAlpins stay in the abandoned castle forever. Folk might muster sympathy for a family of orphans, but she imagined they'd be hard-pressed to allow a spinster to live out her dotage there. Dunnottar might be in near ruin, but someday some wealthy clansman would appear to set it to rights.

Could the girl not even *want* a husband? Marjorie could certainly understand it. She'd given the cold shoulder to many a suitor, and despite the fact that she was perilously close to spinsterhood, she couldn't imagine ever wanting to encourage a single one. To her, city men were fops and dandies all.

There'd always been only one man for her.

She shook her head to erase the thought, but it clung to the back of her mind. That the man in question currently hovered at her back did nothing to help matters.

"Come on, come on." Bridget grabbed her arm.

Furrowing her brow, Marjorie followed willingly, thinking there was more to Bridget than met the eye. Though the MacAlpins had been nicknamed Dunn's Devils, with her black hair and mischievous dark eyes sparkling like the night sky, it was *Bridget* who might turn out to be the most devilish of them all.

Bridget resumed her brisk pace, towing Marjorie alongside. "I'll show you where you'll be sleeping."

The thought made her blush. She heard Cormac following behind them; now that she knew he was there, he was all she was aware of. Would *he* see where she slept?

Suddenly, she needed to know. Did *he* sleep nearby? "I don't want to put anyone out. Where does everyone else slee—"

"Och, you're putting nobody out. We're giving you Anya's room."

They were making their way down a narrow gallery. Squares of watery light pierced the windows. A shadowy cluster of rooms spoked out from the end of the corridor.

The bedrooms. There appeared to be four of them. Which one was Cormac's?

She tallied the MacAlpins in her head. Youngest to oldest: *Bridget, Declan, Cormac, Gregor, Anya.* Five siblings, four bedrooms. *Who sleeps where?*

"You keep a room for Anya?" Marjorie asked, her voice hoarse.

"You've seen the place. I'd say we've rooms to spare."

Cormac was still behind them. She felt the heat of his body radiating at her back. Marjorie struggled to make conversation. "And how is your sister?"

"Her?" Bridget shrugged. "Anya abides."

"And whatever is that supposed to mean?"

Bridget shook her head, stifling an impish grin. "Our Anya . . . She seems to bear her life in silence, aye? Except when she was married off." She beamed admiringly. "Oh, but the fit she pitched when Father sent her all the way down to Argyll! But she seems to have accustomed to married life. Her husband, Donald, he was injured you know, in the wars. Terrible thing. But she has her wee Duncan. Though he's not so very wee anymore. He's . . ." She looked over Marjorie's shoulder. "How old is he now?"

"Nine." Cormac bit out the word as though pained.

She felt a little flutter of optimism. What was he doing, following and listening? It didn't seem like something a man would do if he wanted to rid himself of you. Perhaps she could convince him to help her find Davie after all.

Marjorie cleared her throat. "Do you sleep up here, too?"

Though she'd hoped Cormac would answer, of course it was Bridget who replied, "Well, of course I do. And where else? Mine's just here." She pointed to the neighboring door before swooping into the room on the end.

Bridget began to bustle around at once, running a

finger along a dusty side table, slapping at the bedclothes. She waved a hand before her face at the cloud of dust that swirled to life. "We'll need to air it a bit. But a broom . . . a candle and a washbowl, and it's easily put to rights."

Marjorie couldn't help but cut her eyes to Cormac. He was rigid as a post and eyeing her bed as though it was on fire and he'd been forbidden to put it out.

The bed was big, but not big enough for one so tall as Cormac. What would it be to share a bed with such a man? He'd sit at the edge of it. Gather her onto his lap. He'd kiss her. It would be her first.

She coughed, but it did nothing to slow the shallow racing of her heartbeat. Where had such thoughts come from?

He was staring at her bed. How big would *his* bed be? She fought to breathe. Cormac's bed. Where was his room? Did he sleep close by? She *had* to know. "Where—?"

"I don't know why we even keep it for her. It's not as though Anya ever comes to visit. Her hands are full, nursing that crabbit old numpty she married."

"Mind yourself, sister dear," a voice boomed from behind them, "or *I'll* marry *you* off like Father did Anya."

"Gregor!" Marjorie brightened in surprise at the sight of the eldest MacAlpin brother striding toward them. Though it was Cormac who had her heart, his dashing brother never failed to make it skip a beat. Gregor MacAlpin was light and easy, and he maneuvered women as smoothly as a drover his flock.

He went straight for her, taking her hands in his. "Marjie, love!"

"Marjorie," Cormac growled under his breath.

Cormac's voice reverberated up her spine. His gaze caught hers, and for a thrilling instant she glimpsed a familiar flash in his eyes. One that she hadn't seen since he was a boy. What would he be thinking to have such a look?

"Here's the *true* devil of Dunnottar." Bridget nodded her chin toward Gregor.

"Aye, you'd best watch me, Marj." Gregor leaned down to plant a lingering kiss on her knuckles.

"Watch *you*, Gregor?" She pulled her hands away to study him. He was tall, with the lighter coloring of the MacAlpins' mother, and his blue eyes crinkled as he smiled. Gregor was handsome and gallant, and yet he'd never made her tremble as only Cormac could. "Last I heard, you returned from the wars a noble and conquering hero. As I understand it, maidens have naught to fear from chivalrous knights like you."

Gregor's laugh boomed in the small stone chamber. "Oh, Marjorie, Marjorie," he said, shaking his head. "Just look at you." His eyes swept her up and down, lingering on the cut of her bodice.

Somehow, suddenly, Cormac stood closer among them.

She stole a glimpse. She'd feared he hated her, but it certainly didn't appear the case. If anything, in that moment, it was Gregor who seemed to be the object of Cormac's contempt.

So, he didn't seem to hate her, and that was a good sign. The Cormac she'd known was in there somewhere. But there was something different there, too, and she was unable to read it. Would she be able to convince him to help her find Davie?

"I'm humbled by how beautiful you've grown," Gregor continued. "You don't bless us with your presence nearly enough."

"I . . . I live in Aberdeen, with Uncle." This put her in mind of something she'd meant to ask. "As for Aberdeen, I was under the impression that you—"

"Pray tell, love," Gregor interrupted, "but I must know. Whatever brings you to our wee pile of rubble?" He cocked a brow. "And *how* can we keep you?"

Bridget beamed. "Oh, we're keeping her."

"No, we are not," Cormac muttered.

Bridget put her hands on her hips. "Don't you be ungracious."

Marjorie ignored them. If only they weren't all standing

in her *bedchamber*. "I've come . . ." She glanced at Cormac's stoic profile and girded herself. "To ask for Cormac's help."

"He'll provide it, of course," Bridget said briskly.

"Aye," Gregor added. "Bridge apprised me of your situation just after you came up from the beach. I insist you rest here a while, and then Cormac will return with you to Aberdeen, to help."

Cormac's eyes narrowed. He wouldn't be helping Marjorie, because he *couldn't*. He'd tried such a thing, years ago, tracking Aidan—it was the reason he'd become a scout. And now, one more boy, among hundreds of boys, stolen from the streets of Aberdeen? It'd be easier to find a Covenanter in the king's court. "I'll do no such thing."

Bridget's jaw dropped. "Why ever not?"

"Because I . . ." He hesitated. Then he mistakenly turned to look at Marjorie. She tried to keep a brave face, but Cormac alone could see the despair in her eyes. He wanted to fold her into his arms and stroke her hair until the lines smoothed from her brow.

No.

He wanted to grab her and hold her and kiss her until she forgot this Davie's name.

"Is it because you're busy fishing from dawn till dusk?" Bridget asked, crossing her arms defiantly. She stomped her foot at the answering silence. "No, Cormac. Tell me why you can't take a few days to help Marjorie find this boy of hers. Gregor, tell him."

"Well . . ." Gregor cleared his throat. "Our brother will do what's right. Now I'm afraid I must take this up later. 'Twas lovely indeed seeing you again, Marj, but—"

"Marjorie," the other three corrected in unison.

"Aye, of course, *Marjorie*, but sadly, I must be going. I . . ." Gregor appeared to be fishing for some excuse. "I'll go just now to send word to your uncle that you'll be staying on." He flashed them a broad grin.

Cormac grimaced. *Staying on.* Having Marjorie in their home felt as natural as breathing. Worse, it felt *right*.

And it made him angry. He resented that she'd appeared, making him feel things he shouldn't be feeling.

The pain and shame of Aidan's loss, his mother's death, the hideous and meaningless years at war . . . it had taken him years to inure himself to it all. But he'd finally found solace in his solitary life. And here was Marjorie, ready to shatter that ordered solitude. Like a numbed limb prickling back to life, the sensation was unpleasant.

Their older brother bowed from the room, managing to look both nonchalant and vaguely alarmed.

"Typical Gregor," Bridget muttered. At Marjorie's quizzical look, she clarified, "Our brother avoids any form of conflict. Unless, of course, he's donned in armor. In which case, he postpones his grand exits until he finds himself awarded full military honors."

Cormac needed to escape, too. He didn't see how it'd be possible to help Marjorie, yet he could no longer bear the feeling that he'd somehow betrayed her.

"Not you as well," Bridget said as he turned to leave the room.

Marjorie merely stared intently at the floor. He forced his eyes from her. She'd recover. Her grief was still fresh. Until now, the only hard lesson she'd experienced had been years ago, with Aidan's capture. Eventually she would learn that the world was cruelly able to heap a mountain of suffering onto one's shoulders.

"Don't you fret, Marjorie," he heard Bridget tell her as he left the room. "We'll get Cormac to help you."

Chapter 4

Marjorie slept fitfully, and by dawn, was wide-awake. Though the MacAlpins hired occasional help from the village, they relied only on themselves to do things like stoke the morning fires, and her bedroom was as frigid as one would imagine a wind-whipped cliff-top castle to be.

She needed to feed and water her horse, though, and so she braced herself for her bare feet to hit the slate floor. She hurriedly dressed, and by the time she got outside, she found the morning air invigorating and the stroll a restorative one.

Though the palace ruins and the stables bracketed Dunnottar Rock along either edge, the plateau between was smooth and grassy, and Marjorie stopped, closing her eyes to savor the sensation of being so far above the sea. She felt it to her core; the scent, the sound, and, she imagined, even the pull of the tides, penetrated down to her bones.

Cormac's voice carried to her from inside the stables. A mix of nervous anticipation and simple pleasure rippled through her. She'd spent years coveting each sight of him. To have him so close now was a luxury.

She headed toward the sound of him. He was talking to somebody, and Marjorie deflated, waiting, wondering whom.

Nobody responded.

She reached the barn and paused, leaning in the entrance, canting her head to listen. He was speaking to a horse.

She marveled at the sound of him. His was a man's voice now, and it was a low sound, a confident sound, and she felt the echo of it deep in her chest. It was a stranger's voice but nearly familiar, too, as though, if only she tried harder, she'd be able to hear and recognize the boy she once knew.

What was he saying? She strained and plucked a single word from the soothing hum. *Ree.*

The thrill of it momentarily stole the breath from her lungs. He spoke of *her.* Whatever could he be saying? The thought of it was too much, and she tiptoed in.

A pony chuffed in his stall. He glanced a bored, waiting nod her way, before looking away again. A larger mount filled another of the stalls, a big chestnut, and as he tossed his head at her, Marjorie willed the animal to silence.

She strained but still couldn't parse Cormac's words. He barely put two words together *for* Marjorie. What would he have to say *about* her, and to her godforsaken horse no less?

There were windows along the back wall. She edged out of the stables. She'd hear better from there.

The building was a long rectangle perched on the edge of Dunnottar Rock, and Marjorie knew a moment of hesitation. It was a sheer tumble from the cliff top to the crashing waves far below. But she was no fool. She'd be careful. The windows toward the end weren't so very close to the ledge.

With a hand steadied along the yellowed stone walls, she stepped carefully along the side, quietly nestling her footsteps down into the calf-high tangle of weeds that fringed the stables. Wind whipped in from the sea, and she felt exposed, perched so close to the ledge and so high in the air. Nerves prickled up the backs of her legs. She estimated the distance between the barn and the drop below, assuring herself that a safe amount of land stretched between her and a fall from Dunnottar Rock.

She took a deep breath and pressed on, step by slow step. By the time she passed around the back, her heart was pounding in her throat. But, sure enough, Cormac's voice came to her louder than ever. And though it was still an aggravating mumble, she plucked more words from the air. *Aberdeen . . . lass . . . learn . . . vexation.*

Vexation? She glowered, eyeing the ledge. It was even wider than it had appeared from afar, and it gave her confidence. All she needed to do was make it a few more steps, and she'd be able to peer in the last window.

Slowly she reached along the wall, curving her fingers around the crude stone sill. It framed a square of shadow from which Cormac's voice resonated. Would she be peering into his stall, or a neighboring stall? Would he smile or frown as he spoke?

The window was her sole focus, and she was so shocked when the rock crumbled underfoot that a scream lodged in her throat. She clung mutely to the windowsill, her foot scrabbling for purchase.

A single train of thought swamped her mind: she was ever a girlish fool, she'd messed it all up again, she was about to fall to her death, and she'd never find Davie.

And then an image came to her, in a flash, and the grief was unbearable. Her bed, Cormac's dark stare.

Cormac. She'd never know what it would be to kiss Cormac.

Marjorie gritted her teeth and scrambled for footing. Curse it, but she would find Davie *and* she'd steal a kiss from Cormac when it was all through.

An arm reached roughly around her waist. Astonishment released her voice from her throat, and she shrieked.

She knew a moment of pure fear, and then she recognized the feel of him. *Cormac*.

"How," she gasped as he pulled her tightly to him. He edged back along the side of the barn. Tilting her head up, she caught sight of his face, and she drank it in, fascinated. He exuded anger, possession, and strength. It was a side of him she'd never seen. The boy she'd known was long forgotten. It was a *man* who held her now. "How did you know . . . ?"

Rage twisted his features into a dark mask. "Good Christ, woman. What were you doing?"

She felt strangely pleased. He wanted to wring her neck, but she didn't care. His face was infused with something she hadn't seen there in years: *life*. Cormac was animated and angry and alive. It must've meant something. He *would* help her; she was certain she could wear him down. Perhaps it'd even bring them closer again.

"I came to check on Una."

"From the edge of a bloody cliff?" Wrapping an arm around her back and one beneath her knee, he scooped her up, his movements angry and abrupt.

She'd thought the look in his eyes had been foreign, but *him*, his body, this was more foreign and more thrilling than anything she'd ever imagined. He smelled faintly of sweat and leather, and his chest was a wall of rock against her side. Her Cormac, a *man* now.

She wrapped her arms around his neck. His hair brushed at her sleeves, and she wished her arms were bare. She longed to touch that hair, wondered if it would feel soft or coarse at her fingertips. "How did you know I was out there?"

"You can't spy on me." His words were sharp, staccato punches. "It's impossible."

"Why is it impossible?"

Cormac glared straight ahead, seeming unable even to look at her in his fury. "I was a scout. Nobody gets by me. It's what I do."

"That only confirms it."

"What?"

"That I was right. You are the only man who can help me find Davie."

Scowling, he strode more purposefully onto the green. She chuckled at his obstinacy. This only seemed to rile him more.

"You can put me down now." They were far from the cliff's edge, yet he showed no sign of slowing.

"No."

Slowly she turned into him. She took in the set of his jaw. The morning sun hit the stubble on his face, lighting it to a glowing brown. "No?"

"No. I'll not put you down until I get you safe inside. Where I will make certain that you gather your things. And then you will return home."

She stopped breathing. She didn't care what his intentions were. He was carrying her to her room. Would he truly sweep her up the stairs like a knight? Whisk her into her room like a husband?

A muscle twitched in his clenched jaw. She stared, mesmerized, studying the strong planes of his face. Her eyes returned to the brown stubble shadowing his cheeks. It was thicker and darker at his chin and upper lip.

"Ree, lass, what were you doing climbing along the ledge like that?" The anger had leached from his voice, and Cormac simply sounded tired.

Ree. He'd called her by the old nickname. The sound of it eased her heart. Their eyes caught. His were a sad blue-gray. She wanted to make him smile.

The silence hung, and she inwardly shook herself. Cormac had asked her what she'd been about. Whatever could she tell him and still keep hold of her dignity? She decided simply to avoid the question. "Thank you for tending Una."

"I care for the mounts every day. One more is no trouble."

"I . . . I didn't see you this morning. I didn't know you were already out." Marjorie cringed. Such nonsense spilled from her mouth, but this was her chance to speak with him. Cormac's long strides were quickly taking them back to her room, where he'd put her down and say good-bye.

His eyes narrowed. "I don't sleep near the others."

"Where do you sleep?" She cringed again. A ridiculous and improper question, but she was desperate to know. She felt the blood flooding her cheeks and darted her eyes away, making as though to study the MacAlpins' main lodgings. They lived in what was the old palace, and though much of it was crumbling, the centermost building was sound and watertight.

"Just there." He nodded to a low stone cottage, standing apart to their left. "Off the old smithy."

So he didn't stay in the main building after all. She longed to peek in and see how he lived. Would he have simply a cot and a washstand? Or would there be a desk? A book or two maybe? "Why don't you stay with the others?"

Marjorie sensed his shoulders relaxing, and she risked another glimpse at his profile. She was startled to find him staring at her. His expression was unreadable, his eyes no longer quite so sad. She made the mistake of looking at the set of his mouth. His lips were slightly parted, and he seemed to be contemplating her in some profound way. Her heart gave a sudden thud.

He looked away. "The others are close enough."

He still held her close, unmoving. It struck Marjorie that he'd sensed she was outside the stables and had somehow known she was in danger. Cormac had come and whisked her from the ledge as handily as plucking a flower from a field.

He'd been enraged, but he was composed now. His features were smooth, tranquil even.

She'd been in jeopardy, and *that* is what had upset him.

He felt something for her.

Marjorie's arms tightened around him. She couldn't

stop herself. She had to touch him, to ease the set of that jaw, to feel the scrape of that stubble. Slowly, she pulled her hand up and tenderly cupped his face.

Cormac put her down so swiftly, she almost tumbled to the dirt.

"I cannot help you." He gave her a single horrified look and then walked away.

But it was fine with her. She bit her cheek not to smile.

Marjorie had spied some of the old Cormac lurking deep in his eyes, the boy who'd never liked to see her in danger.

And it gave her an idea.

Chapter 5

Marjorie managed to avoid Cormac the rest of the day. Granted, at one point, she'd heard him approaching and had to duck into what appeared to be an old root cellar—it'd taken her a good half hour to brush all the cobwebs from her clothes—but he'd been set on seeing her leave that day, and Marjorie simply refused. Cormac had the skills to find Davie, and she wasn't going back without him.

She had a plan, and it would unfold here at the dinner table.

She stabbed at her plate of finnan haddie, trying not to look at him seated at the end of the dining table. He'd shaved since the morning, and the fringe of his hair was still damp where he'd splashed water. He wore it long, but not so long that it grew past his shoulders. It became him.

She kicked herself under the table. She couldn't let her mind wander. She needed to stay focused on her goal: finding Davie.

"Do you not like the fish, then?" Bridget asked.

"Aye, I like it fine," Marjorie said, mustering a smile.

She wiped her mouth and reached for the loaf of bread. "You prepared all this yourself?"

Gregor beat her to the bread, slicing off a thick hunk and handing it to her with a flourish. She nodded her thanks, and he winked in return.

Sighing, she glanced at Cormac. There'd been a day when all she would've needed to do was taunt him, saying *Gregor* would help her, and Cormac would've risen to the bait.

And Gregor might've helped her now. But in her short time at Dunnottar, she'd become convinced that she needed *Cormac's* help. At first she'd made excuses to herself. Cormac alone could help because he'd understand; he'd known the pain of losing Aidan. Cormac alone had experience, on both water and land, suited to spying around the Aberdeen docks.

She studied him from beneath her lowered brows. He was intent on exacting the meat from a crab claw, pretending not to listen to their conversation. But Marjorie knew he'd be picking up every word. He was attentive, steady, and strong, and she was certain she needed Cormac—*only* Cormac.

"Well, our Cormac catches the fish, of course. Even though he usually *never* joins us at the supper table like this." Bridget gave her brother a wicked smile, but he didn't look up from his plate.

Something fluttered in Marjorie's belly. Cormac had joined them at dinner, when normally he didn't. With a clean shave, no less. It had to be significant. She reached for the butter, biting her lip not to grin. Her plan would definitely work.

"But, aye, I do the rest. And who else? Not this one, certainly," Bridget added, swatting Declan's hand. "Don't you take that butter before Marjie has a go first."

"Marjorie," she muttered for the thousandth time since her arrival.

Declan passed the butter along with a rueful shrug, and his light brown hair flopped in his eyes.

"Thank you," Marjorie told him, thinking how much he'd grown to favor the MacAlpins' mother. Unlike Gregor, Declan's likeness to her went beyond the mere fact of his lighter coloring. There was something of Mary MacAlpin there in the set of his full mouth and the far-away look in his eyes, as though one corner of his mind were always occupied elsewhere. At twenty, he was young yet, and an unconventional sort of handsome; Marjorie imagined he'd grow into a striking man.

"And Declan, I've been meaning to ask you . . ." Marjorie cut her eyes to Cormac. He appeared to be focused entirely on his supper, but she knew him better than that. She spied a minute stiffening of his shoulders when she spoke. The digging of his knife slowed ever so much. He was listening. Time to fire off a broadside, as Uncle would say. "We're of a size. I'd like to borrow a pair of your trews, if I may."

Declan's eyes widened, Bridget's hands froze over her plate, and Gregor burst into loud laughter. Most of all, she was gratified to see that Cormac nearly choked on his crab.

"My . . . my trews?" Declan looked to their eldest brother for help. Gregor merely shrugged, leaning back in his chair as though to enjoy the show.

"Aye, your trews." Marjorie carefully buttered her bread. She used her peripheral senses trying to gauge Cormac's response. "I'd like to fashion myself a disguise."

Gregor grew instantly serious. "Does this have to do with your Aberdeen boy? Bridget was telling me—"

"I ken what you're about." Bridget put her cutlery down with a clatter. "A disguise? I suppose you'll be wanting to find this Davie yourself? Well, we'll be allowing *no* such thing. *I'll* borrow some trews as well, and go down to the docks with you."

Gregor sat up, his face stern. "Bridget Mary MacAlpin, the only folk who'll be gadding about Aberdeen wearing trews are me and your brothers."

Marjorie ignored him. "Really, Bridget, you don't need to come. I'll be perfectly safe." She waited a beat for Cormac to protest, but none came. "I'll go during daylight hours," she continued. "I'm thinking perhaps I'll overhear something down by the docks."

Still not sensing any movement from Cormac, Marjorie risked a glance his way. He was chewing slowly. *Silently.*

"The *docks*?" Bridget's voice came out as a shrill yelp. "Cormac, tell her how we'll be allowing no such thing."

There was a moment of quiet, then he simply said, "The boy is gone." He chewed and swallowed another bite. "I'd be of no help. I'm needed here." He finally looked up. "To feed the lot of you."

"Cormac." Everyone stilled at Gregor's dangerously low tone. The eldest MacAlpin wasn't much for conflict, but when he pushed up his sleeves and got in the fray, unpleasantness generally followed. "I'm expected elsewhere, or I'd help her. And Declan is too young."

"Elsewhere?" Bridget exclaimed.

"Young?" Declan slammed his fist down on the table. "I'm a man grown!"

"Where is this *elsewhere* you're suddenly needed?"

The table had erupted, and Marjorie was mortified. She hadn't expected his family would need to *beg* Cormac to help her. The blood pounded in her cheeks.

"Declan's place is here," Gregor continued firmly. "And so it falls to you, Cormac. In any case, you, more than any of us, are suited to this. The famed scout and spy? Who better to trawl Justice Port for rumors of a shipload of indentured laborers."

Marjorie studied Cormac's face. The candlelight caught the scar at his temple. It winked in the light, before falling back into shadow.

Cormac curled his lip. Slowly, he shook his head.

"Marjorie's mother was our mother's dearest friend. You will do this for her." Gregor leaned forward, his usually jovial manner forgotten. "Mother would have wished it."

This was going too far. Marjorie had simply wanted to make Cormac think she'd put herself in danger. Spur him to action.

Cormac tensed. "Think twice before you invoke our mother." He blinked for a long moment. "You know as well as I that the boy is gone."

Such dark words, so casually spoken. It shot a fresh spear of dread through her belly.

"He might not be gone." Bridget reached over to pat Marjorie's hand.

"No," Cormac said evenly. "The boy is gone. The world is cruel. It's time for Marjorie to accept it once and for all."

He only spoke *about* Marjorie, not *to* her. Why wouldn't he address her? Did he blame her that much, hold her that accountable for the loss of Aidan? The loss of his mother?

"You will take a few days," Gregor ordered. "Go with her to Aberdeen, have a look around the docks."

Marjorie sat frozen. She couldn't endure the fact that he wouldn't voluntarily help her. "No, truly," she stammered. She'd wanted his help, but not like this. "I'm able to do this myself."

Gregor stared at his brother. "He'll come to his senses, won't you, Cormac?"

Cormac gave her a cold look. If he hadn't hated her before, he'd surely hate her now, for putting him in this position. He was a proud man, and she'd set him up to take orders from his older brother.

Whatever it was she'd started, she needed to follow through now or seem a fool. But first she needed to get out of there. Cormac's glare told her there was no changing his mind. It seemed she really was going to the Aberdeen docks. By herself.

She dabbed her mouth then meticulously folded her napkin. "I'm afraid I shall have to excuse myself."

"Marjie, wait," Bridget said.

Marjorie got up quickly, meeting nobody's eye. She managed a shaky laugh. "Thank you for your hospitality. I'll be returning to Aberdeen . . ."

When?

An image of Davie came to her. Two missing teeth and perpetually soiled cheeks. His eyes were bright, always with a smile for "Marjrey."

She needed Cormac's help, no matter the cost.

She braved a glance his way. He fisted his dinner knife as though ready to run someone through.

She had no choice but to force his hand.

"I'll leave tomorrow. If you'd be so kind as to lend me those trews?" She flicked a glance at Declan, catching his wide green eyes, and then fled the room.

———————

Cormac stalked to the kitchens to forage for food. His appetite had fled the table with Marjorie, and now his empty belly was paying the price.

But he'd been furious. Furious his world had been so upended. That his entire family appeared set on forcing him to do their will. Furious at Marjorie's daft plan. And furious at himself for not being the man worthy of her.

Because he would make all her pain go away if he could. He'd take her and help her, and make it all better. But he was unable. He was his own mass of pain, a great black nexus of despair. Were he to go with her to Aberdeen, he'd be the one forced to show her how this Davie was gone forever.

And were he to go so far as to claim her as his own? To take her and claim her as he'd wished for his entire life? His own darkness would eventually destroy her.

He was about to step through the door when he heard hushed voices.

"Truly, I will," Marjorie said.

The sound of her stilled him, as it always did. Like a damned buck catching a scent, Cormac froze.

"Are you certain you won't let me help?" his sister asked her. "I'll be simply devastated if something untoward comes to pass." There was a rustling. "I am so sorry about Cormac. He really hasn't been himself since coming back from the wars."

He fisted his hands, lips curling into a scowl. *He's* not acting *him*self? What do they call a lass in trews? Marjorie was acting rash, foolhardy, and it made him angry.

He knew she acted thus to spur him to action, but he wouldn't be swayed.

He had a quiet life, alone. He *had* returned from the wars a changed man. Bearing the scars of what he'd seen, what he'd done. He'd come back and worked hard to carve out a piece of solitude in a world that made no sense. Though his seclusion hadn't healed his wounds, it had numbed them. And here was Marjorie, dredging up old feelings, conjuring the old impotence of that day, the unendurable pain of it.

And this other boy who'd been taken? Cormac was unwilling even to *let* the child pierce his consciousness. Pain would only beget more pain.

"Don't worry for me," he heard Marjorie say. The words echoed down the empty stone hallway.

"But you can't go alone."

Cormac began to walk away. He refused to be pulled into her crisis, refused to be a party to it.

"Don't fash yourself on my account. I confess"—Marjorie laughed nervously—"I'm a bit frightened to go it alone. But I've thought of someone who can help. There is a man."

Cormac stopped dead. *What man?*

"A physician surgeon from Marischal College." Marjorie's voice was tentative. Cormac leaned a hand against the cold stone of the corridor, listening. "He comes to help at Saint Machar. That's where we met. He's offered his . . . support in the past."

Cormac's body went rigid. What kind of bloody *support*?

"I think Archie . . . that's his name . . ."

Archie. He balled his hands into fists. So they were on intimate terms. *How intimate?* Rage coursed through him at the prospect. He'd find and kill the man who'd touched her.

"I don't think he'll let me go to the docks alone," Marjorie continued. "He'll come with—"

Cormac burst through the door, slamming it open hard. Marjorie and Bridget sat on stools by the cook fire, their hands earnestly clasped.

Marjorie stared at him, the words frozen on her lips. Her large blue eyes were all the more vivid for being so bloodshot. She'd been crying.

The sight of one plump tear rolling down her cheek cracked his resolve.

Damn the woman. And damn his pathetic weakness for her.

Cormac took a step toward her. "I'll take you to Aberdeen."

Chapter 6

She awoke wanting a bath. But hauling fresh water to Dunnottar Rock was a luxury she'd not ask of the MacAlpins, and so Marjorie bent for a brisk splash along the shoreline.

The water was frigid, but she made quick work of it, chafing her face and darting her hands beneath her gown to scrub under her arms. Low, uneven waves slapped and ebbed, sucking at her feet. A breeze found the damp patches on her bodice, pebbling her skin tight, and she shivered with the pleasure of it.

Her last seaside wash had been with Davie. Stripping the boy down and tossing him in the waves had been the most effective way she'd found to get him cleaned. He loved splashing and dunking, grabbing for the small silvery fish that darted between his feet.

Dread turned her heart to lead. Davie surely wouldn't be enjoying any seaside baths now. What would he be doing? Was he unhurt? Warm and fed?

She haphazardly scoured her ankles and calves. They

had to get on the road quickly, before Cormac changed his mind.

Cormac. They had a long day's ride ahead of them. How would it be to travel with him for an *entire day*? Would he finally talk to her? How much did he resent her? The prospect made her queasy.

A distant splashing mingled with her own, so at first she didn't notice. But then Marjorie sensed a presence on the edge of her vision. She knew before she looked whom she'd find.

Cormac had haunted her thoughts and now seemed even to materialize like a ghost at the strangest of moments. On the edges of cliffs. During private talks. Of course he'd appear for her seaside wash.

She straightened, steeling herself for the sight of him. What would be the look on his face this time? She wondered if an easy smile would ever be waiting there to greet her, or if he'd always bear his grim mask.

Like iron to a lodestone, her head turned toward him. He was higher up the beach, but still close enough to see.

Cormac was emerging from the waves. Nakcd.

Oh sweet Lord. She blinked. She wasn't prepared for *this*.

It was improper to look, yet she couldn't bring herself to turn away. The early morning sun was low on the horizon, and his body glistened with light. Water drizzled down his shoulders and chest, disappearing into shadowed valleys of hard flesh. His hair was plastered to his brow, and the water made it appear almost black.

Her eyes went to his face, and he looked away before their gazes could catch. He bore a dark scowl.

Of course. Why would he be friendly? She'd forced his hand. She'd all but made him accompany her to Aberdeen.

He bent to retrieve his plaid from the rocks, and her gaze slid to the flex of his taut haunches. She gasped, widening her eyes. She'd never seen a naked man before. And Cormac wasn't just any man. He was lithe and muscled, confident and comfortable in his skin.

"I . . . I'm sorry," she managed, grateful for the freezing water that numbed her feet, though it was her whole body she needed to dunk. Maybe then she'd be able to cool the hot flushing sensation that suffused her. "I didn't know you'd be here."

He wrapped and tucked his plaid, and even though her cheeks burned hot, she couldn't look away.

"I could say the same to you," he said blandly. "It's no' my beach."

Finishing, he walked toward her. There was such purpose in his stride, his body all fluid power.

She held her breath.

His eyes flicked to her bodice. She was exquisitely aware of it clinging damp and tight to her breasts. Her belly quivered with something that reached even her numbed toes.

"We leave once there's food in our bellies," he told her. And then he simply walked on past.

—————

Cormac tucked the reins under his thigh and laced his fingers, stretching his arms before him. He flexed his wrists to the point of discomfort, but still, mastering his body was taking a conscious effort.

"So strong you are," Marjorie cooed, her voice sounding low and sultry next to him.

He mumbled a curse. She'd been purring, whispering, and just about moaning at that damned mare all morning, and it was driving him to distraction.

"So, so strong." She ran her hands along her horse's neck in long, languid strokes. "You were lonely in that stall. But you like when I ride you, don't you? Yes you do. You like having me on your back."

Cormac flexed until his knuckles popped.

He looked out of the corners of his eyes, watching the

sway of her hips in the saddle. The sound of her bedroom voice was a reverberating hum through his body. What would she look like riding *him*?

His mind returned to the image branded there: Marjorie, standing in the shallows. Her wet bodice had clung to her, revealing every curve, every dip and swell of her soft flesh. And then she'd looked at him, and there'd been a darkness in her eyes, a wanting that he recognized as his own.

It'd taken all the concentration he had not to go hard at the sight of her. If there was anything that could make his cold cock rouse, it had been the feel of Ree's eyes on him, roving his naked body as though she'd a right to.

Her horse began to flag, and Marjorie made soft kissing noises to liven up the animal's gait.

"God help me," he breathed. He adjusted himself on the saddle, forcing himself to focus on the path ahead, on the sway of the horse beneath him.

It should've been a decent ride. Gregor had shocked Cormac when he loaned his braw chestnut gelding, but not even the superior horseflesh at Cormac's seat could distract him.

Marjorie. Marjorie was the distraction.

"Ohhh, that's the way," she murmured.

Cormac's groin tightened anew. He scowled. *Agony.* What could've been a pleasant enough ride had become his own personal hell.

He held his body stiffly, putting his mind to other things. Fishing. Hunting. The fine horse he rode. He patted the animal's neck, willing thoughts like the mending of boats and the gelding of horses to wipe the wayward images from his mind.

"What's his name?" Marjorie asked, trotting to catch up to his side. The sea breeze had pinkened her cheeks. She'd always loved riding, and she bore the hint of a smile on her face. Her breathing was up, and her bodice strained with it. The sight silenced him.

"Cormac?"

Marjorie was waiting for his response, and the only

words that surged to mind were how lovely she looked
with the wind in her hair. He shook himself. It was too
dangerous to entertain such notions. "Name?" he said,
coming back to himself.

"Aye, Gregor's horse. What's his name?"

He looked down, contemplating the animal's coat, dark
russet with sweat. He shrugged. "I don't ken its name."

"You didn't ask the horse's name?" She nudged her
mount closer to his. Her skirts rustled against Cormac's
calf, and he stifled a shiver.

Fishing. Hunting. Boat mending.

"He's a braw one," Marjorie said, leaning toward the
animal. Her bodice tugged lower, revealing the gentle
swells of her breasts.

Boat mending. Hoof trimming. Stall mucking.

She murmured to the beast in a low, sultry voice,
"Aren't you just a big, braw boy?"

"Why?" Cormac asked abruptly, his voice barking out
like a muted shout. "Why would I need its name? It's not
as though he'll come if I call."

"But you'll be riding him all day. Don't you want to
know?"

Cormac was completely off his guard, and so his
response was something his younger self might have said.
"He and I, we weren't formally introduced, Ree."

Suddenly silent, Marjorie let her horse fall behind.
Cormac grew curious after a moment, and twisted in the
saddle to study her. A puzzled look wrinkled her brow.

"What is it?" he asked, concerned. "Are you not comfortable?"

Her puzzled look intensified. "No . . . I . . . why do you
ask?" Her features hardened. "I'm perfectly comfortable.
Don't forget, Cormac. I have made this journey before,
and I am perfectly capable of making it again."

"Och, that's not what I was saying at all." What had he
unwittingly stepped into? "That'll teach a man," he added
under his breath.

Now she just looked hurt. He rued his words.

"That's not what I'd meant," he said, trying again. "You simply . . . you've got a look about you. I thought you might be uncomfortable, is all."

"Oh." She thought on it for a moment, then gave a brisk shake to her head. "I'm perfectly comfortable. It's simply . . . you foxed me some, with your jesting." She gave him an uneasy smile.

"Aye, I've not jested much," he admitted.

"Not jested? Cormac, you barely speak."

"Aye." He stopped himself from saying more. Marjorie's bright blue eyes were guileless and her face open as she watched him. She seemed to be waiting for something to happen. He needed to stem such ideas. *Nothing* would ever happen. How had he even found himself this far into the conversation? Nothing could come of such talk. Naught could ever be between them. "Aye, 'tis true," he said again, and left it at that.

The brief exchange had charged their silence, and he regretted ever saying anything in the first place. Her horse caught and then passed his on the path.

"You're angry at me," she said after a time.

"Oh aye?" The lass was such a mystery. He didn't recall her being so perplexing when they'd been children. He studied her back as she rode before him, watching as her muscles tensed, imagining the look that might be crossing her face. "Angry, you say?"

She gave a tight nod. "For making you come with me to Aberdeen."

He thought on it. It wasn't anger but dread that he felt. He dreaded Aberdeen. Cormac didn't want to face the ruffians of Justice Port; they had naught but fights and death in their eyes, and he only recognized himself in their cold, flat gazes. He dreaded revisiting her uncle's town house. Most of all, he dreaded facing the memories of another missing boy, one who'd never been found.

But Marjorie would be dreading Aberdeen as much as he did. She'd come to him for help, and he'd been acting the boor.

He felt guilty, and it warmed his words. "It's not that I'm angry, Ree." He sighed. He'd never been able to stay angry with her anyhow. Like it or not, they were traveling to Aberdeen together, and he might as well make the best of it. Inhaling deeply, he announced, "We'll need a plan."

"A plan?" It was *Marjorie's* voice again, the voice he knew, straightforward and without hesitation.

He hadn't realized his shoulders had tensed until he felt them unclench just then. "Aye, if we're to search for the boy, we'll need a plan. We're up the coast to Aberdeen, and to your uncle's by dusk. We'll take a turn around the quay tomorrow, at first light."

She nodded and stilled her mare for him to catch up.

Cormac felt a fraction lighter inside. Empathy was too painful, but this planning, this he could do. He was in it now, and if he was going to do a thing, there was no sense in not doing it right. His words came more easily. "I'll need to know about the boy. You'd said he's a wee lad, just five?"

"Aye." Her voice cracked. She cleared it and started again. "He didn't know exactly, but he thought five. I'd say not more than six."

"What's he look like, then?" He braced himself. He would hear her response and parse it as though devising a military campaign. He'd not let himself imagine this boy too vividly. This boy who would never be found.

"He's a wee rascal."

Cormac heard the smile in her voice and kept his eyes trained on the path ahead. He gathered his nerves. He'd not let himself grow attached to the thought of a missing child. And more even than that, he'd not allow concerns for Marjorie to penetrate his defenses.

"He's a little ginger-haired boy," she continued, warming to the topic. "Smaller than the others. With freckles, and a pointing chin, and mischief to spare. From the start, he seemed to me a fey creature."

It was clear she loved the boy. It suddenly struck him

how much she'd enjoy raising a child of her own. He wondered why she hadn't yet married.

And he realized he was oddly glad she hadn't. Deep down it pleased him that there was someone out there who'd turned to *him* for help. More so, that it'd been *Ree* who had. The thought that she might've married, might now be relying on another man for support, sent a plume of instinctive, protective anger snaking through his belly.

He let the sensation hang briefly before pushing it away. It'd do no good to dwell on such things.

"And you're certain he wouldn't simply have wandered off?"

"I'm certain of it," she said with a steadiness that made him feel a strange wash of pride. "Evening was his favorite time of the day. Supper at Saint Machar isn't a grand affair, by any means. But there's a pack of them, the youngest boys, who play in the evenings. Such grand stories they enact for themselves. Davie's favorite is to relive tales of the Campbell, just as we did. Remember?"

"Aye," he said quietly, feeling a small crack in his heart. Of course he remembered. It'd been his favorite thing as well.

Cormac's expression softened almost imperceptibly, and Marjorie swelled at the sight.

She let herself relive memories of Davie. "They'll play at the same stories for days," she said, smiling wistfully. "Such elaborate campaigns with pretend armaments and battle plans. Fights with the Marquis of Montrose are a particular favorite. Except when Davie has to play the Campbell. Och, but he hates being the Campbell, just like—"

Marjorie stopped herself short. She glanced at Cormac, but his face was shuttered. She grew cold. Just when he'd begun to open up, she went ahead and spoiled it by speaking without thought.

Such thoughtless chatter. She cringed.

"Just like Aidan," he finished for her.

His comment took her aback. The look on his face was calm but not cold, and her relief was profound.

"Aidan always hated playing the Campbell, too," he said.

He wasn't smiling, but he was speaking, and it gave her courage to press him. "Do you ever think about him?"

He was quiet. The only sound was their horses' hooves in the gravel of the drover's road. Geese called overhead. If she listened for it, she could hear the hiss of the sea in the far distance.

Just when nerves once again began to chill her blood, he spoke. "There isn't a day goes by that I don't think about my brother."

"Of course," she said quietly. Such an understatement. Of course he'd think of Aidan. Every day. But did he blame her for it? He'd endured such pain. His whole family, such pain. *She* blamed herself. He must damn her as well.

But would he speak of it? Never. He only stared, silent accusation in his eyes. She'd lived for thirteen years with the guilt, and she refused to keep it in a moment longer. It needed to erupt, here and now, to the surface. "I know it's my fault."

"It's no' your fault," he said, his voice flat.

"Aye, it was my fault." As she brought her darkest thoughts to light, she realized the words couldn't come fast enough. So much time had passed; she needed desperately to talk about it. "I dared you boys to climb the chimney. You must blame me for it."

"Ree . . ." He scrubbed a hand over his face. "Ree, I can't speak of this now. If you must talk, talk to me of the Aberdeen quays. If there were any ships newly docked, we must—"

"But I *want* to talk about this, Cormac." She'd rather have his shouts of anger, of hatred, *anything* but his dreadful silences.

"No."

He halted his horse, and she fumbled to bring her

mount to a stop. She turned in the saddle to find his eyes flat and steady on her.

"I agreed to come help you," he said. "And that is all I agreed to."

His brooding hurt her, and now it was beginning to anger her as well. She would hear him give voice to his accusations, hear his sharp words, if she had to provoke them herself. "We *have* to talk about this."

He merely looked at her blankly, and her fury erupted. Marjorie swung off her horse and stalked to him. She felt the words begin to boil from her and did nothing to stop them.

"We have to talk about this, but instead you just glare at me. You're like a silent, glowering man of . . . of *stone*. All these years!" She slapped his horse's belly just behind Cormac's calf, and the animal skittered beneath him. He swung off and stared, standing still as granite before her, silent as stone. It made her want to rave. "All these years and never a word from you. I was left to wonder, for *years*. I felt like some . . . some pathetic spy, forced to skulk in the shadows, begging word of you from your sisters, gathering news from town."

The memory of it brought her emotions to a fever pitch. But still he remained quiet, and his silence dragged words from her lips she'd never dreamed she'd utter. She knew she'd regret airing such secret, shameful thoughts, yet she couldn't seem to stanch her outburst.

She stepped closer to Cormac, until they stood, both ramrod stiff, mere inches apart. "It's like *I* disappeared that day. You were my . . . my . . ." She faltered at the sharp pain in her chest. He'd been her *what*? Her dearest friend forever? Her treasured knight and protector? The boy she thought she'd wed? Her one true love? "You were my *friend*."

He just looked at her mutely.

Tears stung her eyes. Such pique, such humiliation, such agony clenched her chest, bringing her breath in short gasps. She cast off what last scraps of dignity she had left. She slapped her hands at his chest. "Say it! Just say it, Cormac! Say you hate me. Tell me once and for all."

His hands gripped her shoulders, and she realized she was trembling. Slowly she dared to look up, fearing what she'd see.

His eyes were intense, the blue subsumed by gray, like clouds over a stormy sea. "Ree," he rasped, and something in her slackened. "Och, Ree, it's not you I blame. Can't you see? *I* bear the shame of that day."

She shook her head sharply, for once speechless. It was *her* fault. Naughty, willful, sweet, darling Aidan *kidnapped*. It was unthinkable. And it had been all her fault. She trembled, shaking her head harder. *Her* fault.

"Hush, lass," he whispered. He cupped a hand to her cheek, stilling her. Gently, Cormac touched his forehead to hers. "I could never hate you," he said, his voice the barest whisper.

At his words, his touch, relief swamped her, melting something deep inside. Marjorie wilted toward him. Her breasts brushed against his hard chest, and relief changed like quicksilver into another thing entirely.

Desire shocked through her, sharp and hot. Her knees buckled, and she grabbed Cormac's arms to steady herself. The feel of his hard muscles in her hands only intensified the feverish buzzing throughout her body.

Before, she'd needed to purge the words that had festered for so long inside. But now she needed to release an entirely different demon, something that had haunted her for years. She *wanted* Cormac. She'd always wanted him near, but now that she was a woman, that craving had transformed into something hotter, darker, more powerful. She wanted to give herself to him, to make her body an offering, just for him. The desire stole the air from her lungs.

His breath was warm on her face, his mouth a whisper away from hers. *Kiss him.* She could kiss him. She slid her hands up his hard arms, stroked them up his neck. A fantasy flashed in her mind: Cormac, naked above her. What would it be like to lie beneath him? She'd seen his chiseled arms; they'd flex as he held himself over her. She'd kiss and bite that strongly corded neck. The thought made her gasp.

Abruptly, he tried to pull away.

She almost let him. But the residual fury and shame that had been simmering, battling deep within, caught into a rapid boil, making her feel as though her heart would roil from her chest. She grabbed his shoulders, flexing her fingers into rock of muscle and bone. "Cormac," she said, her voice a scold, a plea.

He seemed to stop breathing. He held himself stiffly before her. She'd surely scandalized him, but Marjorie felt beyond fear, beyond shame.

"Cormac," she breathed. She felt his muscles slacken beneath her fingers. "Cormac, I want you . . . I want you to—"

"Hush."

She swallowed the words she'd been ready to say, wondering if she'd later regret or be grateful for the discretion.

"Ree, lass, we . . ." He lowered his head, whispering into her hair. "*This* . . . this cannot be."

This . . . them. He was right. There was too much between them. Too much fault, too much blame. Much too horrifying a history. Cormac might say he didn't hate her, but she couldn't believe he didn't bear some small kernel of contempt in a distant corner of his heart.

She could never have him. Because, on some level, never would he fully accept her.

Marjorie nodded mutely. She might never have him, but she could steal something of this moment instead. She tucked herself into him.

He froze for a moment, but then his arms folded around her as effortlessly as a puzzle piece falling into place. She shuddered in a deep breath.

He held her carefully, and she let her gaze drift to the

distance. They were close to the coast, and she stared blindly at a faraway and fathomless gray sea diluting into gray skies above. She thought of Cormac's eyes.

They stood there for a time, in silence.

Cormac spoke finally, and his low voice reverberated in her chest, soothing her. "Some mornings, when I set off in my boat, I wonder what it would be to go and not turn back. Just keep going. Sailing away, with Scotland at my back."

He paused for a time, and she remained utterly silent, wanting the moment never to end.

"Do you ken," he said finally, "that here we're closer to Scandinavia than we are to London? If you sailed straight from here, you'd land in Norway. And sometimes I do set off, and for a time, I don't turn back, thinking I'll find some icy rock where I can live out the rest of my days."

"But you always turn back," she said, subdued.

"Aye. So far I've always turned back."

He pulled away then, and this time she let him, with more peace in her heart than she'd known in years.

"Thank you," she said.

"For what?"

"You ease my mind, Cormac." She wasn't convinced he didn't blame her. Deep in Cormac's heart, he surely held her accountable. But he at least cared enough to *try* to make her feel better. "You ease me, and it's always been thus."

She might not have believed his words, but she'd take them. For now.

Chapter 7

They handed their tired mounts off at the Broad Street mews and headed toward her uncle's Aberdeen town house. Marjorie was stiff from the day's ride, but she saw from the corner of her eye that Cormac walked with as much fluid ease as ever. He seemed aware of everything around him, and she wondered once more what he'd been like as a soldier.

They reached the house, and he paused on the street to stare up at it. Her uncle's home was much the same as it'd been thirteen years ago: a stone facade harled white with lime, black-painted window sashes.

A dark cloud passed over Cormac's features. He'd not been back to her uncle's since the day Aidan was taken. She followed his eyes up to the second-story window. Her stomach turned, remembering the last time they'd stood together at that window, looking down at a cart full of sweeps below.

"Come," she said quietly, touching his arm. Ghosts abounded in the old house. He'd best inure himself to them now.

She'd been in her great-uncle Humphrey's care since her mother died. It'd been just the two of them for some time, and she knew that, after supper, her uncle would be found in one place, and one place only. Marjorie walked in and headed straight for the library, Cormac stalking silently at her heels.

Though the room had high ceilings, its dark paneled wood and rows of leather-bound tomes made it feel smaller than it actually was. There were only a few candles and a fireplace, and warm light danced and flickered, cutting swaths of orange through the thick black shadows. "Uncle!" she cried as she entered.

Humphrey bent over a book, his reading glass in hand, mouthing silently to himself. His hair was a fine, fuzzy halo of white atop his head. Her uncle was getting on in years, and the sight of him gave her a pang.

"Uncle?" she said again, walking to him with outstretched hands.

Humphrey looked up, a finger marking his place in his book. It took a moment for his eyes to come into focus, but after a moment's perplexed goggling, the man smiled broadly. A splotch of ink stained his cheek with an indigo-black oval. "Marjorie, dearest."

A clock chimed the late hour, and her brow furrowed, part of her aware of Cormac looming uneasily in the shadows. "Shouldn't you be abed? It's so late, and you know sitting for too long in your chair is no good for your gout."

"Aye, I'm going, I'm going. But I'm afraid I've misplaced my *Botanicals* again." He rifled through his cluttered desktop, moving piles on top of piles. "Do you know where volume four is?"

Shaking her head, she shot Cormac a wry smile and walked to the far corner of the library. She stepped on a small stool, reaching for a thin sheaf of papers bound by a leather cord. "It's between volumes three and five, as it always is."

"Oh Marjorie, dear, what would I do without you?" Humphrey beamed, taking the manuscript from her. He gently untied the cord, his face softening with relief. "But whatever brings you here at this hour? You can't simply have sensed that I needed your assistance."

"You know how I cannot stay away from you, sir," she jested. She plopped on the edge of his desk and began to straighten his piles. "I've just now returned. And I wanted you to know I'd arrived back safely."

"But . . . back from where?" The old man bore a look of good-natured bewilderment. "You were away?"

Cormac saw Marjorie's shoulders slump just the slightest bit, and anger washed over him. Could her uncle truly not even have noticed that she'd been absent from the house?

"Yes, Uncle. I've been away. Visiting the MacAlpins. But Gregor told me he sent word. Did you not get his message?" Marjorie unearthed a small envelope from one of his stacks.

"Och, girl,"—Humphrey took the letter from her hand— "you know I can't find a thing without you. But where did you say you were?" He glanced at Cormac, seeming to see him for the first time. "You visited a gentleman?"

"No. Well . . . yes. I suppose. But not like that." She stopped fiddling with his papers to look her uncle in the eye. "Not a gentleman. Just Cormac."

Not a gentleman. Cormac frowned. He didn't know whether to view it as a compliment or an insult.

"Cormac MacAlpin?" He leaned forward, his eyes narrowing. "Truly?"

Cormac gave a brusque but respectful nod. "Lord Keith."

"Come here, lad. Step into the light." Humphrey cleared his throat roughly and pulled a handkerchief from his pocket to cough into.

Stepping closer to the firelight, Cormac could see that the years hadn't been entirely kind to the old man. He was thicker at the waist than was healthy, and Cormac wondered how often he left his desk.

He supposed he should make polite chatter, asking

about Humphrey's never-ending scholarly investigations, but the sight of him so aged stuck in Cormac's craw. What would Marjorie do after her uncle's death? The man hadn't even known she'd been gone. Was there anyone who looked out for her?

"But it is you." Humphrey adjusted his glasses. "A man grown now! And with the look of your father, I daresay. And yet nothing like the man, I'm sure," he added quickly.

Cormac didn't care to think what he'd meant by that last statement. "Aye, and as a man grown, I couldn't allow Marjorie to make the long ride home by herself."

What he wanted to add was, "Unlike you, who let her embark on a day's journey, alone." But then Cormac gritted his teeth, ashamed that, were it not for his family, he'd have allowed that very thing.

"Hm." Humphrey absentmindedly rubbed the crown of his head, his joviality momentarily faded. There was a slight tremor in the man's gestures, in the pursing of his lips and the wavering of his hand, making him seem frail, despite his weight. "Well, I insist you stay."

"I'm afraid I cannot—"

"Of course he'll stay." Marjorie was at his side, her hand on his arm. Her touch scorched him, and Cormac forced himself not to flinch away.

"Angus will show you a room," Humphrey said, nodding at a wizened footman hovering just outside the door.

"Oh, good evening, Angus," Marjorie said warmly.

Cormac also nodded a greeting. Angus had been in her uncle's employ for as long as he could remember.

But he was losing focus. He'd seen Marjorie safely home, and it was time for him to find a room elsewhere. "Really, Humphrey, I canna—"

"Cormac MacAlpin." Marjorie's grip cut into his arm, startling him to silence. "You have ridden all day, and now you will rest."

He glanced down, taking in her profile. Her jaw was

set, and her vivid blue eyes glittered in the ambient light. She was thinking of his comfort. And yet there was no one in the world who seemed to be doing the same for her.

He didn't know why he was fighting the invitation. He'd be just as happy to be spared the hassle of finding a room at this late hour. There was nothing improper about taking Humphrey up on his hospitality.

Cormac decided to let himself get swept along in Marjorie's undertow. Just this once.

He kept his mouth shut, and amid bids for good nights, let her tug him from the room.

It wasn't until later, by the fire, that he regretted his decision. Regretted it deeply. His eyes burned from staring at the flames, and yet naught could dispel the memories that played over and over in his mind.

Him and Ree racing through the house at a game of lummelen. Challenging her at draughts, at chess. She'd clap and squeal when she won, and Cormac never begrudged her—he'd loved the triumphant flush of her cheeks too much.

How many hours had he, Marjorie, and Aidan spent playing rounds of hid? They'd each try to top the other, finding increasingly obscure hiding places. Places like the buttery, her mother's wardrobe, the privy.

The chimney.

He stared at the hearth, remembering a pile of cold ashes. An upturned grate. The screams of his brother.

Clenching his eyes shut, Cormac dropped his head against the chair back. He'd lost so much that day. His brother. His innocence. His joy.

His Ree.

"Cormac?" Marjorie's voice was muted, but he'd become so attuned to her, she could probably whisper from far away, and he'd still hear.

He braced himself for the sight of her. Attuned indeed. He was *painfully* aware of her, and it wasn't a pleasant sensation. "Aye?" he asked, raising his head slowly.

It was late, and the fire had burned low. Marjorie stood in the doorway, shrouded in darkness. Her hair was long and loose, and she'd dressed for bed. Though she had a tartan shawl wrapped tightly around her, a white night rail billowed about her legs. The fabric was fine, and it clung to the slope of her thighs.

He could pull her to stand before the fire. He could push the shawl from her shoulders. She'd stare up at him with those mysterious eyes. The gown would be sheer.

Cormac clenched his hand hard around his glass of brandy. *Damned brandy.* Whiskey was what a man really needed. What he wouldn't do for a bottle of whiskey and a good clout over the head.

"I wanted to make certain . . ." She hesitated, and then stepped into the room. Her bare feet were pale and delicate.

"Of?" The word came out sounding gruff. He slugged back the rest of his drink, welcoming the burn in his throat.

"Do you have all you need, then? Are you hungry?" she added in what struck him as a hopeful voice.

Damn her hope. Damn him and her both. He cut his eyes back to the fire, away from the sight of her. "Not hungry, no."

"Can you not sleep?" Her voice was gentle. She stepped closer, and he smelled the fresh, floral scent of her bath.

Shutting his eyes, he leaned his head back against the chair once more. He'd never be able to sleep now. "Please, Marjorie. Go back to your room and do not fash yourself on my account."

She didn't leave, though. He could feel her. Her presence charged the air, like a coming storm.

"Not once have I sat in this room and not thought of him," she said.

The rustle of her nightclothes told him she was sitting in the chair opposite him. The firelight would illuminate her. Would he be able to see the color of her skin beneath the white gown?

Cormac couldn't help but open his eyes. She was watching him. Good Christ, but she was beautiful. Orange light warmed her skin. He dreamed of touching it, just a quick stroke with the backs of his fingers. She'd be soft, like the petal of a flower.

"Why do you do this to yourself, Cormac? Sit here like this?"

"Nursing my demons." He raised his emptied glass in a mock toast. He wanted to get up and refill his brandy, but his body betrayed him. He'd stiffened the moment she walked in the room.

"Go rest now." She gently took the glass from his hand. "You said yourself, it's up at dawn to explore the docks."

He studied her, staring at him so unabashedly. Marjorie knew him well. Speaking of the task at hand was probably the only thing that could tear him from his reverie. "Aye, I'll be off to the quays at dawn."

Her eyes narrowed. "*We'll* be off at dawn."

He'd be damned if he let her risk her pretty hide down at the Aberdeen docks. But he was tired. Tired to his bones in a way that had naught to do with any physical exertion. He refused to let her go with him in the morning, but he'd not fight that particular battle with her just then.

"Ree." He let himself say her nickname, low and intimate, and it felt illicit on his tongue. Apparently there were a few things he was incapable of fighting that night.

"Cormac." She watched him expectantly, her chin jutted high, and it reminded him of the girl he'd adored. But there was nothing girlish about the way her shawl slipped further from her shoulders.

He couldn't stop his eyes from grazing down. With the firelight behind her, Marjorie's legs were outlined clearly through her gown, nude flesh beneath gossamer white. His groin tightened further. Clenching his teeth, he looked back at the fire. "Good night, then."

"Good night, Cormac," she whispered softly and drifted from the room.

He stared at the flames, listening to Marjorie's light tread on the stairs. He stared long after she'd have gone to bed. Staring at the fire reminded him of who he was. Of his mistakes, of his sins. Of what he was incapable of having.

Most importantly, staring at the fire kept him farther away from the temptation waiting upstairs. A beautiful woman, who'd be a balm to his soul and a spur to his loins.

A temptation he feared he was neither strong enough nor brave enough to withstand.

Chapter 8

"How does this . . . ? Fiona, do you know . . . ? How do you . . . ?" Marjorie wriggled, trying to hike Declan's breeches up over her hips. She finally just flopped onto the bed, scooching her bottom into the seat.

The maid stepped back, looking disgruntled that her bed-making progress had been interrupted. "I wonder how much of a gentleman your Cormac is."

"Got it!" Ignoring her comment, Marjorie popped up and bounced on the balls of her feet. "Oh, Fiona, this is lovely. So freeing. Is this what it feels like to be a man, I wonder?" She marched a few steps in place, lifting her feet high off the ground. "All women should be allowed to wear trews."

The maid shook her head disapprovingly. "What kind of gentleman allows a woman to wear his trews? No gentleman, I say."

"Oh, pish. You're too young to be such a wet rag." Marjorie wound her hair into a loose bun. "Besides, they're not Cormac's trews. They belong to his brother."

"But what sort of gentleman encourages a lady in his care

to stroll about town like a common . . . *commoner*? 'Tisn't seemly."

Marjorie's hands froze over her head. Fiona had been her maid since they were young girls, and so she allowed many liberties. But this was approaching the line. "It isn't town," she said warily. "Just down to the docks. And Cormac's not *encouraging* me."

"What business do you have down at the docks that you need to dress as a boy? And . . . wait." Fiona aggressively plumped a pillow. "Does Cormac even know what you're about?"

"Well, he's going to the docks, and I'd like to go with him. But if he says no, he can't stop me from following."

She heard Fiona gasp, and Marjorie sighed. She shouldn't be telling her maid so much. "You don't need to know any more than that. It's a private matter." She switched her focus to tucking her hair beneath a man's tartan bonnet. "There!"

"Not my business, she says." Behind her, Fiona snapped the bed cover, an indication of her pique. "It's unsafe. What would your uncle say if he found out?"

"Don't be silly. I'll be completely safe." Marjorie put her hands on her hips, studying her front and sides in the mirror. She'd bound her breasts as best she could—it wasn't perfect, but the man's shirt and vest did a good job concealing her form. "I think I'll pass. What do you think? Do I pass for a lad?"

Fiona made a choking noise. And then, realization washing over her face, she asked slyly, "Is this about that boy who went missing?"

"I'll just have to imagine that's your assent." Marjorie strode to the door, feeling lighter, unencumbered . . . *free*. Halfway out, she paused, turned. "And Fiona. I'll have you know, Cormac is every bit the gentleman."

She descended the stairs with a smile on her face. Dawn was just beginning to warm the sky, and she felt her way down, navigating the old steps through the gray half-light.

Reaching the landing, she stopped to adjust her outfit. She'd never thought herself overly curvy before, but the boxy trews were intended for someone with the silhouette of a tree. She plucked at the seat. The feel of such sturdy fabric between her legs was strange and uncomfortable, almost a transgression. Wiggling, she tugged them down, pulling them as low on her hips as she reasonably could.

The movement loosened the strips of woolen cloth she'd used to bind her breasts, and they tickled, making her senselessly itchy. She swayed a bit, jiggling her torso, trying to chafe the fabric along her skin. She felt a breast begin to slip free.

"Criminy." She smoothed her hands up her sides and along her breasts, trying to settle herself back in place. She frowned at the results. She'd never make it to the docks if she needed to stop every five 'minutes to readjust.

The sound of metal scraping on stone came from above. She looked up, startled. Cormac stood there, staring daggers down at her. He'd fastened a sword at his waist, and it rasped along the narrow stairway.

"You startled me," she said, a hand still clutched at her breast. "Losh, Cormac, where did you get that sword?"

"Where did you get those clothes?" Anger was plain in the set of his jaw, and waves of power rolled from him, as if he'd summoned some dark force to him, all vigor and strength.

A frisson of excitement shivered through her.

"I borrowed them from Declan." The statement was met with grim silence. "Your brother? Remember?"

"Would that I could forget," he grumbled.

Sensing a disagreement, she straightened her back, gathering her wits. Davie needed her, and she'd not fail him now. "I told you. I'm coming with you. I'm readying for the quays."

"And I told you, you're not." Every muscle in his body seemed to be flexed taut. Ready.

The thought flashed to her that she'd chosen the exact right person to help her. She'd woken nervous of the prospect of trolling the docks. But this man would protect her. He'd know how to handle any trouble that might come their way.

"Then I'll simply follow behind." The clock was ticking—they needed to find Davie fast, before whatever ship held him sailed away, if it hadn't already. The thought sent black spots across her vision. She turned and strode to the door, lest her knees buckle beneath her. "Two pairs of eyes are better than one. Davie is my lad to look after, and look after him I shall."

"You're staying," Cormac snarled.

She stopped in her tracks. "No, I am not."

"I'll be damned if any harm comes to you. How am I to sniff around the docks while keeping an eye out for your safety?"

"I don't need a nursemaid, Cormac." Setting her shoulders down and back, she spun to face him. "I will absolutely *not* stay here whilst you gad about the docks in search of a boy you wouldn't even recognize."

"You . . . you . . ."

She stared. "I *what*?"

"Och, woman, you try me. Listen to reason for once, would you? You need to be safe."

"You're the one with the great, big sword," she said with mock innocence. "Won't I be safer with you?"

"Aidan wasn't safer with me." The retort cracked rapidly from his mouth but then hung frozen in the air.

As sharp as any blade, his words gutted her. It came down to Aidan. Always Aidan.

Blame. Distrust. *This* was what it was all about. Marjorie had failed the boys so many years ago. Cormac feared she'd fail him once more.

"But—"

"Enough," he barked, cutting her off before she could speak. He hissed an exhalation, considering her. "I suspect I could tie you to a chair, and you'd still find a way to follow me to the docks."

Cormac could blame her all he wanted, but Davie was *her* responsibility. Davie was all that mattered. "I suspect I would."

"Fine."

"Fine," she repeated, giving him a triumphant nod. She turned to the door and was stopped by his hand on her shoulder. The heat of his touch imprinted upon her.

Cormac flinched away as though burned. "You may come. But you will not go dressed . . . like . . . that."

"Dressed like *what*?" She put her hands on her hips. The gesture had the unfortunate effect of straining the buttons along the front of her vest. Marjorie kept her voice steady, despite the furious blush she felt suffuse her entire face. "I'm pretending to be a boy."

His eyes flicked to her chest for the barest moment. "If you pass for a boy, I'm the king of England."

"This is my disguise, and I think it a very clever one."

"Clever?" His eyes went to her legs, and his whole body seemed to stiffen. "You can see . . ."

The feel of his eyes roving over her so boldly made her insides go weak. "See what?" she asked, her voice grown unintentionally husky.

Does he like what he sees?

"Your . . . legs. One can imagine . . ."

She became overly conscious of the trews. She'd felt so free before, but all she felt now was the fabric hugging tight between her thighs. "Imagine what?"

"One can imagine a lass getting her own self taken, wearing such a thing," he said, his voice finally finding its strength. "I'd never dreamed . . ."

"It's a disguise." Marjorie raised her chin high.

"It's indiscreet." He turned his back to her and seemed to be adjusting his sword belt. "Go and change."

"I know you, Cormac MacAlpin. If I go back up to my room, you'll leave without me."

"You're not safe dressed as you are."

"I'll be perfectly safe."

"Mind me, Marjorie," he gritted out. "And stop this stubbornness."

"*Mind you?* Mind *you*?" Her heart beat double time with her pique; she felt it glitter in her eyes, suffuse her cheeks.

"Aye." He spun to face her but then froze. He consumed her with his gaze, and her skin seemed to tighten over her body in response to the predatory scrutiny. Finally, he spoke again, and it came out a snarl. "Mind *me*."

"I promise to mind every word you say, the moment we set foot through these doors." She placed a hand on the heavy iron latch as though ready to begin then and there. "But as for my clothing, folk might recognize me from the work I do at Saint Machar, so no, Cormac," she said, backing against the door to shove it open. "A costume makes sense, and a costume I shall have."

He growled in frustration. "You're stubborn and impudent and . . ."

"And? And what, Cormac? I'll have you know I am still the same Marjorie after all these years."

"But you're not the same Marjorie," he shouted. Taking a deep breath, he devoured the sight of her hips, her legs. He spoke again, this time more subdued. "Believe me, the years have brought quite a few changes. Changes that aren't nearly hidden enough."

She sputtered, battling embarrassment, shame, and hot awareness. She remembered an older, greater shame, from that day so long ago.

"At least find yourself a cloak," he said.

"Fine. I'll wear a cloak." She'd weather his blame for the loss of his brother, but she'd not abide his intolerance. She would help find Davie. She *would* redeem herself. "But I don't trust you won't leave while I search for one. You may ask Angus to fetch me a man's cloak. One of his should suffice."

And, in the end, she was glad she had it. The thick wool of the man's bonnet and cloak didn't just warm her, they made her feel safer, too; the docks were a much grittier and more frightening place than she'd anticipated.

They'd reached the head of North Pier, stone pilings topped with rotting wooden planks that stretched like an arm into the sea. A sloop had newly docked, and he wanted to investigate.

The wind whipped off the water and found its way straight to her bones. The place smelled thick and briny, like sea creatures caught and left to rot. The morning sky was as gray as the water.

She was thankful it was daylight and thankful she had Cormac by her side. She thought about wee Davie. He was somewhere out there, facing all this alone. She was a grown woman, in daylight, and still the docks made her nervous. Young Davie, alone for days, and God only knew where? The boy would be terrified.

"Wait here," Cormac told her.

She gripped his arm. "Can't I come with you?"

"They have the look of smugglers about them." He nodded to the end of the pier. "I'd feel better if you stayed back."

"Is it safe for you?"

He barked a cynical and incredulous laugh. "Aye, lass, safe enough. Now truly," he added, scanning the area one last time, "you'll be fine for a few minutes. I'd not have a boatload of smugglers lay eyes on you. One clout on my head, and they'd have you on board before you knew what they were about. And then it'd be *you* I'd have to come searching for."

The thought terrified her. She'd never felt in true peril before in her life. At least not since the day Aidan was taken. But then she registered his last sentence. "You'd come to search for me?"

"Come for you?" Something gentle flickered in his eyes for the briefest of moments. "How could I not?"

The words warmed Marjorie to her soul. If he'd come for her, he didn't hate her. He might bear her blame, or resentment, but somewhere down deep he still valued her. "Fine, then. I'll wait here. But don't be long."

With a brisk nod, he was off down the pier, and in no time she was watching him talk to a shadowy figure on board the sloop.

A rustling of activity slowly emerged behind her, but Marjorie pretended to be engrossed only in a single point at the end of the dock. It wasn't so much an act, either. She refused to let Cormac out of her sight. And to think she'd threatened to come down here by herself.

A legless man on a cart rolled himself in front of her, staring up for a time before moving on. Shivering, she pulled the cloak's hood lower over her head. She wondered if, when they returned safely home, she should swallow her pride and thank Cormac for making her wear it.

"Aren't you a pretty laddie?" The voice was a slurred rasp, coming from over her shoulder. There was a laugh in response.

Her heart kicked against her chest. She felt the presence of two men standing behind her. She refused to tear her eyes away from Cormac. Surely he'd be done soon.

A hand brushed at her cloak. "What brings a pretty boy like you to the quays?"

"What are you looking at, laddie?" the second man asked, coming to stand shoulder to shoulder by her. Eyeing the sloop, he told his companion, "If laddie here has business with those runners, he's got money in his purse."

She ducked her head. So these men knew about the smugglers. Might they know something else? But how could she ask?

His companion came to stand on her other side. She could see both of them in her peripheral vision, one hulking, one tall and rangy. They smelled of ale gone foul.

"I'll wager we've got a wee lordling, fancying himself in for some sport, eh, Fergal? You don't mind if we have a look-see, do you now?" A hand tugged the hood from her head.

"Well, would you look here? 'Tisn't a laddie at all!" The tall man gripped her chin and gave it a wiggle, and she bit her lip not to scream. "What's a lovely crumpet like yourself doing here? Why don't you give us a peek under your coat, eh?"

"I am not a crumpet." She pulled from his grip, fighting to regulate her breathing, refusing to panic.

Cormac. Come back to me, Cormac.

Her fingers were numb from the grip she had on the front of her cloak. She definitely didn't want these men seeing her in the trews, which felt suddenly, scandalously too tight. "And what do you know of smugglers?" she challenged. "Do you know of men in these parts who . . . smuggle people?"

The men laughed. "Smuggle *people*?"

The voice of a third rose dark and menacing over the others. "What's a wee thing like you want to know about smuggling people?"

Terror prickled up the backs of her legs. *Three men.* How many more were there? She felt like a piece of raw meat that'd been tossed into a pit of dogs. The scent of blood was in the air, and there'd be no stopping the rush.

She poured her whole self into staring at Cormac, willing him to look at her. And look he did. He instantly stiffened, seeing the gathering around her. He said some final thing to the man on the boat and strode directly toward her. He rested a hand on his sword, and though the gesture was nonchalant, it was loaded with meaning.

She fought crumpling with relief.

"And who's this, then?" one of the men wondered, spotting him coming up the pier.

Worry slithered cold up her spine. What had she gotten them into? Surely these men had knives or even guns. Cormac was armed, but how would he fare against three men? They'd kill him and then take her.

Smuggling people indeed. Cormac's words came back to her, something about a lass getting her own self snatched from the docks.

Could she not do anything right? Because of her, Aidan had been taken. Would Cormac be killed because of her, too? She fisted her hands even tighter in her cloak.

"Seems we're not the only ones interested in our fine lass here. But she's so quiet." Someone tugged the bonnet from her head. Waves of long, light-brown hair spilled out, and they all laughed. "Such a fine thing you are, I might just smuggle you away myself. Why so quiet, luvvie? You won't be so quiet when I get you under me."

Cormac walked straight to her. His face was a mask of barely checked rage, and she knew a flicker of hope. They just might manage a way out of there. Their eyes locked, and he seemed to be trying to communicate something.

"Gentlemen," he said in a low, tight voice. He didn't take his eyes from her. "I see you've discovered our little secret."

The cold menace in his voice made her tremble. Shaking his head imperceptibly, he mouthed, "Hush."

"Who are you?" one of the men demanded.

"Aye, perhaps we'd like a wee cut of what you're about," another added with a nod toward the smuggler's boat.

"What we're about?" Cormac's voice was steady and calm. "Lass, are you ready to tell them what we're about?"

Her every muscle vibrated with tension. She didn't understand what he was trying to tell her.

There was a scraping of steel as one of the men unsheathed a blade.

"Are you ready?" Cormac asked her again quietly.

Ready? What could he possibly mean, *ready*?

The man with the rasping voice stepped just behind her. Marjorie shot him a backward glance. He looked mean, with black hair and murder in his eyes. He spoke through gritted teeth. "I said, who are you?"

Stricken with terror, she looked back to Cormac. The blue-gray of his stormy eyes grew eerily tranquil. They didn't waver from her. "Ready, Ree?" he asked in the barest whisper.

And then he winked.

She fought not to gape, wondering who this stranger before her really was. He'd disarmed her, and her voice cracked, "Aye, I'm rea—"

"Duck."

Chapter 9

Marjorie's knees buckled instinctively, and in the space of a heartbeat, Cormac's calm transformed into something else, something feral and raging.

She'd ducked, leaving Cormac facing the man who'd been standing behind her. A sword appeared in Cormac's hand, and in one stroke, he slashed the man's throat and swung around to thrust at another.

She covered her head as blood spilled on her shoulders and hands. Marjorie buried her mouth in the crook of her arm, fighting not to scream.

The man crumpled just behind her, and finally she squealed, spinning around to skitter backward down the pier, where she knelt with a hand to the ground. She didn't trust her legs to stand.

Fighting to control her fear, she made herself watch. Her Cormac, the boy she'd loved, had become some other creature: powerful, brave, strangely placid—and ruthless.

One man was down, and Cormac had just stabbed one of the two remaining. It was the burly one, and his torso was so thick, the slash to his chest incapacitated him for only a moment. He quickly regrouped and was coming at Cormac with vengeance in his eyes and a peculiar sword in his fist.

She put a hand to her mouth, frozen in terror. How had she not seen the man's sword before this? It was enormous and curved, a terrible, foreign thing, looking like something from Arabia, and it was ugly, too, its blade gray, with ghastly dings along its surface.

Would this be how Cormac met his end? On a sordid pier, at the end of a ruffian's blade? It would be her fault.

The thought was so painful, she shut her eyes for a moment to withstand it. She couldn't bear another life on her hands. Not Cormac's. She opened her eyes. She wouldn't let him face this alone. Slowly, Marjorie stood.

"Stay down," Cormac growled. He took a quick step, placing himself between her and the two men. He blindly swung a hand back to push her to the ground, but she bobbed out of the way.

The gesture opened Cormac's chest to his attacker, and the man lunged forward, throwing his whole body behind his sword. Broadsword held close to his chest, Cormac blocked the thrust, grunting with the effort. He edged backward, swinging his blade in short slices, but his opponent kept parrying and hopping closer, too close for Cormac's sword to find momentum.

While Cormac and his opponent fought, the other man homed in on Marjorie. He was gangly and smiling, and it sent a chill up her spine. He nodded at her, waggling his dirk playfully.

Narrowing her eyes, she shuffled slowly to the side, to the man lying dead and bloody on the ground. Swallowing back a rush of bile to her throat, she squatted, snatching a dirk from the scabbard at the dead man's waist. She'd not let Cormac fight alone.

Cormac saw what the fool woman was about, and he snarled. He looked away quickly, not wanting to call attention to her. But he vowed, if they got out of this alive, he'd take great pleasure in tanning her hide. *Braw, fool lass.*

He redoubled his attack. His opponent struck him as a dim sort, but a canny fighter. Cormac had fought against a few curved sabers in his time, but never a scimitar. Its inner edge was blunt, and his opponent cradled the blade close, thrusting with his whole body.

It wasn't the typical clashing of swords that Cormac was used to, and he couldn't step back far enough to get a good strike in.

"Say a prayer," his opponent rasped. "'Tis a heathen weapon, but sure." Steadying his scimitar below his forearm, the man made a short stab at Cormac's chest.

"A pretty blade," Cormac managed, dashing the thrust away with the flat of his sword. The man jumped forward, and Cormac edged back, feeling the lip of the pier at his heel. He spied a low post for tying up boats and spun around his opponent toward it. He slashed as he went, grazing the man's calf with his blade. "But pretty is as pretty does."

The man looked down at his leg, incredulous. "Enough chatter." He ran to Cormac, his scimitar hugged diagonally across his chest.

Just then, Marjorie screamed.

Cormac would die before he let anyone hurt her. But he couldn't spare her a look. His fight had reached a critical point. He had to keep his focus. He'd get only one opportunity, and that but a mere flicker in time.

Balancing along the edge of the pier, Cormac rushed the man. Slamming his free hand onto his opponent's shoulder, he vaulted past him, onto the post.

The man spun, momentarily startled, and Cormac didn't lose a moment. He leapt back down, arcing his sword through the air, cleaving the man between neck and shoulder.

The dead man toppled into the water with a loud splash, and Cormac instantly turned his attention to Marjorie. The last attacker held a knife to her throat. Though her chest shuddered with fear, she held her chin high.

They locked eyes, hers brave and vivid blue. Pride filled him. Pride and terror.

"I ken you," the man told her with surprise in his voice. "You're the pretty piece from Saint Machar. Ye gave me sommit once. A heel o' bread." The man waggled his brows. "Time tae give me more than that, aye?"

The last of Cormac's patience flamed out in a blaze of anger. Not taking his eyes from her, he calmly resheathed his sword.

The movement caught the man's attention. "And what's this pretty piece to you?" he asked, giving Marjorie a shake.

Cormac remained silent, his eyes only for Marjorie. She remained stoic, her blank face belying the shuddering rise and fall he saw clear in her chest.

The man jerked his head to the end of the dock. "Move along, you."

"Move along?" Cormac asked placidly, shifting a blank-eyed gaze to the man. Making his body loose, he casually reached behind him, to the dagger he kept tucked in the small of his back. It was long for throwing, but he'd no other choice. Besides, he was confident fury would guide his aim. "Aye, I'll move along."

Cormac's slackened muscles hardened in an instant, and his arm lashed out, his blade landing with a dull suck into the flesh of the man's shoulder. "But I'll take my woman with me," he said with utter serenity.

The man shouted, letting go of Marjorie to pull the blade from his body. He was injured but not downed.

Marjorie spun, and Cormac spied the blade glittering in her small hand. The fool woman was meaning to charge.

"No," Cormac snarled under his breath. He couldn't let her fight, couldn't let her spill a man's blood. He knew Ree; her conscience wouldn't bear it.

Marjorie pulled her arm back and lunged for the man, crying out with the effort.

"No!" Cormac shouted. He couldn't let her sully her soul; his was sullied enough for the two of them.

He sized up the scene in the fraction of a heartbeat. He'd no time to draw his sword, nor could he risk Ree getting in its trajectory if he did. He had his hands, though.

Cormac leapt, tackling the man around his upper thighs just as Marjorie's blade arm swept down. She missed, spouting a brazen curse that shot a surge of inexplicable delight to his heart. *Always a spitfire, Ree was.*

He rolled on the quay, tussling with her attacker, finally managing to pin him from above. And then the man's feet hammered against the rotted wooden planks as Cormac choked the life from him.

Cormac sprang up and ran to her. "Ree, look at you." She was trembling and covered in blood. Pulling her to him, he refused to think on the sweet wonder of her in his arms. "You braw, wee thing."

He'd almost lost her. The thought was unbearable. The lass had placed herself in harm's way because she was stubborn, and she was impudent. *And brave, and magnificent.* Hugging her closer, he let the entire length of her soft body cradle close against his.

"He recognized me," she said, her voice shaking with shock. She pulled away, and he saw the fear in her eyes. "He knew me, Cormac."

He took in the two bodies littering the rotted wooden planks. "Aye, lass, I know it. Come," he said, leading her from the pier. "Cover yourself with your cloak. We must be away from this place."

"I . . . I'm worried." She tucked back into him as they walked, her breathing gradually slowing to normal. "What if someone else saw me? What if this leads back to my uncle's house? We have to keep him safe." She bit at her lip. "Oh God, I can't believe little Davie is out there with men like *that.*"

"Aye, we'll need to keep your uncle safe," Cormac told her. He glanced behind him, casting one last look at the dock. The smugglers' boat bobbed, heedless of what'd been just another fight along the quay. "I need a plan good enough that all eyes turn from him."

He gently pulled her chin up to look at him. She'd foolishly dressed herself in men's clothing, in trews that had revealed scandalous curves, clinging to her long, firm legs like sin itself.

When he'd come downstairs that morning to find her rubbing her breasts beneath her vest . . . He scowled. He had almost spilled his seed at the sight. How would a boatload of lecherous sailors react to the sight of her?

"You must stay out of this from now on."

"What should our plan be?" she asked, dismissing his last statement as he knew she would.

"*My* plan will be to continue hunting the docks for information, while you're safe at home." He directed them up a side street, toward the direction of Market Green. He felt too exposed near the docks and would have them surrounded by the morning's market bustle instead.

"I thought we just agreed we needed to keep away from Uncle Humphrey's house."

"No," he said, stiffening. "We just agreed that *I* will devise a plan while *you* stay safe."

"But—"

"But nothing, Marjorie."

She raised her brows in challenge at the formal sound of her name on his lips.

"You try me, woman." He pulled them into the shadow of a tavern that'd already begun to hum with the day's business. "Was that scene by the docks not enough for you? I refuse to see you in harm's way. One more man, and I might not have managed them."

"I helped," she protested.

"You did indeed." He let out a disbelieving chuckle and took her hands in his to study them. Using the edge of his plaid, he wiped a smear of blood from her palm. "But at what cost? Heed me," he said, waiting for her eyes to meet his. "From this moment on, I go alone. I will keep you safe, and that means keeping you away from smugglers and dock men."

Her countenance brightened, remembering something. "Did the smugglers give you any information?"

He narrowed his eyes. The smugglers had told him much, and God help him, their words had stirred the embers of hope in his chest. But it was a dangerous game they played, and he'd keep her well away from it. He studied her, staring up at him expectantly, her eyes fever bright. He'd need to sneak away from her somehow, deal with this alone. "They say there's a ship docked in Justice Port."

She gave a grim nod. Justice Port was infamous for being the roughest, the foulest of all areas in Aberdeen.

"They say it's stocked with folk to be sold as slaves in America." Her face fell, but he kept her chin cupped tenderly in his hand, not letting her look away. "But Ree, don't you see? You were right. Your wee Davie just might be alive after all." He nodded to the distant waters of the North Sea, lightening to a steel gray in the morning's haze. "Alive, and out there. Somewhere."

"Will you find him for me, Cormac?" She sniffled and stood up straighter. She had a look in her eyes that stilled him. A look of hope, of trust, of admiration reserved for him alone. No one else had ever looked at him that way. "Please?"

"Aye, lass," he said, knowing he was lost, knowing he'd do anything for this woman in his arms. "I'll find him for you."

Chapter 10

Marjorie was changed and out of the house in no time, off to see what she could discover about Justicc Port from the most wayward, unlawful folk she knew: the boys of Saint Machar.

They were close to finding Davie, and she hadn't a moment to spare. She'd forsaken the midday meal for a slice of bread and bit of hard cheese, which she carried with her to eat while she walked. If she got too hungry, she could always grab something from the ministers at Saint Machar. There was always a pot with stew to spare at Westhall Manse, part of the cathedral complex, and the mainstay of their charity work.

Westhall stood at the end of Chanonry Road, nearly in the shadow of Saint Machar, which was a granite sprawl in comparison. It was a stout building and one of the few that'd been left largely untouched by the wars. They used the triangular upper story as a dormitory, while the ground floor saw to the vast cooking, feeding, and general tending necessitated by all those boys.

She was proud of what they'd built. She'd been coming

to Saint Machar for years now, and before she'd begun offering her assistance, Westhall had offered nothing but a few cots and the occasional cold rations for the wayward poor of Aberdeen's streets.

She spotted a close-cropped head of black hair among the boys seated at a long dining table. Marjorie smiled. She'd never known Paddy to miss a meal.

Before he sat down, she swooped in from behind, grabbing his attention by mussing her hand atop his head. Soon he'd be too big for such a gesture. All the boys seemed to grow like weeds once they got regular food and rest. "Just who I was looking for."

Paddy looked up, and his eyes widened. "But today's not your day," he exclaimed. The boy was surprised, and she saw both pleasure and anxiety on his face. She surmised the latter came from pure instinct. He'd lived for years on the street, alone and on guard, and some habits were hard to break. "You're not supposed to be here on Saturday."

"Perhaps I came just to see you." His prickly response had put her on alert. Paddy was one of her most challenging cases. He'd been like a feral thing when she'd found him, but years of tough love—not to mention daily meals—had begun to turn him around.

"Though I wonder . . . have you done something wrong, Paddy?" Her hand shifted to pinch one of his ears between her fingers. They protruded comically, sticking out like two Spanish apricots from either side of his head. She leaned closer, eyes narrowing as she registered the fresh scab on his face. "And pray tell, *what* is that on your cheek?"

"I've done nothing wrong. I swear it!" His eyes darted right and left, and she knew he'd be eager to map his escape. He'd been doing it all his life. He'd come with his family from Ireland when he was but a wee thing. Typhus had taken his parents not long thereafter, and Paddy soon learned how to fill his belly by picking pockets. Marjorie had just about gotten the boy turned around, but success was a fragile thing, and he was still one of the toughest, most fight-happy kids at Saint Machar.

"Don't panic," she assured him, guiding him from the dining hall. "You're not in trouble. In fact, there might be a bit of steak pie in it for you." She patted her pocket, gesturing to the carefully wrapped packet she'd hidden there. She wasn't above treating—or bribing—the boys with extra food and regularly brought goodies from her uncle's home. "I merely have some questions that I think you might be able to answer. *While* I tend to your cheek."

Stools before the kitchen fire marked the warmest spot in Westhall, and as the cooking was finished for the time being, that's where she settled them. She handed him the meat-filled pastry, and he pounced on it with relish.

"How'd you manage this one, Paddy?" Marjorie scooted her seat closer to his. "It has the suspicious look of a fist to it. Ah, yes." She tilted his cheek toward the firelight for a closer look. "I see the scrape of . . . I daresay that might be the mark of someone's *ring*?"

He shrugged, chewing an outrageously stuffed mouthful of food.

She set to swabbing the cut clean with a damp rag. "How did you get it?"

He merely shrugged again.

"A ring." She looked closer at the imprint of a perfect red circle. A signet ring, she'd wager. "Fighting with men now, are we? Paddy, what am I to do with you? I swear it, you are the brightest lad here, but you won't make it to your fifteenth birthday if you keep this up."

Swallowing, he murmured, "I mighta accidentally stepped in front of a fist."

"You weren't playing the cutpurse again, were you?" She lowered her voice. "You made me a promise."

He pulled his chin from her hand, suddenly earnest. "Oh, no. Losh no! I promised, and I'd never break a promise. Not to you, Miss Marjie."

"Yes, I know." Smiling, she scruffed his short hair. Her boys were the only ones she'd let call her Marjie.

And Paddy could call her whatever he liked, just so long as he stayed alive and out of trouble. "But you must think of what's good for yourself, too. Not just what I might think."

Glancing down, she saw a tear in his breeches. "The knee, too, Paddy? Truly. This was a perfectly sound piece of clothing just yesterday."

"I'm sorry."

Her shoulders fell. Sometimes it felt like she was fighting a losing battle. "No matter. I'll stitch them for you—"

"Don't be mad at me, Miss Marjie. I was just trying to help, really I was."

She stilled. "Help what?"

"Well, I knew you've been sad about Davie. And I thought . . ."

"What did you think?" she asked, her every nerve thrumming with alarm.

He froze, eyes widened like a deer scenting danger.

"Answer me, Padraig, and don't think I won't tweak that ear of yours again." She reached her hand out, waggling her fingers menacingly. "It stands out like a flag in the wind, just begging to be—"

"I'll tell, I'll tell! I went down to the docks is all. I was careful!" he added quickly, seeing the scold in her eyes. "I just asked some questions, you know, of some of the other lads."

"I told you to stay away from there. After Davie . . ." She tapered off. Her legs felt weak, and she was glad she was seated. If any harm came to any of the other boys in her care, she didn't think she could survive it.

And then fear flicked into hard panic. When had Paddy gone to the docks? What if she'd been discovered? She dreaded the thought of what would become of her if Archie or any of the other Saint Machar folk got wind of her traipsing around the docks in men's clothing.

Paddy chewed thoughtfully, and the look on his face went from worried to thoughtful to confident. He swiped his hand across his mouth, wiping away the last of the pastry crumbs. "What questions?"

"What?" She focused, unwilling to lose the upper hand in the conversation.

"You said *you* had questions for *me*." He lifted his chin. "And so I said, what questions?"

"Changing the subject, are you?" She pursed her lips, fighting not to smile. He certainly was one of the brightest boys she'd ever met. "Deftly done, Paddy. I've always said you're a canny one."

He raised his brows, still waiting for her to answer.

She took a deep breath, conceding. "Fine. We shall address my questions first. But don't you for one moment think I'll forget about this business with you down at the docks."

She waited for him to nod wary agreement, then continued, "I came to ask you once more about the morning Davie disappeared. If you remember *anything*."

"I told it all, Miss Marjie. I seen him with the other lads in the alley," he said, repeating by rote what he'd told her a dozen times already. "They'd worked a bit of rawhide into a ring, and they'd gotten some sticks, and were having a game of quoits. And then I seen him later. With . . ." His voice tapered off, cutting his eyes shyly to hers.

"I know it. You saw Davie with me. He disappeared just after he'd been with me." Pain lanced her, and she pushed it away. There must be something from that day she'd missed. Some clue. She leaned down, taking Paddy's hands in hers. "Think on it, sweet. For me. Think on it one more time. Was there anyone strange? There'd have been the other lads. There'd have been a few folk like me. There would've been market hucksters. Some dockmen, mayhap. But anyone else? Do you recall anyone strange?"

He scrunched his brows in deep and apparently painful thought. "There was one man. I didn't think on it then . . ."

A man. It couldn't be so easy. Her heart beat faster nonetheless. "What makes you think on it now?"

"Well, I seen him yesterday. At the docks. And I remembered him from that day with Davie."

"What made you remember?"

He pulled his hands from hers and stared sullenly at them, flexing and fisting them in his lap.

"Paddy?" She knew boys well, and she knew this one was holding something back. "What aren't you telling me?"

"Well . . ."

He picked at the skin around his nails, and she reached for him again, squeezing his fingers to quiet him. "It's all right, Paddy. I won't be angry. Please, though. You must tell me."

"He looks like all the other men. Just some middling lord. But then I saw the coin purse tied at his waist. And I remembered, I'd seen him that day, too, the day Davie was took. I didn't do nothing wrong," he added quickly. "I swear it. But even if I don't do no cutpursing no more, don't mean I don't have eyes, and this were a big, brown pouch, sure filled with coin. I saw it that day, and I saw it again yestreen. I'd swear it was the same man, both days."

"What'd he look like?" she asked steadily. Energy crackled to life, zipping up her spine and to her fingertips. She was onto something. Paddy was a sweet boy, and he'd turned his life around, but he had seen some tough times and had a nose for trouble like no other.

"He . . ." Paddy shrugged. "He looked like other men."

"He looked like other men," she repeated. "So, an average-looking man? Was he the one who hit you?"

"Aye." Paddy reached up, running his finger over his scab. "He thought I was after his purse."

Was he? She'd need to think on that later. First, she needed to find out what Paddy knew. The pertinent clues that he didn't even realize he knew. She leaned closer to start her interrogation.

Cormac leaned in the doorway watching Marjorie tend

some alley rat. He folded his arms at his chest, marveling at her spirit. If he'd expected her to cower at home in fear after the incident at the docks, he realized now he'd been gravely wrong.

The news he'd gathered at the docks gave him hope that this Davie still lived. He'd come to Saint Machar to question the other lads, but blast it if she hadn't beat him there. He fought the aggravating sensation that once again he found himself following in her wake.

Westhall Manse. His eyes scanned the kitchen, a grim chamber bearing sooty walls and the smell of charred meat. *Manse* indeed.

His eyes went back to Marjorie. She hadn't seen him yet, so engrossed was she with the boy. Clearly she'd come for her usual charity work. He realized he'd never asked her exactly what that work entailed. He watched as she gingerly swabbed the boy's cheek.

So good, so true. That was Marjorie. She'd always been thus. Full of vinegar she might be, but she'd always been kind to the core. Most lasses would've been broken after Aidan's kidnap. But Ree was made of stronger stuff. She'd turned her pain into something else, directing it to good and charitable works.

He watched her take the boy's hands in hers. Her manner was easy, unthreatening, like he might be with a skittish horse. The expression on her face was heart-breakingly tender. The two of them sat before the fire, and a warm, orange glow played over her gown, casting deep amber shadows beneath curves that he suddenly longed to touch, to trace, to cup in his hand.

Marjorie sat in a grim, reeking kitchen, yet somehow she still managed to appear elegant. She still managed to be the most beautiful creature he'd ever laid eyes on.

Cormac shook his head. He needed to focus on the task at hand. Such foolish, boyish notions were not for him. He came for a reason: to question the other lads. Not to get swept away by base urges or by feelings that threatened to unman him.

Still, he stepped toward her helplessly, eager to prolong the moment. He wanted to overhear the gentle words she'd be speaking to the boy. He felt a stab of anguish, mourning the boy *he'd* been.

"So out with it," she was telling the lad. "What did you discover at the docks?"

Cormac's stomach fell. It wasn't the tenderhearted Ree caring for this alley rat's wounds; it was the brazen one. Charitable she might be, but he'd never known the woman to step down from a challenge, and it was *that* woman who'd be the death of him.

He marched over to them. "I told you *I'd* find the boy for you."

"Cormac." She looked up with wide eyes.

She was clearly unsettled to see him, and he felt oddly gratified. The woman could use a good dose of apprehension. She had entirely too much pluck. It was what had led to the fight at the docks. The memory recalled his surliness with a vengeance.

"Westhall," he said flatly, looking around him, gathering his wits. "Not much of a manse, is it?"

"It suits our needs." She dabbed the boy's injury one last time. "That's all for you, Paddy."

The lad glanced nervously between them, lifting his chin at Cormac's answering glare. Damned if the gesture didn't put him in mind of Marjorie. Much to his aggravation, the boy looked to her for direction.

"It's all right, sweet." She patted his knee. "You can go. And thank you."

Her quiet smile for the boy made Cormac even angrier. "What are you about, sending mere lads to investigate for you at the docks?" he asked the moment the boy disappeared from the kitchen.

"I did no such thing." She stood, outraged. They were closer than he'd realized, and she had to tilt her face up to hold his gaze. He felt the maddening urge to cup the back of her head.

"Paddy went to the docks of his own accord," she said

sharply. "I was merely asking him what he'd learned. You said yourself that I was right, that Davie is alive and out there somewhere."

"Aye, but I didn't mean *you* should be the one to chase him down. It's a man's job."

Her face was blank for a curious moment, and then Marjorie startled him by laughing. "You don't know me very well if you think I'll just sit by and wait for you to save Davie."

She was right. He'd underestimated her. He had no idea whom she'd become. He found he wanted to know.

Instead, he only stepped closer. "That's exactly what I think."

Someone entered the kitchen, and she pitched her voice to a low, angry whisper. "Don't misunderstand me, Cormac. I appreciate your help. But if you won't let me be a true partner to you, then I will be forced to pursue this on my own as well."

Someone cleared their throat. "Pardon, mum?"

"What?" she and Cormac snapped in unison, still staring daggers at each other.

"Lord Murray was looking for you."

Cormac's eyes narrowed. "Who's Murray?"

"Archie Murray." She told him in a tight whisper. "A friend."

Archie. He recognized the name from the conversation he'd overheard. It was the man who'd supposedly sworn to help her. "Is that the fop who lets you lead him about by the nose? What does *he* want?"

"Archie is no fop!"

"Well who is he, then? Some pretty lordling? Can he protect you?" Cormac felt chagrin at the nobleman he'd never be and shame at his inability to protect his own loved one so many years ago. The raw emotions made his words come sharp. "Answer me."

"*He* appreciates the work I do."

"You haven't answered the question." Some foreign emotion burned through him, turning his blood to acid.

Jealousy? he wondered distantly, and dismissed the thought at once. It was vexation he felt. That was all. Marjorie was a vexatious, exasperating, uncooperative, senseless woman. "Who in hell is he?"

"He's training to be a physician surgeon," she announced proudly. "He offers his help each week, tending to the physical ailments of the poor folk of Saint Machar."

"A student?" he scoffed. "And what? He'll throw books at the smugglers and dock men? You honestly think this Archie will be of help to you?"

"Yes."

He turned to stalk out. "Then to the devil with both of you."

"The devil," she called after him. "Why, Cormac, I'd thought that was you."

Chapter 11

"Archie!" Marjorie exclaimed, sweeping into her uncle's drawing room the following morning. The day was overcast, and watery light filtered in through the windows, but Archie's easy countenance perked up the dreary room.

He came to her side, taking her hands eagerly in his. "Marjorie, my dear."

"Archie, what an unexpected surprise." He was so tall and lean, and his long, thin hands were always so chilled. She paid mind to not letting her smile flag.

Her maid bustled in close behind, bearing a tray of refreshments.

"Ah!" Face brightening, he let Marjorie's hands slip from his. "Your lovely maid."

Marjorie could've sworn she heard Fiona mutter, "Now *there's* a gentleman."

She frowned. Fiona was right. If only *Cormac* would show her a warm greeting once in a while. She surreptitiously scanned the room, but he was nowhere in sight.

Good. She'd seen him only once since their conflagration in the Westhall kitchen, and the silence between

them had been deafening. He didn't want her help, and it
goaded her. The man was brooding, and he was just as
stubborn as he'd ever been as a boy.

Archie gravitated toward Fiona and the tray of food.
"Shortbread. How delightful. There's nothing better than
a bit of mid-morning sweet."

Fiona blushed.

Marjorie wandered to the tray, eyeing it blindly. Could
it be that Cormac wanted her to stay away because she'd
mucked things up so horribly in the past? With Aidan,
and now again with Davie?

She must've made some inadvertent sound, because
Archie turned to her as he swallowed his shortbread, concern clear on his face. "Marjorie, my dear. You must tell
me how I can be of service."

She took in the sight of him. Upright, clean-shaven,
well-dressed . . . the man practically glimmered with
principle. Would that she could preoccupy herself with a
man like *Archie*.

Blasted Cormac.

She harrumphed. Blast that she even thought about
blasted Cormac.

Well, she didn't give a tinker's curse about his censure.
She'd work to find Davie on her own. Still, it wouldn't hurt
for him to see her efforts and successes. She pitched her
voice a little louder, in case Cormac was within hearing
range. Even though she hadn't seen him, she suspected he
was lurking somewhere close at hand. "Oh, Archie, it's
always so nice to see you."

He seemed surprised by the enthusiastic statement.
With a nervous smile, he brought his hands protectively
to her shoulders, and she felt a rush of affection. Dear,
awkward Archie. Their mutual charitable interests had
led them both to Saint Machar, where for the past few
years she'd assisted him in treating the many boyhood
injuries and illnesses that appeared on their doorstep. She
fancied she had quite the knack for it.

"I came the moment I heard," he told her earnestly.

"There'll be trouble for sure," Fiona said, busying herself straightening chairs that didn't need straightening.

Marjorie gently pulled free, darting a sharp look at the maid. "What did you hear, exactly, Archie?"

"I heard you spoke with Paddy. That there was some distress by the docks." Pulling his shoulders back, he stood even more upright than he'd already been. "I, of course, came here straightaway. Fiona has told me everything."

An alarming clattering noise came from the maid's direction. Marjorie cut her another glance. When had she and Archie had an opportunity to talk? The young woman flushed pink as a radish and proceeded to give her complete attention to dusting a set of glass bowls displayed along the hearth.

She'd been around since they'd both been girls and were of an age. That Fiona would spill secrets to Archie came as an intriguing surprise. As intriguing as that telling blush.

"What do you mean, everything?" She looked from the blond physician to her busty, blushing maid, and back again.

"Marjorie, dear Marjorie," he scolded. "What were you thinking to go down to the docks like that?"

"'Tweren't thinking at all, more like," the maid said under her breath.

"That will be all, Fiona." Marjorie gave her a meaningful look, and the young woman scampered from the room. She turned to face Archie with her chin held high. "It's not as though I was alone."

"Who is this man you went with?" he demanded. "Where is he?"

Yes, Cormac, where indeed? She glanced at the doorway. It'd do Cormac good to hear another so concerned with her. Unlike Archie, Cormac managed to be protective yet somehow dismissive at the same time.

"I'd meet the scoundrel who'd lead you into such peril."

"Be easy, Archie." If only *Cormac* felt such enthusiasm—above and beyond his usual litany of grim protestations. "Cormac fought in the wars. He knows what he's about."

"Why did you not ask *me* to help? While at Marischal College, I met many men in positions of great importance. The bailie himself is a friend of my father's."

Marjorie spotted a shadow cross the doorway. She knew it. "Cormac will no longer allow my interference," she told him, casting her voice loudly enough for their eavesdropper. "Perhaps *you'd* be so kind as to bring me to the docks."

Archie looked instantly alarmed, and so she quickly amended, "To meet your many and varied important contacts, that is."

But still, neither word nor movement came from the hall. Gathering her nerves, Marjorie reached her hand out and allowed Archie to take it. "I know you'll keep me safe."

Behind the doorway, Cormac flinched.

He'd heard a man enter the house, heard Archie announced. And damned if he hadn't come straightaway to get an inkling of their conversation. Lurking like some spy, instead of entering with ease, interacting like any other man would. Scouting, spying . . . killing in the shadows. It seemed all he'd ever been good for.

"Aiding you, my precious Marjorie?" Archie proclaimed, gripping her hand in both of his. "Protecting *you*? 'Twould be my greatest honor."

He's more earnest than a vicar on Sunday. And the weasel was holding her hand like a greedy schoolboy. Cormac glowered. *Archie the physician surgeon.*

He'd die before letting such a man take Marjorie to the docks. He looked to be a weak bastard. There was not a strand out of place in his shining yellow hair. Cormac raked his hand through his own hair. When was the last time *he'd* had a good barbering? He shrugged it off. A real man paid more attention to the safety of his family than to his damned coiffure.

Marjorie pulled her hand away, and Cormac grinned.

She turned to the window, and he watched as Archie quickly smoothed and adjusted his waistcoat. *The weak bastard would never be able to protect her.*

"I would love to take you to the docks." Archie followed her like a besotted spaniel. "I've been waiting for you but to say the word."

I'll imagine you have.

"You must let *me* protect you," Archie said. He moved closer to her.

Cormac bristled. *Step back.*

"Not this ruffian, this scoundrel, this . . . MacAlpin fellow. I don't even see him," Archie exclaimed, incredulous, sweeping his hand to gesture across the room. "The tragedy writ on your bonny face, dear Marjorie? Well, it breaks my heart. But this *Cormac*? He doesn't even care enough to be here. To turn your frown into a smile." He chucked her chin, and Cormac's stomach turned.

Marjorie edged away from him.

There's my Ree.

Archie studied her back, and his flat eyes reminded Cormac of a pig. A lanky, glassy-eyed pig. The swine hesitated for a moment and then went to stand beside her, bringing his hand to rest at the base of Marjorie's spine. "I'll be in touch with my contacts forthwith."

Cormac's entire body seized. *The gall.* To touch her so. To touch Marjorie where *he'd* always dreamed of touching her. Who was this man to grope her so? Cormac made a sound like a growl, low in his throat.

There was an infinitesimal shift in Archie's features. The man was considering something. He shifted. And then he swept his arm up and all the way around Marjorie's shoulders. "*I* will take care of matters now."

That was it. Cormac strode into the room, grabbed the popinjay by the shoulders, spun him around, and punched him in the jaw.

"Cormac!" Marjorie screamed. "What are you doing?"

"I'm doing what should've been done ten minutes ago."

He flexed his fist. The contact was deeply satisfying. He wondered if he should opt for a second.

"Are you all right?" she exclaimed, rushing to the other man's side.

Cormac instinctively hugged her from behind, pulling her away. Abruptly, he let her go. "I can't believe you let this man touch you."

"Get a hold of yourself this instant!" she ordered.

Ignoring her, he leaned in, snarling in Archie's face. "You will leave here. You will never touch Marjorie again. Never will you even *think* of touching her again."

Archie stumbled backward. "I . . ." he gasped. "I'm afraid I should be going. I simply wanted to help. I shouldn't have interfered so."

"Oh, Archie." Marjorie slumped. "Are you all right?"

"Yes, fine, fine." Archie coughed. "I'm afraid I really must be going. But my offer stands. Despite what this barbarian might say to you."

She nodded grudgingly, her eyes lingering on the angry welt blooming on his jaw. "Find Fiona on your way out. Mayhap cook has a bit of Solomon's seal for that bruise."

Cormac shook his head in disgust as the coward left the room.

"What were you thinking?" He felt Marjorie storm up to his back. "Why ever did you do that?"

He wasn't entirely sure. "I didn't like the way that man gaped at you," he told her, unable to meet her eyes.

"And what's it to you how men look at me?"

What indeed? He took a deep breath and turned to face her. She'd stepped up into his face, her little spitfire body threatening his, and though the difference in size should make her intimidation absurd, her proximity nearly unmanned him. "It's unseemly."

"Are you saying *I'm* unseemly?" She pointed her finger into his chest, and the heat of her body roared like a bonfire, searing straight to his bones.

"I'm saying he had no right to touch you."

"It was innocent!" She flattened her hand, her pointed finger becoming a palm flat against his chest. "*You've* touched me."

"No. Yes. Mayhap." He took a step back, knocking his heel against the wooden baseboard. *Touch her.* He *could* touch her. He could grab her hand from his chest, twine her fingers with his. He could bring his hands to her shoulders to pull her close. What if she let him?

"So *you* do have the right?" She edged even closer, and this time he let her.

He stared at her mouth. What was she saying? How should he respond?

"Do *you* have the right to touch me?" Her hand curled, his shirt fisting in her hand. "You certainly don't seem to have any problem ordering me about."

"Because you're reckless, lass." It was reckless to stand so close to him. Didn't Marjorie know he was a dark shell of a man? He was all anger and emptiness and wanting. It was risky even to be near him, unsafe to press her body so close. "You don't listen, and it's dangerous."

Her face fell, and he regretted his words at once.

"I'd thought you could forgive me," she said quietly. "But I was wrong. You blamed me then, and you blame me still."

She turned to leave. He'd spoken without thought, and she'd badly misunderstood. Cormac wanted to take back his words, to tell her this had naught to do with Aidan nor Davie nor any boy, but with her own safety. But by the time an apology came to him, all he saw was the slow swing of the door.

Marjorie had slipped from the room.

Hours passed, and finally Cormac could bear it no longer. He'd been a boor, and he sought out Marjorie to apologize. He didn't for a minute regret punching Archie, but damned if that fool lordling didn't made him feel like less than a gentleman in comparison.

And so Cormac had been to the library, the solar, the

gardens, and now the sitting room, but the woman had simply disappeared.

It made him angry. He'd been back in her life for less than a week, and it seemed all he did was chase after the lass. She was always scampering one step ahead, and it was driving him mad.

It'd been that way as children, too. Though he'd been enthralled then. Now he just found this . . . absorption . . . galling. He slammed his fist against the doorway and then, scowling, shook it out. He'd not punched anything in some time. How was it he found himself two for two by noontime?

He'd simply go to her rooms. He nodded and headed to the stairs. Surely he'd find her there. It was improper, but the woman had gotten under his skin. He felt the clumsy brute, and the urge to make his peace with her had grown maddening.

He knocked. Silence.

Banging harder, he cursed under his breath. If she wasn't in her room, it meant she'd left the house altogether.

He frowned, instantly angry that yet again she'd risk her safety and leave the house unchaperoned. Assuring himself it was for her own good, he decided he'd simply go out, find her, and retrieve her.

And then Cormac frowned some more, scolding himself that she was an adult who likely spent much time on her own. Marjorie was a grown woman, for some reason still unwed, living very nearly independently.

The thought gave him pause.

He found he was suddenly curious for a glimpse of her world.

He told himself he needed some idea as to her whereabouts. All he really needed to do was ask one of the household staff where she might have gotten off to, but still, he told himself it was her bedroom that held the best clue.

He turned the knob, and the door opened to reveal a modest, airy room, with walls painted a cheery butter-yellow. Though it was a simple space with only a bed, side table, and small desk, it didn't feel austere. Small personal touches were scattered about the room: a handful of books, knots of dried flowers, a smattering of seashells.

Cormac stepped inside, fascinated. He sat on her bed and knew a moment's guilty thrill, which he dismissed at once. He was a man grown now, no longer a smitten ten-year-old. There was a task at hand, and he would concentrate on it. He would be logical, impervious, like the scout he'd been trained to be.

A strange starburst pattern on her bedside table drew his eye. It was a collection of shells, arranged so deliberately. He realized it was of more import to her than he'd originally thought.

He picked up a shell. He'd had no idea she was so fascinated by the seashore. The notion sent a peculiar thrill through his belly. He thought on his own affinity for the sea, of his love for the gray, blustering, lonely promise of it.

He carefully fingered each one. There were limpets the color of sand. A top shell with a flawlessly smooth mother-of-pearl lining. Black periwinkles. The long, twirling white shells they'd called twisties as children.

And in the center, a perfect mermaid's purse. He picked it up, rocked by the rush of memories. Smooth and black, it was nearly the size of his palm. He traced his finger along the straight edges to the curls at its top. Until that moment, he'd forgotten that they'd always been her favorite. Though merely the seed sac of some creature, it'd been the stuff of magic to young Ree. She'd swear selkie brides carried them with their grandest finery. Cormac remembered now how he'd comb the beach, proud when he found one perfectly intact to give her.

He carefully set it back in its place. Astonished, he wondered what it all meant. What the strange tug in his chest meant.

The door swung open, and a woman's gasp tore him from his reverie. Guilt twisted his stomach, and he quickly submerged his errant feelings in the familiar cold, hard exterior he wore as comfortably as his plaid.

"What are you doing?" the woman exclaimed. "Who are you?"

"Me?" He rose from the bed to glare down at her. "Who are *you*?"

Chapter 12

"I'm Marjorie's maid," the woman said. "Fiona."

Though she didn't strike him as nervous, her cheeks flushed immediately and thoroughly. Cormac placed her at once.

He shook his head in wonder. "Fiona." A girl named Fiona had come into the Keith family household when Marjorie was eight. *Not long before,* he thought, his every milestone in time falling either *before Aidan's capture* or *after.*

Cormac hadn't been much interested in the girl at the time, though he had noticed her peculiar habit of blushing at the slightest provocation. "The same Fiona?"

She shrugged, wandering in to straighten the bed, blushing anew. "Same as what?"

"Aye, you'd be the same Fiona, then." He shook his head. *Lasses and their ways.* It aggravated him. "Be easy, woman. I'm Cormac MacAlpin."

"Oh aye, Cormac. Aye. Of course." A strange look crossed her face, and he could've sworn she muttered, "Finally decides to appear, he does."

Cormac stared. "What?"

The girl stared back, then, like water come to a boil, she exploded into chatter. "Marjorie said she'd find you. That she'd bring you back. She knew where you lived, you see. Your sister tells her everything. Bridget, I mean. Oh, and that dear Archie"—she sighed, pressing a hand to her breast—"he wants to help."

"Archie." Cormac didn't realize until he heard his own voice that he'd growled the name. Did this Archie captivate *every* female he came into contact with?

"But Marjorie'd have naught to do with his plan," the maid prattled on.

Cormac tried to keep up, parsing her nonsense, wondering what cursed plan she could be referring to. She was nodding meaningfully, and he found it inexplicably irritating.

"Oh, but I told her she should," Fiona said with a scold in her voice. "Archie knows all manner of noblemen. But, she wanted *you*. You know she thinks . . . that you are . . . well . . . never you mind *that*." Her eyes suddenly widened. "But you were sitting on her *bed*!"

Her words echoed in his head. *She wanted you.*

"I need to know where she is."

"Well it wouldn't be her day for Saint Machar," Fiona mused. "Likely she just went to her place."

"Her place?" he prodded impatiently.

"Why, the shore, and where else? Aberdeen Beach. She fancies the waves. Says they're bigger there." Relaxed now, the maid bustled around the room, straightening the bedclothes where he'd been sitting.

"Is that where she got all these seashells?"

"Oh, aye. She finds them along the sand. It's fair soft there. Our Marjorie likes to take off her shoes and walk by the waves."

Our Marjorie. What did she see, standing in the surf and looking to the horizon? Did she feel the same pull, find the same lonely solace as he?

My *Marjorie*.

"The whole thing strikes *me* as a fool silly thing to do. Her hem when she gets home—it's a mess!"

He could imagine it in his mind's eye. Marjorie walking along the shore, the wind whipping her hair, her cheeks flushed from the brisk air. She wouldn't be a mess. She'd be beautiful.

He had to go to her. He had to see her for himself.

"Well, I never . . ." Fiona sputtered, as Cormac stormed past.

He fled from the house and didn't even think to fetch his horse from the mews. Instead, his feet devoured Aberdeen's winding streets in long strides. Navigating mucky wooden cobbles, over Hangman's Brae, past Gallowgate, heading eastward.

To her.

Gray granite buildings, gray sky, gray sea—gloom surrounded him. And so he barely noticed the rain at first, when it came. Cold, thin drops pricked his face.

Marjorie was out there, somewhere, feeling this same rain. Did she lift her cowl against it, or turn her face in welcome?

His feet moved faster, until he found himself running. That gray sea loomed larger, closer. An eerie light hit it, the sun breaking through clouds, even as it rained. It cast the sea in a strange, luminous blue. He ran faster.

Aberdeen Beach swept before him, the stretch of it much wider than his own sliver of rocky Dunnottar shore. The waves were higher here, the sand soft underfoot. Something visceral shot from his feet to his core: a recognition, a homecoming.

A lone figure walked along the sand. A woman, with a dark cloak whipping about her legs. Her hair tangled long and loose behind her. She held it tucked behind one ear.

Ree.

Marjorie dug in her toes. She wished the waves could smooth the thoughts from her mind as predictably as they washed her footprints from the sand.

Cormac's words had rocked her. She'd thought nothing could be worse than weathering his blame, enduring his cruel silence, until he'd put voice to his cruel thoughts.

Unseemly. Reckless. Dangerous.

That last had been the worst of all. She'd been a danger to Aidan. A danger to Davie. Cormac thought her foolhardy, that her recklessness made her a danger still.

She'd only wanted to make him jealous. It had worked before, at Dunnottar. Or so she'd thought. But she'd clearly miscalculated.

It seemed Cormac had only accompanied her to Aberdeen because of his sense of duty. She'd been a fool to hope otherwise. *Of course* he'd offered his help. He was a man bound by honor. The years had hardened him, his time in the wars hammering all but that sense of duty from him. What she'd hoped might be tender feelings for her had merely been a sense of obligation.

Marjorie felt something, a shift in the air around her. It made her turn.

Cormac strode to her. Intent darkened his face. He was power and conviction and anguish, too.

He came to her in anger. He came to berate her and belittle her. Pride sputtered up from someplace down deep. Marjorie stiffened her back, bracing for his attack. "If you've come to—"

Cormac slammed into her, crushing her body close to his, and his mouth stole the words from her lips.

Wrapping an arm at her back, tangling a hand in her hair, Cormac kissed her, roughly, deeply, his mouth hard and hungry. She let her head fall back, feeling her heels leave the sand as he pulled her up and into him. She'd been gripping the sides of her cloak tightly, but her hands slackened. She let go, her arms stretched down and out at her sides, as though poised to feel a storm's wind rush over her body.

She'd felt ripples of desire tease through her before, but it'd been nothing compared to this. Need flooded her, crackling up and between her legs, lighting her belly on fire. Marjorie brought her hands to him, desperately clutching at Cormac's arms, his shoulders, his face. Whatever could get her closer to him.

His tongue took her mouth, exploring her, owning her, and she thought her heart might explode in her chest. She opened herself, trembling from the sheer bliss of it.

She'd never kissed a man before. She'd always known it could be only Cormac. But she hadn't dared hope. She barely dared believe it now.

She stroked her hands along his arms, more mindful now, needing to feel him, to convince herself this could really be true. He wore only his linen shirt and his plaid, and the fabric clung to him, wet under her fingertips. His muscles were solid, as though his entire body was clenched for her, fighting either against his desire or for it.

Her fingers curled into those hard muscles, and he pulled her closer still. His hand tightened in her hair, cradling her head as he pulled his mouth from hers, only to come down hungrily on her neck, her throat, her jaw. He rained kisses over her face, tender kisses, hard kisses. Both angry and loving, and she wondered what demons he fought. Did Cormac's kisses overcome them, or was this his submission?

He clutched her tightly to him, and the feel of his strong arm braced along her back, the broad span of his hand on her waist, made her feel tiny, insubstantial. She was no longer a woman plodding through the world but had become instead some other, more transcendent creature, the sum of her now simply the fluttering of her heart in her breast and this tremendous need vibrating through her veins.

His hand roved her, along her side, over her breast, up to cup her cheek, and then back down again. She sank into Cormac, her legs molten, held upright only by the muscular arm at her back.

A crash and hiss, louder and closer than before, burst through to them, and frigid seawater broke and swirled over their feet.

He pulled away, staring at her, their faces a breath apart. His eyes were half-lidded, his dark brow furrowed almost as though in pain. In that moment, she found Cormac unbearably beautiful. He bore such secrets, such hidden depths. She wanted to understand them all.

She saw something else on his face: a wanting, raw and potent.

His intent, for *her*.

Could it be possible? Battered hope sprang to life in her heart. She blinked the rain from her eyes, fighting to breathe.

He was silent, and fear speared her through. Would he feel regret? Was this kiss to be her first and her last?

"Cormac?" she asked, her voice tremulous. Cold rain spilled down her cheeks, and she felt chilled for want of him.

"Ree," he said simply. "You. It's always been you."

Slowly he eased closer, ever so slowly his mouth came back to hover just over hers. She felt his breath on her lips, and she knew such a rush of pleasure, of completion, it was like her soul expanding from her body.

He gently wiped wet strands of hair from her face, their gazes locked.

Could this mean he was to make her his? That he'd include her in his life? "Does this mean you'll include me in your . . . plans?"

Shaking his head, Cormac let out a low laugh. "Does it mean you'll not let that swine Archie touch you again?"

"Never. Never will any man touch me. Any *other* man," she amended with a smile.

She'd spoken lightly, but he grew grave. He gave her a tight nod, the look on his face inscrutable.

"So?" She reached up and cupped his cheek, giddy

with the freedom of it, the intimacy. The faint scrape of stubble was rough in her palm. He'd never be so shining and clean-shaven as one like Archie, and it made the heat in her belly rage anew. Cormac was rough and raw and all man. Her next words came breathily. "Can I stay with you?"

"Aye, Ree. You'll stay with me." He kissed the top of her head with a husky laugh. "Woman, I ken you, and if I don't keep an eye on you, you'll be back in those trews and trolling the docks by yourself."

She'd tasted his jealousy and found it irresistible, and so she couldn't resist jibing him. "I always had Archie to help me."

"The devil I may be, and I'll be damned twice over if I let that ninny help you."

"Archie's not a ninny. He's merely—"

"I know. A *physician surgeon.*" He gave her a mock glare, and she giggled despite herself.

"No lass, I've had enough of this Archie. Knowing the bailie," he muttered under his breath. "As though that's of any use." He inhaled, touching his forehead to hers. "It's not child's play we've ahead of us, Ree. Do you swear to mind me? There'll be danger, and you'll need to trust that I know how best to protect us."

Ahead of us. She nodded. *Us.* She swelled at the thought.

"You'll need to take a different name," he went on. "It's too dangerous. I'll not let you be recognized."

"Of course." The excitement stole all other thoughts from her head. She and Cormac would work together. They would find Davie. *Together.*

Cormac cared for her, wanted her even. Did it mean he forgave her everything? She pushed away the thought, unwilling to let it pierce her joy.

Because he would help her, they'd find Davie; she knew it. How could they not? Such a joining felt too perfect for failure.

Cormac turned his head to look out at the waves. She

watched him deep in thought, waiting patiently, trusting him.

"Your uncle will be safer if this doesn't lead to him." He looked back at her, and resolution had smoothed his brow. "You'll need to tell Humphrey, and tell that meddling maid of yours, too, that my sister has invited you for a prolonged visit to Dunnottar. I'll not have you compromised. We can't be discovered off alone together; the scandal would be too great. Tell them you need to go away for a time."

"Go away where?"

"With me, lass." He placed his finger gently beneath her chin. "Away with me."

Chapter 13

Fiona stood on the threshold of Westhall Manse, meticulously dusting and straightening her skirts. It was strange, Marjorie's request that she deliver news to Archie. But it meant Fiona could see Archie once more and on her own, so she'd leapt at the chance.

She was to inform Archie that Marjorie was going away for an extended visit to Dunnottar. Only on the walk over did it strike her what an odd turn of events it was. Why was Marjorie leaving now?

And why didn't her mistress tell him herself? Was it to distract Fiona from something? Or did Marjorie simply suspect the fancy she harbored for Archie?

Fiona couldn't imagine why any woman wouldn't be fascinated by the young physician surgeon. Archie was proper and kind, and though he was beyond the reach of a mere maid like her, she relished every chance she got to see him. Marjorie could have a man like him in an instant, and it baffled Fiona that she'd chosen not to.

"Just knock, chit," she scolded herself, her heart

thudding in her chest. She grew light-headed trying to catch her breath, and that made her even more anxious.

But then again, if she fainted, *Archie* might be the one to resuscitate her. Quickly, she fingered the pleats in the front of her skirts one last time. She knocked hard, before she had a chance to think twice. "He's a physician, and I'm a fool."

The rectory housekeeper ushered Fiona into a tiny receiving area off the main entrance. Fiona's eyes widened as she entered. The Keith family had bigger closets than this.

"We've no showy solars or sitting rooms here," the old woman told her. "Lord Murray puts every space to some use."

Lord Murray. The woman had meant Archie. Fiona gulped. Because of his close association with Marjorie, he'd always insisted Fiona call him by his given name. But she was a mere maid, just like this housekeeper.

Had she overstepped all this time? She felt a rush of heat to her cheeks. "Thank you," she said as primly as possible.

Though she'd visited Saint Machar before, it'd always been with Marjorie, and the instant the housekeeper bustled out, Fiona looked around eagerly. The room was narrow, furnished only with a padded bench and side table. A cross hung on the wall. Distant bustle echoed from the rear of the building, and she peered back out the door, wondering if it was the next meal's preparations she heard.

She met with Archie's chest as he strode around the corner, and she pulled back with a start. "Oh! Losh, I . . . my apologies . . . I had no notion . . ."

Archie caught her arms to steady her. "Oh no, no. I'll not hear of it, Fiona. You must accept *my* apology."

He put her at her ease, as he always did, and she gazed up at him. So tall and chivalrous, just what she imagined a lord should be. Lean, well-spoken, and neat as a pin— not rough like Cormac. His hands lingered longer on her arms than was strictly proper.

"I have news, Lord Murray." She made herself say his correct title, and self-consciousness inflamed her cheeks.

He gave her a scolding look. "Archie. I've told you. You must call me Archie."

"Archie, then." She gave him an adoring smile that she thought might split her face in two. "I've news from my mistress, Archie."

He swallowed hard, seeming unsettled. He was pleased to see her, but he looked a little nervous, too. The thrill of it swelled in her breast.

Slipping his hand around her elbow, he guided her to sit next to him on the bench. "First, we must see to your wound."

"But that was so long ago." Weeks back, she'd cut herself badly with a kitchen knife. As luck had it, Archie had been visiting Humphrey's house at the time. It had hurt something fierce, but it'd been worth it to experience his tender ministrations.

"Aye," he said, taking her finger, "but I'd like to see how it healed."

His hand was cool cradling hers. He nestled his thumb in her palm, tilting her finger to the light. She thought her heart might fly from her chest.

"Perfect," he said, his voice husky.

She had to clear her throat to reply. "I've you to thank for it."

"It was truly my pleasure." He brought her hand down but didn't let go. "And now what can I do for you, my dear Fiona?"

"So . . ." It took all she had not to sputter. She cursed her hot blood, feeling a flush rise from her breasts all the way to the tips of her ears. Her eyes met his. The silence hung between them, and finally she shook herself. She was here for a reason, as much as she wanted just to sit and gaze into his expressive brown eyes. She'd always dreamed of finding a man with expressive brown eyes.

"So?" he asked gently.

"So . . . Marjorie wanted that I tell you. She's going away for a time."

"Where?" Archie sat up, immediately concerned.

She knew a flare of jealousy, and fought to tamp it down. It'd do no good to envy her mistress. God had given Fiona her lot in life—maids who yearned for more only ended up heartbroken. "She says it's to visit the MacAlpins, but . . ."

"Aye?" he asked, anxiety pinching his brow.

It was a rare treat to have news to report, and she prolonged the telling of it. "But I don't believe her."

Something shifted in his tone, from apprehension to intrigue. "Do you think something else is afoot?"

She shrugged, giving the gesture as much meaning as she could without seeming a gossip.

"Do you think she's going with that MacAlpin devil?" He leaned closer. "Does this have to do with Davie?"

"I don't know," she whispered. His conspiratorial posture excited her. It was impossible to think that a man like him could ever be interested in a mere maid like her, but huddled close, his eyes alight with shared secrets, suddenly a maid and the physician surgeon seemed the rightest thing in the world. "But there's one thing I do know," she said breathlessly.

He squeezed her hand. "What is it?"

"He's no gentleman like you, Arch."

Chapter 14

Marjorie leaned against the counter of the Cross Keys Inn, trying to appear more self-possessed than she actually felt. She hadn't been able to stop thinking about that kiss.

She cut her eyes to Cormac, negotiating with the innkeeper in his typically curt manner. Her eyes went to his hands, braced on the table before him. She remembered the feel of them, so rough from fishing and weathered from the sun, and yet they'd been so tender on her cheek, possessive at her back. She wanted those hands, wanted to feel them in other places. On her bottom, her breasts . . .

Blushing, she looked away.

Cormac had *kissed* her, and it had set her body on fire in ways she'd never before imagined. She knew what happened between a man and a woman, had even tried to picture it. But the reality was so much more. She felt agitated, unsatisfied, like there was an itch inside her body that only he could reach.

And here they were, in a rough, dockside area far from any Aberdeen she'd ever known. He'd given the innkeeper false names. He'd asked for a room for himself and his *wife*.

Her heart kicked in her chest.

They were about to share a room. Would that mean they were to share a bed? Would he hold her close, kiss her as he had on the beach? They hadn't spoken about it since—in fact, Cormac hadn't spoken about much of anything—but the tension between them was palpable.

Had it been a one-time weakness? Could it mean something more? Was his silence regret? Anticipation? Or was it just his way? She couldn't imagine.

She hoped it meant he was as eager as she to try one more kiss. Only this time, she'd be braver with her hands. On the beach, she'd touched his arms, his back, but now she wished she'd had nerve enough to explore his chest. It had felt so firm and strong against her breasts. How would it feel without his shirt? She inadvertently gasped at the thought.

Cormac gave her a peculiar look and took her arm. "We'll take dinner in our room," he told the innkeeper as they headed up the stairs.

Our room. She clung to the banister to catch herself from stumbling. *Dinner in* our *room.*

Davie, she reminded herself. This was about Davie, not the devastating man looming on the stairs above her.

He unlocked their door, revealing a small but tidy room. With one lone, small, but tidy bed. An entire flock of birds fluttered to life in her belly.

About Davie, not Cormac.

"Will we be going to investigate straightaway?" she asked, affecting a studied bravado.

"So ready to storm the docks, are you?" Tossing his small satchel on the floor, he sat on the bed to pull off his boots.

The bed frame creaked with his weight. Would it creak when they lay on it together? When he turned over in the night?

Marjorie strode purposefully to the window, suddenly

feeling very warm. She struggled to unlatch the narrow shutters, trying to picture Davie. She focused on a memory of the boy—his freckled nose. Unfortunately, she could only picture Cormac, and the masculine look of his once-broken one.

"It seems to me that we could get many questions answered whilst the sailors"—she pinched her thumb in the latch and, hissing, sucked it quickly into her mouth—"whilst they go to drink at the taverns."

Cormac rose and, reaching around her, easily unhitched the rusted hook. She felt the heat of his body along her back.

He was as cavalier and as impervious as ever, and it was maddening. Didn't he feel this, too, this *itch* that consumed her?

"We'd be welcoming trouble if we did," he said matter-of-factly. "I'd rather let the blackguards drink and carouse their fill, then investigate in the early hours while they're sleeping it off. So no, *Lady Brodie*, we shall stay inside until the morrow."

"That's another thing," she said, grateful for a new topic to gnaw upon. Specifically, the ridiculous name he'd come up with for her. She spun to face him. "Gormelia? Really, Cormac. Did you have to christen me *Gormelia*? Gormelia Brodie," she mused, shaking her head.

He shrugged. "From the Gaelic, lass. For those blue eyes of yours."

That silenced her. She couldn't figure out if there was a compliment in there or merely a statement of fact, and it made her peevish. "How is it you get to be a nice, steadfast Hugh, and I get saddled with Gormelia?"

"We needed fake identities, Lady Gormelia." A smirk flickered across his face. "If we're to pose as a wealthy lord and lady in search of servants, we should have appropriately grand names."

"If this is what constitutes your sense of humor, Cormac MacAlpin, I don't much care for it."

He merely shrugged, the barest ghost of a smile on his

face, and it unnerved her. She glanced to his bare feet and decided if he was going to make himself so casually at home, then she could, too.

"Next time, I'll choose the names, and we'll see how you enjoy being called *Lord Boniface Humperdinck.*" She bent to pull the leather slippers from her feet, though her fingers were trembling as she did so. She and Cormac would both have bare feet. Would they touch under the sheets? Would his warm hers? Finally, she managed to unknot her laces and stood. "I can think of a dozen—"

Marjorie's tongue froze in shock to see Cormac undoing the leather thong that tied his plaid at his shoulder.

"A dozen . . . ?" he prompted as the wool slid from his chest.

What had they been discussing? She cleared her throat. "A dozen other names. But what . . . Cormac, what, pray tell—"

He unbuckled his belt, rolled it, and tossed it into the corner.

Her mouth went dry. She wanted to look away, should look away, but she couldn't bring herself to. Too vivid was the memory of him, emerging naked from the sea.

"Aye?" He slowly unraveled the *breacan feile* from his waist. All that wool fell heavily to the floor. Stepping from it, he gathered the handful of dark green, blue, and black plaid. "Pray tell what?"

He shook the wool out, surely unaware of the slight tensing of his muscular calves as he did so. Unaware that the flex of his thigh was visible under the linen of his shirt.

Her skin felt stretched unbearably tight over her body. Was this what it felt like to want a man?

Because she wanted Cormac. She wanted to pull that shirt up and once again see the naked flesh of those thighs. To run her hands over them. To feel them braced around her legs, his body heavy over hers.

But she felt a little frightened, too. What would she do faced with a naked stretch of man? What would Cormac want her to do?

He bent to unfurl the plaid on the ground, unaware that she could see straight up into the dark shadows between his . . .

"What are you doing?" she blurted.

He looked up at her, seemingly oblivious.

And why wouldn't he be? His tunic reached almost to his knees. He was nearly as clothed as he'd been before he'd removed his *breacan feile*. No, *she* was the shameless one, with all these unseemly imaginings.

"Making a pallet." He pointed to the enormous swath of his plaid, laid in thirds at his feet.

"A . . ." She looked down, and the fluttering in her chest thudded to a halt. "You're sleeping *there*?"

"Don't worry yourself," he said with a laugh. "You get the bed, lass. But, aye, I'm setting a place for myself on the floor."

"Well . . ." She put her hands on her hips, disgruntled. She'd imagined their kiss had been a preview of things to come. She'd been fantasizing about feeling his body next to hers for the whole night. "Don't be foolish, Cormac. You can sleep on the bed."

"Och, and have *you* on the floor? What do you take me for?"

"No, not that. I mean . . ." *You could sleep by my side.* She looked from the pallet to the bed, refusing to meet his eyes. She'd been disgruntled and was quickly becoming annoyed that she'd be forced to set aside her pride to put a fine point on the matter. "That is to say . . ."

Finally, she met his gaze, and her nerve failed her.

He stood stiffly, staring at her, waiting. His eyes were slate and indigo in the growing dark. The look on his face was hooded, and as unreadable as ever.

Even so, she tried to read him, desperate to understand. She saw the same shadow that always loomed there: his loss, his pain. She knew a part of it was the same anguished memory she carried with her always.

Was it resentment she saw there, too? She'd spent years blaming herself, and it had sown doubt deep in her soul. And so, though they'd kissed, she couldn't help but wonder what was keeping him from being with her. Was she a reminder of bad times?

She fumbled for something to fill the silence. "I suppose you're used to sleeping on the ground." And then she realized how true that was. Though her memories of him were so vivid, and their friendship had been so close, those first ten years had been the barest fraction of his experience. After that, Cormac had become a soldier, something that'd marked over half his lifetime.

"Aye," he replied simply.

She studied his scars, the faint spidery lattice of tissue on his brow, the slight crook to his nose. The loss of his brother might be a scar on his heart, but he bore the marks of battle on his body.

Cormac had been a warrior, a hero. He'd endured unfathomable things, things she couldn't begin to contemplate. And it was clear that it had altered him, transformed him irrevocably. There was a darkness in his gaze deeper and more poisonous than the loss of his brother as a child. She was desperate to know how it was that he'd grown from an anguished boy into the dark, forbidding man before her.

"How . . ." she began quietly. What feats had he performed? What bravery? At what reckless disregard to his life? She stepped closer, gingerly stretching her hand toward his face. "How did this happen? Your nose. Was it in battle?"

His laugh startled her. "Such sweet torture on your face, lass. All this and you ask about my nose?"

"I thought it the best place to start."

Shaking his head, he plopped on the edge of the bed. "Ree, you're too much. I'd thought you were going to ask . . . well . . ." He sighed, giving another wistful shake to his head.

She sat stiffly beside him. She felt abashed, and then she simply felt put out because he even had the power to make her feel thus.

"'Tis a remarkable tale indeed," he began. "You guessed correctly. My nose was broken in a serious battle." Leaning his elbows on his knees, he struck a relaxed pose.

She couldn't relax, though. The cursed man had her thoughts running every which way.

She tried to gather herself. He was going to tell her about his battles. She'd longed to hear about them. The notion that he'd share such a personal thing, that she was about to get a glimpse into his shadowed past, made her restless, excited. She folded her hands in her lap, schooling her face to emotionless quiet.

"The day began like any other. There was naught but dried oats to break our fast. 'Twas hardtack to eat in the morning and, with naught but a bit of bread and cheese to hand, iron rations when the sun grew high. Bellies were gnawing and moods were frayed by the time the enemy approached."

"When did the battle begin?" she asked gravely.

"Just after midday, and och, Ree," he said somberly, "it was a terrible sight. They came with a mad glint in their eyes and a wild howl on their lips."

Marjorie scooted closer, mesmerized. He must've been terrified. She couldn't imagine the horrors he'd faced in his years away.

"And this enemy," he said, "you'll not credit your ears when you hear their name."

"Was it the Campbells?" she asked, spellbound. Finally, she'd learn some of the secrets of his past. "Argyll himself?"

"No. Worse than the Campbell. 'Twas a demon, shooting straight for me as though fleeing the mouth of hell. Indeed, folk have been known to call this enemy a devil. But I tell you, it was even more frightening that that. Even more terrible."

"Why?"

"This enemy . . ." His voice grew to a whisper. "My dreaded foe, and the author of this broken face of mine . . ."

"Who? Tell it, Cormac, what was this enemy's name?"

"My enemy's name was Bridget. Bridget MacAlpin."

Marjorie's mind went utterly blank for a moment, and then she swatted Cormac as hard as she could. *His sister.* This was a story about his sister.

"You see!" Grabbing her hand, he broke into loud laughter. "You are proof of it yourself. The female of the species is the most dreaded enemy of all."

"Be serious, Cormac." Though her tone was stern, she bit her cheek not to smile. She hadn't heard him laugh since they were children.

"Oh, I am as serious as the grave. You'd be serious, too, had you seen my sister. Wee, wild Bridget, coming at me with a wooden sword. A man tries for a mid-afternoon nap in the stables, and next thing he knows, a berserker in an *arisaid* sets upon him, flailing a boy's weapon as though it were on fire and she alone could wave it out."

Marjorie could no longer help herself; she had to laugh. "Bridget *attacked* you?"

"Indeed." He rubbed his nose. "She had it in her head that she could learn to fight as well as any lad. She went at me with her . . . her cudgel, and I wasn't about to strike my very own sister. Next I knew, the lass cracked the thing over my face. And damned if my cursed nose didn't bleed like a stuck hog for hours."

Marjorie didn't know if she wanted to swat him again or laugh even louder than he had. All she knew was, sitting there with her hand in his, she felt warmed to her very soul.

The moment was broken by a knock at the door.

Telling his story, he'd momentarily forgotten his miseries, but the intrusion brought him back to himself. Cormac caught her gaze, and she could almost see the joy bleed from his face, see the shadows seep back into his eyes.

"That'd be our meal." He rose from the bed to swing open the door, and by the time he spoke again, his voice had grown rough. "What?"

"Your supper, milord." A serving girl stood there, and the smell of ale and roast meat wafted into the room. The girl didn't raise her eyes.

"Aye." He took the tray from her hands. "That'll do."

"That smells lovely," Marjorie said, wondering which demons she'd lost him to, and why. She'd do anything in her power to eradicate them and resurrect the old Cormac for good. For now, that meant continuing her bright chatter. "I do believe I'm quite hungry."

"Aye. Beef stew."

She watched him survey the small room. Without a stool, the only places for them to sit would be on the floor or on the edge of the bed. Cormac's eyes went to her on the bed, and he stiffened.

He set the tray on the floor.

"Oh, this is lovely," she said, determined to normalize the situation. She wouldn't let him descend back into his darkness. Hearing his laughter had been too much of a revelation. She moved to sit beside him on the floor, imagining they were on a picnic. Taking a delicate bite of the stew, she hummed her content. "Ohh, I'm a woman starved."

He looked away.

Damn him.

But she refused to give up, and so asked the first question that popped into her head. "How's the rest of your family?"

"You saw for yourself, aye? When you showed up at Dunnottar." He'd chewed, swallowed, spoken, then resumed chewing.

Difficult man. "Yes. But I didn't see your older sister. How is Anya?"

He shrugged. "She spends her days tending her husband."

Silence again.

Would he help her even a little bit? Why did the laughter of just a moment before disappear? "What happened to her husband?"

"He lost a leg. At Carbisdale." Fork halting in midair, he asked pointedly, "Did you ever meet Donald?"

She hadn't, though she knew it'd been far from a love match. Anya's heart had always belonged to another. "No. But he was from a wealthy family, right? In Argyll?"

"Aye, he's got land and money to spare. A good thing, that. The man is good to no one, particularly my sister."

"Cormac! That's a horrible thing to say."

"Nay, not horrible, simply the truth. Man's lucky to be alive, though he doesn't see it so." He took another bite, chewing thoughtfully. "And now Donald rules the household—and my sister—from his bed. Or so Bridget tells it."

"Bridget?"

"She's never much liked our brother-in-law. Girl's got some fool romantic notions about love and marriage." He shook his head. "She's young yet. She'll see."

"So Bridget *is* interested in marriage. And a love match," she mused, surprised. "Well, I think it's a lovely thought. *Fool notion*, indeed. Truly, Cormac, you can be so gloomy."

He shrugged a shoulder. But Marjorie had spied a smirk, too, and took it as an opportunity.

"That's you. A real wretched beast." She blithely rattled off a litany of complaints, feigning distracted intent on her stew all the while. "Rich folk are suspect. Love is for fools. Your sisters are doomed to lives of disappointment, misery, and dashed hopes. Oh, and please to be leaving your legless men on the battlefield. Did I miss anything?"

He exploded into laughter.

Stilling, she looked up and was greeted by a wicked gleam in his eye. The man perplexed her utterly.

He nodded at her food. "Your mum used to scold you for that."

Marjorie looked to her hand, still poised in her bowl, where she was swabbing up the remains of her stew with a hunk of bread. She finished mopping the bowl and took a bite. "She did at that. But soaking your bread with the sauce is the best part."

"I'm not disagreeing," he assured her. "She was merciless, as I recall it."

"My mother?" Marjorie gave a rueful laugh. "Aye, the woman prized her manners."

There was a moment's companionable silence, and then he asked, "How did she die?"

She sighed. "A fever. When I was sixteen. It happened quickly."

"I don't imagine it was easy for a young girl to weather such a loss. You'd have been just beginning to think about a husband."

She merely shrugged. It *had* been hard—incredibly so. But life in the Highlands was. As for the other, she'd made the decision never to marry long before her mother died. She had been ten, in fact, and her best friend Cormac had just turned his back on her.

"You'd have made her proud," he told her.

"A titled husband and a gaggle of bairns is what would've made her proud," she retorted. "No, I'm lucky Uncle Humphrey is so patient with me. Though I suppose it's less about his patience and more that he likes keeping me about to fetch the more obscure tomes from his uppermost shelves." She gave a resigned shake of her head. "Either way, I'm thankful. There aren't many men who'd abide a self-appointed spinster for a niece."

His eyes narrowed thoughtfully, and the scrutiny unnerved her. She shifted her attention back to her meal, needing to break the connection.

Cormac gestured to her bowl. "You've a bit of dinner on your knuckles," he said, a broad smile spreading across his face.

She groaned. Finally, the man smiles, and the only cost had been her dignity.

Marjorie pulled her hand up. Dark brown sauce

glistened on her thumb and two of her fingers. She hesitated. She had no napkin, just the clothes on her body. With a defiant shrug, she simply raised her knuckles to her mouth and quickly licked them clean. She shot Cormac a challenging look, daring him to say something.

His face went blank. "You liked it, then? Your stew?"

"Yes, thank you," she replied in an exaggeratedly lady-like tone.

He stood abruptly, gathering the bowls and placing them outside. "I imagine the day has caught up with you," he said, bustling around her.

She stood and dusted off her skirts. "I suppose it will eventually, but I don't seem to be tired yet."

"Good night, then." He lay on his pallet with his back to her, his movements stilted, as he pulled his plaid over his shoulder.

She plopped onto the bed, stunned at his sudden shutdown. Could it mean that this arrangement unsettled him as much as it did her?

You'll not get off so easy, Cormac.

A purposeful smile curved her lips. She'd enjoyed their conversation and wasn't nearly done. She lay on her belly, pulling the last of the pins from her hair. She tossed them haphazardly, one by one, onto the side table.

"Would that we were having a grand Aberdeen adventure, rather than searching for Davie," she ventured. Though silence greeted her comment, she hadn't really expected him to answer. Which was fine—as long as he was listening.

She contemplated her clothing for a moment. Finally, at a loss, she simply blew out the stub of candle on the side table and stretched out on the bed. Her outfit was restrictive, but she was uncertain what to do about it. She hoped she'd eventually fall asleep despite the uncomfortable bodice and layers of skirts. At least the heavy *arisaid* would keep her warm.

"This inn is more pleasant than I expected." She shifted, feeling free to give a sharp and unladylike tug to her bodice in the darkness. *Better.* The dried heather of the overstuffed mattress crackled as she scooted under the blanket. "And it's more comfortable, too."

She attuned her ears to the silence, taking in the sound of distant voices downstairs, the creak of timber as Cormac turned, the rhythm of his breathing.

"Gormelia," she mused after a time. "It's a strange thing. Having a new name like this. Almost as though we could be anybody, do anything."

She brought her hands to her belly, tracing up and down the hard lines of her stays, wishing she could be free of the blasted things altogether. At least what she currently wore was far simpler than some of her gowns. Tomorrow, though, she'd need to dress in her best, if their act was to be convincing. She looked forward to the pretense. "I wish we really were a wealthy lord and lady. Not in search of slaves, of course."

The thought brought her mind to an inevitable place, a place she'd gone to innumerable times before: her, married to Cormac, a half-dozen children between them.

It was Cormac's own fault, mentioning his sister's notions of marriage as he had. Marjorie wavered, but she had a question she simply *had* to ask. And although she knew the real truth of the matter, she had to know if he'd face that truth, if he'd answer her honestly.

"Do you ever think what might have happened if . . . well . . . if Aidan were still here? Do you think . . . Cormac, would *we* have wed, you think?"

The only response was his muted snore breaking through the silence.

———

He woke that night, his heart pounding. The memory of Aidan's scream echoed in his skull. It was a dream he hadn't had in a while, but he supposed all this talk of saving Davie had brought it back.

It had taken him hours to fall asleep, in truth. Marjorie had been going places in her mind that pained him, and so he'd feigned sleep in order to find some measure of peace.

But peace had been long in coming.

Sharing a room with her had been a critical error. The place was entirely too small. When he'd opened the door to see the lone mattress, dark thoughts spilled into his mind in a crazy rush. The mere sound of that mattress giving beneath her weight had been enough to pull the blood to his groin, hardening him to the point of distraction. Rolling Marjorie onto that bed was all he could think of. Pinning her beneath him, kissing her as he had on the beach. Only next time, he wouldn't stop kissing her.

Next time, he'd push the cloak from her shoulders, shuck the bodice from her breasts. Would she giggle and be playful, or would desire simmer in her eyes?

He sat up in the darkness and wiped the sweat from his brow and tried to wipe the dream from where it lingered in his mind. He was a boy again, stuck in blackness, hearing Aidan's terrified cries.

"Cormac?" Marjorie's voice was such a familiar thing, but she spoke now in a drowsy whisper. It was a novel sound, tinged husky and mellow. "Cormac, are you all right?"

He looked up at her. The moon had risen full and high, and it shone in their room, casting a white light on the side of her face, down the side of her body.

Desire ripped through him.

No, I am not all right.

She'd forsaken her Aberdeen finery for the day, dressing instead in a simple *arisaid*. He sucked in a breath. She'd somehow managed to remove all that tartan wool in the night. His eyes roved down her body. The blanket clung close to her legs, and he realized she'd stripped her layers of petticoats as well. *And her bodice, too?*

He swallowed hard. Marjorie lay there, staring openly down at him, wearing only her sark and the moonlight.

Desire tore through him at the sight of her, but so,

too, did fear—fear for his very soul. Because he'd never stopped caring for her.

Only now he was a man, with a man's needs.

"Cormac?" she asked again.

"Good night, Ree," he said, his voice tight. "Get some sleep."

Chapter 15

Marjorie fell back asleep almost at once. But Cormac had tossed and turned with the sleep of the damned, as though he were off to face the hangman in the morning instead of the Aberdeen quays.

Finally, he rose to look at her. Her bare arm stretched across the bed, silvery in the moonlight. It was lean, pale like ivory, and it mesmerized him. For all her posturing, she was so delicate, so vulnerable.

He longed to touch her, to feel the velvet of her skin under his fingers. He could stroke that arm. He'd draw his hand to her shoulder where he'd pull her blanket down, reveal the rest of her. He could climb into the bed, pull the blanket over them both. Beneath the bedding, she was barely clad . . .

He clamped his eyes shut.

He needed to remain focused, on his guard, which meant not imagining her naked body beneath gauzy linen. It meant not kissing her, not dreaming of holding her close in bed.

Gathering his wits, Cormac wandered to the window,

estimating dawn was still over an hour away. Marjorie's breathing was slow and even, so quiet he needed to strain to hear. He'd let her rest a while longer.

He shut his eyes and leaned his head against the windowpane, tilting it to catch the light of the setting moon on his cheek. He recalled the madness that had accosted him earlier, just there at the window. Like a fool, he'd gone to stand behind Marjorie. The mere feel of her before him, jiggling and grunting to unlatch the damned glass, had him yearning and ravenous, like some cursed rutting beast.

And then she'd pinched herself and sucked her thumb into her mouth, and the look of her rounded lips had been so erotic, it'd been all he could do not to pull her tight to him and grind his base flesh into her backside. Later, too, she'd licked her food from her hand like some sort of wild, carnal creature. Just a mouth, merely her fingers, and yet the sight of each had his thoughts spiraling to dark places where her tongue played along *his* flesh.

The young girl he'd once adored had grown into this spirited, impassioned woman, *this sensual woman.* And she was driving him mad, igniting desires he thought he'd doused long ago.

She'd always been a wonder to him, her boldness and her bravery, and so the adult she'd become was no surprise. He considered her laughter, her crusading ways, her passions.

Her kiss.

He'd been forced to recount that ridiculous incident with Bridget to get it off his mind, grasping at humor to eradicate the pain of his longing. And then she'd asked about his battles, and he'd clung to that same humor to hide the pain of his past.

She'd sat so close to him on the bed, though, and she'd kept edging closer still, until she was laughing and swatting at him as she'd done as a child. Only this time, Cormac wanted to do much more than simply engage Marjorie in a playful tussle. What if he'd simply grabbed her and crawled atop her? Would lust have replaced the laughter in her eyes?

Those eyes. Her eerily vivid blue-green eyes had been riveted to him for the telling of his tale, as intent on him as when he'd taken off his plaid.

His muscles clenched with the memory. The way she'd watched him had nearly been his undoing. He'd wanted to ask *her* to undress him instead. To *tell* her to undress him.

And how she'd stared at his pallet, as though it were evil itself. Had he read disappointment on her face? For the briefest moment, he hoped she'd say something. Invite him to her bed. But she didn't.

And of course she didn't. She was good and proper. *Too* good and proper. Too good, at least, for one such as him. He could spend a thousand lifetimes atoning for his sins, and still he'd never deserve her.

He scrubbed at his face, longing to see an absent sun peek over the horizon.

What was he doing sharing a room with Ree? He was a brute for putting her in this position. An unmarried lass in the company of a creature like him?

He'd taken advantage of her on the beach. And she'd been as perfect as a spring morning. Opening to him, touching and whispering, in ways so sweet and hot that he thought he'd died and landed in paradise. She'd been such a revelation, he *wished* he'd die, so that he'd no longer have to face this torture, the beautiful woman who'd never be his. He was darkness and killing and shame, and he'd never be worthy of her.

Marjorie was dredging up painful, dangerous notions. Sympathies he'd thought long ago extinguished stirred to life in his chest. Feelings for her, for others like this boy Davie. He'd spent a lifetime building walls against such emotion. He needed to fight it harder than ever now.

He'd loved this woman as a child. But children were fools, with no idea about the real world and its suffering. It was all disappointment in the end. He imagined

Marjorie's only encounter with such profound sadness had been thirteen long years ago, when Aidan was taken.

She'd learn the lesson again, though, soon enough. And he hated the prospect. He'd help her search for the boy, but he braced for the inevitable despair they'd find at the end of the road.

He attuned himself to her breathing. It felt like a transgression, like he was spying on her. But the sweet sound of her was an irresistible balm to his soul.

Poor, lovely Ree. For all her mettle, she was still such an innocent. There was no way to protect her from it all. Would that he could've left her at home and searched for the boy on his own. But he'd known he had no choice but to bring her with him. If he hadn't, she'd surely be storming the docks this very evening, and all alone.

Or worse, with that sodding Archie character. *Archie* would've figured out a way to help her without sharing a room, without compromising her.

Rich men and friends in high places. He scowled. He knew in his heart that Archie's way wouldn't have kept her safe.

No, keeping Marjorie close like this was the only, best way to keep her from harm. And more than finding Davie, more than Cormac's own safety, Ree's welfare was paramount. If anything were to happen to her, he'd become completely unmoored.

That there was someone as good and as kind as Ree in this world had been the one thing keeping him going all this time. Cormac had seen such horrible things; he'd give his life, sacrifice what little humanity was left to him, to protect her from it all.

As though summoned by the intensity of his thoughts, she sighed and muttered in her sleep. There was a rustle and a shifting, and then the rhythm of her breath once more.

He girded himself. Her sighs were quiet, but they reverberated like thunderclaps through his core. He imagined he could detect even the smell of her, permeating their small space with the intoxicating scent of sleeping woman. She'd seared him through, and not even the cold, bare timber underfoot was enough to ease the heat of his body.

He knew he shouldn't look. He should give her some semblance of privacy. But Cormac couldn't stop himself from stepping closer to her.

He felt his feet moving before he knew what he was about. And then he did realize, and still he paid it no heed. Rather, he imagined himself a man moving through a dream, his movements inexorable, him helpless to stop them.

His first sight was of her lips, parted slightly. Soft and full, they appeared dark in the shadows, the shade of a ripened plum.

She lay on her side, her hands pressed palms together, resting under her cheek. Her hair lay strewn behind her, and curls that shone light brown in daylight spread across her pillow, streaking behind her like a dark wing. Her, an angel in flight.

Slowly, he reached out. Gingerly, he traced a lock of hair from her brow. He froze, waiting, but she didn't rouse.

Then Cormac smoothed his hand over her hair. It was coarse but somehow smooth, too, skeins of uneven waves tickling his palm.

And still her breathing didn't alter, and so he grew bolder, bringing his hand to her shoulder. Her bones were sleek and delicate, too fine for the weighty burdens she bore. He'd always thought of her as such a dauntless, braw thing, but truly she was a fragile creature.

He stroked his hand lower, and his groin tightened at the feel of her torso, the soft curve of it, the gentle rise and fall of her chest. He imagined the bare skin beneath the fabric. Her breasts would be pale and perfect. They'd fill his palms, neither too big nor too small, and he'd bury himself between them, a man come home.

He stroked lower still, his body humming now, alive. If before he'd imagined he was asleep and dreaming, there was no fooling himself now. He was awake, alert, and entirely aroused.

He dragged his hand over the blanket covering her legs, and the wool rasped against his fingers. He remembered those damned trews. They'd outlined her curves, hugging her legs, clinging in the cleft between. It had been all he could do to keep his wits about him and not come at the sight.

He stroked along her thigh. It sloped elegantly down, to bended knee, then to lean calf. Carefully he cupped her ankle, and the bone seemed perilously frail. Never before had she struck him as more a woman than she did in that moment. Never had she seemed more exquisite, more precious.

A vision came to his mind of taking both his hands, gripping those calves. Flipping Marjorie flat on her back, spreading her, mounting her.

He pulled his hand back as though burned.

The game he played was more dangerous than any wartime spying or any dockside brawl.

Hissing a breath, Cormac took up his plaid. Wrapping it about himself, he curled on the floor once more, where he'd wait for the sun to rise and the angry flesh of his body to retreat.

———————

Marjorie woke strangely energized. She stretched, and despite the tension of the past days, her muscles felt invigorated, her mood light.

She flipped onto her back, staring at the wood beams overhead. She flexed and pointed her toes, thinking it was no wonder she was in such high spirits. They were to go to the docks today. Cormac was helping her, and they had a plan.

Cormac. A little flare of excitement ripped through her belly.

She rolled onto her stomach, looking over the edge of the bed. He was gone. She knew a rush of disappointment and tamped it down at once. He was his own man, who surely had business in need of tending, concerns having naught to do with her or Davie.

Unfortunately, she had well over an hour to consider that fact, and she was dressed, staring idly out the window, and feeling just on the brink of impatience when he finally returned.

"We need to discuss the plan," he said baldly, bolting the door behind him.

"And a fine morning to you as well, Cormac." Moving from the window, Marjorie gave him her best dazzling smile. She wasn't about to let him sully her curiously bright outlook. "I'd thought we *were* enacting our plan. Posing as a wealthy lord and his *lady*." She stepped closer to him, wondering if he was immune to the tease in her voice. Pretending to be Cormac's wife was already proving to be quite the diversion.

"I've made inquiries," he said, looking away quickly. "I've identified a contact at Justice Port."

"Did you go back to that smugglers' boat?" Her voice grew sharp. She didn't know which she felt more: fear for his safety or resentment that he'd leave her out of something. "Without me?"

Disregarding her question, he continued, "We will go, claiming we'd like to purchase a boy."

"That sounds . . ." She shuddered.

"A horror. I know it, Ree." He was silent for a moment, and just when she thought he was done speaking, he inhaled deeply and said, "But I've thought on this long and hard. It's the only way."

She turned her back to him and leaned against the windowsill. Pretending to *buy* a boy. Did people really do that? It was unthinkable.

His voice gentled. "Listen, Marjorie. There are many horrors out there, which I fear you're not ready to face. You must consider this and tell me truly. Will you be able to—"

"Able to do my duty here?" Did he doubt her? She

spun to face him, hands on hips. "I can be just as strong as you are. You aren't the only one capable of subterfuge, Cormac. Just because I find this whole business dreadful does not mean that I cannot do what's necessary to find and save Davie."

He merely shrugged and, maddeningly, seemed to be fighting a smile.

"What is it?" she asked, in no humor to brook any more of these inscrutable shifts in mood. And to think she'd started the day so cheerfully.

His eyes roved down her body and then back up. She resented the rush of blood she felt in her cheeks. For once, could she bear his gaze on her without blushing like an unschooled maiden?

Not that she *wasn't* an unschooled maiden. She'd reached her twenty-third birthday an unschooled maiden, and would likely see her *seventy-third* the same way. She pursed her lips into a frown.

His eyes lingered on her shoulders. "Aren't wealthy married ladies supposed to . . . to do something with their hair?"

She'd donned one of her finest dresses, but she hadn't given much thought to her hair, leaving it long and loose instead, as a young maid might. And although she supposed he had a point, she was feeling contentious. "I'm a spinster, Cormac." The word *spinster* spat from her mouth like venom. "I can do what I like with my hair."

He opened his mouth, then shut it again, the look on his face unreadable. "A spinster, eh?" He shook his head.

Whatever did he mean by the headshake?

She lifted her chin, feeling ready for battle. "What did that mean?"

"What did what mean, Ree?"

She glared, unwilling to let him distract her with that blasted nickname. "The . . . *this*," she said, mimicking the slow shaking of his head with wide and impatient eyes.

A smile spread slowly on his face. He scanned his eyes once more along her body.

She thought her heart would hammer out of her chest. *Unreadable, unpredictable, unnerving.* The man was throwing her off balance.

"Only that I find it amusing." He shrugged. "Marjorie Keith, a spinster."

"Fine," she snapped. "I'll pull my hair back."

"Not on my account."

"Oh no, Cormac," she said with mock sincerity. "You are absolutely correct. I mustn't forget, I am playing the part of a wealthy lady. I shall immerse myself entirely."

He gave her a quick nod. She imagined she saw a flicker of unease on his face, and it gratified her.

"Though, Cormac," she said sweetly, "I will, of course, need your help."

"You need help?"

"Oh yes, I usually have a maid for these things." She wandered to the small mirror that hung by the bedside and, gathering her hair at the nape of her neck, studied herself intently. "If we're playing the part of a wealthy couple, and I find myself traveling without my maid, why then, you will need to act the part."

"Of your maid?" he said incredulously.

"Well . . . not that precisely." It took effort, but she tossed off her best carefree giggle. "But the part of a dutiful husband, certainly."

Dutiful husband. Marjorie couldn't tell if his answering silence was fury or if it might possibly be related to the strange internal quivering she knew *she* felt at the prospect.

"I've brought my ivory comb for just such a purpose." Letting go of her hair, she lowered her arms, and she caught sight of his reflection in the mirror. Though she'd been having a hard time reading him, she thought Cormac's current look was decidedly *not* fury.

She dug her comb from her satchel and tossed it on the mattress. "I can gather my hair into a knot," she said, willing her voice to calm. "I'll just need you to tuck it for me."

Reaching her arms behind her head, she felt her bodice pull tight. And though she studiously avoided looking at him, Marjorie felt Cormac's eyes on her. Her heart pounded mercilessly. "The angle is too awkward for me, you see."

Fighting to master her suddenly inept fingers, she smoothed her hair, winding it into a bun at the base of her neck. She swallowed hard. "Now if you'll be so kind . . ." She nodded to the ivory comb on the bed.

He picked it up, and all she registered was his large, strong hand on the mattress where she'd been sleeping just hours before. Marjorie blinked hard. Why had she put the comb on the *bed*?

She curled her fingers tightly into her bun. She'd remain composed. She wouldn't let him see her fingers tremble.

"All you need to—"

"So how do I—"

They each spoke over the other. She laughed nervously, but Cormac remained as stoic as ever.

"Simply make sure the hair is smooth," she said, sweeping her hand up from the bottom of the bun.

He reached out with the comb, and their hands brushed. His was warm, and she pictured the broad strength of it. She imagined that hand stroking her hair, cupping the back of her head.

"Yes, that's it." She cursed the breathy sound of her voice. "Now simply push the comb down, securing it . . ." She tapered off, feeling the gentle touch of his fingers.

It was such a novel thing, his touch. New and unfamiliar, yet she imagined she'd somehow recognize the feel of his hands anywhere.

She realized he'd finished and experienced a peculiar moment of loss.

"And there!" she exclaimed overly brightly. She gave herself one last look in the mirror. "I am a wealthy lady."

She turned to face him, but Cormac was already halfway across the room. She felt her shoulders slump.

Strange, surly, *incomprehensible* man. So much for her *dutiful husband.*

Husband. Marjorie's eyes narrowed. The man avoided her gaze and instead bustled about their tiny room as if suddenly plagued by a battery of menial tasks.

A slow smile dawned on her face. *Husband indeed.*

If Cormac wanted her to play a part, a part is exactly what he would get.

Chapter 16

"Oh, *Hughie*," Marjorie cooed, "I couldn't possibly set foot on such a filthy boat."

"Hughie?" Cormac muttered. He began to pull away, so she leaned in, gripping his arm more tightly. He scanned the harbor and its bustle of people, and then shot her a wicked look. "'Tis known as a ship, *Gormelia*, not a boat." He hadn't bothered to pitch his voice lower.

She frowned. Cormac would be harder to bait than she'd thought.

Shielding her eyes from the glare, Marjorie took in the massive vessel at the end of the pier. Of the ships newly docked in Justice Port, only two were large enough to accommodate a hold full of slaves: the *Oliphant* and the *Venture*.

She'd thought the *Venture* had sounded the likelier of the two for nefarious dealings, but subtle inquiries and a few strolls nearby had turned up nothing more suspect than a gaggle of missionaries bound for the tropics.

They wandered toward the *Oliphant* instead, and as

they approached, she stared, goggle-eyed. As a resident
of Aberdeen, Marjorie had seen ships before, but as a
gently bred woman, never had she dreamed of seeing one
this close. It was vast, with three masts, a battery of can-
nons, and a belly easily broad enough to accommodate a
cargo full of slaves.

A shiver ran up her spine. *Davie.*

The *Oliphant* was grand indeed, and she felt sure
Davie was on board. She stared, trying to imagine
where he might be and how they might get on board to
save him. They were close now, and the thrill of it was
exhilarating.

The ship buzzed with activity, an entire world unto
itself. Sailors busily loaded supplies, wheeling carts and
rolling barrels aboard, preparing for what appeared to be
a long voyage. There was so much hustle and bustle, if
their initial plan pretending to buy slaves failed, surely
there was some way she and Cormac could simply sneak
onto the ship and find him.

On deck, sea-weathered men shouted orders, cleaning,
scurrying, and most startling of all, climbing. "Look!"
she exclaimed, pointing to the men clambering up amid
the sails. "There are men up high. They look so tiny and
faraway, like wee birds flying up the ropes."

She tightened her grip on his arm. "I'm certain Davie
is on board. I can just feel it. How I wish we could just
storm aboard this instant and get him."

She glanced up at Cormac, and the blank look on his
face squelched her excitement.

"They're called lines," he told her flatly. "Not ropes.
Lines. 'Tis the ship's rigging."

"Oh." They continued to stare, quiet for a moment,
and then she sighed, *"Rigging."* Marjorie shook her head
as though dumbfounded. "Oh, *Lord Brodie*, you are so
very wise. Indeed, the cleverest of all men. I thank you
for enlightening your dimwitted bride."

His lip twitched. *A smile?*

She appreciated the gravity with which Cormac approached their mission, but they were so close now, there was no reason it couldn't be an adventure they shared. Last night's laughter over his Bridget story had been too great a pleasure—she wanted more. Marjorie decided she'd get her ill-tempered *Lord Brodie* to smile before the day was through.

"But what a name," she said, turning her attention back to the ship. *"Oliphant?"*

"Aye, like that comb in your hair."

She gave him a quizzical look.

"Ivory, lass. Tusks . . . ivory. Oliphant, as in . . ." His voice petered out, and she felt as much as heard his distraction.

"You mean ele—?"

"Ist."

Normally she might have badgered Cormac for so rudely ordering her to silence, but that had been *before* her last visit to the docks. Every muscle in her body froze, except for her heart, which thudded powerfully in her chest. *Not again.*

She eased closer to him, grateful she had his arm to hold. At least she wasn't in men's trews this time.

"Don't move," he whispered. "A man stands behind us."

Moving was the farthest thing from her mind. In fact, merely breathing had become an effort.

"I daresay, you two make an unlikely pair of visitors."

Cormac stiffened at the sound of the stranger's voice.

"You've taken a fancy to the *Oliphant*, I see."

Placing a steadying hand at her back, Cormac slowly faced the newcomer. The man was not much older than forty, solidly built, with dark hair. And, Marjorie realized, he wasn't unattractive. He had quite a pleasant face, really. Smiling, her shoulders eased in relief.

Cormac, however, remained tense at her side. "You are . . . ?"

"Why, I suppose I could ask the same thing." The stranger broke into a broad smile, which he aimed right at Marjorie.

Frowning, Cormac sidled closer to her.

"But it is *you* who are the newcomers to my wee corner of Aberdeen, and so I shall be the one to bid welcome." He swept a bow. "Malcolm Forbes. Aberdeen bailie, at your service."

"I am Hugh Brodie, and this is my wife, Lady Gormelia."

The sincerity bled from her smile. *That ridiculous name.*

"Forbes," Marjorie exclaimed, the pieces falling into place. He must be the one who was a friend of Archie's father. "But of course I've heard of you."

While she returned the man's smile, Cormac's hand slid to grip her waist. Firmly.

She cursed her eager—and unthinking—response. She'd heard of Forbes because she hailed from Aberdeen. Lady Gormelia, however, could claim no such thing. She decided to amend the error at once. "Are you the Forbes from Lanarkshire?"

She'd caught Cormac's grimace, and she stood a little taller. She thought hers a fine enough ruse, as ruses went.

"Oh dear no," the bailie said. "I and my five magistrate peers all hail from Aberdeen."

"Did you hear that, my little trout?" Cormac said tightly. "Aberdeen has *six* bailies. Truly we're far from the banks of the Clyde now."

Little trout? Little trout? Did he just call her his *little trout*? She could concede that referring to him as *Hughie* might be construed as goading, but the maddening man just raised the stakes.

"Ah, you're Lowlanders, I see."

"Aye, from a village east of the Clyde," Marjorie said. "But not for long—"

"Not for long, however," Cormac interrupted, "as we find ourselves on the brink of a great move. My wee trout here"—he gave an exaggerated squeeze to her shoulders—"has a sister who just married into a Jamaican coffee plantation."

Marjorie shrugged, attempting to jostle Cormac's arm from around her shoulders. Clearly, he wanted to speak for both of them. The thought that he might believe her incapable of sustaining their drama vexed her.

"Jamaica. Of course," Forbes said with a knowing nod. "Croydon, is it? I've an uncle who's spent much time in the Indies."

Marjorie saw Cormac's jaw tighten. They were on dangerous ground. They'd armed themselves with rudimentary information about the coffee business in the West Indies, but they'd also known that nothing could prepare them for the detailed questions that would invariably arise.

She decided that, as a woman, her mistakes would be seen as excusable, expected even. The notion galled her, but she dove in all the same. "Yes, in Croydon. My brother-in-law will be pulling Hughie in as a partner."

"Aye," Cormac broke in quickly. "'Twas most generous of my in-laws. Though it's a bigger enterprise than I've ever faced before. 'Tis why we came here . . . for . . ." Cormac looked meaningfully at the ship.

"Ah. You'll be wanting introductions, of course." A smile spread across the bailie's face. "I'm hosting a dinner tomorrow, and I insist you come. There will be folk in attendance whom you must meet."

"I'd be honored." Cormac glanced down at Marjorie and gave her an assessing look. She imagined she saw a warning in his eyes, and it rankled. "Though I imagine yours isn't an affair for women."

She glared back up at him. "But *Hughie*," she said through gritted teeth, "I would simply *adore* dining with the bailie."

"And so you shall," Forbes said merrily. "Wives are most welcome at my affairs. In fact, you'll have much to discuss with the other women. It's a whole new world in the Indies; there will be much for you to prepare for, my lady. There is the intense heat, for one. And such a remarkable variety of flora and fauna!"

"Oh! Flora and fauna?" Marjorie clapped her hands. Hughie's *little trout* wasn't done yet. "How uniquely fortuitous! My husband does adore our feathered kin."

"Truly?" Forbes looked taken aback.

"Truly," Marjorie replied before Cormac had a chance to. She avoided his gaze and the daggers she felt pointed her way. But really, she couldn't abide being silenced or shut out.

"Any particular . . . species?" Forbes asked Cormac. "That is the correct phraseology, is it not?"

Marjorie wrested the attention back to her. "Rare varieties of duck are an *especial* favorite. A veritable duck *expert* is my husband. Isn't that right, Hughie?"

She finally spared Cormac a glance, deciding he looked not unlike a cat ready to pounce. He managed a tight twitch of his head, which she imagined could be construed as a nod.

"Ducks . . ." Forbes mused. "Are there ducks to be found in—?"

Marjorie didn't know the first thing about ducks. Nor did she, at the moment, know just how she might go about bringing her extemporaneous ramble to a close. "Oh, sadly it's no more ducks for Hughie. My Lord Brodie finds himself eager to move on. He's greatly anticipating recording the various tropical species found in the Indies."

She and her foolish temper had her talked into a corner. Forbes seemed to be formulating a question, and the prospect alarmed her.

Just when she began to worry that Cormac was going to leave her hung out to dry, he chimed in. "That's quite enough about me, *trout*. I'm certain our new acquaintance has no interest in the banalities of my pastime."

He gave a patronizing—and, she'd daresay, overly firm—pat to her arm.

Forbes looked visibly relieved. "Well, I must admit to a dreadful lack of knowledge where . . . uh . . . birds are concerned."

Thank goodness. Marjorie breathed a quiet sigh of relief. Her whimsical speech had really been quite reckless. She was certain she'd hear about it later.

She glanced up at Cormac and pursed her lips not to smile. Reckless maybe, but how it had been worth it. The man needed to learn a little humor, and if ducks were the thing to chisel through that stony facade of his, then so be it.

"I may not know birds," Forbes continued, "but I do know business. And the plantations of the Indies are quite the opportunity. Your brother-in-law sounds like a very generous man indeed. But I'm afraid I didn't catch his name . . . ?"

Panic skittered up her spine. She hadn't reckoned on the bailie actually knowing anyone in Jamaica. She forced a brittle smile onto her face. "His name is John. Oh, John! Our dear, lovely John!" With exaggerated dismay, Marjorie brought a hand to her nose and mouth. "But Hughie, I'm afraid this stench is getting to me. Shan't we be on our way?"

As much as Cormac wanted to watch her flail in her own verbal traps, he knew he needed to get them away from there as soon as possible. "I see I've been remiss, my wee trout. If you'll excuse us, Forbes."

"But of course," he replied grandly. "The docks are no place for the fairer sex. I shall send my own carriage for you, tomorrow at six, at the . . . ?"

"Cross Keys Inn. Dockside." Cormac whisked Marjorie around, putting space between them and the bailie. *Fairer sex? How about more unruly, more taxing, more maddening* . . . He strained to keep their charade while Forbes was still in sight. Mustering affected cheer, he called over his shoulder, "Tomorrow at six then!"

When they were out of view, he dropped her arm as though she were leprous. "What in blazes were you thinking?"

"Well, nothing, obviously." She shook her arm, flinching away from him even though he'd already separated from her. "Seeing as mere *wives* are good for naught but thinking about the weather and—"

"And don't forget flora and fauna." *Blasted woman.* He didn't know where she came up with such nonsense. "Seems as though you had much to say on *that* particular topic."

"You provoked me."

"I?" Cormac stopped in his tracks. "*I* provoked *you*?"

"Yes. You've been goading me since we left Dunnottar, in fact."

He merely stared at her. She'd dressed as a wealthy lady would, in a blue-green gown that set off the color of her eyes. The tight bodice pressed her breasts into two perfect globes; all day it had been an effort to keep his gaze above her chin. And she claimed *he* provoked *her*?

She stormed on, toward the inn, and he jogged to catch up.

"How, exactly, have I managed to so bedevil you? By helping you on this mission of yours? By keeping you safe? Or was it when I fed you and gave you a bed while I slept on the floor?"

"You didn't have to—" She stopped herself from saying something, and Cormac couldn't help but imagine her completed thought.

"Didn't have to what, Ree?" he asked in a low whisper. Stepping closer, he took her arm, and he might as well have stepped before an open flame, so much did her proximity scorch him. "Sleep apart from you?"

She blushed, giving him a breathless look that made him wild and wishing he *had* crawled into bed with her.

Marjorie pulled away and strode on, entering the inn

with an angry sweep of her skirts. "You didn't have to speak for me at the docks. I am perfectly capable—"

"Of getting yourself into trouble." He lowered his voice so as not to be overheard, nodding a perfunctory greeting to the innkeeper as they passed.

"Oh *Hughie*, I know a fine husband like you would never allow that to happen." She stormed up the stairs to their door, fumbling with the lock.

Cormac snatched the key from her to open it.

"And Hughie, how wonderful that your little *trout* has such a great man like you to open doors for her." She stomped into their bedroom. "To make her decisions, and to speak for her."

"Och, Ree, stop this." He closed the door. The woman had lost her head. *Force decisions upon her?* The concept was laughable. Cormac would be first in line to swear there wasn't a man alive capable of taking control of Marjorie. "I only worried—"

"You worried I'd mess it up, didn't you?" She struggled to unlace her shoes and finally just kicked them off. Standing, she panted before him, lips parted and cheeks flushed. "You worried I couldn't handle a simple act."

He worried she'd get hurt. He worried she'd never find her Davie. He worried the lad was already dead. He worried her heart might break as irrevocably as his had so many years before.

He worried that the sad look in her eyes would never go away.

"That's not it at all."

"You worried I'd ruin everything like I always do."

"Stop it, Marjorie." She was intentionally misunderstanding. She'd whipped herself into a lather, her breasts rising and falling with each breath. He stepped closer.

"Isn't that it, *Hughie*?" She tore the comb from her hair, and slammed it down on the table. Long curls cascaded over her shoulders. "You didn't think I'd be able to carry on a simple conversation without—"

"Stop." He took another step.

She sneered. "Oh *Hughie*, am I bothering—"

Another step. "Stop it with this *Hughie* business."

"Make me!"

He did—with a kiss.

Chapter 17

He couldn't fight it. Feeling had seared back to life in his numb heart, and he'd awoken ravenous. Ree was nothing *but* feeling and passion, and it set him on fire.

He kissed her, pouring the whole of his godforsaken soul into it.

His mouth took hers fiercely, and she opened to him, twining her tongue with his, all eager innocence. Her hair had gotten trapped under his hand, and he laced his fingers through the long, silky waves. The scent of her filled his senses, and his body responded, quickening, straining against her. The press of her belly against his hardness taunted him, and he grabbed her bottom with his other hand, holding her tighter, closer.

She moaned in response, melting into him as if there were nobody and nothing else in the world, and the glory of it broke the last of his resolve. His hand roved to her breast, and she was soft and full in his palm, just as he'd always imagined she'd be.

What he'd never imagined was just how fiery, how desperate, her response would be. She writhed for him, swiveling her hips, rubbing into him, her nipple stiff and eager in his hand.

He stroked and pinched her, and her breath caught faster. Her heart hammered furiously against his chest. And the closeness felt right. She felt right.

It *was* right.

She was so soft and so sweet.

And she was his.

He knew in that moment that it had always been that way. Ree had been his when they were children. And now that he was a man, she belonged to him more than she ever had.

After years of numbness, she made him feel such violent emotions. More than that, Marjorie made him *feel*.

There was a commotion outside—shouts bantered across the alley, followed by a clattering.

Reluctantly they parted. She whimpered a protest, but Cormac forced himself to focus. He needed to remain on alert.

He went to the window, sensing her following even before she touched him. For a moment, he held his breath, savoring only the heat of her at his back.

A pale and tender hand stroked up and under his arm. And another, from the other side. Gently, Marjorie wrapped her arms around his stomach, and standing behind him, she rested her head on the side of his arm. "The sweepers."

A handful of raggedly clad men were clearing offal and refuse from the alley below. Left unsaid was the distant memory of gazing out a different window, at a different brand of sweepers. "Aye, just the street sweeps."

"Would that the city could sweep the docks clear of *all* its horrors," she said.

"Aye. Would that." Cormac brought one of her hands to his lips, kissed her palm, and replaced it at his belly. She'd only just begun to lose her innocence, and it pained him.

In the meantime, there was much work to do to prepare

for their next meeting with the bailie. "It seems we've a dinner to attend tomorrow."

She deflated. "We need to think up names for my imaginary sister and her husband."

"Don't fret on account of that. 'Twill be easy enough. New money and enterprising new faces abound in the Indies. We've simply to choose a common enough name and then bandy it about with all the confidence of a preacher on Sunday."

"Is that a skill you learned in the wars? How to deceive?"

He thought for a moment she was speaking facetiously, but Marjorie waited attentively, still hugging him from behind.

Deception. She had no idea the treachery he was capable of. It was a gulf that would be forever between them. Sometimes it felt like a gulf that lay between him and the rest of the world.

"I don't know that I'd call it a skill so much as a curse, but aye, deception is some of what I learned at war."

He reached around to pull Marjorie by his side. He'd bridge that gulf as best he could. Only for her.

Tucking her under his arm, he kissed her lightly on the crown of her head. After a while, he chuckled. "Now, what I didn't learn was *birds*. It looks as though I need to brush up on my mallard facts before tomorrow evening."

"I know. I'm sorry." She turned her head into him, hiding her face for a moment. "But, you know, a man can never know too much about the world around him."

He laughed outright, and it felt strange and good. "I see."

"And besides, if women will be there, mayhap there will be dancing, too." She reached up to pat his cheek. "I do fancy a good reel."

Possessiveness coursed to life in his veins. "You're only allowed to dance with me."

"Oh really?" She shook her head, but there was humor in her voice. "Cormac MacAlpin, is there any man in this world whose company you *do* accept? You detest Archie, and you seemed ready to throttle the bailie."

Anger flared, recalling both of those fools. "Forbes smiled too much. It wasn't right. He struck me as over-familiar. They both do. So, no, lass. I'm afraid there's not a man in the world I'd let you dance with. But I'll not be accused of small-mindedness." He paused for a moment, letting himself truly think on it. "Fine, I suppose you could dance with my brother Declan. In a pinch. If you must."

"Not Gregor?" She practically purred the question, and envy clenched his chest. Women adored his older brother, for whom life, love, and many a reel came easily.

"Och, never Gregor. You stay away from Gregor. The man's a rakehell."

"I see." She grew reserved. Just when Cormac feared his response had been overly vehement, she asked, "But you? Will you dance with me, then?" Her voice was deceptively mild, and he imagined he heard some uncertainty there.

The bold and lovely Ree, insecure? He couldn't credit it.

He'd not danced in years, but in that moment, he thought he could put aside their troubles, could forget the despair of his years and the certain suffering of this world, to dance with her till the end of time.

"Aye, lass, I suppose someone has to keep you from dancing with the bailie."

Chapter 18

The moment they stepped into the hall, Marjorie was captivated. Malcolm Forbes hailed from a well-to-do family, which his surroundings made no pretense to deny. The great hall had been transformed into a grand dance floor, with torches, candelabra, and a giant fireplace all illuminating the scene with warm, amber light. Musicians played in the corner, and knots of dancers whirled and laughed before her. It was like glimpsing a fairy tale.

Momentary panic clenched her chest. Their plan was to gather as much information as possible, which might make them conspicuous. She'd had occasion to meet folk who moved in Aberdeen's finer circles—would anyone here recognize her?

But, looking around the room, she eased. More than unfamiliar, these lords and ladies struck her as utterly foreign. The men dressed in waistcoats more luxurious than Aberdeen fashion typically allowed. And the women were downright flamboyant, with jeweled gowns and elaborate plumage sprouting from their heads.

She bit her lip not to smirk. Hopefully none of the

ladies would have occasion to discuss said plumage with her allegedly bird-loving Hughie.

"The look on your face would frighten a lesser man." She felt Cormac's hand come to rest at her back. Marjorie glanced up at him and wondered at the strange light that danced in his eyes. Perhaps it was the exotic setting, but his guard seemed temporarily down.

"Remember, Ree, I'll ask the questions. Don't say it," he added quickly, obviously seeing temper furrow her brow. "I know you are capable of more, but tonight you have only to look your bonny self."

"Yes, we went over the plan." She sighed. She'd reluctantly agreed that, while she should stand by Cormac, gleaning as much as possible, the moment would likely come when he'd go off with the men. He'd use the opportunity to learn as much as he could.

Davie. They were so close now. It was only a matter of finding out how to penetrate the *Oliphant*, and they'd find Davie. And so her own inaction was fine with her.

Just this once.

She pulled her shoulders back, adopting the mien of a wealthy lady set to embark to the Indies.

"That look again," Cormac muttered. He brought his lips to her ear. "What wickedness are you devising now, Gormelia?"

Wickedness. The notion had her looking away, studying the dance floor with feigned intent. She blushed to think it, but she'd been devising all manner of wickedness since they'd shared their first kiss.

He'd slept on the floor, but she'd get him up and off that deuced pallet yet. Her pulse leapt at the thought.

"I'm imagining the fresh torments with which I can assail you."

Cormac didn't immediately respond, and so she looked back up at him, expecting to be met by his glower. But instead, he was watching her with hooded eyes.

"Torment me?" he asked, his voice husky. He had

leaned close, and she felt his breath along her neck. The pleasure of it shivered across her skin.

Awareness of him shimmered to life. As if a veil had lifted from between them, she became keenly aware of the heat of him, the scent of him, the rhythm of his breath and heart.

She generally felt in control of situations, but this repartee had her scrambling. Feigning nonchalance, she scanned the room, taking in the swirl of strangers in shimmering skirts and velvet coats. "Aye, you. I intend on persecuting you mercilessly—"

"How I tremble." His hand snaked down to her lower back, scandalously close to the swell of her bottom.

She would not let him gain the upper hand. Setting her shoulders, she continued, "Until either you concede my superior intelligence, or . . ."

"Or?" His voice was bemused.

Curse him, she could be just as casual. She forced her voice to steadiness. "Or you agree to a dance."

"When will you learn, Ree?" He chuckled low. "You're no match for me."

She gasped as he took her hand and led her to the dance floor. As far as she knew, Cormac's feet hadn't seen a dance floor since he was a boy. And yet his movements were commanding, his hand on hers calm and assured. It was exhilarating.

"I challenge you to do your worst," he whispered, finding them a place near the center of the floor.

She darted a quick glance around. Surrounded by all these outlandish strangers, she felt as though the two of them had become a single unit circumnavigating some strange new world. The other men cut fine forms on the dance floor, and yet they seemed to define the term *popinjay*, all grand birds in their jewel-toned velvet coats. They struck her as far inferior compared to Cormac. He wore only a plain brown waistcoat, a simple shirt, and muted tartan trews, and yet he made all these men in their peacocks' clothing appear weak and simply . . . less.

The reel was transitioning into a strathspey, and the music slowed, drawing couples closer together, the dancers gradually organizing into pairs rather than groups of four or more.

She and Cormac came together side by side. He brought his arm over her shoulder, taking her right hand in his right, and left in left. He stood so handsome and tall, held her so close, their real names forgotten amid this roomful of strangers, and it was a thing of magic. Marjorie imagined she could be this other person, could be simply a woman enjoying a dance with her husband. Her shoulders eased, savoring this brief respite from her worries, from her very reality. There on the dance floor, all thought about the night's goal faded from her mind.

The music began, and slowly they walked forward, their steps taking them across the dance floor. The heat of his thigh blazed along her own until it rippled slow and sultry between her legs, leaving her feeling agitated, breathless.

"Ease yourself, lass." The edges of his profile caught the firelight—his strong jaw, the uneven line of his nose—and his bearing struck her as especially powerful in the shadows. And yet she saw an uncharacteristic lightness, too, playing in his eyes.

She managed a nod, pretending to concentrate on the dance.

He gave her hands a squeeze, and the heat between her legs spread to her belly, melting her from within. The floor was filled with couples, but for her, Cormac was the only other person in the room.

"You'll want to breathe, aye?"

Her eyes narrowed at the humor in his voice. "It's merely the cut of my gown that restricts my breath so."

"Ah, is that the only matter, then?"

The dancers began to pivot, and just as she wondered how her stunned body might manage to shift positions, he spun her, his movements sure and confident but gentle, too.

The only matter? Not nearly, she thought, trying for a

deeper breath. "I had no idea you knew how to . . ." Her voice tapered off, thinking about all the things she had no idea about. She thought she'd known Cormac, until she'd experienced his skillful kisses, his confident dancing.

Had he been doing more than waging war in their years apart? Jealousy dumped into her veins like sour milk.

"No idea how to dance?" Cormac pulled her tightly to him. The tempo shifted, and couples came together, chest to chest, to waltz about the room. "We danced as children, do you not recall?"

He held her close, closer than was proper, and though her cheeks blazed red, she couldn't bring herself to push him away.

"I remember," she said, recalling the many playful reels danced at the adults' heels. It had never been like this, though. Not even close. Even when her little-girl thoughts of him had turned to imagined smiles and kisses, she had never felt this. "But . . ."

But had he danced with other women? Had he held others in his arms like this?

"But . . . ?" he mused, crushing her chest closer to his. Cormac's hand glided from her waist to rest low on her back. If not for the layers of skirts, his fingers would be splaying just over the crest of her bottom.

A peculiar urgency bloomed to life in her core, pushing thoughts of other women from her head. She knew better than anyone: the only mistress in Cormac's life was the sea. But, in this moment, his body was hard against hers, and for now that was all she'd have a mind for.

As he swung her about the room, her breasts chafed against him until she thought she'd die from this feeling. This unspeakable, almost angry need for him simply to stop, for all the others simply to disappear, and for him to get on with doing everything his body threatened to do.

He must've felt it, too, for he managed to pull her even nearer, cradling his manhood against her. He looked down at her, his slate-blue eyes dark with lust, and she fought to stay on her feet in time to the music.

"But it was never like this," he said, giving voice to her thoughts. "I'd always—"

The strathspey ended, and the guests cheered to hear the band breaking into the jaunty opening bars of "Strip the Willow." They were forced to part, and the moment her hand slid from his, Marjorie's chest felt hollowed.

She faltered, stunned from the intensity of their last dance. Reluctantly, they joined the others to form two rows, a line of men facing a line of women.

What had he been about to say? Always *what*?

Her careening thoughts distracted her, and when their turn came to meet in the middle, linking arms to spin down between the lines of dancers, she was a beat behind. She skipped a step forward to catch up, and when Cormac laughed outright, the delight in his eyes disarmed her.

When was the last time she'd seen such easy pleasure on his face? The sight of it startled a carefree laugh from her.

Always what? she mouthed when next she caught his eye.

The corner of his mouth lifted in a smile, but there was darkness in his eyes. Her laugh stilled as that dark intensity wended its way straight to her belly. How did he manage it? How could a simple look from him stagger her so? Dancing with Cormac was by turns pure joy and utter disquiet, her body and heart experiencing such uncharted heights and wants.

Their turn came again to twirl arm in arm down the center column, and as he spun her, she fought to maintain composure. "Always what, Cormac?" she managed breathlessly.

"Always wondered . . ." They approached the midpoint, and he slowed their steps, prolonging their contact. He canted his head down to hers. Instead of finishing his thought, the completion of an earlier conversation came out in a rush. "You'd said you asked after me. Did you truly, Ree? Did you think of me, all these years?"

Their hands parted as they reached the end, and they

returned to their rows, their eyes locked as they took their places in the lines.

He was asking for no less than a glimpse into her soul. It felt like a critical moment, a leap into the unknown, a moment to be reckless with her feelings or to tread with care.

There was nothing to consider. Had she thought of him? She'd done nothing *but* think of him. She nodded slowly, and a smile spread wide on his face.

A truly unfettered smile from Cormac. She hadn't seen the sight in nigh on thirteen long years. She beamed back at him.

The dance became a blur around them, and soon their turn came again. His strong arm linked with hers. The smile was gone from his face now, his tone fierce and low. "I thought of you, too, Ree. Asked after you, too."

Could it be? Could he care for her as she did for him? The mere thought made her tremble.

All the couples paired off as the dance approached its finale. And as the music sped, Cormac braced her elbow with a firm hand, spinning her faster and faster till she thought her feet would leave the ground.

He laughed aloud, and the exultation on his face made her heart soar.

The music stopped abruptly, and they fell into each other, their hearts pounding an erratic beat against their chests. He held her longer than was strictly appropriate, but the couples shifting and rearranging around them seemed oblivious to two lovers on the periphery.

Reality slowly pierced Marjorie's consciousness, and she began to pull away, but Cormac gripped her arm, stilling her. His breath stirred her hair, and she felt warmed utterly from within. As she gradually caught her own breath, she realized Cormac stood frozen, his body seized, breathing measured, and every muscle tense and still as granite.

"Cormac?" she whispered, unlinking her elbow from his to run her hand up his arm.

He turned into her to hug her close, caressing his hand up the side of her torso. He stroked his thumb scandalously along the edge of her breast and shuddered in a breath, and she became aware of another aspect of his body grown terribly hard.

"Oh . . ." she gasped. She nestled closer, his manhood digging into her belly, and she felt wicked and free. "Oh."

"Come, Ree," he told her, his voice husky. Their eyes met, his blue-gray gaze turned dangerously intense in the shadows. "Come with me."

Chapter 19

Marjorie looked up at Cormac, her heart skittering madly. She curled her fingers into the sleeve of his coat in an effort to steady herself. "Where are you taking me?"

"Why, all this dancing is making you faint, aye?" He brushed an errant lock from her damp brow. Putting his hand over hers, he pulled her grip from his sleeve, twining her fingers with his. "It seems to me I need to take you to find yourself some sort of . . . salon in which to recover."

"Ohh. I see." She bit back a smile. She put a dramatic hand to her chest. "Why yes. I think I *am* feeling a bit light-headed."

"Damn," Cormac whispered, his features sharpening.

"What is it?"

Pressing his hand on her shoulder, he attempted to steer Marjorie to the left, but it was too late. A knot of dancers had parted to reveal the bailie. He'd spotted them and, with a broad grin, was heading straight toward them.

"Damn," she repeated with gusto, and Cormac's startled laugh almost made the disappointment worth it.

"Why if it isn't Lord and Lady Brodie!" Forbes extended his arms in a hearty greeting. "Welcome, welcome."

His gaze shifted from Cormac to Marjorie, a question in his eyes.

She schooled her features, realizing she must look the picture of stunned outrage.

"But is aught the matter?" he asked them.

Marjorie deflated. *Aught* indeed. She'd been about to get Cormac alone.

She steeled herself. The bailie was the whole reason they were there. Never would they get a better opportunity to gather information, to find Davie. And, as much as it vexed her, she knew Cormac was the one to do it. She adopted what she hoped was the expression of a fainting flower.

"I'm afraid I'm feeling light-headed." She gave Cormac a pointed look, hoping he'd understand her message: it was up to him now. "Perhaps I shall seek out the company of the other ladies?"

"Ah, yes," Forbes said, understanding her dilemma at once. "The fire blazes high, and what with all the dancers, women with such fine constitutions as your own are wont to need a rest."

It took an effort not to swat the bailie's arm and give him a dose of her *fine constitution*. She nodded weakly instead.

"You'll find a number of the wives in a small sitting room just beyond the library," he continued. "And might I recommend a sip of my wife's ambrosia? Don't fear," he added in an aside to Cormac. "It'll be sure to put the color back in your wife's cheeks."

He turned back to Marjorie. "It's a recipe from her aunt. From the Indies, of course. There they distill the most decadent spirits. Rumbullion, it's called, and I daresay it tastes as dark and as dangerous as the tropics themselves."

An elegant, black-haired woman floated up to his

elbow, the cobalt-blue feathers in her hair a perfect match to her low-cut gown. She was more exotic than beautiful, with a prominent nose and a small, pursed mouth.

"Ah, but here is my dearest Adele now." The bailie put his arm at his wife's back.

The woman sketched them a flirtatious curtsy. "You were speaking of Aunt Sesane's punch? Or by 'dark and dangerous' did you mean me?" Her laughter trilled over the din. She spoke in a peculiar accent, and Marjorie wondered if she was the most appealing or most *un*appealing creature she'd ever met.

She eyed Adele, and suddenly the prospect of sampling a forbidden drink lifted her mood considerably. "Your husband spoke to me of your aunt's rumbullion, and dare I say, it sounds lovely."

Cormac shot her a warning glance, but Marjorie only smiled. She was no stranger to the occasional brandy; surely she could handle a taste of some tropical concoction. And besides, she'd likely get more information from a roomful of punch-drunk ladies than Cormac ever would from the bailie and his cronies.

"Fine, fine," Forbes said at once, clearly eager to be done with the wives. "Come, Lord Brodie, I know just the men you need to meet. Tell me, how are you at the billiard table?"

Adele linked arms with Marjorie, sweeping her from the room. It was a promising start, and Marjorie estimated she had approximately one hour and no more than two of these rumbullions to wrest as much information from the woman as possible.

"Adele," she mused. "It's such a lovely name. French, is it?"

"Well reckoned, Lady Brodie." The woman bowed her head, a kittenish smile curving her thin lips. "My mother was French, the daughter of a well-to-do plantation owner. She met my father in Barbados. He hailed from Edinburgh, a worker from one of the more . . . how to say *mal famé*? . . . from one of its dodgier neighborhoods. A servant dallying with his master's daughter? It was quite the *affaire*."

It seemed owning slaves was routine practice. Aidan popped into mind, and Marjorie wondered if Adele's father had been transported by force or had gone to Barbados willingly.

The bailie's wife flicked open her fan, its mother-of-pearl handle glittering in the candlelight. A wicked smile lit her eyes. "But who could blame my mother, *non*? A sheltered girl, but with *Parisian* blood in her veins, meets a handsome field worker with thick arms and an equally thick . . ." Her laughter chimed like crystal bells. "*Bien sûr que oui!* A healthy dowry, a generous inducement to shut the mouths of the other workers, *et voilà*, I appear seven months later."

Marjorie hung on her every word. At first she'd found Adele vaguely unattractive, but charisma alone was transforming the woman into something fascinating and oddly beautiful.

She swept them down a marble-tiled hall into a small room. Thick, smoky scents and the chatter of a dozen women assailed her. Gold-embroidered pillows in dusky colors littered the place, a patchwork of rugs and animal skins underfoot. The wives all lounged on sofas, reclining informally, despite the elegance of their gowns.

Marjorie couldn't stop her gasp.

Adele laughed her peculiar, harmonious laugh. "Perhaps my husband warned you, my lady. In the Indies, you shall find a world quite unlike any you've known before."

"Indeed," she responded, and before she knew it, a cool pewter tankard was placed in her hands. It was large and heavy with drink, its contents smelling of sugar and sin. She sipped, and a shiver ran up her spine.

"Come," Adele said, leading her to one of the sofas. "I insist you tell me where you are from, where you are going."

Marjorie sank into the feather-stuffed silk upholstery.

Concerned she was in over her head, she took a fortifying sip of her drink. The rumbullion tasted of exotic fruits, and it went down surprisingly easily. She sipped again, this time for the flavor of it.

She decided to be as vague as she could. Though, with her luck, Malcolm and Adele Forbes owned a summer home on the banks of the Clyde.

"Hugh and I hail from the south, near the Clyde." She drank again, and the alcohol buzzed up the backs of her legs, rendering them warm and loose. She eased back into the pillows. "But we are very excited to be embarking on this new chapter in our lives. *Jamaica*. The name alone is magical."

"Ah, off to our corner of the world?" another woman chimed in.

Marjorie nodded her response, judiciously sipping rather than speaking.

"And you've never been?"

"No." Marjorie shook her head, and it set a little wheel spinning deep in her skull. She took another sip of her drink in an effort to quiet her mind. "This will be our first trip."

A chorus of exclamations went round the room, the women chattering all at once about the heat, the help, the sun, Scotland, and everything in between.

"This is my first trip back to Scotland in twenty years," one said.

"Imagine!" a few exclaimed in harmony.

"We needed help," another began, "and I'd almost forgotten what strapping lads there are to be found here. My Arthur has become a bit . . . doughy in his later years."

"My husband, too."

"It's native life, you know. And the heat. The men pay to see the work done from the comfort of their hammock, drink in hand."

They couldn't truly be so idle as all that, could they? Marjorie couldn't imagine Cormac indolently issuing orders from the comfort of a hammock.

"I'd forgotten what a *real* Scotsman was like," someone said with a naughty tease in her voice.

Marjorie cringed. These women were all married, and yet they spoke of Scotsmen as studs in the field. What of their husbands? If *she* were married, she couldn't imagine ogling anyone but her own man.

She'd sworn herself to spinsterhood, though, so that meant if she were married, the man in her bed would be *Cormac*. Ogling Cormac at her leisure? She took a cooling sip of her drink, forcing herself to follow the conversation.

"Highland stock *is* quite . . . strapping, no?"

A wave of lascivious giggles swelled through the room. One of the women clapped gleefully, sending an armful of bracelets clattering. Marjorie's eyes were drawn to the obscene array of rubies and gold glittering in the firelight. Just one of those bracelets would feed a poor Aberdeen family for a year.

"But we have simply to ask Adele's mother for the answer to that!"

"Oh indeed," the bailie's wife purred. "You have simply to ask *ma mère*, and she will tell you of a Scotsman's superior flesh."

These women. They had such elegant veneers, and yet deep down they were common, as crass as wenches in a dockside pub. But they were worse still than that, because they pretended to more. And though they *could be* more, they were too selfish, too shallow for their scruples ever to come in line with their elevated station.

"But truly," an older woman added seriously, "there is no better help to be found. And so convenient to be able simply to *choose*."

To choose. Marjorie's stomach turned.

"We found a fine Glasgow boy years ago," someone said. "He'd been begging on the streets."

There was a round of exclamations before another asked, "How did he do with the transition?"

"Oh, you have to be careful. Sometimes the lads adopt

quite the attitude and need a firm hand to lead them straight."

Fury wavered Marjorie's vision, her outrage fueled by the liquor in her veins. She bit her tongue not to lash into all of them.

"The Scottish blood," someone tsked knowingly.

"But our lad has grown into quite the piece." The woman smiled proudly. "I daresay, my maid can't take her eyes from him."

A disgrace. Marjorie's mouth opened, then she snapped it back shut again, worrying for a moment that she might've accidentally barked her thoughts aloud.

"It's the tropical air," someone agreed. "It's much healthier for them than playing catch as catch can in a filthy alley somewhere."

Marjorie's blood pounded until the women's voices blended together into an amorphous hum.

"Oh, indeed. These lads go from climbing chimneys—"

The hum of conversation translated into a buzzing in her skull. *Climbing chimneys.*

God help you, Aidan.

Had Cormac's brother ended up in some man's field? As the curiously coarse dalliance of some lonely plantation wife?

"So dreadful!"

"Yes, and so many die! But, with us, the lads have their fill of fresh air and sunshine."

Marjorie put her fingers to her temple. She needed to focus. Aidan was long gone, but not *Davie.* She could still help Davie. *Concentrate.* She needed to ask something.

"I . . . I should like to find some help, too," Marjorie said, her voice cracking.

"Not with that fine cut of meat you came in with!"

The women tittered wildly.

"Cor—?" She caught herself and forced a saucy laugh, sounding tinny in her ears. "Do you mean my Hughie?"

"Hughie?" Adele mimicked, fanning herself. "Don't

be coy, *ma chérie.* Surely you know the fine specimen
your husband to be."

Fine specimen? Is that how women saw him? Had he
ever taken advantage of what would be women's obvious
interest? Her jaw clenched, and she adjusted herself on
the sofa, attempting to sit straighter in the deep pillows.
"No, I need help of a different sort, for the plantation
work. Where does one . . ." Marjorie faltered, unable to
bring herself to use the word *buy.* She cleared her throat.
"Wherever does one secure such a boy?"

Her eyes scanned the room. These women, who'd
seemed such exotic birds of paradise, now struck her as
merely obscene. To steal children, to make five-year-old
boys do their work for them. It was unconscionable.

"Oh my dear, your husband will be the one to set it up
for you."

"Yes, I'm certain Malcolm will help Lord Brodie with
all the arrangements," Adele assured her.

So the bailie was involved. The realization rocked her.
She brought her cup to her mouth, then thought better of
it, realizing the smell of the rumbullion had gone from
sweet to nauseatingly cloying.

And why wouldn't the bailie be involved? she decided.
According to Parliament, procuring slaves wasn't simply
legal, it was encouraged. More workers in the Indies was
good for the economy. Less loitering poor was good for
the streets.

Just how many people *were* taken? How many boys
stolen from their mothers? Or, God forfend, how many
mothers from their children?

Marjorie's hands began to tremble. She tried to put her
cup on a side table, but it slipped through her fingers and
tumbled to the floor, falling with a muted thump on a
brightly woven carpet. She realized she'd consumed the
entire tankard.

Despite the hush that fell over the room, the buzzing in
Marjorie's head grew deafening.

"Are you all right?" someone asked.

The silence broken, a chorus of voices joined in at once. "Are you feeling ill?"

"It's the drink, I'm sure," someone said, taking Marjorie's hand.

She flinched away, not wanting any of these horrid women to touch her. "I'm fine, truly."

"Adele, lend us your fan." A woman began fanning her, sending bursts of heavily scented perfume swirling.

The smell disgusted her. *They* disgusted her. Clutching her stomach, she scooted to the edge of the sofa. "That's unnecessary, really."

"Did you see, the poor creature downed the entire thing."

Marjorie's stomach roiled, and she swallowed convulsively, her smile feeling like a grimace. "I will be fine, I assure you."

"Who gave her such a serving?"

"Should we fetch the physician?"

She couldn't bear the thought of meeting another person that night. "I . . . I'm fine," Marjorie said, lurching to her feet. *Cormac.* Cormac was the only one she wanted to see. She needed to get out of there. She needed to find Cormac.

"Are you certain?" the bailie's wife asked tentatively. "Perhaps I should accompany you."

The last thing Marjorie wanted was to spend another moment in Adele's company. She forced a smile on her lips. "By no means will I allow you to leave your guests. No, I'm afraid . . . the strain of our travels has finally overcome me. If you'll please excuse me. Your company has been most . . . illuminating."

She reeled from the room, leaning against the wall in the dim hallway. The marble was cool, the tiles and floor appearing as uniform shades of gray in the shadows. It was a relief after such a riot of color and sensation.

There was a moment's silence, and then the ladies' chatter resumed almost instantly.

Cormac. She had to find Cormac. She longed to see

him, hoped the sight of him would reassure her. She couldn't have borne being in the same room as those women for a minute longer.

Holding the wall, Marjorie edged along, eager to get away from the roomful of wives, away from their decadent splendor, from their cruel excess.

The sound of men came to her from the end of the corridor, and she headed for it unthinking. Her footsteps slowed as she approached, realizing she didn't hear the clack of billiard balls or the benignly amicable babble she'd expected. She tiptoed closer. There were just two voices.

One struck her as oddly familiar.

She crept to the doorway, peeking in. The room looked like a small solar, empty now but for two men speaking in earnest.

Marjorie furrowed her brow, not believing her eyes.

A man was speaking furtively with the bailie's butler. The butler reached under his coat to a coin purse tied at his waist. There was the clink of coins as money exchanged hands. The second man took the money, tilting his head as he readjusted his jacket, and the candlelight caught his cheek, illuminating it. Illuminating his perfectly combed hair to a fine sheen.

Marjorie's gorge rose.

Betrayal speared her. And then fear, quick on its heels. She and Cormac needed to get out of there before they were recognized.

Because there in the solar was the last man she ever imagined she'd see.

Chapter 20

"I say!" The bailie froze, hovering over the billiard table, his cue poised in midair. "Lord Brodie, you may want to tend to your wife," he said with a nod toward the door.

Cormac looked, and his heart lurched to his throat. Marjorie stood trembling in the doorway. The hall's dark shadows clung to her, making her wide eyes appear ghostly in the candlelight.

Forbes took his shot, and the balls clacked together and then thunked against the rails. "Seems like she's taken a turn."

"Aye." Cormac handed his cue to one of the other men in the room and went to her at once. Her skin was clammy, and he chafed her arms, trembling and so delicate in his hands. "What's happened?"

"'Tis the rumbullion, I'll wager," the man said with a knowing smile.

Forbes leaned against the table, taking a contemplative sip of whiskey. "She's a delicate constitution that one."

Cormac glanced back at the billiard table. He'd esti-mated he had only one more round of the deuced game before he could broach where one might acquire a smuggled boy from the Aberdeen docks.

"Cormac?" Marjorie's voice cracked, and all thoughts of smugglers and slaves flew from his mind.

"If you'll forgive us," he said, even though he was halfway out the door already, his back to the bailie and company.

As they left, somebody mused, "*She's* off to Jamaica?" and was answered by a round of skeptical clucking.

"What is it, Ree? Are you ill? Did the women say something?" Cormac whisked her down the hall, practically carrying her as he went. He wished he *could* simply sweep her into his arms, but they'd drawn enough attention to themselves already. He saw the set to her jaw and realized it might be anger, not fear, that had her trembling so. "What's happened?"

"We must go," she said, coming to herself. She looked around frantically, tugging his arm to spur him on. "It's Archie—he's here. We must go, Cormac. Now, before he sees us."

"Archie?" Cormac asked, confused.

"Yes," she hissed, her face in a snarl. "He was taking"— she glanced around—"taking *money*. From the bailie's manservant."

"Archie," he repeated, understanding dawning. What business would the hallowed physician surgeon of Saint Machar have with Malcolm and Adele Forbes? Marjorie had said Archie's father was friendly with the bailie, but just how friendly did one have to be to mingle among this eccentric crowd, or worse, to have some reason for the bailie to pay him off?

He resumed his stride, supporting Marjorie with an arm at her back and one at her elbow. "Money? Are you sure?"

"Yes, I am certain—"

They reached the foyer, and their conversation ground to a halt at the sight of said butler. They requested their return carriage and finally were able to bid a stiff and hasty farewell.

"I saw it," Marjorie said the instant the carriage door closed. "The butler dug something from his coin purse and gave it to *Archie*." She paused for emphasis.

"Popinjays with their bloody purses," he mumbled. "A real man would carry a sporran. I knew I didn't trust the look of him."

She glared. "Be serious, Cormac."

"Och, calm yourself, Ree. We mustn't make assumptions," he said steadily, even as he was coming to the same conclusion. "There might well be another reason Archie was there."

"What?" She scooted as far from him on the carriage bench as she could. "Another reason? I thought you despised Archie, and now all of a sudden you're standing up for him?"

"I'm not standing up for him." Cormac fought not to crack a smile at her vehemence. "I'm simply saying, perhaps we should find out all the facts before—"

"And to think he comes each week to work with the boys. He knows everything, about every one of them. Their health, their history." She stared out the window, worrying her hands in her skirts. "If Archie is involved in nefarious goings-on . . ."

"Nefarious, is it? How are you so certain it's as depraved as all that?" Sighing, Cormac sidled closer. Taking Marjorie's chin in his hand, he turned her to face him. "Don't forget. The slave trade is entirely legal. Sanctioned by Parliament, forbye."

"So it is. But last I checked, parleying with smugglers and pirates is decidedly *il*legal." The last thought seemed to break her, and her chin began to quiver. "I think we have to tell my uncle."

Tears pooled in those vivid blue eyes, her face a sweet ruin. *Dear, innocent Ree.*

He had to get this Davie back for her. He couldn't

abide her tears. He knew, if pain shattered her heart for good, he'd not survive the sight. He needed to calm her, to remind her of their goal.

"Panic won't help us. Think on it." Putting his hands on her shoulders, Cormac swiveled Marjorie to face him. "Aye, Archie could be involved. But there's naught we can do about it tonight. Our priority is to find Davie. Spoiling our disguise to confide in your uncle Humphrey won't help matters."

The carriage rolled to a stop outside their inn.

"Promise you won't jump to conclusions. We're close to finding the boy. If he's alive, and if he's in Scotland, I'll find him for you." He tenderly smudged the tears from her cheeks. "I will always help you; I swear it. But you must promise you'll trust me."

She was quiet for a moment, searching his eyes. He forced himself not to look away. Though it was Ree who was in need of solace, never had he felt so vulnerable.

"I trust you, Cormac," she told him in the barest whisper.

And with those few words, a foreign sensation found purchase in his desolate heart. She needed him. Over all other men, Marjorie had chosen *him*. The feeling was heady.

All his years of warring, of scouting and killing in the shadows, could they actually be put to some good? Might he actually be able to find the boy, to help Marjorie?

Would it redeem him if he did?

He helped her down from the carriage, letting his hands rest overlong on her waist.

Marjorie looked up at him, a sort of distressed bewilderment replacing the ire wrinkling her brow. "I'd thought Davie's kidnap was mere chance. Bad luck."

"I told you to take your mind from it, Ree." He guided her inside. "We will find him."

"No, but Cormac, listen to me. If there is someone actually preying on the boys . . ." She shivered. "And if it's Archie, I swear, I will stop him. I won't let this happen again."

"First we focus on Davie," he said, ushering her up the inn stairs.

"But what of the other lads in the meantime? How can I keep them safe?"

He gave a comforting squeeze to her shoulders, then quickly unlocked their door. "There's naught we can accomplish tonight."

"Archie will still come round to Saint Machar. He was supposed to be helping." Renewed indignation flushed her cheeks red. She tugged at her gown for breath. "The damned blackguard. I trusted him."

She was growing riled again, and Cormac blamed it on that accursed foreign liquor. It had intoxicated her, rousing her with this wildly careening alarm.

By the time he settled them in their room, she was all swirling skirts and fisting hands. Her body quivered with fury, and she wriggled and plucked at her bodice. "But how in the world—?"

"You don't help Davie when your head is going in other directions." He needed to take her mind from it all. "It's the drink, Ree. You must calm yourself."

"I *can't* calm myself. And it's *not* the drink." Reaching awkwardly behind her, she struggled with the ties of her gown, trying to loosen them. "Cormac, I can't seem to—"

"Hush, lass." He turned her away from him and slowly began to pick at the laces running up the back of her dress. "Catch your breath."

"Catch my breath," she grumbled. "I'll tell you what I'll catch. I'm going to catch that Archie and . . . and I'll shove *him* up a chimney."

Cormac worked at her laces, letting her rant. He understood her state of mind all too well. She was right—it wasn't the drink that was the cause. It was hard not to get swept away by a tide of outrage and dread. Only through years of hardening his heart had he learned to master the tumult of feelings. A baptism of blood and gunfire had taught him how to focus his mind utterly, how to numb himself to the chaos and despair all around.

He knew, though, if he were only to let go, if he let his own mind drift for but a moment, he'd invariably end up in a dark place. A guilty, anxious place filled with morbid imaginings. *Aidan kidnapped, Aidan beaten, Aidan killed.*

"I'll find the smugglers, too, Cormac. If I have to go down to the docks myself, I swear I will find every last one of those pirates, and I will chain *them* up and send *them* away to a tropical isle."

Concentrating only on the woman before him, he tucked his grim thoughts into the farthest corners of his mind and continued to pick at her laces. "I know you will, Ree."

She jiggled her torso and shuddered in a breath as her bodice began to loosen. "Those women, too. *For the boys' own good.* Can you imagine? I'll send those horrible women away to live on an island for *their* own good, and I'll send the smugglers, too, and see what those nice wives think about *Highland stock* then."

"So many ties," he muttered. It was no wonder she couldn't breathe; women's clothing was preposterous. Just when he thought he was finished, another knot or another layer would appear. "How do you women manage it?"

Finally, her bodice sagged, and she took a huge and shuddering gulp of air. His muscles relaxed, his body easing when hers did.

Cormac's eyes grazed up her spine, and his body quickened at once. He'd been so busy practicing his damned focus, paying mind only to the endless series of ties, he hadn't realized her sleeves had slipped low and her gown gaped open at her back.

"You've got that big, long sword, Cormac."

He coughed. *Sword indeed.*

"Aye," he managed. Her back was laid bare before

him. His eyes devoured the creamy length of naked skin, the elegant stretch of neck. He longed to sweep his hands down her, finding each bone and muscle with his thumbs and rubbing her cares away.

"You'll fight them for me, right?"

"Of course, Ree," he rasped. Even though there were no ties left to undo, he placed his hand at the small of her back. He longed to feel her naked flesh just where spine curved into bottom.

"What will you do when you get your hands on them?"

He couldn't think about his hands anywhere but right where they were at that very moment. "I . . . I'll . . ."

Her beautiful shoulders slumped. "Oh Cormac, tell me I didn't make a hash of things yet again."

A few long strands had spilled free from her knotted hair, and their light brown waves against the ivory of her skin mesmerized him. "Whatever can you mean, Ree?"

"Did you manage to arrange a meeting with Forbes, before I . . ." She visibly deflated.

"Hush." How smooth those curls would be if stroked between his fingers, how delicate if they were to brush against his chest. "I've made the connection, and that's enough. I've good reason to go meet Forbes at his office now."

"I suppose he will want to know how your ailing wife is." She straightened her back, sighing deeply. "We'll find Davie, won't we? We're close to finding him?"

He traced the slope of her bare shoulders with his fingertip. "Aye, Ree."

He drew in a sharp breath. His heart, his body—both knew.

There was only one thing in this world that could banish the darkness, all the rage and the fear, from both their minds.

Chapter 21

Cormac laced his fingers through a wayward lock of hair, and Marjorie's breath caught.

Oh dear Lord. She was half naked. While she'd ranted, Cormac had nearly undressed her.

There was a curious moment of stillness at her back, and then his hand swept over her shoulders. Breath whooshed into her lungs. And like that, anger transformed into desire, raging like a storm-swollen river.

"Cormac, I . . ." She turned to face him. Her gown sagged, and she braced the heavy fabric against herself with a hand at her breast. "I seem to be undressed."

"Not quite yet," he murmured, and the sound of his low, rasping voice set something to quivering deep inside. His eyes flicked to her bare shoulders, and awareness burned through her.

She returned his rapt stare, and something in her shifted. It was as though Marjorie were watching the actions of another woman. She became desperately curious to know what would happen next to that woman, what that woman might dare. Perhaps traces of the rumbullion still buzzed through her veins, perhaps that's what was to blame, but she let her gown slide ever so slightly from her grasp. "Better?"

Cormac exhaled sharply, and she felt its echoes in the heat pooling between her legs. "Not yet," he said hoarsely.

She let her dress creep lower still, and cool air kissed the top of her bosom. Her breasts tightened until they ached, and the feeling was wicked and sensual. "How's that?"

His eyes swept down, and he lingered this time, leisurely dragging his gaze along the front of her. "More," he told her.

The ache she felt in her most private of places spread, until she felt the intensity of it lance deep into her soul.

Marjorie realized then, she wanted to forget.

Marjorie Ellen Keith, self-avowed spinster at twenty-three. Hounded by tragedy, plagued by poor luck and poorer choices.

Just this once, she wanted to *feel*.

She let go of her gown.

Cormac moaned, and the raw sound of it slammed Marjorie back into herself. No longer did she watch her actions as if from afar. She was completely in her body now, and it clamored for him.

His eyes flew to hers, his look almost angry, vehement with want. He seized her waist and pulled her close. This was the moment. She parted her lips, waiting for his kiss.

He swung her onto the bed instead. The breath left her lungs with a startled gasp as she bounced on the thin mattress. He stared down at her hungrily. "We shouldn't do this."

She spread her legs to feel the cool between her thighs, but her flesh there was thick with a damp heat only Cormac could ease. "Lie down," she told him in a sultry voice that surely wasn't her own.

He landed on her, tugging down her gown and kissing her hard. The wash of chill air made her heated skin pebble, and the sensation was delicious.

He pulled away to look at her and then he succumbed again, plunging his mouth to hers to take her in a fierce kiss. Blanketing her upper body with kisses, he murmured, "I can't stop, Ree. I should stop, but I can't."

"Don't stop," she said, knowing she'd never been more certain of anything in her life. "I need to forget. Make me forget."

"Aye, I will. I will." He rolled to his side to fumble with his waistcoat, his boots.

"Cormac," she said breathlessly. She reached to undo his trews, and he froze, watching her with hooded eyes. "Can I . . . ?"

Speechless, he gave her a slight nod. Marjorie fumbled with the buttons and, feeling uncertain, stopped for a moment, looking at him with a question in her eyes.

"Yes." He sat up to tear off his shirt, then lay back, angling toward her, offering his hips at a better angle. "You do it."

It was an order, and it made her feel sinful and naughty, his gruff words heightening her arousal to a maddening pitch. She hitched her gown down and kicked it off from where it had tangled at her feet, and then scooted down on the bed to get closer to her goal. He wedged a leg between hers, and the chafe of rough wool on her bare skin shot a fresh wave of aching between her thighs.

"All right," she murmured, splaying her hands on either side of his hips. She stroked both thumbs close to the line of buttons, her rapt attention on the thick swell in his pants. "I'll unbutton you, then."

She traced her finger along the top of his waistband.

"Ree," he croaked. "What do you do to me?"

She realized her control over him, and it was heady. To have Cormac so close, after so many years, was heady.

"You told me to undo you," she said, feeling wild and uninhibited. She hesitated for a moment, then traced her finger down the line of his manhood.

His breathing caught, and he fisted his hands in the sheets. "Christ, woman."

Smiling to herself, she undid his first two buttons, revealing the tip of his manhood. The head of it looked like a ripe fruit, and mesmerized, she traced it with her fingertip, spreading damp along its hard ridge.

"Good . . . God." Cormac moaned and hitched his hips as though in pain. "You'll kill me."

Each button she opened revealed more of him, smooth and dark in the candlelight, until his pants were loosed about his hips and his erection was stiff between them. She reached out to stroke him, amazed at the size of him, at the silken smoothness.

"So wicked you are." Eyes narrowing, he pulled Marjorie back up to him. "I'll kiss that wicked smile from you, woman," he said, before parting her lips in a slow, deep kiss.

Their kiss grew frantic, hands twining in hair, skimming along legs, clutching at arms and shoulders. A feral urge overcame her, and with it a hunger so powerful it blinded her, blotting out her reality.

She welcomed this darkness. For one night, she'd jettison her life of empty solitude. She'd reject her virginity as meaningless; virtue was for naught. She was and would remain a spinster. Her maidenhead was worth nothing without a husband to take it. And the only husband she wanted was Cormac.

Her hands were restless, kneading his waist, his hard shoulders, and the tensed muscles of his arms. She pulled away to kiss along his jaw. She whispered in his ear. "I can't touch you enough." He sat up, trying to gain the upper hand, and she pushed him back onto the mattress. "No. I want to watch you."

They shucked off his trews, and he groaned, seeming to grow stiffer and larger, if that were even possible. Joy bloomed to life in her breast, mingling with her arousal. She felt mischievous and freed, and she wanted to laugh. And then she shifted, realizing she wanted to do more still than that. "Lie still, Cormac."

"Och, woman, what are you—"

She kissed down the hard plane of his chest, down his belly, and he groaned in surrender.

His erection jutted between her breasts, and it set her legs to trembling. Bracing herself over him, she kissed lower and then paused, amazed to be so close. An urge struck her, and she thought surely she was the most corrupt of sinners, because she wanted to kiss him *there*. She leaned down to taste the very essence of his manhood.

"Not yet," he growled, startling her. He grabbed her, swinging her up and onto her back. He crawled over her, and she instinctively wrapped her legs around him. With a low laugh, he ran his hands along her arms, spreading them up over her head. His eyes devoured her face, her breasts. "Look at you, like a wanton."

"Now, Cormac." Some primitive instinct told her relief was near, and she arched her back, eager to feel the hard length of him brush against her. Finally, his erection grazed her, so large and heavy at her cleft, and she gasped with the pleasure of it. But then he shifted away, and she moaned her displeasure. "Now, Cormac. Please."

"Easy, lass." He nipped at her neck, rained kisses down her throat, until he reached a breast. He brought a hand down to cup it, stroking and kissing her softly, teasing around the edges until she thought she might scream with want. "This is about you. All for you."

He took her nipple in his mouth, and ecstasy like none she'd ever imagined rocked through her. He moved to the other, sucking hard, until she felt the pleasure of it pulse all the way down to her womb. He pulled away. "I've dreamt of this, Ree." The feel of his breath on her damp breasts brought them to exquisitely tight peaks. "Dreamt of you."

She knew she should be pleased, but for now his words were meaningless. All she understood, all she knew, was this maddening want. "Then take me," she said, her need for relief grown urgent.

She swiveled her hips higher, desperate to rub against him. Finally, he rested his weight between her thighs, and she thought she might weep with delight.

"Cormac," she gasped. "I know what it is, between a man and a woman. I want us to . . ."

Reluctantly he pulled his mouth from her breast and brought his face level with hers. Cupping her cheek, he stroked her lower lip with his thumb. "What is it you want, Ree?"

"I want you."

He kissed the corner of her mouth. "And so you have me." He kissed the other corner. "But I told you. This is only about you. I'll not take your virginity"—she began to protest at once, and he silenced her with a finger to her lips—"but I will do something else for you."

A moment's disappointment skewered her, thinking he might not want to lie with her. But it was replaced just as quickly by titillated curiosity. "Do what for me, Cormac?"

Cradling her body between his legs, he knelt over her, making her feel as though she were an altar he bowed before. He stroked his hands down her torso, lingering over her breasts, and then caressed slowly downward until he reached the apex of her thighs.

He shifted, settling lower on the bed. Gently, he parted her legs, idly stroking his thumbs along the top edges of her inner thighs. "I'll make you come."

Chapter 22

Marjorie didn't quite understand. She didn't want to leave this bed. "Come where? Where are you going?"

He merely chuckled, and then maddeningly, he rose from the bed. Where was the blasted man off to?

She looked him up and down and, like an eager pup, she couldn't stop looking. He stood so tall over the bed, and with his hard-cut body and the fine webbing of scars that shone in the flickering light, he looked so dangerous. His manhood jutted ominously in the shadows, and her eyes went wide. She fisted her hands in the sheets as if that could slow down her careening heart.

And yet she wasn't afraid. Nervous, yes, that she wouldn't know what to do or how to act. But not *afraid*, never with him. She knew, better than she knew herself, that Cormac would never hurt her. She wondered how it could be possible that she always felt so safe with him, this man who claimed to bear such darkness in his soul.

She just wished she knew what he was about. "Where could you possibly—?

"Cormac!" she yelped, as he grabbed her knees and tugged her to the edge of the bed. "What are you doing?"

He knelt before her, spreading her legs.

Her pulse throbbed in her neck, and she tried to swallow. What was he doing? What was *she* supposed to do? "I . . . I—"

He went straight to her inner thighs, spreading hot, openmouthed kisses along her skin.

Her mouth went dry. He was so . . . *close* down there. Close to . . . *down there.* "What are you—?"

His hand swept up her belly, straight for her breast, finding her nipple with his thumb.

"Ohh," she moaned, "Oh my."

Against her better judgment, her body relaxed, until she found herself lying back on the bed. She shut her eyes and let herself enjoy the feel of his hands on her breasts and his mouth along her legs. *Come where?* she wondered distantly.

He shifted. There was a moment's chill on her thigh where his mouth had been. And then she felt his tongue lick her *there.*

"Cormac!" Her head shot up, but he ignored her. "Cor—"

He latched onto her.

Oh sweet heavenly . . .

"Oh . . ." Such rapturous warmth spread from his tongue to the very tips of her fingers and toes. He moaned, sounding pleased. Could he actually be enjoying it? "Cormac?"

He slid a finger into her.

"Oh dear," she muttered, dropping her head back.

He crooked it deeper, working her with fingers and tongue, and all notions of embarrassment fled her mind. She twined one hand in his hair and flung the other over her head, loose and languid, like butter melting in his touch. She swiveled her hips, pitching herself closer to his mouth. "Ohhh. Oh my . . ."

Cormac's low chuckle reverberated through her core. He *was* enjoying it.

"That's good," she murmured. The feeling of warmth grew intense, the sparks in her belly quickening to flame. And the sensation grew more powerful still.

"Come back," she pleaded, a little frightened she might lose control. His mouth felt miraculous, but she was ready to kiss him again. She gave a little tug to his hair to nudge him back over her. "Kiss me again."

He unlatched to say in a ragged voice, "I am kissing you," and then nestled even deeper in the crook of her thighs.

"Really," she said, growing nervous. She didn't want to hurt his feelings, but this was growing too intense. "You can stop now."

The arm she'd splayed so languidly over her head tensed. She felt agitated, her body too hot, and it frightened her. The heat from his mouth seared her, flowing molten in her veins.

She realized she was panting for air. "It's too much," she gasped. "Cormac, please. Cor . . . *oh*."

Something deep inside her hitched, held taut, and she held her breath to match. *Too much*. It was too much, and she was afraid she might die of it. "Cormac, I can't . . ."

She gulped in a single breath, then stilled again, her whole body rigid. Marjorie shouted as her body seemed to explode. Her lungs loosened, and with it came a tremendous release, sweeping her into momentary oblivion. She trembled; she was shuddering, mindless rapture, a thousand shards of glittering crystal suspended in darkness.

She'd had no idea.

She became aware that he was laving kisses all along her inner thighs, stroking her legs, her belly, her breasts. He paused, and she felt his words blow across her damp skin. "I'm sorry, Ree. I couldn't stop."

Sorry? She swallowed, trying to reacquaint herself with the use of her tongue. Oh yes, she'd asked him to stop. What had she been thinking?

"Again, please," she said weakly.

He laughed outright, climbing up her body, reveling in it as he went. He greeted her with a slow, deep kiss. Her own musk filled her senses, and she was startled at the new sparks crackling through her body in response.

His erection brushed against her hip, still hard and angry, and she grew serious. "But what of you?"

Though it'd been made clear she didn't know *exactly* how matters proceeded between a man and a woman, Marjorie did know the male of the species derived some sort of physical release from the whole endeavor. "I thought we might . . . Can we still? Ohhh," she cooed, realizing maybe there was more in store for her. Now that she'd recovered from her . . . *coming*, she was realizing her body was not quite done.

"Aye, we could *still*," he conceded, repeating her implication. "But no, Ree. I'll not take that from you. You should be a maiden on your wedding day."

Wedding day. She'd have neither a wedding day nor a wedding night. This time with Cormac, *this* was what mattered. There was no other man for her. She knew that, certain above all things. This was her one opportunity to experience true passion, and she had to seize it. Seize *him*, while she had the chance.

Glaring, she sat up. "I told you. I'll not have a wedding day. I'll not wed, unless . . ."

Unless it's you I wed. She trailed off, leaving the words unspoken.

He either didn't catch or refused to acknowledge her implication.

She hoisted herself onto her elbows. This experience had changed her. In fact, it wouldn't be an exaggeration to say it had changed her whole understanding of the world. But the echoes of bliss had left her feeling hollow, as though only now did she realize how much he belonged inside her.

She still had needs, and she *would* see them satisfied. She just needed to make herself more clear.

"My life is full and rich," she told him briskly. "I've decided to remain unmarried. So you see, it would be no problem for you to . . . for us to . . ."

"Why'd you never marry, Ree?" He tucked a damp tendril of hair behind her ear. "Why will you not?"

The maddening man needed to get back to the topic at hand. She avoided his question, gesturing instead to his still-erect flesh. "Isn't that uncomfortable?"

He laughed. "I asked you a question. 'Tis customary to answer before posing your own."

Her eyes narrowed. Cormac had spent the past however many years glowering in silence, and now suddenly he wanted talking. "Is it *customary* to talk so much in the midst of . . . of such proceedings?"

"One could argue this is a part of such proceedings." He drew his hand in one slow stroke along her cheek, down her neck, and over her breast to her belly. He watched the path of his hand with single-minded intent.

Her breasts pulled taut, her whole body quivering in response to his attention.

His attention. She sighed. How many years had she longed for such attentions from Cormac?

He gripped her hips firmly, staring at her with such purpose. He pressed close to her, and then abruptly he pulled away.

She studied him, his strong profile in the guttering candlelight. Folk had likened him and the other MacAlpins to devils, and Cormac was certainly as handsome as one. But his scarred brow bore so many secrets. What had dragged him from the darkness of Aidan's kidnap into such grave depths?

She could talk, she decided. For now. But she *would* convince him. Cormac *would* lie with her before the night was over.

"I'd like to answer your question with a question, then." She'd grown chilled and reached for the sheet. With a gentle hand to stop her, Cormac leaned to the floor, retrieving his plaid to cover them. "Thank you," she said as matter-of-factly as if she'd been at a banquet table.

"So." She pinned him with a steady look. "I'd like to point out that you're not wed either."

He regarded her quietly, and uncertainty assailed her. Why hadn't he wed? Was there a woman out there some-where whom he'd loved? Who'd hurt him? Was Marjorie not the only woman who waited for him?

"Oh." Her voice was tiny. *She* felt tiny. She wanted to change the topic. Blast him, she wanted to flee from the damn room. But she had to know. "Have there been women?"

"I'm human, Ree."

She blinked back the sting from her eyes. He was human. What could *that* possibly mean?

He touched her chin tenderly. "But have any found their way into my heart? No, Ree. None since you."

"Oh," she said again, and then grew brighter, consid-ering the thought. Did that mean she'd been in his heart? Was she in it still? She gave him a tremulous smile. If he wanted to talk, she'd be happy to plumb *that* topic for all it was worth. Cormac would have all the discussion he wanted.

But she would have Cormac before the sun rose.

Chapter 23

Into my heart? How had *that* slipped from his tongue?

He took in Ree's tousled hair, the sight of her lips swollen from his kisses. He'd kissed her and touched her, had tasted the most intimate parts of her. No, he knew exactly how he'd let it slip out. His resolve had shattered the moment she'd dropped her gown.

Her breasts had taken his breath away, full and flawless, her body glowing golden in the candlelight. And now this precious creature lay with him, their naked legs in a tangle. He held her close, stroking her pale skin, softer than any satin in his hands.

"Not since me?" She repeated his words with a smile.

He should've known she'd cling to that statement. "I suppose that's what I said."

She pursed her lips. "You suppose?"

"Yes. No. I mean . . ." He couldn't help himself from stealing another touch. He rubbed his hand over her belly, letting his fingers sweep down to graze the small triangle of stiff curls. She was so gorgeous, so perfect, and she'd let him taste her.

He clenched his eyes shut—he couldn't concentrate with the sight of her naked shoulders to distract him. What had he been saying? "Aye, in my heart," he confessed. "It's always been so."

Cormac dropped his head to the pillow in defeat. He was doing it again, saying more than he should. Turning onto his side, he shifted away, but the rich, musky scent of her only rose to him from the sheets. "Och, Ree, you have me at a disadvantage."

She gave a sultry little laugh, and the sound terrified him.

"Then *I* suppose I'll just have to keep you here." She traced her fingers down his arm. Her touch was so soothing, so delicate, and yet so arousing.

His skin was on fire. He took a deep, measured inhale. He'd not steal her maidenhead like some undisciplined boy.

Talking. More talking might take his mind from it. "You're still avoiding my question."

"Am I?" Her delicate fingers roved to his leg, outlining a pattern along the tartan draped over his thigh. She opened her hand, giving him a gentle squeeze.

He hissed out his breath. She *was* avoiding his question.

The look she gave him belied her inexperience. It was the look of a seductress. "But Cormac, I thought we were talking about your heart."

"No," he said in quick reply, eager to draw the subject away from dangerous waters. He couldn't remember the last time he'd thought of his heart as anything but a practical organ, good only for pumping battle lust through his veins. But that heart was waking back to life, and he realized Ree had been lodged just there for longer than he could remember. He'd dreamed of her for years. He'd cared for her—aye, if he had to admit it—*loved* her for years.

He couldn't let her know that, though; he couldn't let her in. The thought of it frightened him more than any battlefield. To be so vulnerable? He'd experienced loss once before; he'd not survive loving and losing her.

"We were talking about why you've not married," he said firmly.

"Mm." She may have sounded her assent, but Marjorie's mind was clearly on other matters. She shifted closer and slipped her arm beneath his plaid, placing her hand where she'd had it a moment before, only now it was the skin of her questing fingertips he felt on his leg.

"I wonder. Whyever have I *not* married?" The pattern she traced along his thigh made her words an innuendo. Her lips parted in the wicked suggestion of a smile.

He flexed his muscles, girding against Marjorie's onslaught. All he'd need to do was tilt his pelvis to her. She'd know what he wanted. She'd wrap her cool, soft hand around him. He could teach her how to stroke him.

The mere thought of it made his cock pulse. Though he willed his flesh to calm, his blood pumped hot, leaving him hard and wanting. If she were to touch him, he knew there'd be no going back. And she deserved more than him. More than this lie they enacted, more than Lord and Lady Brodie in a seedy, dockside inn. He'd not take her innocence from her.

Her touch drifted perilously close to his erection. He gently took her hand and tucked it along his side. "Why choose to live alone?"

"I don't live alone." Slipping her hand away, she reached around to idly stroke his backside, bringing his cock to stand at happy attention. She rubbed a thumb along his hip bone. "Why, only just last month, Uncle Humphrey—"

"You're *alone*, Ree." Tenderly, he lifted her chin to look her in the eye.

Her hand stilled. Sadness flickered in her eyes, and the sight of it speared him. He regretted his honesty, but she deserved more than this life she'd chosen for herself. And she deserved more than *him*.

He carefully removed her hand from where it rested

heavily on his hip. "Humphrey's an old man whose only concerns are his books and botanicals."

"He takes care of me."

"*You* take care of *him*," he insisted. "You take care of everyone, Ree. But who is there to care for you?"

Cormac thought of his own situation. Waking, fishing, feeding his family, and sleeping alone once more. A life alone—hadn't they both made the same choice?

He'd embraced his solitude as a sort of penance. Is that what Marjorie did? The difference was, unlike him, she bore no sins on her lovely shoulders.

He pinned her with an accusing look. "Do you think by working with the folk at Saint Machar, you can right the wrongs of all Aberdeen?"

"I'm just trying to help." Her voice trembled.

He should've let it be, but he couldn't bear the thought of Marjorie choosing such a lonely life. It was fine for a worthless soul like him, but *she* had a right to more. "What imagined sin do you atone for?"

"What imagined sin?" She pulled away, tugging the plaid up to tuck it over her breasts. "How can you, of all people, ask that, Cormac?"

"Good Christ, Ree, is this about Aidan? You isolate yourself because of something that happened when we were children?"

"And what is it *you* do?" She propped herself up on her elbow, her voice finding its strength. "What do you call living alone in some tumbledown pile of rock, fishing alone all day?"

"This is about you—"

"You keep saying that, Cormac. You keep saying it's only about *me*. How could you possibly think this"—she gestured between them—"has naught to do with you?"

"You speak truly." He grew subdued. He *was* there, lying with her, God spare him. He sent up a desperate plea for forgiveness. "But I gave up on my life long ago."

"You gave me up," she whispered, sinking her head onto the pillow.

"Aye, I gave *you* up. I'd failed Aidan, you see, and I saw suffering in solitude as a sort of penance. And then the war happened."

"What happened in battle to change you so?"

"You have no idea the sins I have to atone for. But you, Ree, you've committed no such sin. Are you to grow old, alone, and with no one to care for you?" The thought infuriated him, lighting tinder beneath his words. "You need more. A home of your own, bairns aplenty."

Her loneliness was a tragic waste. She was a woman of such passions. The way she ignited at his touch, it was clear she longed for completion. *She should have a man to share her bed.* He scowled, despising the thought as it came to him. "Don't you want a man about?"

"Perhaps it's the man who'd never want me." She leaned up, angrily plumping the pillow beneath her.

"No man would ever—" Realization dawned. And it was devastating.

Cormac had once thought he'd never be worthy of her. He once thought he'd never be capable of feeling the joy of it if he did. But now he knew differently.

Though he couldn't imagine himself ever being deserving of Ree, now he had a fantasy of *what it would be*. He remembered the sight of her splayed before him, innocent in body but with lust in her eyes.

"Och, Ree, to be with you . . ." He considered it, and he knew joy and loss in the same instant. "'Twould be wrong. To sully your pure soul with my dirtied hands."

"They call you the devil, Cormac, and I think you are. Who are you to say what I need? What happened to you at war? What are the shadows in your eyes? Who are you now? When did you become this"—frustrated, she adjusted herself, kicking the sheets from her legs—"this . . . man?"

He'd kept his past cloaked in shadow for so long now, he no longer knew who he was protecting with his secrecy. He was too tired to fight it any longer.

"Fine, Ree. You wish to be my confessor; so be it." He

lay on his back, bringing his arm to rest over his head, stealing a glance at her from the corner of his eye. How would she hear his story? Would she offer perfunctory reassurances with eyes gone cold and a smile grown false? There was only one way to find out. "I became this man when I went to war, a boy of thirteen."

Marjorie's stomach fell.

Thirteen. The bald fact of it gutted her. She remembered Cormac as a boy of ten. Just three years after Aidan's disappearance, and he'd gone off to battle? She tried to picture him as he'd been, all lanky limbs, a fringe of long eyelashes around grinning eyes.

She pictured the boys of Saint Machar. How might Paddy look, a musket slung over his back? To imagine young Cormac trudging far from home, off to God knew where, to fight in the Civil Wars . . . her stomach churned at the thought.

She schooled her face. She was being squeamish. Many boys fought for their clan at such an age. "So young," was all she managed to say and keep her composure.

"Young," he agreed. "But not in my own head, aye? It always was vinegar not blood that coursed through my veins."

She gave him a gentle smile. "I remember."

"But it turned sour after Aidan." He stared blindly up at the ceiling. "After I couldn't save him."

"How could you possibly have saved him? You were only ten—"

"Hush, Ree. You asked my story, and it's my story I'm telling."

She nodded mutely, wondering how he could blame himself. It was a wonder they hadn't lost *Cormac* that day, too, suffocated in that godforsaken chimney.

But hadn't she also been blaming herself all these years? The thought was too painful to touch. Instead, she gently prompted, "So you had something to prove, then. When you went to war?"

He shot her a look with brows raised, as though she'd

just given voice to the greatest of all understatements. "I always had much to prove. The battle, *this* battle," he amended, studying the scars on his arm, "was in '51. That's one year after my da died."

"You'd have thought you were man of the house," she said, understanding. She struggled to make sense of males, and yet sometimes their reasoning could be so simple. "You and Gregor both. You'd have thought you needed to prove yourselves men."

"Aye, there was that. And I was fair guilty, too." He inhaled deeply, shutting his eyes against the pain of it. "Don't forget the guilt."

"Guilt?" she asked quietly.

"That it'd been Aidan, and not me, who was taken. The fates had ignored me, and so I *dared* death to take me. I courted it. I accepted every fool's errand. Any danger I could embrace, I did. I ran off to spy when others were too scared. Part of me thought, if I were good enough, I'd someday find Aidan. But I never found him, and death never found me." He shrugged. "And so I was just fourteen when they made me a scout."

"Your courage made you successful."

He gave a bitter laugh. "'Twas *folly*, not courage. A lad's bravado and a goodly dose of luck are what brought me success."

He seemed to run out of words then, and she let him have the silence. What lifetimes he'd lived, all by the time he'd become a man grown.

She turned onto her side to face him. Reaching a hand out, she outlined the fine tracery of scars along his forearm. Though he stiffened, she persisted, running her fingertip along the uneven surface, over unnaturally smooth knots of flesh, across small discs of satiny-thin skin. "You were telling me about these."

"These," he said simply. They both studied his scars until he brought his hand over hers to conceal them. "You wish to know about these, Ree?"

"Aye, Cormac. And be serious this time." She smiled, trying to break the tension. "I assume Bridget can't claim these wounds in addition to that crooked nose of yours."

"It's not as crooked as all that." Though there was humor in his words, he seemed to be having trouble summoning it to his features. "No, my sister can't claim these. Though mayhap if *she'd* been on the battlefield, the Royalists would've fared better."

She edged closer to Cormac, reassured by his attempts to lighten the mood. She'd not let him feel alone in the telling of his tale. "Which battle was it?"

"Do you remember Worcester? 'Twas in 1651."

She groaned inwardly. Of course she remembered the Battle of Worcester. It marked the end of the wars. "Aye, I recall it. The Royalists lost."

"No, Ree, the Royalists were *decimated*. Thousands of Scotsmen killed to Cromwell's two hundred." Cormac grimaced. "The bastard called it his 'Crowning Mercy.' "

She registered the reality of what he'd told her. "But Worcester is so far away. You were only fourteen."

"Aye, we'd covered nigh on forty-five leagues in a week, marching deep into England. I told you I was a scout, traveling with Rothiemay's Foot, out of Aberdeenshire. And march we did, straight into a rout . . ."

He grew silent, and she waited. She wouldn't push him; rather she'd let his story rise to the surface as slowly as he needed it to.

She brought her fingers to his brow. Their candle had long since guttered out, and she studied his face by moonlight. Gently, she combed her fingers through his hair, drawing it back from his forehead. A strand had tangled in his lashes, just as it used to do when he was a boy. Feelings of unutterable tenderness swelled within her, clutching hard at her throat.

She waited and stroked his hair, and finally his story came.

"As a scout, I didn't see much of the battle. I had other

duties." Something dark flashed in his eyes, and the notion of what some of those duties might've entailed made her flesh crawl.

"I knew, when the officers sent me off, that we were destined for a crushing defeat. And yet, it had lit something in me. I suppose I thought there was something more I could do for the cause. I snuck farther afield than any of the other scouts had before. I was deep in Cromwell's camp when I discovered something."

"What?" she asked, her voice barely a whisper.

"The Parliamentary soldiers . . . Cromwell's *'New Model Army,'*" he amended sarcastically. "They were gathering up innocents. Later, I found out that, by the end of the battle, they'd taken ten thousand prisoners. All men and boys, every last one shipped off to Barbados or to the colonies."

She couldn't help her gasp, knowing at once what that would mean for him. "So you were afraid they'd take you, too?"

"No, I was *not* afraid." His body stiffened, a burst of savage energy vibrating through the room. "I *longed* for them to take me. But I had a job to do." Sighing, he came back to himself, his fury spent as quickly as it'd come. "No, Ree, I wasn't afraid they'd take *me*. I was afraid for the others. They'd hundreds of lads in the camp by then, all well guarded."

His eyes went distant, lost to some horrific reverie.

She was hesitant to speak for fear he might stop talking altogether, but even more so, she feared letting him sink too deeply into the pain of his memories. Finally, she asked, "What happened?"

"What happened," he repeated, his tone flat. "Well, there was no help for it, of course. They were as good as slaves already. And so I went back to report."

His words began to lag, and she reached for his hand in encouragement. Seeming bolstered by the gesture, he sighed deeply and continued, "I'd been told to keep to the trench road, through a place called Pirie Wood. But something told me to leave the path. Sure enough, I found an old barn. At first I congratulated myself on my great good luck."

He shot her a self-mocking smirk. "The honorable scout would return with word of refuge. A roof overhead for our wounded . . . *Fool*. Do you ken what I found instead, Ree?"

She shook her head mutely, mesmerized and yet utterly terrified by how his tale might unfold.

"'Twas a damned barn full of Irish."

Her eyes went wide with disbelief. *"Irish?"*

"Aye, 'tis true. Did you know the soldiers travel with their families? The men had gone off to skirmish, and damned if I didn't open the barn door to the sight of a dozen women and their bairns."

"Good Lord," she exclaimed, her voice finding strength. "They bring their babes into battle?"

"They bring them *all*." He turned to face her on the bed, and the cold steadiness of his gaze chilled her. "And these women, they'd heard tell Cromwell was rounding up all the boys."

"Oh . . ." Marjorie couldn't imagine such terror. The last days of the wars had been distant to her, living in Aberdeen with her uncle. What would it be to squat with your children in a barn, praying to God to keep them safe and alive?

"They were mad with terror. Some of the boys were babes yet, and too young to be taken. But there were a handful of older lads . . ."

Marjorie held her breath. She'd thought she wanted his stories, but she didn't know anymore that she could hear them. What had she asked him to tell her? What had she asked *of* him, to remember it in the retelling?

He watched her. Curled on his side in the darkness, he looked so alone, nervous even, and in need of reassurance. Who had reassured him after Aidan? And then who'd been there for him after his mother had died, so shortly after?

He'd turned his back on Marjorie before, but she was there now, and the only thing she wanted was to share his burden. *She* could be the brave one, this time, for him. "Tell me, Cormac. You can tell me."

He nodded, and she imagined she saw his shoulders ease. "There were a few lads. They were . . . I don't know . . . nine? Ten? About the same age Aidan had been."

"Of course you'd want to help them."

"It's true." He nodded, replaying the memory in his mind. "But I think what really got me was that they were about the same age as my younger brother."

"Declan," she exclaimed. "Where *was* Declan, all that time? With you and Gregor at war, who was home to mind him?"

"*Declan* was home to mind Declan. Why do you think the villagers call us a pack of demons?" He cocked his mouth into a humorless smile. "Deck didn't get to foster away like other boys. He didn't have a mother to teach him manners and whatnot."

"He hasn't seemed to suffer for it," she said, recalling the odd manner in which Declan always seemed to be lost in thought. "I think he's quite bright, actually."

"Aye, between my sisters and whatever books he could get his hands on, Deck's done just fine by himself. But you see why the sight of these boys touched me so. I couldn't see them taken."

It was obvious to her. "You couldn't allow it."

"No, Ree. I couldn't. The pain of Aidan . . . it was too fresh."

"And so you fought," she concluded.

"Not at first. At first, I ran. I took the boys and hid them in the gorse."

"It was a brave thing to do."

"It was a *fool* thing to do." He scrubbed at his face, as if he wished he could wipe his mind free of the memory. "I should've taken them all."

"*All* the women and children?" She sat up, astounded at the ridiculous notion. His plaid slipped down her chest, and she folded it back under her arms. "You couldn't have taken a barn full of Irish with you through the woods."

"Aye, well, in any event, I didn't. I came back, and they'd been slaughtered."

"Oh, dear God," she blurted. He'd stated it so simply, was watching her so warily. Was *this* his great confession? Did he think *this* would frighten her from him? "Oh, Cormac."

"Every last mother, every last babe, killed. Except for a few of the . . ." He raked his fingers through his hair, leaving his head cradled in both hands. "I think a few of the older girls were missing. I can only imagine what came of them."

"Maybe they got away."

"And maybe I'll be the next Stuart king." He looked at her, his eyes empty of emotion.

She knew better, though. His gaze might appear blank, but the flatness in his eyes stanched unbearable emotion. He'd seen so much with those eyes, it broke her heart. A lad of fourteen had no business bearing such tragedy and such responsibility on his shoulders.

"What happened to the boys you'd hidden in the gorse?" They still hadn't gotten to the topic of his scars, and she dreaded his reply.

"The boys," he said, his tone gone icy. "Well, I went back, of course. Straightaway. Some of Cromwell's men had found them; they were there still, rounding the Irish lads up, meaning to truss them like a drove of cattle. I lost my mind then. I'd taken the soldiers by surprise and managed to kill a few of them." He tried to look away, but she slid her hand around his neck, the taut column of it hot under her palm.

He held her gaze, unspeakable sadness darkening his features. "I should've let them just have the boys. Maybe they'd be alive today. But the lads saw my fight, and fancying themselves men, they joined me. They were cut down, every last one."

She cleared her throat, desperate for her voice not to crack. She would be strong for him. "And your arm?"

"Ah, yes, my arm." He held it up, examining it in the moonlight. "I got this defending a lad. I was just a scout, you see. Thankfully I had a sword, but there was no shield to hand. I did the best I could, but my arm got in the way. Grazed by a redcoat blade." He flexed his fist.

She took his hand and, with a kiss to the broad span of his palm, turned his arm to study the scars. "It's a stroke of luck that it wasn't sheared straight through."

He grimaced. "Luck. My life seems to have been luck and more luck. Or perhaps it's that I'm bad luck for the ones I come near."

"You can't say that, Cormac."

He only shrugged.

"Where did you go after it all happened? What did you do?"

"Do? You wish to know what I did next? I ran, Ree. It was chaos. I saw the boys lying dead, I saw the soldiers' ropes, and then I saw a path through the trees." Words picking up pace, his story barreled on, unstoppable now. "I ran and ran. Because I *didn't* want to be taken. I'd thought I did. I thought I'd wanted to die. But you see, I didn't. I was too selfish. In that instant, all I wanted was to live, to be free. And it felt like a betrayal. Like I'd betrayed Aidan."

"But you were only fourteen. Your brother never would've wanted you to suffer his fate."

"We'll never know, aye?"

"No, Cormac. I know. Aidan loved you. He'd never have wanted you to be kidnapped or killed merely out of your own guilt." The notion was preposterous. She slid closer to him on the bed, needing to convince Cormac, to make him see. "It was an impossible situation," she insisted. "You were a child, against a troop of redcoats. You might as well have found a barn full of Irish, dead already. There was naught you could've done."

"No," he said, sounding wrung out. He'd been holding his story in for so long, the loosing of it had rendered him completely emotionally spent. "I should be dead. Those boys, at least, should be alive."

"As forced laborers on a distant continent somewhere?"

"They could've been with Aidan," he muttered. He shut his eyes, and only then did she see the exhaustion that had smudged them black.

She watched as sleep pulled him under, hoping it was dreamless, praying he'd exorcised his tale. It had devastated her, but rather than wanting to push it—and him—away as he'd feared she might, Marjorie wanted only to share his pain, to convince him, to absolve him.

She curled closer, longing to hold him tight. There was no shutting her out now.

Cormac had thought this was the thing that'd drive her away. Little did he know. His confession was what would bind her fast to him forever.

Chapter 24

This dream, again. Cormac's hips ground forward, his body searching for release. Marjorie's daydream hand circled him more firmly, moved with more intent. In the place between sleep and reality, he was only this: only wanting, and this hard, aching knot between his legs.

The sweetest of dreams.

An alarm sounded in a corner of his mind, how fragile this sleep. He moved slowly, carefully, holding on to his slumber. This fantasy of her hand on him was too erotic, too sweet a pleasure to forgo.

He rolled onto his back, but he didn't wake—or didn't think he did. Instead, the sensations intensified, until he imagined the soft weight of her long hair feathering against his belly, his legs. There was a lick of warmth, and he imagined her mouth—

Cormac's eyes flew open.

Not a dream. He froze. Marjorie knelt over him, her hair a wild tangle in the early morning light. She was touching him, exploring him, laying such sweet kisses all over him.

He needed to stop her. He'd sworn to keep her virginity intact. Marjorie's virtue, above all things, was to be preserved.

But the feel of her, it was too exquisite. He held his breath. Her small hands lit along his skin, so delicate, like the touch of a bird.

But there was confidence there, too. Eagerness and questing. She took his shaft in her hand and tentatively kissed all around him. He gave an involuntary shiver. He should stop her, but it was so good. She lifted her head, and his skin was cool for a moment, and then her lips encircled him, and the wet heat of her mouth pulled him in.

He fought not to gasp. Too good.

Soon, he'd feign waking and stop her. But not yet. Slowly, she drew him in and then took him out again, her movements exploratory, untutored. Just a few moments more. A dreamlike hush enveloped the room, quiet but for the sound of her lips and tongue.

He should let her know he wasn't asleep. But she was rearranging her body over his, and he had to see what she did next. He slanted his eyes down, careful not to move.

With her mouth still on him, she began to slide her legs apart, slowly guiding her cleft closer to his leg, her hips arching down, seeking her own release.

His back flexed, heels digging into the mattress. *Too much, too good.*

She cradled his leg between hers, grinding into him. He felt her hum of pleasure on his cock. It was a force of will not to explode on the spot.

She wants this. It was a revelation. Ree had seen his desolation, and she still wanted to lie with him.

She wants me. And what if he were to give in, to surrender himself to her? What if he simply let go? In asking to share his memories, she'd requested nothing less than a glimpse into his soul. Could she withstand the bleakness she saw there? Could she stanch his hopelessness, eventually blot out the pain?

Would she save him?

He'd been a desert when she'd arrived back in his life. But as feeling returned to his heart, he marveled to realize, it wasn't that bad. He was surviving it. Could he survive her?

Could he be with her?

He remembered the steadiness with which she'd heard his story. The same hand that brought him such pleasure now had last night curled so tenderly around his neck. He'd shown her his despair, and she didn't flinch away.

He watched her tentative movements. She pulled away, kissing him, learning him, in the hazy morning light. Then in a single motion, she leaned closer and sucked him deep into her mouth.

"Oh, Ree," he whispered finally. He reached down and gave a single stroke to her hair. If she wanted his bleak and godforsaken heart, then hers it would be.

Her fingers curled into his thighs, holding on, protesting his interruption. He brought his hand under her arm and nudged her toward him. "To me, love."

"Cormac . . ." She wiped her mouth with the back of her hand, and his blood surged at the wanton sight of it. "I know you said—"

He stopped her words with a kiss. He held nothing back. The raw needs of a man, the tender affection of a lover—the lifetime of his wanting went into his kiss.

She was wildfire, on him in an instant, the bright flame of her searing over his body, tangling her hands in his hair, writhing her hips against his. She cupped his face in her hands, and the look in her eyes was triumphant and fever-bright. "I want you."

"Patience, Ree." He forced himself to slow down, moving his hands over her body in long, languid strokes. It was her first time; he would do this right.

He kissed her again, his tongue exploring her mouth with deep, lazy thrusts. He slipped his fingers between their bodies, finding her. He moaned to feel how slick she was, how ready for him.

He kissed her more, and it set his blood on fire, until he

couldn't stop kissing her. He didn't know where to move his hands—he wanted them everywhere. He wanted to feel her everywhere, to know and pleasure every last inch of her body. And so his touch roved all over. Tangling in her hair, down her lithe arms, to her breasts. They were so tight and firm. He chafed and squeezed them, and her wild moans sent a shock of pure lust to his groin.

"Now, Cormac," she begged, and her hands wrapped around his buttocks to pull him closer. "Please. I want you. Now."

He gritted his teeth, drawing deliberate breaths. He would not rush this; he had to be the disciplined one. "I don't want to hurt you, Ree. I want to make sure you're ready."

She wriggled atop his body, nestling his shaft just right, until he was poised in her slick folds. "I am ready," she insisted.

"Not yet," he told her and retook control. Clutching her with one arm, he swept her beneath him on the bed and set to devouring her neck and breasts until he thought he might see red from his need to take her.

With a frustrated whimper, she tilted her shoulder, urging a breast back to his lips. "I've been ready."

He hated the thought that this might cause her pain; he'd do everything in his power to ease it for her. Once again, Cormac brought his hand between them, his finger finding her and sliding in with ease. And then he slid in another. She was tight, but so wet.

"Aye," he couldn't help but laugh low into her neck through his kisses. "You are ready at that." He crooked his fingers and felt a rush of masculine satisfaction at her little cries of pleasure. "But you're so tight."

"Wait." He felt her body stiffen the slightest fraction. "Will it hurt very much?"

"Relax, love. Look at me."

She looked. Daylight caught her eyes at an angle, lighting them the eerily vivid blue of stained glass. Her mussed light brown hair reminded him of the color of wet sand.

"It will. But I think it's just for a moment, and then you'll feel the pleasure."

"You think?"

He kissed the crooked half-smile from her mouth. "The pain will go quickly."

"Wait," she said again. "Cormac?"

He froze. "Anything, Ree. What is it?"

"I trust you, you know. And I want you very badly. Please do it now."

"I'm trying, love." Chuckling, he kissed each corner of her lips. He nipped at her earlobe. "Now may I get back to it?"

Feeling her nod against his neck, he eased inside her an inch, and then another, all the while nuzzling and murmuring at her ear to distract her from the pain. He wanted nothing more than to plunge himself deep inside her, and the muscles in his back and thighs quivered with restraint.

He pushed in deeper and felt her sharp intake of breath. He paused, searching her eyes. "I don't want to hurt you."

"You can't hurt me, Cormac. You'd never hurt me." She canted her hips toward him, and he could no longer fight it. With one hard thrust, he drove all the way into her.

She cried out, and he froze.

Marjorie caught her breath, and then gave a quick laugh. "Go on, Cormac." She shifted suggestively beneath him. "I know that's not all there is to it."

And then he laughed, too, with relief, with disbelief.

Their gazes locked, and his smile faded, his mirth hardening into something darker and more primitive. His cock pulsed inside her, and he began to thrust. She gasped, shutting her eyes, clutching at his shoulders.

Cormac had one last flickering thought before losing himself to her. "I think I'm still dreaming, Ree."

And then she loosened, and finding his rhythm, joined him. Time fell away, until Marjorie shouted her climax, and Cormac's deep groan of pleasure wasn't far behind.

He held himself over her, bearing his weight on his

arms. He rained tender kisses over her face as they caught their breath. "There's no going back," he told her, his voice husky with emotion. "For either of us."

"I don't want to go back, Cormac." She drew a strand of hair from his sweat-dampened brow. "Ever."

His heart clenched. Was it possible for a man like him to find redemption?

Cormac rolled onto his back, tucking her in the crook of his arm so they could doze in the late morning. But lying there motionless proved as turbulent as being tossed about in storm-roiled surf, his heart pitching in his chest like flotsam. He prayed he could keep her safe and that he might keep his soul safe in the bargain. But he knew it was too late now. He was too far gone.

He thought she was dozing, and so when she spoke, her clear voice pricked his consciousness, sounding through his reverie like the chime of a bell.

"I don't want to leave you," she murmured, tracing lazy lines along his chest with her fingertip. His skin was damp, and her touch drew gooseflesh in its wake. "I don't even want to fall asleep."

"You won't be leaving me," he said groggily. With a firm arm, he nestled her to him, stroking her hair. Sated exhaustion pulled him down. "Ree, don't you know?"

"Hm?" She snuggled closer.

"I find you when I sleep." He let himself begin to drift, filling his head with the scent of her, filling his hands with the wavy silk of her hair. It was peace. "Always."

Chapter 25

They stood arm in arm at the foot of the quay. Marjorie's legs still trembled from yesterday. Merciful sweet heavens above. *Yesterday.*

She looked up at Cormac, remembering. They'd lain abed much of the day, simply exploring each other. He'd wake her up with his wanting and send her back to sleep sated, repeating it over and again until her thighs ached from their lovemaking.

Finally, in the late afternoon, he'd left her to pay a visit to the bailie, and then to the docks. But he'd come back. She sighed dreamily. He had most certainly come back.

And though her body was still tender, he had awoken deep and slumbering places she hadn't known existed. She gave him a coy but suggestive smile. They were places that wanted to be explored again, and soon.

"Are you ready?" He stared down at her, the usual steadiness in his eyes.

She could face anything by this man's side, so implicitly did she trust him and rely on him. She'd never stopped relying on thoughts of him to get her through. "I'm ready for anything," she said with her jauntiest of grins.

"Anything, eh?" He gave a surreptitious pinch to her rump.

Swallowing a squeak, she grabbed his arm. "Anything *on board ship.*"

He shook his head in mock ruefulness. "That's what scares me. You must let me do the talking, Ree. These men . . . they're killers, with icy water in their veins."

She gave an abbreviated curtsy. "The Lady Brodie is ever careful."

"Mind you, I had to do some very pretty talking for the sailors to agree to let you board. They're dreadfully superstitious, and women are a particular menace for any sensible seafaring man."

"A menace, am I?" She stood a bit taller, pleased with her newfound status. "How did you manage to convince them?"

"Once I *managed* to leave the bed yesterday"—he paused to give her a teasing wink—"'twas easy enough to find Forbes at his office, under the pretense of bearing tidings of the ailing Lady Brodie. Your 'illness' proved a most convenient explanation, by the by. My weak lady wife must hire a boy for her obvious needs."

"Why, I *am* a menace." Her eyes narrowed, and he chuckled.

"Those were the imaginary Lord Brodie's words, not mine," he was quick to assure her. "And it was all the excuse we needed. I gather Forbes is new to this particular enterprise. He told me whom to contact dockside, and here we are."

"Enterprise," she muttered with a frown. "As though we're discussing a new sweets shop instead of folks' lives. You're certain Davie's on board?"

"We can't be certain of anything. But if Davie is on the *Oliphant*, we'll find him." He let go her arm to slip his hand behind her, hugging her close to reassure her. "Now, shall we?"

They were about to enter another foreign world. She thought of eccentric wives and their uncharitable husbands. A wave of nausea swept her, as though she'd just had another tankard of that hideous rumbullion. "I don't want to see any of those people ever again, Cormac."

"Don't fret," he told her, leading them down the pier. The walkway was spindly and precarious, reaching far into the inky water. Its wooden planks creaked underfoot, and she gripped him for balance. "'Twill be simple sailors we find on board. A coarse lot, but at least they don't come clothed in velvet."

Slowing his pace, he stroked her hand with his thumb. "Are you certain you're prepared for what awaits us?"

"Never more certain." Standing tall, she eased her grip on his arm to prove her point.

"I promise there will be no more feather-wearing harridans to provoke you. You'll be the only woman aboard. And I doubt Forbes or any of his cronies will make an appearance. I gather those sorts of men don't like to sully their good names by standing witness to the vulgar exchange of goods and money."

Goods. The word made her shudder. It was boys they were talking about. "No, he simply enjoys the profits after the fact."

Cormac stopped in his tracks. "It's the last time." He turned, leaning close to her, his voice a whisper even though none could possibly hear. Cupping her chin, he told her, "We'll get Davie and go far from here."

We. His hushed promise gave her strength. Marjorie gave him a definitive nod. She could weather anything as long as she was by his side.

"Ho!" he cried when they got to the end of the dock. The *Oliphant* cast a long shadow, its hull looming thrice her height overhead. Was Davie just on the other side of that timber, imprisoned in a darkened, vermin-infested hold? Cormac chafed her back, and she realized she'd shivered. "Ho there!"

There were distant shouts, and a head popped over the

side to look down at them. A young boy, no older than thirteen, studied them skeptically. His head popped back out of view, replaced a moment later by a grizzled man in want of a full set of teeth. "You be Brodie?"

"Aye." Cormac's voice was clipped, and Marjorie was astonished to watch his transformation. The man who'd soothed her chill a moment before had, with a word, turned into a creature of all mettle and no heart. "We come aboard."

The man sucked on his rotted teeth and spat into the water. His eyes went to Marjorie, scanning her intently. She was proud she flinched from neither spittle nor stare.

"*She's* no' comin' aboard. No womenfolk." His eyes lit, glimmering with suggestion. "Not unless she's—"

"No," Cormac said, his voice sharp. "She's coming aboard or your man sees none of this." He lifted the edge of his waistcoat, flashing the coin purse tied there.

Scowling, the man disappeared.

"I wish it weren't this way . . ." Cormac muttered.

"I *have* to come with you. How else to be certain we retrieve the right boy?" She nodded to where the coin purse was nestled beneath his coat. "So," she said, with a quick change of subject, "I thought you said true Scotsmen carried only sporrans."

He shook his head in disbelief. "You're not very afraid, are you?"

She inhaled deeply, contemplating his question. "We're close to finding Davie. And when I consider that, I feel bravery enough for the both of us. Right now, the concern foremost in my mind is"—she eyed the side of the ship—"how precisely are we to"—a rope ladder tumbled over the side—"ah."

The flimsy ladder swung in the air, and he grabbed the side to steady it. "In the mood for a climb, Ree?"

"Come aboard," a voice shouted from above. "The both of you."

Even with his help, it was a struggle to mount the ladder. Finally, she pulled herself completely onto it.

Between their adventure and the fact that they were about to save Davie, a wave of giddiness overtook her. Standing on the swaying rope ladder, she looked back over her shoulder and told him saucily, "I don't know if my legs can handle any more strenuous activity."

When she glanced up, though, spying some of the ladder's more threadbare footholds, her high spirits flagged. She glanced back down to see what a fall would look like. A gap between the dock and the side of the ship wavered like a great flapping maw. "Would one survive the fall, do you think, or be crushed between ship and pier?"

"Courage, lass." With a wicked gleam in his eye, he placed his hands on her rump and gave her a push up to get her started. "Nobody will be doing any falling this day. And anyhow," he added with a wink, "as for the strenuousness of the activity, 'tis I who's had the most exacting time of it."

His ribald comment erased her trepidation long enough for her to scale to the top. He climbed right behind her, helping to guide her up and over the side.

After Marjorie gathered her wits and dusted her skirts, she raised her head to see dozens of gape-mouthed faces staring at her. The stench of unwashed men hit her like a wall. She forced a prim smile onto her face.

Davie. They were so close. And the first thing she would do was give him a bath. Or feed him and then bathe him. Perhaps she could feed him *while* he sat in the bath.

She remembered they played a role—she was supposed to be a wealthy woman, generally entitled, and keen to hire help. She stood taller, adopting her best haughty mien.

Shading her eyes from the sun, she took a step forward, staring wide-eyed at the dense webbing of lines overhead. It seemed an impossible tangle of ropes and poles. She took another step, watching as a sailor climbed high, edging out along the top of one of the sails to tie something off.

"Mind the boom, mum."

Marjorie looked down to see who'd spoken, and she had to bite her lips not to gasp. A young boy stood there, and he was the strangest, most beautiful creature she'd ever laid eyes on. His skin shone dark as ebony, his shy smile baring teeth like small pearls.

She'd heard tell of Moorish folk, and here was one before her, a lad with such a peculiar inner stillness combined with the most incongruous Scots brogue spilling from his lips. She wanted to ask who he was. Did he remember his mother? Was he safe? "Thank you," she said simply instead.

She didn't understand this world, didn't want to contemplate boys stolen from faraway lands. She felt Cormac at her back, and something eased deep inside. They were in this *together*.

There was a shout, and the sailors scattered like marbles, scurrying in dozens of different directions, back to their posts.

Another man appeared before them, and he stood out dramatically from the rest of the crew. Unlike the majority who wore loose-legged sailor slops, this man had donned fine tawny-colored britches and a simply cut black waistcoat. An oily smile spread across his face. "Welcome aboard. I confess, my men are in quite a dither. The last woman aboard was a pretty little native rowed out to us as a gift when we were docked off the coast of Dominica. You can imagine they wonder if the appearance of another female might mean—"

"Let's just get on with this, then," Cormac snarled. "We are the Lord and Lady Brodie."

"Oh, I know who you are, or you wouldn't be standing here. And you may call me . . . Jack." The man's smile grew broad, but it didn't reach his eyes. He winked, and her skin crawled. "You must understand I'm not in the habit of handing out my Christian name to strangers, no matter how pretty a king's subject she might be."

"Aye," Cormac rasped. "A pretty subject who happens to be my *wife*."

With a nonchalant shrug, Jack turned and strolled toward the rear of the ship, his clear assumption being that they'd follow. "I'm told you want a younger lad, but there's not much promise in that group. You might find more satisfaction with—"

"We want a younger lad." Cormac didn't follow. Instead, he stood firmly, legs apart and arms crossed at his chest. He was a man who'd brook no disagreement, and the vision of him made Marjorie swell with admiration.

Jack stopped. Looking between Cormac and Marjorie, he shook his head ruefully. "'Tis your coin." He nodded to the front of the ship, at a structure standing one deck high, nestled in the bow. "We keep the young lads there."

"In the crew's quarters?" Cormac looked suspicious, and it put Marjorie on alert. "Why not the hold?"

Jack sighed dramatically. "There was two or three of the men what was beginning to pay the lads too much mind. We had to stow them in the foc'sle instead."

Marjorie shivered. If Davie had been touched or harmed in any way, she'd come back and personally send each and every one of the men to find their fates on a foreign plantation.

Jack's eyes flicked to Marjorie, and for a second, some vile thing glimmered there. "Come on, then," he said, strolling to the forecastle.

"No." Cormac stood firm. "We'll not go below."

Jack sneered. "Just you then, if the lady wife is too afeared."

"The *lady wife* doesn't leave my sight." He stepped beside her. "You'll bring the boys above deck if you want to see your coin."

It struck Marjorie that these foul men could simply *take* their coin, and there'd be none to stop them. Cormac was right; there was no way she was going down into the crew's quarters. Who knew what awaited them there. She sidled even closer to him.

"The boys are tied," Jack protested. "You canna

expect me to drag the whole line of squirming, wee pests on deck, like a drove of cattle to market."

"That's precisely what I expect." Cormac rubbed the side of his coat, and seeing the bulge, Marjorie realized he had a pistol holstered there.

The man's eyes went flat, and then, with a single resentful nod, he headed to the front of the ship and disappeared into the hatch.

"Thank you," she whispered.

"No worries, Ree." He affected a smile that she suspected was purely for her benefit. "Neither of us will be going belowdecks. I can assure you, I've had my fill of tight spaces for one lifetime."

The comment threw her for a moment, until she realized the episode with Aidan surely would have traumatized him in more ways than one. "Is it because of the chimney? Do you not like to be enclosed?"

He only looked at her, but his gaze was distant, some faraway memory replaying in his mind. Finally, he said, "You could say I'm not overly fond of confinement, no."

Cormac tossed the reply off to her with the same nonchalance he'd been feigning all morning. Though he'd been pretending calm, he'd been on alert since the moment he'd shouted a summons to the hands on deck.

He hadn't wanted to alarm her. Though true, he hadn't exactly been comfortable in tight spaces since getting stuck as a boy, the real reason he didn't want to go belowdecks was far more pressing. The deckhands needed but one sharp hit to the back of Cormac's skull, and they could be off with Ree, away to do the devil knew what with her. And when they were done, he imagined she'd fetch a pretty price in the middle of the Indies.

Just the thought of it had his hand touching the weapon at his side, an old wheel-lock pistol that'd belonged to a grandfather he'd never known. God spare him, it was good to be wearing a pistol again.

Then a hopeful thought flickered bright in the recesses of his mind. Might they truly be close to retrieving Davie?

Subterfuge, idle threats, and a whole lot of confident posturing had gotten them this far. Could his godforsaken gifts for killing and spying actually be used for good?

Perhaps he was redeemable after all. The notion brought him closer to Ree's side. She looked up at him, and though she had a quizzical look on her face, she remained silent. He put his hand at her slender waist, giving her a gentle squeeze. She had her own sense for subterfuge, God love her, though the poor thing must be a bundle of nerves inside, despite her bravado.

Redemption. The thought made his heart clench. If such a thing were possible, he had Ree to thank for his soul.

There was a ruckus, and he felt her stiffen at his side. "Steady, Ree."

"Settle yerselves!" The grizzled man with the missing teeth emerged from the forecastle, shouting orders down the ladder. "One by one, or you're all in for a flogging."

She took in a sharp breath, and Cormac whispered, "Be calm."

A half dozen boys gradually spilled one at a time onto the deck, all filthy and squinting as though they hadn't seen the sun in days. The biggest of the lot couldn't have been older than ten.

Cormac scanned the group, and Davie stood out at once. A little ginger-haired boy, just as she'd described. He hoped the lad had sense and didn't give them away.

Ree gasped, and he was quick to steady her with a firm hand at her elbow. It would do them no good if *she* were the one who spoiled their disguise.

He saw the instant Davie spotted her; the boy's mouth gaped, and his freckled cheeks turned apple red. Cormac watched Ree in his peripheral vision as she silenced the lad with a sharp shake of her head.

"These are them." Jack was back among them, watching Cormac and Marjorie very carefully. "And a sorry lot they are."

Cormac's mind raced. He needed to improve upon

what was a threadbare story. Jack was growing suspicious, and the last thing they needed was a suspicious smuggler.

Jack stared Marjorie up and down, as though he were trying to work something out. "If you decide you want older—"

"No," Cormac interrupted, choosing his strategy. "These lads are just what we had in mind. My wife . . . a bairn has yet to quicken . . ." He mimicked hesitation. "She's been unable . . . you ken my meaning."

"Ah," Jack said simply.

"Aye. That's why so young." Cormac heaved a sigh of relief that wasn't entirely pretense. "Lady Brodie has a fancy for ginger-haired lads, so we'll be taking—"

Marjorie stepped forward. "We'll take them all."

Chapter 26

Cormac's eyes shot to Marjorie in disbelief. Had she really just said what he thought she'd said? She stood, staring at the smuggler. He recognized the tilt of her chin.

"Och, good Christ . . ." he hissed under his breath. So much for allaying Jack's suspicions. "All"—he quickly counted—"six, love?"

"Aye." She gave one resolute nod, avoiding his gaze. "My . . . sister has needs as well."

"Mm-hm." Cormac's eyes narrowed, focusing on Jack. They definitely didn't have coin enough for all the boys. But Marjorie had made a decision, and they were in it now. "The lady has spoken."

Jack had a strange, fixed look on his face, considering his next move. His arm angled up, hand poised over the sword on his hip. "I'll see the money, then."

"Aye, the money." Taking Marjorie's hand, Cormac took a step back toward the ladder. How was he to get all the boys *and* her off the boat safely? "First, my lady wife takes the boys off the boat. Then we deal with the money."

Marjorie gasped. "But—"

Cormac squeezed her hand, giving her a pointed look. "I'll not have you a party to our *transaction*." He purposely stressed the last word, as though to imply the exchange of coin was a dirty thing unfit for feminine eyes.

Jack wrapped his hand around the hilt of his sword, well past pretense now. "There best be gold in that wee pouch of yours."

"You'll have your gold." Cormac scanned the deck, tallying the number of deckhands posing a threat. Jack had a sword. The old man wore a rusted fish knife in a scabbard at his waist. And there was one sailor standing alongside Jack—likely his first mate—and though he bore no visible weapons, there'd be at least a dirk tucked in the belt at his back.

The other crew members were either too far away, in the rigging, or simply not paying them any mind. Even so, Cormac imagined the moment he made a move on their captain, they'd become an issue soon enough.

He had to better his odds.

"You'll get your payment belowdecks," Cormac said, his voice steely. He shot Marjorie a meaningful look. "But first, you *will* get off the ship. You and the boys."

The look she gave him was terror and anger and regret. He had time for none of it.

"Now." Cormac swaggered over to the boys, mimicking contempt. "It seems I own you now."

Jack watched quietly, momentarily appeased by the prospect of money. Or maybe the smuggler was simply appeased by the thought of getting Cormac below, where he'd knock him senseless and whisk *him* into indentured servitude.

Cormac scowled. Either way, it was just one more concern he had no time for.

His only care was for Marjorie . . . and the lads, he unwillingly admitted to himself. He glared at them with mock disdain. Cords bound their hands at their bellies, with each boy tethered to the next by a single stretch of rope. Unsheathing the tiny *sgian dubh* from his leg, he began to saw at the first of the bonds. "I'll not know what my wife sees in you ugly lot."

The first to be freed was a lad no older than ten. The picture of Aidan popped into Cormac's mind, and he shoved it away again. He kicked the boy toward the side of the ship. "If you don't hasten down that ladder, I vow I'll leave you behind, paid for or no."

He hated to be cruel—he'd tried to be as gentle as possible—but they had a ruse to maintain. It was life or death now. He prayed they lived long enough for the boy to thank him later.

He loosened the next few, and they scuttled toward the side, limping in a way that made his heart crack. Cold single-mindedness mellowed into calm resolve. If he ended up dying to save these boys for Marjorie, so be it. He'd known all along his life was forfeit.

"You," he barked at the eldest. "You go down and hold the ladder for Lady Brodie." Marjorie would just have to manage the rungs on her own. He had enough to contend with on board.

Cormac watched as Marjorie and the last of the boys disappeared over the side, and then he turned his attention to Jack. He'd need to better the odds, which meant splitting the captain off from the rest of his men.

The captain's cabin would be aft. It'd be a small cell, small enough to accommodate only a few sailors at a time, minimizing the number of men Cormac would have to face at once. He flexed his fingers, anticipation heightening his senses. Despite what he'd told Ree about an aversion to confinement, he fought well in enclosed spaces.

"To your cabin," Cormac said and then realized he should temper himself so as not to arouse suspicion. A man in *Lord Brodie's* position—a wealthy noble dealing with smugglers, presumably for the first time—would express caution. He added, "You'll get the money when I'm not feeling so exposed."

Nodding, the smuggler led them to a small cabin at the rear of the ship.

As they crossed the deck, he studied Jack's back. Cormac was the taller man, but the captain wasn't exactly small. And the man had a sword, while Cormac had only his pistol. Which was a handy weapon indeed, if one had the time to load it, and time was something Cormac wouldn't have.

He rubbed his fingers together, deep in thought. He'd need to disarm Jack and muscle his way out. His elbow grazed the knob of wood and steel holstered at his side. A cold smile cocked the corner of his mouth. Pistols were capable of more than just firing bullets.

He'd have only one opportunity to act. Smugglers or no, ships like these were run with clocklike precision. Every moment he hesitated invited interruption.

Cormac didn't hesitate. Jack entered the dim cell. It was just as he'd imagined it: a narrow rectangle of a room featuring a bunk, a small table and bench, two portholes, and a lantern bearing an unlit candle.

Cormac stepped in right behind him, and then stepped even closer still, until he could smell the man's sweat and feel the heat of his body radiate to his chest.

Jack stopped, stiffened, began to turn. "What do you—"

Cormac slammed his pistol down onto the captain's temple. Jack grunted, and Cormac caught him before he toppled noisily to the ground. Hugging the man awkwardly to him, he kicked the door shut behind them, shuffling Jack forward and dropping him onto his cot.

He was back out the door at once, Jack's sword in his hand. Though he held the blade as low and as inconspicuously as possible, it was only a matter of time before some canny sailor recognized their captain's blade in this stranger's hand.

A few sailors looked at him, and he held their eyes, giving them a brazenly confident nod. It was apparently an attitude they were comfortable with, because nobody raised any alarm.

He walked briskly to the side of the ship and had almost reached the ladder when he heard the old man's voice. "Ho!"

Cormac picked up his pace, and the man shouted again, "You there!"

He sensed the activity on deck come to a standstill. There was a loud thump behind him as a man jumped from the rigging, landing just behind his shoulder.

Cormac sprinted to the edge of the ship, looking over the side for Marjorie. The boys had congregated at the head of the dock, and she stood alone, staring up at him. The anguish on her face broke something in him. He hated bringing her pain, and he'd do his best to survive this. But if he didn't, he'd know he'd given his all, and all for her.

His years of killing, of watching the killing, all would be redeemed today, on this ship. All his terrible knowledge, his *talents*, would finally be put to a good end.

"Cormac," she screamed. "Behind you!"

He tossed the coin purse down to her. "Go!"

She caught it, but then simply stood, paralyzed, on the quay.

Panic seized him. "Run, now!"

He hated leaving her alone. And then he remembered there was one person in Aberdeen, outside of her uncle's home and apart from her charity work, whom Marjorie could count on. "Run," he shouted again. "To your maid, lass! Hide with your maid!"

As he watched her eyes flicker bright with understanding, he heard a footfall behind him. Raising his sword, he spun, blocking a young sailor's blade with a sharp clang, stopping it just above his collarbone.

Chapter 27

She raced up the quay, thoughts careening wildly in her head. She'd done it again. She'd made a dreadful decision, a deadly decision.

A low keening sound escaped from her lips, and she bit it back. The boys were waiting for her at the head of the dock, terrified. She needed to be strong for them. Cormac would want her to be strong.

A loud crack sounded at her back. She'd never heard gunfire before, but the menace and the power of it was unmistakable.

Her legs pumped faster. She reached them and, barely slowing her pace, snatched Davie's hand and another of the smaller boys.

"Marjry!" Davie cried, his tiny fist damp in hers. She clutched it even harder, terrified he might slip from her grasp. "You're hurtin' me, Marjry."

She shushed him, and panic made her voice stern. "Run! We must run!"

Run. It was the last thing Cormac had told her to do. Would those final words echo forever in her mind, haunting her? *Go . . . run.* This time she couldn't stop the short, sharp cry that tore from her throat.

Cormac was the one who should've run—from the sight of her. He'd known it that day on the beach at Dunnottar. He'd wanted nothing to do with her, but she'd forced herself back into his life. He'd been wary, skittish, as though only he had been able to see the clouds of tragedy looming over her shoulder, just on the horizon.

Cormac. A sharp cramp in her side stole her breath. She embraced it and ran harder. What pain was Cormac enduring even now, for her?

She'd impetuously demanded all the boys. They hadn't discussed it before. She was sure he would've done her bidding, had they only discussed it, planned for it. Instead, she'd made the decision for them rashly, and it was costing Cormac his life.

She could see no way out of his situation. She'd gotten away with the boys *and* the money. All the fighting talent in the world wouldn't save him from a shipload of furious smugglers.

He had no way out.

She stopped, leaned over, a hand on her knees. Gasping for air, she clutched at her belly, feeling like she might be sick right there in the street.

She felt a small hand stroking awkwardly at her hair. *Davie.* Wee Davie. She had to get him to safety. It wasn't about her now, nor Cormac. He'd known that; it was why he'd forsaken his life to save theirs.

Convulsively swallowing back the bile in her throat, she looked up. The boys were staring at her expectantly, alarm and confusion furrowing their poor, filthy faces.

She glanced around to get her bearings. The docks were far at their backs now, and in her panic, she'd led them down a warren of side streets. She needed to gather her wits, or it'd mean the death of all of them. Not wanting to invite too much attention, she forced herself to walk again.

Fiona. Cormac's last intention had been that she find her maid, Fiona, and that was exactly what she would do.

Pulling her shoulders back, she picked up her pace, but not so much as to raise suspicion. "Come now, boys."

One of the younger ones was crying silently. She gave a perfunctory pat to his head. "Steady on, lad. You're safe now," she assured him, wishing she spoke the truth.

She racked her mind, trying to get her bearings and recall where exactly Fiona lived. How could it be that the maid had been in their employ for over a decade, and yet Marjorie had never once been to her house? She scolded herself. All her talk of the importance of charitable living, and here she'd never expressed enough of an interest in Fiona's life to pay her family a single visit.

She remembered the lass had once told her of life in the vennel, a narrow lane off Huckster Row and one of the poorer spots in Aberdeen. Marjorie girded herself, hoping Fiona still lived there. Braving the vennel was bad enough; she prayed it wouldn't be in vain.

They came to the head of the alley. Buildings hovered close together, casting the place in cold shadow. The boys edged away, outright panic on their faces.

"Come on," she urged, tugging at Davie's hand.

One of the older boys came to a full stop, his arms crossed over his chest. "No, mum."

The pose reminded her of Cormac, and a needle of pure anguish pricked her chest. Marjorie pursed her lips. She had no time for boys' nonsense. They were in grave danger, and doubly so now that they were standing exposed and unprotected before who knew what manner of unsavory elements there were to be found in this neighborhood. "No, *what*?"

"I'll not go there." His face took on a look of utter indifference, as if he had something better to do, and Marjorie were merely the pest keeping him from it.

"You listen to me." Every ounce of fear and regret poured into her voice, sharpening her tone into something that'd tame even the most headstrong of Saint Machar lads. "I'm saving you, if you haven't noticed. You *will* do as I say, you little wretch, and right this instant. And what I'm saying is that you will"—she let go Davie's hand to tweak the older boy's ear—"follow"—she stepped into the lane, dragging him close behind—"me."

Marjorie herded them along, feeling more alone than ever. The vennel matched her despairing mood. Dilapidated houses crammed the alley cheek by jowl, each shoddier than the last, all listing walls and windows stuffed with rags. But it was the silence that struck her the most. The place was silent and menacing, as though people skulked behind closed doors hiding and scheming.

This was where the blushing Fiona lived? Marjorie shivered. It was a horrid place. She took in one appalling structure after another, wondering how she would ever find her.

A few of the boys apparently felt more secure, though, because they split off from the group, scuffling and running along the lane, shouting threats at each other.

Her face flushed hot with anger and fear. The boys were innocents who had no idea what they were dealing with. Little did they know, if overheard by the wrong person, they'd find themselves back on the *Oliphant*, but this time she'd be trussed up right alongside. "Get back here now."

But it was too late. There were sounds of murmuring and of creaking shutters, and the hard scuff of warped wood against stone, as folk looked out their doors to see what the ruckus was about.

"Miss Marjorie?" The voice was tentative, and hearing it, Marjorie nearly crumpled in relief.

Turning around, she spotted a linen-capped head peeking out from a doorway behind her. *Fiona.* Once this was all over, she vowed she'd double the girl's pay. "I . . . *we* need your help."

"I imagine you do at that." Fiona darted a look up and

down the alley. If she had any questions, she held her tongue, and Marjorie was grateful.

"My da's out." The maid paused, a peculiar look flickering across her face. "But you've come in perfect time. I'm about to put supper on." A few of the boys hesitated at the sight of her cramped, one-room dwelling, but Fiona shooed them in. "In you get, then. So many of you . . ."

"Quickly now," Marjorie added, cramming them all inside and following close behind.

She pulled the door shut behind them and cringed, fighting the urge to put a handkerchief to her nose and mouth. Not because of the filth, for a single glance told her that Fiona kept a spotless home, but because of the cook fire. The room was cramped, and the fireplace not well ventilated, and the charred odor of woodsmoke gave a twinge in her lungs.

"Not what you're used to," the maid muttered matter-of-factly. She began bustling around at once, leading Marjorie to a small washbowl in the corner, arranging the smaller boys around the hearth, and pointing the older ones to a corner. "But we'll all fit in, we will."

She went to a table along the side of the room and, hands on hips, contemplated the food spread before her. She snatched up a skinned hare, holding it by its hind paws. "I've a fresh-caught mawkin."

"A rabbit?" Davie popped up to marvel at it. "He's so pale and wee without his coat."

"Aye, wee indeed." Fiona laid the rabbit out along a modest table, its wooden slab top scarred from years of use. She took up a knife and set to dressing the meat. "Too wee for all these bellies," she noted, scanning the room. "But I've a bit of barley . . . mayhap in a broth, 'twill stretch it."

Marjorie was amazed that, with nary a question, the young woman determined she'd give up the full bounty of her family's supper, sharing it instead with a houseful of strange children. Yes, she decided, she'd insist they begin paying Fiona more. Much more. "I'll not take the food from your table, Fiona."

"I'll pretend I didna hear that, and you can pretend you didna say it."

She continued to prepare the meal with deft hands, and eventually the smell of rabbit soup filled the room. The rich aroma had a calming effect on all of them. The boys gradually relaxed and began to chatter quietly among themselves. Marjorie's panic had dulled, and all that was left were thoughts of Cormac and a thick ache in her throat.

Wiping her hands on her apron, Fiona turned her focus to a meager pile of vegetables. "So, then."

"So." Marjorie sighed, preparing for an onslaught of questions.

"Does this have aught to do with that Cormac fellow?"

Marjorie blanched, unable to speak through the grief thick in her throat. *Cormac.*

Fiona hesitated, a faint blush pinking her cheeks. Meeting Marjorie's eyes, she said, "I seen him, you know. Cormac was rifling about in your room, mightily bothered he was, and quite keen to find you." She focused on her food once again, chopping turnips with great intent. "Trouble follows them MacAlpins," she mumbled. "Like smoke from fire."

Marjorie sat up straighter. "What did you say?"

Fiona paused to study Marjorie, gauging her, and must've seen something that gave her enough courage to continue. Putting her knife down, she announced confidently, "I didna like that you went away so close after *he* appeared. Your uncle said you'd gone to visit that Bridget lass, but I think you should have a care when it comes to those MacAlpins."

Marjorie swallowed hard. *She* was the trouble now—not the MacAlpins. And she'd brought it under Fiona's own roof. She eyed the boys, wondering how to explain them, and what to say about her sudden appearance on her maid's doorstep. "It's not Cormac . . . or . . . well, 'twas Cormac who helped me." Her tongue felt thick, and she looked down, worrying the fabric of her skirts in trembling hands.

Fiona turned to stir the soup. She allowed a few minutes of silence before asking, "When will you take them to Saint Machar?"

"The boys?" The maid was right—Saint Machar would be precisely the place to drop them, if she hadn't spotted Archie that night at the bailie's party under such suspicious circumstances. But she dare not confess her doubts about Archie, and so she lied instead. "There's no room there for now."

Fiona's eyes widened. "No room at Saint Machar?"

She nodded, despising her deception. *A full heart never lies,* she thought, considering the old proverb with regret. "I'm hoping to find their families. And I'm hoping to find them work."

Both statements were true, in their way. Working in a Scottish kitchen had to be far preferable to toiling on a distant plantation. And who was to say she wouldn't find their families? She'd need to begin at once, querying the boys as to their origins. For all she knew, they hailed from as far away as Glasgow.

The door screeched loudly as it scraped against the stone floor. A heavyset man stood in the entrance, glowering.

"Good Christ preserve us," Fiona whispered.

What little light there was in the vennel hit him from behind, casting strange shadows on an already hard and ugly face. The room fell silent. "What the devil . . . ? Who let these vermin in?"

The words tripped uneasily from his tongue, and Marjorie thought it might be whiskey that dulled the man's speech.

Slamming the door, he stormed to Fiona, hovering over her, the rage plain on his face. "What are you up to now, you silly chit?"

"I . . . I . . ." Fiona's cheeks turned crimson as she sputtered for words. "Da, this is—"

Her father? Marjorie bristled. Father or no, Marjorie wouldn't sit idly by as a drunken sot bullied her maid. He struck her as a tyrant who hadn't a care for any but himself. A man like that would not only balk at having folk under his roof, he'd turn the lot of them out on the street without so much as batting an eye. Drawing her shoulders back, Marjorie spread her grand skirts around her. She knew his type.

She'd put the situation into language he'd understand. "My name is Lady Brodie, sirrah, and your daughter is a clever *chit* indeed."

"Brodie," he said, and then belched. "I've not heard of no Brodie around here."

"I'm a woman of great resources, though I insist on a quiet life. But now I find myself in a crisis, and your daughter offers a means to my preferred ends." Marjorie pulled the coin purse from where she'd hidden it in the skirts of her gown. "Her wily tongue talked me out of nigh close to my entire savings. It's all arranged, though." Waving the pouch enough for the coins to clink enticingly, she cocked a brow in challenge. "Unless you disagree?"

Shaking her head, Fiona tsked quietly. "A full purse ne'er lacks friends."

The sound of money stopped the man, as Marjorie had known it would. He stepped closer. "What are you talking about, woman?"

"I've important business to attend. In . . . Glasgow," she improvised, realizing perhaps she was onto something. If she could hide the boys away here with Fiona, it would buy her time to . . . *What?*

She'd saved Davie. That had been her sole intention. She'd had no plans after that.

Without Cormac, things felt so incomplete. What did she need to do now? She'd have to travel back to Dunnottar, of course. Deliver news of his passing. Tears stung her eyes, and she forced herself to focus on the moment.

She'd also need to sort out the Archie . . . situation.
Fury spiked her veins, and it was almost refreshing.
There was no way she'd allow a predator back into Saint
Machar, where he could cull the strongest of Scotland's
lads for a profit.

"I've asked your daughter to attend my charges for me."

"Your . . . *charges*?" A bit of spittle flew out of his
mouth at the last word.

Grimacing, she flicked a bit of food where it'd landed
on her arm. "Aye, they're students of mine. They'll be no
trouble. And it won't be long until I return. I've offered
her coin for her trouble."

He steadied himself with a hand on the table. "They're
to stay *here*?"

Fiona gaped, no less shocked. "Lord love her."

"Aye, *here*." Marjorie sat up, trying to look as much
like an affronted lady as possible. "I offered your daughter one bawbee per day for each lad, but she asked for
two bob, to which I said *no indeed*, and I went up to a
shilling, which wasn't good enough for the likes of *her*,
and so we finally ended up at half a crown for minding
the lot of them."

Fiona's father gawked, clearly not following, which
had been Marjorie's intention precisely. She willed the
man to shut his mouth, though. He was exuding a powerful stench, and it was beginning to turn her stomach.

Schooling her features, she slipped the pouch back into
her skirts. "I should be gone no more than a fortnight."

Fiona's father stared, astonished. "A half crown comin'
to me, eh?"

"To *you*," the maid scoffed under her breath.

"To your daughter," Marjorie snarled, losing patience.
She felt the desperate urge to escape—from the stench,
from this man, from her loss.

She rose and marched to the hearth, pinning him with
her haughtiest look. "You will receive payment *only* upon
my return, and *only* when I see that neither these boys nor
your daughter have come to any untoward harm."

He shrugged, his face a simple, thuggish grimace. He may not have understood her words, but it appeared he at least understood their gist.

Marjorie knelt down to cup Davie's chin. "I'll be back for you, laddie," she whispered. She kissed him on his forehead and then cleared her throat, willing her voice to steady. "I swear it."

She swept out the door, trembling violently. She needed to weep, to scream.

Davie, Archie, Fiona . . . life had handed her a series of appalling revelations, pulling the shades from her eyes. She'd been naive and foolish for so long. To think there was true charity in the world. To think the world made any sense.

And she was a fool now if she thought a life without Cormac would ever make sense again.

Her gorge rose. *Cormac.*

She tugged at her bodice, half walking, half running to the head of the alley. She knew she should exercise caution; she should be more circumspect, less conspicuous. She was a woman alone, and with a pocketful of coin, no less, racing along as though she were a child. But she needed to flee. She was going to be sick.

Cormac was gone, and she'd never be right again.

Hands grabbed her roughly from behind, clapping over her mouth and hard around her belly.

Terror exploded, blurring the edges of her vision. Marjorie's heart pounded in her chest, as she was dragged back into the chill shadows of the vennel.

Chapter 28

"Hush." The lass was squirming like a fresh-caught haddie, and her squeals were beginning to attract unwanted attention. Cormac's profound relief at being reunited was momentarily eclipsed by concern. Unwelcome eyes meant danger. Gripping her more tightly, he put his mouth at her ear. "Hush, Ree. It's me. It's Cormac."

She froze for a split second. Spinning in his grip, she flung her arms around his neck, crushing her body to his. "Cormac!"

He kissed her hair, agonizingly aware of her soft breasts pressed into him. The moment he got her someplace safe, he'd not waste a moment before he had her lying naked before him.

Her squeals of terror had turned instantly into sounds of delight, and she let loose a stream of nearly unintelligible exclamations and apologies, alternately cupping and kissing his cheeks.

Cormac couldn't help but laugh. Seeing her was a revelation. Being parted so violently had plunged him into cold darkness; he'd been terrified for her safety, terrified he'd not survive to see her again. "You're a glorious sight, Ree."

"*You're* the glorious sight!" She patted his arms, his chest, as though he might be concealing some hidden injury. "Thank God you're safe." She curled her fingers into his shirt and, with a laugh, gave him a little shake. "We saved them! We did it, Cormac, we saved the boys."

"Where are they?"

"I left them safe with Fiona, just as you told me."

"Good work," he told her, and she beamed. "But now we must save ourselves." He couldn't stop his eyes from grazing down her body. Her low-cut gown revealed the tops of her pale breasts, and she was breathless and flushed with the excitement. Laying one last rough kiss on the top of her head, he pulled her into a brisk walk. First he'd assure her safety, and then he'd claim his reward. "We must make haste. Jack's men are out looking for us."

"But how did you escape? I thought you'd been killed!" She swatted him on his arm in mock anger. "How did you find me?"

"One question at a time, Ree." Though there was humor in his voice, the look in his eyes grew deadly serious as he led them from the alley, warily charting a path into the heart of the city. "I'm a highly motivated man, you see."

"What do you mean?" She looked up, innocence in her eyes.

He'd get her safely tucked away, and then he'd show her *exactly* what he meant. But for now, he said, "It means I'll not stay parted from you, whatever the cost."

"What happened?" she demanded. Fierce emotion lit her eyes, her expression intense. "I thought surely those smugglers would kill you."

"Once I knocked Jack out, his men didn't put up much of a fight. A hoary old ship's mate and a deck full of greenhorns armed with naught but rusted fish knives and empty muskets held in trembling fingers? They weren't too tricksy a gang from which to escape. And the younger sailors have their own reasons to be on board, none of which appear to be fealty to the captain."

"Had they been kidnapped, too, do you think?"

He shrugged. "Indentured, enthralled, or simply out for trouble, the lads apparently valued their lives over a load of stolen boys and a fistful of coin. I was forced to . . ." He paused, considering his words. The deckhands had attacked him, and it was kill or be killed. He regretted that a few of them had been no older than Declan. "I took a few out of the mix," he said carefully. "Seeing their mates go down was enough to take the wind from their sails."

"But how did you find me?"

"Och, lass, if only I'd kept a bit of the coin I'd tossed to you, it wouldn't have taken me quite so long." He hugged her playfully to him. "But not to worry. A few well-placed questions was all it took. Pretty lassies like Fiona, who are maids to even prettier ladies, tend to attract attention."

She glanced around, flush from the compliment. "Where are you taking us?"

He'd chosen an out-of-the-way path, turning up a side street, steering them to walk in the shadow of a row of buildings. "I'm afraid we can't go back to the inn."

"Then where should we go?" She stopped, perplexed, and he tugged her back into a walk.

"I'm afraid we have no choice but to go to your uncle's."

He felt the tension drain from her shoulders. "Oh, that's wonderful. We can ask Humphrey for help with—"

"No," he interrupted, regretting what he was about to tell her. "There can be no *we*. You've been in too much danger as it is. The ruse of Lord and Lady Brodie is at an end."

"But we still need to understand what Archie's involvement is," she exclaimed.

"Quiet now, Ree. We won't be safe until we're out of sight." He made sure he had her full attention. "*I* am the only person who will be investigating Archie."

"*We'll* investigate Archie. But," she quickly added, looking baffled, "I still don't understand why we can't ask my uncle for help."

Humphrey was a doddering old man above suspicion, and that was precisely the reason Cormac didn't want him involved. He worried her uncle might forget the need for discretion and blather the wrong thing to the wrong person. Rather than sharing that fear with Marjorie, though, he appealed instead to her sense of propriety. "I can't stay indefinitely at Humphrey's. Your uncle is a peculiar old duck, but even he'd raise a brow at that."

"Och." She smiled broadly and waved a dismissive hand. "*That's* your concern? Humphrey won't even know you're there. We simply won't announce your presence. In any case, the man is much preoccupied with other things of late. You've seen him. He didn't even notice when I'd left Aberdeen. In fact, I'd bet we could install ourselves there for a fortnight before he'd even notice my return." She sidled closer to him, giving his arm a quick and suggestive stroke of her fingers. "And besides, your staying at my uncle's has the additional advantage of extending our time together. You'd not deny an innocent lass that, would you?"

The seductive shadow in her gaze made his body quicken. She had the right of it: staying by her side would forever be his heart's only desire. He'd tasted paradise, and it was in her bed. "Innocent, eh? I thought we'd left your innocence by the wayside. Quite enthusiastically, as I recall."

Giggling, she leaned into him. He felt the soft give of her bosom on his arm. Drawing in a sharp breath, he quickened their pace. This woman was exquisite, and she was *his*. And the moment they returned to her room, he'd make very certain she knew it.

Which, at the pace he set, was not long.

"I swear to you," she whispered as they scampered up the stairs to her bedroom on the third story, "Fiona is the only person who will know you're here."

"And you trust her?"

She gave him a scornful look. "Cormac MacAlpin, as I remember it, *you* are the one who instructed me to trust her in the first place."

"Enough of your sass, woman. Just get us to your rooms." He swatted Marjorie on her bottom, hurrying her along.

With a delighted squeal, she spun, catching him around his neck. "I do love you, Cormac MacAlpin."

The words stole the breath from his lungs.

She stood on the stair above him. They were face-to-face, mere inches apart. In the shadows of the staircase, her magnificent eyes glimmered dark as sapphires. Her arms tightened around him. "I love you," she whispered.

Passion—and some bit of fear, too—stole the words from his throat. His own feelings overwhelmed him, remaining unspoken. He locked his mouth on hers instead and, sweeping her into his arms, stormed to her room like a Viking. He broke the kiss only to kick the door shut tight behind them.

Cormac strode to the bed and tossed her down. She laughed, bouncing on the heather-filled mattress, but the look in her eyes soon grew dark, watching him as he began to strip.

His shirt, his boots and trews—one by one his clothes dropped to the floor. And she stared hungrily all the while, her breath coming short. He thought his cock could get no harder, until he saw the stark desire in her eyes.

"I need you, Ree," he rasped. He needed her by his side. He needed to bury himself between her legs.

He needed her in his life forever.

He crawled on top of her, and the rustle of her clothes against his body was a maddening tease. His desire was sharp, and sharper still, until he thought it wouldn't even be enough for him to have her.

"You've brought me to life." He kissed her gently along her jaw, her forehead, and then, after tracing a path along her lips with his thumb, kissed her mouth. He'd been coming slowly back to life, until he discovered himself a feeling man again, a man capable of joy in her arms. "You've made me happy again, somehow."

A lifetime of pain and their shared hours of joy—everything that had passed between them—crystallized in that moment. He was a man redeemed. "My heart hadn't beat since that day," he said, knowing he'd not need even to speak Aidan's name for her to understand. "But it beats again, Ree. For you."

Her small hands stroked down his back, cupping his ass. His skin shivered. "I just thank God you're safe," she said, raining kisses over his face and neck. Her touch was tender and loving but ardent, too, and it ignited him.

She pulled away, and he saw uncertainty flicker in her eyes. "There's just one thing."

His body strained hard, an eager knot of flesh that addled his mind and fevered his flesh. But still, he'd stop if she wanted him to. "What is it, Ree?"

"I fear I need a bath."

He barked out a laugh. "A bath, is it? This is your great confession?" Nuzzling and nipping at her neck, he inhaled with exaggerated deliberation.

She yelped, squirming beneath him. "Stop that!"

"Ree. Lovely Ree." He pinned her beneath him, chuckling. "A bath you shall have. *After.* But for now, you're perfect." He nestled himself over her, coming to rest in his rightful place, in the cleft of her thighs. "Och, Ree," he whispered, his voice hoarse. "You're *so* perfect."

And she was. Marjorie had taken him to a place he thought he'd lost, and he'd be forever grateful, forever hers. He rolled onto his back, swooping her up onto his belly, and she gave a little cry of pleasure.

"Cormac . . ." She pulled up, tracing a seductive finger along her lacy neckline. "Don't you think I'd be more perfect if I were naked, too?"

"My thoughts precisely, love." He made quick work of the laces up her back, and she wriggled eagerly out of her gown. The moment her breasts bobbed free of her tight bodice, his breath caught. *Perfection indeed.* Would he ever get used to the sight of it?

"Come to me, Ree," he said, his voice low with desire. He pulled her up so she straddled him, and then he eased her slowly down onto him.

"Always," she whispered, and the word made his heart clench.

With a deep, shuddering sigh, her eyes fluttered shut. But he kept his own eyes riveted to her, straining to take in her every aspect in the dying light. Her slim shoulders beneath the wavy curtain of her hair. The blush of her nipples, dusky in the twilight.

He reached up to knead her breasts. They stiffened under his palms, and she moaned, mindlessly parting her lips with her pleasure.

"I need you closer," he said, his voice husky. He shifted onto his elbows, kissing his way up her torso, until he sat upright with her in his lap. "You're never close enough."

He rubbed his hands up and down her back, and then eased her backward so that he could taste each breast. She writhed over him, and he pumped and ground her closer, until she flung back her head, crying out. Raking his hand in her hair, he kissed her, the thrust of his tongue echoing the rhythm of his cock, until his climax pulsed deep inside her.

They collapsed sideways, lying in a tangle on the bed. Marjorie idly traced the damp hair from Cormac's cooling brow, until their heartbeats gradually slowed. "I know what we must do now," she said at last.

"Am I permitted to guess?" He playfully swept his hand down to fondle her backside. But he quickly grew intent, kissing along her neck, down to her breasts, his body stirring again already. "If you must have it again just *now*, love, we'd best get started."

But she remained serious, and Cormac grew serious, too, sensing her resolve. He pulled away and sighed, meeting her gaze. "Out with it, Ree. What is it we must do now?"

"The ship." She gave a slight nod, and the distant look in her eye worried him. "We must destroy the *Oliphant*."

Chapter 29

"We?" He disentangled himself from her, moving to sit on the edge of the bed. *"We* must destroy the ship?"

"Of course *we*. I can't very well do it by myself." Marjorie extracted the sheet from the rumple of bed linens and covered herself, her body chilled without him. "Have I upset you?"

He appeared to give the question thorough consideration, and then, inexplicably, he began to laugh. His easy, lopsided grin put her at her ease. "Not in the slightest, actually," he said, standing up. "I'm feeling difficult to upset."

She sat straight up. "Where are you going?"

"Don't fash yourself, Ree. I'll not leave the premises." He stepped into his trews and then strolled to the side table. "Unless you wish me to race down to the docks immediately and set fire to the ship. Or were you of a mind for something more along the lines of, say, an explosion? With black powder perhaps?"

"I hadn't considered something so spectacular as all that. Where would someone even get black powder?"

He gave her an amazed look.

The man was joking. She pouted back at him. "Cormac, be serious."

"Oh, I am." He retrieved a chipped white and blue basin. "We have terribly serious business to attend."

His body was taut, and she stared, enthralled by the minute flex of muscles in his back and arms as he walked to the door. She regretted mentioning the ship. She should've held her tongue and kept him in her bed a while longer. Though he couldn't get far with his shirt trapped beneath her leg. "What business? What are you doing?"

He paused in the doorway. "Earlier, you'd asked for a bath. Before we pursue any nonsense pertaining to ships or smugglers, I'd honor your request."

"But Humphrey doesn't know you're here. You can't just—"

He opened the door, and somebody gasped and stumbled backward. Marjorie swiftly pulled her sheet higher, covering her shoulders, and craned her neck to peek. It was one of the girls Fiona kept about to help with the washing, a young dark-haired wisp of a thing, and she'd been listening in the doorway. How Cormac knew the girl would be standing there, she had no idea.

His body altered slightly, and Marjorie was mesmerized to watch his metamorphosis from lover into threat. "You work for Fiona?"

Cowering, the girl gave a panicked nod. The poor creature was likely no older than twelve. Marjorie rolled her eyes—it was a young age at which to be exposed to the full force of Cormac MacAlpin.

"And you value this work, do you not?"

She gave him another fretful nod, this time accompanied by a curtsy.

"Then you'll fetch us water. Warm, mind." He handed her the basin. She reached for it, but he held it in place as he added, "And if anyone becomes aware of my presence here, I'll know it was you who told them. Just as I knew you were listening outside this door."

Nodding frantically now, she edged backward before spinning and dashing down the hallway.

He shut the door, saying with a smile, "You'll have your bath directly. Well, not a *full* bath, but I've my ideas." Stalking to the bed, he peeled the sheet from her torso and ran a possessive hand down her body. "I assure you, it will be a *thorough* one, at the very least."

She spied the thick bulge in his trews, and goose bumps rippled across her skin. All thoughts of the *Oliphant* fled to the back of her mind.

By the time the girl returned, Cormac had found a linen washcloth, a new cake of Marjorie's favorite rose soap, and he had her spread across the bed like a holiday meal on the table. Before the maid had a chance to knock, he opened the door, just a crack this time.

"Put the bowl down. Aye, that's the way," Cormac said in a low voice. His body blocked the door, and Marjorie could only imagine the terror on the poor girl's face. "I've told you what'll happen if folk find out I'm here, but would you like to know what will happen if they don't?"

There was a rustling, a pause, and then he continued, "Your mistress Marjorie is a good woman. I'm only here because she needs help. She's done no wrong, and you do no wrong if you choose to help her, too. If you mind me, I've a thruppence in my sporran, and it'll be just for you."

Marjorie heard a childlike gasp.

"But heed this," he added sternly. "If I catch you listening at this door one more time, the thruppence is mine."

There was the pattering of bare feet as the girl dashed away.

"Your touch with children is magical," Marjorie said with a laugh. "All glowering and bribes. How'd I not think of it myself?"

"Easy, lass. I ken you're not above bribery." He came

to the edge of the bed, basin in hand. "I've seen you dole out your wee packets of steak pie to the Saint Machar lads, who, by the by, could do with a fair spot of glowering besides."

Stripping off his trews, he knelt before the bed, and excitement thrummed through her. Whatever did he have in mind? Slipping his hands beneath her calves, he pulled her to the edge of the bed. The thrumming intensified to fire crackling in her belly.

He stroked his hands up her legs, and with a gentle squeeze, parted them. She lay naked before him, and the cool air on her bare skin made her breasts pull tight. The wickedness of it made her heart skip.

"Now, enough of your ships and your plans and your sass." He rubbed his thumbs in languid circles on the insides of her thighs. "You'd longed for a bath, and I'll not allow anyone to say I'm not a good man to my woman."

His woman. She thought her soul would burst from her body, so exhilarating did that sound. "*Your* woman, am I?"

Rather than answer, he studiously dipped the cloth in the water, a wicked grin cocking the corner of his mouth. "You need to lie back, Ree. For the full effect, aye?"

She did as he told her, the thrill of it bringing a secret smile to her face.

She tensed at the first shocking touch of wet washcloth on skin. But the water was warm, his touch confident, and soon she relaxed into the bed. He began at her feet, massaging them, and the cloth was just rough enough not to tickle yet soft enough so as not to abrade. She gave a little hum of contentment.

Cormac methodically washed, rinsed the rag, and washed some more, and she gladly let him. She felt love in his touch, even if he hadn't yet spoken the words.

His woman. He'd called her *his* woman. But for how long?

"What's to come of us, Cormac?" she asked quietly.

She heard the tinkling of water wrung into the bowl.

He rose and sat on the bed, swabbing the cloth along the side of her hip. "Come of us?"

"When all this is done." Her skin was cool where the damp cloth had touched her, but her blood pumped hot, her body responding to the rhythmic stroking of his hand along her torso. "We can't just go on as before."

His eyes met hers, held them. "No," he agreed at last, his voice a low rasp. "Not the same as before."

She saw hesitation in his eyes. "But . . . ?"

"But I don't deserve you, Ree. Look at you," he said, raking her body with his gaze. "You're a treasure."

He pulled the edge of her gown from the floor, rubbing the rich fabric between his fingers. "For me, this"—he held up the hem and, even in the low light, it shimmered— "this is a masquerade. And yet *this* is what you deserve. Wealth and finery." He tossed the dress back down. "You should have a handsome lord with an estate and a fleet of maids at your disposal. Not a poor fisherman living in a tumble of rocks."

Cormac was so much more than a mere fisherman. It baffled her that he didn't see it. "What if I *want* a poor fisherman?"

He gave her a rueful smile. "Then you strike a poor bargain."

"In any case, money matters not. I've money from Humphrey. It simply doesn't matter." She stilled his hand with her own. "Cormac, don't you see? I'd live the rest of my days, happily raising our children in your *tumble of rocks*, if it meant we could be together."

Pain flashed across his face. "Children? How could I ever raise children? Christ, Ree, how could I, of all men, raise a son?"

"I think you'd do a fine job of it."

"Children," he mused, raising his brows as though their existence had only just then occurred to him.

"Aye." She rolled onto her side to face him. "A house full of sons. With your dark hair, and your long, strong bones. They'd have your eyes."

She combed her fingers through his hair, drew them along the side of his cheek, his jaw. She wondered what held him back. Was it the thought of children that made him hesitate, or the thought of children with *her*? "Although they might have a touch of their mother in them, too," she added, looking away. "Whoever she might be."

"But I already know the mother of my children. And I want them to have *her* eyes." Cormac's voice was husky with emotion. He cupped her cheek, bringing her gaze to his. Easing Marjorie onto her back, he leaned his body over hers. He studied her face, tracing a delicate line along the tops of her cheekbones, over her brows. "I'll have sons with eyes that are blue like jewels, vivid and bright. Eyes that see the good in the world. Eyes that smile. Your eyes, Ree, my love."

He kissed her then, tenderly. Mending two hearts that had spent a lifetime broken.

Chapter 30

"What's to say a boy like Paddy won't be next?" Marjorie chewed a forkful of eggs with great enthusiasm. Swallowing, she pointed her fork at Cormac. "I tell you, we *must* destroy that ship."

"Easy, Ree," he said with a laugh. They sat on a love seat before the hearth, and he reached over their tray to grab her waggling fist. "No need to spear me with the cutlery. Fiona had enough to explain this morning, bringing her mistress such a heaping portion of food. Impaling me with the silver will do naught for our concealment."

He took a bite of black pudding and chewed thoughtfully. "*Crivvens* but your uncle Humphrey eats well."

"I've been thinking about this black powder," Marjorie said abruptly. She snatched a triangle of toast, buttering it with great zeal. "How much would it take to explode an entire ship?"

"You wee savage." He put his fork down to study her. If the swirl of emotions on her face was any indication, the woman's mind was spinning like a top. He nodded to her knife. "Is the plan to avenge yourself on the toast?"

Ignoring him, she snapped a bite from the corner and, putting a hand in front of her mouth, she spoke as she chewed. "Of course, we'll need to figure out how to free the men held captive. There are slaves still aboard, don't forget. And then I think the next order of business is for me to go to Saint Machar and confront Archie."

He barked out a laugh—so preposterous was the idea—and promptly quieted himself. It'd do no good to bring the servants running. "Will you indeed?"

Her eyes narrowed at his sarcasm. "Cormac MacAl—"

"No, Ree." Her amateur efforts at spying had been successful thus far. But that'd been before. Now he was certain all manner of ruffians were scouring the streets of Aberdeen for a woman of her description. "There will be no more. I am deadly serious."

She set down her utensils with a clack. "You can't expect me to wait around for more children to be taken."

"Of course not. We will do all in our power to stop it. How could you doubt otherwise?" He stood abruptly to pace a circle around her room, then stopped and pinned her with a look. He felt raw, and he needed her to understand. "Don't think I feel this any less than you. Not a day goes by that I don't remember Aidan. He was my *twin*, Ree. I'd not have another lad suffer his fate."

Her eyes were wide, and he walked back to her, worried that his harsh words had upset her. "But," he said, kneeling before her to take her hands, "I'll not wait and worry that you're out there, alone and in danger, somehow suffering the same fate as Aidan. I *cannot* lose you. I will not."

Her eyes softened. "I can't lose you either."

"And so you won't. I'm an expert. Trust me, I will handle this. I'll not have you flouncing about Saint Machar's, flirting with danger."

"You just don't want me flouncing and flirting with *Archie*." She gave him a wicked smile.

"Not unless you wish me to kill the man," he deadpanned. He sat beside her again, and the dishes on the tray clinked with his weight. "Truly, Ree. Let me do this for you. I spent a lifetime training. I have the devil's own knowledge of how to kill, how to destroy. Let me use it for good. I will destroy the ship. And I promise you, we *will* figure out a way you can help, too."

Marjorie was quiet for a time, and he braced himself for her uplifted chin, for one of her rebellions. Instead, she gave him a thoughtful smile. "I trust you, Cormac. And more than anything, I love you. It will be as you wish it."

The muscles in his shoulders released. She'd let him handle it. In destroying the *Oliphant*, he'd avenge Aidan. But more, Cormac would avenge the evils of his youth, in using his terrible skills for good.

She tilted her head, pensive. "So you'll burn the ship?"

"No, love. I'll sink it."

Fiona had always dreamed of a houseful of boys, but not like this.

"Stop," she ordered them, but it was in vain. She darted to the corner to break up yet another tussle, sighing heavily. She'd wanted to do a favor for her mistress, but this was proving more grueling than she'd anticipated. "How does wee Marjorie manage to keep you rascals in line? Mind me, stop right now."

Ignoring her, they wrestled their way into her worktable, and a wooden bowl clattered to the floor. It was two of the bigger lads, and their size had her at a disadvantage. She flinched away from a flying fist, clearing her throat to shout, "Stop!"

A banging at the door finally put an end to it. She put a finger to her mouth signaling quiet, though it wasn't necessary. They'd all frozen, meeting each other's eyes, stricken.

There was another knock, more insistent than the last. "Fiona? Are you there?"

Archie?

Hastily smoothing her hair, she stepped to the door.

Though she made an effort to be silent, she feared the visitor would surely be able to hear her nervous breathing from the other side.

"Fiona? It's Arch. Are you there? I heard a racket." He jiggled the latch. "Is everything all right?"

Heaving a sigh of relief, she opened the door and whisked him inside. "*Losh*, Arch, but it's good to see you."

He took in the tableau of boys in various states of disarray. Raising a brow, he said, "There was word of some unlawful disputes in these parts, but I see the reports were vastly understated."

She felt her cheeks heat. Even though she wasn't entirely certain what he referred to, she did know the current chaos mortified her. "Disputes?"

"Aye." He pulled the tallest of the boys to standing and straightened his shirt. "I'd heard there was some violence by the docks, not far from here. I knew where you lived. Do you remember? When I came to stitch your wound . . . ?" He trailed off, looking embarrassed. When he spoke again, he didn't meet her eyes. "Och, Fiona, I pray I didn't overstep."

Remember? He came once to dress her cut finger, and she'd thought of his visit every day since. His upright form had filled the small cottage with a gentle, understated presence. He'd been attentive and kind, his manner striking her as protective, taking care of things in such a manly way. He was everything her father wasn't. "I remember, yes, of course," she said quietly.

"But who are these boys? Surely you've never mentioned brothers." Archie scanned the room, and eyes alighting on Davie, he did a double take. "Davie? Could it be?"

A sort of bewildered caution crumpled the boy's face, and he tucked himself behind Fiona's skirts. She twisted back to scruff his red hair. "It's all right, lad. Don't you remember Archie? He's the nice man from Saint Machar's."

Davie gave a wary half shrug and went to sit with the

others in front of the fire for an impromptu game of mer-rills.

"I'll not understand it," she said, referring to the sudden quiet. She chalked it up to Archie's steady presence calming them all down.

"How is this even possible?" He pitched his voice low and had to step close to Fiona to be heard in the crowded space. "I can't believe it's Davie."

"Marjorie saved them all, God love her." Fiona smiled wide. "I'm caring for them, as a favor."

"But surely you can't keep them here." Archie shook his head, perplexed. "They should be with me. At Westhall."

She hesitated. "But Marjorie said there was no room."

"No room?" His eyes softened. "Oh Fiona, dear. Perhaps you misunderstood. There's *always* room at Saint Machar."

Elation filled her. "Oh, Arch, that would be lovely." The boys had been overwhelming. And they'd overwhelmed her father, too. He'd not taken kindly to the lot, despite her mistress's bribe. He'd begun yelling at them, and she worried it was only a matter of time before shouts became hits.

"I can bring them back with me now," he said, his brown-eyed gaze more earnest than ever.

She wasn't accustomed to thoughtful gestures and fought against the sudden ache of tears in her throat. "You'd do that?"

"My dear, my lovely Fiona." Archie's uncertain smile made her weak in the knees. "I'm discovering there's not much I *wouldn't* do for you."

Chapter 31

Cormac turned up the collar of his coat. He'd have preferred wearing his plaid, but a pair of sturdy brown trews was less conspicuous dockside. The afternoon was gray, the sky wishing for rain but unable to muster more than a damp haze, and it was like walking through a cloud.

A new boat had docked—a small, one-mast sloop—just next to the *Oliphant*. It bore investigating. For the plan he was considering, gaining proximity to the smugglers' ship would be key. If the sloop were used for fishing, mayhap its owner would be amenable to a bit of grease in his palms in exchange for turning a blind eye. Approaching, he struggled to read the name, painted dark crimson on even darker brown timber. The *Journeyman*. An odd name for a boat.

Shrugging his chin deeper in the neck of his coat, he strolled closer.

A man sat on the bow, his legs dangling over the edge. Cormac moved closer still, squinting through the mist, some vague intuition pricking the back of his mind.

The stranger leaned back on his hands, swinging his feet in the air, his head canted lazily to the side. And then he rubbed his nose with the back of his hand.

Cormac's knees buckled.

His mind flashed to a boy. A boy who'd wipe his face with the back of his hand till their mother's voice grew hoarse from her scolds. A boy who'd sneak out with Cormac to talk until the wee hours. Cormac would stare at the stars above, but this boy couldn't sit still. He'd sit on a rock, swinging his legs over the edge, ever moving. He'd had hair the color of Cormac's but eyes all his own. And he'd hated when he had to play the Campbell.

Aidan.

The stranger was Aidan. Cormac knew in that instant, as surely as he knew his own self. Aidan was alive, and he sat on the edge of a boat not twenty paces away.

Alive. Cormac knew without a moment's doubt. He'd know his twin anywhere. He needn't study his brother's features to recognize him, to *know* him.

Cormac filled his lungs. He wanted to shout, to run to him, to leap and cry out.

But then Aidan sat up and called to someone. Cormac strained to make sense of details through the fog and the bustle. There was a responding shout from the deck of the *Oliphant*. Jack appeared.

Cormac held his breath, listening.

The smuggler had a bandage wrapped around his head where Cormac had struck him. Jack nodded at Aidan, shouted back. They shared a laugh.

Black wavered on the edges of Cormac's vision. What did Aidan have to do with a smuggler?

He forced himself to draw breath. Turning on his heel, he walked back up the quay, staggering like a drunken man. Aidan had returned—but how and why? Was he indentured still, or did he return to Scotland as a slaver?

Cormac didn't recall the walk back to Humphrey's. Instinct alone saved him from barreling up to the front door, desperate to go straight to Ree's arms. The world made no sense, but *she*, she made sense. All he wanted was to be near her, to get his bearings.

His years of training kicked in, and as he approached Humphrey's street, caution and wile returned, as ingrained in him as his other five senses. Cutting down a back alley, he snatched an untended bucket of coal for an impromptu disguise, and snuck in a back entrance.

Marjorie gasped as he stumbled into her room. "Cormac," she cried, running to him and shutting the door behind him. "What happened?"

How to explain? He stared at her, his mind reeling.

He couldn't tell Ree what he'd just seen. If she knew, she'd only race down to the docks to confront Aidan for herself. His brother might be pleased to see them. But if he'd become a smuggler, might he also flee in panic? Cormac had lost his twin once before; he couldn't risk losing him again.

More than ever, this godforsaken world confused him. And more than ever, there was one thing he knew: family. It'd been robbed from him at a young age, but he knew its value now.

He had to find out the whole truth. He had to make sure. And until he did, he'd protect his brother by keeping his existence a secret.

He seized Marjorie's hands in his, and though she drew a sharp breath at the pressure, the grip she returned was just as firm. *Marjorie* was the only thing that made sense; Marjorie was the only thing that made his world real. Steadfast and true, she'd been in his heart for as long as he could remember.

He'd make her his in truth. He'd make *her* family.

But first there was another truth he needed to discover and a secret he needed to guard, because would Marjorie still want him if it'd been his brother—another devil MacAlpin—who'd been responsible for stealing her beloved Davie?

"Did you do it?" she whispered, brow furrowed with her intensity.

"We can't, Ree. I'll not destroy the ship."

Chapter 32

"What did you say?" Marjorie pulled her hands from his.

"I said . . . Ree . . ." Cormac raked a hand through his hair, fumbling for words.

She tamped down a surge of angry impatience. Now was not the time for the man to return to his silent ways. "Do you mean, we're going to destroy the *Oliphant* in a different way?"

"No," he said, his voice flat. "We'll not be destroying anything."

"Help me understand, love." Surely he didn't mean what he'd just said. He'd made her a promise. "Is it that you've found a different way to save the men?"

He shook his head mutely.

"Just tell me what you mean. What are you planning to do?" Her heart began to pound in her ears. Cormac just stood there, grappling for words. She read the regret on his face, and it spoke volumes.

The truth of it hit her: he wasn't going to *do* anything.

"There are men still on board," she said, incredulous. "*Scotsmen*, imprisoned. We'll save them, right? You must agree."

"I . . . I'm sorry, Ree." He reached for her hands.

"Sorry?" She pulled away from him, feeling numb, unreal. "Are you saying you'll do nothing?"

"Aye, Ree. I'm sorry."

Frustrated, she shot him a look. "Stop saying sorry. Tell the men in shackles, Cormac. Tell the men imprisoned on that boat, who'll never see Scotland or their families again, tell *them* you're sorry."

He stood silently, buffeted by her angry words. It only piqued her anger more. That he didn't argue back meant he wasn't going to do *anything* to help.

"I thought we were of the same mind," she said, edging away.

He stepped closer to her. "We *are* of the same mind."

"Then why?" She paced to the hearth, staring blindly at the fire burning in the grate. "Don't you have any explanation? More than *no, Ree, sorry*?" Her voice rose, anger, confusion, and betrayal all roiling inside her. He was completely closed off from her. "Has it become impossible? I'd understand, Cormac, just give me a reason."

"I think . . . I think we should investigate further . . ."

"Investigate? Investigate *what*? The *Oliphant* has a load of prisoners in her hull, their only crime that they're too poor to matter. They'll set sail any day. What more do you need to know? Just give me a reason why."

"I can't. I just . . . I no longer want to destroy it, Ree. That's all I can say." He came up behind her, placing his hands on her shoulders.

His touch was tentative, and she was too numb to move away. "You promised me," she said bleakly. "I should've done it myself. I'll need to do it myself."

"You'll do no such thing," he said, outrage in his voice.

She spun to face him, galled that he'd use such a tone with her. "You can't order me about."

"I'm sorry, Ree," he said, and the look on his face was one of helpless anguish.

Men. She was the one who was helpless, she the wronged one. Men were such inexplicably foreign animals. She'd prick his male pride, she decided, and perhaps *that* would get at the truth. "I don't understand," she said coldly. "Help me understand. Is it that you're *unable* to do it? Afraid, even?"

"Of course I'm *able.* It's just that . . ." He hesitated, perhaps realizing he'd just admitted he *could* help her if he wished.

The breath whooshed out of her, as another answer occurred to her. "It's because you don't love me enough."

"That is *not* the reason," he said vehemently. "Not nearly. I want us to be married."

"You want to marry me instead of destroying the slave ship?" She put her hands on her hips, trying to discern truth from invention. "Is that a marriage proposal?"

"Aye, Ree, it is." He opened his arms before him as though entreating her.

She no longer knew what to believe. "Are you asking me to marry you because you feel guilty you won't do this for me? Or perhaps it's simply to divert my attention."

"Of course not," he said quickly.

He *was* acting guilty, and her stomach turned. "Do you speak of marriage because you feel guilty you've taken my virginity? Is that it? Is this proposal merely your mislaid sense of duty?"

The truth of things came to her in a rush of clarity. Cormac had never told her he loved her. *She'd* been the one to speak the words. What he felt was simple attraction—his passion for her didn't extend from his body to his heart. He'd surrendered to his passions, and now he acted merely from a sense of duty.

Horror and embarrassment overwhelmed her. She was an *obligation* to be minded.

She'd fooled herself all this time—she'd never be his.

She could accept his proposal, make Cormac lawfully hers. Unutterable sadness filled her—she ached with it—because she knew she couldn't say yes. She'd always dreamed of being Cormac's wife, but she had her pride. She needed to be the bride of his heart, not simply his bride in name. "No, Cormac. I cannot marry you."

"But I love you," he said, and his voice cracked.

She wavered for a moment, wanting it so badly. Wanting his words to be true. But she couldn't trust them. His promise had proven untrue. How could he love her when he didn't care enough even to pretend to help her?

She shrugged. It was his guilt that spoke, not any love for her.

He mistook her shrug. Perhaps he thought it was assent, but he leaned down to kiss her tenderly on each cheek.

Her body hummed to life at his touch, and she despised herself for it. Was she so helpless to him? She felt tears burn in her throat. If she were ever to regain her dignity, she'd need to part from him.

He cradled her neck, and she clenched her eyes shut tight. There was such strength in those broad hands, and yet their touch was so gentle.

She couldn't help opening herself to him, and his kisses grew fervent. Panic drove his passion, she decided, panic at the potential for duty denied.

When she pulled away, his blue-gray gaze was waiting for her. It was a gaze that made her heart break and her body ache with two very different kinds of wanting.

She couldn't fight it. She'd enjoy this for what it was—physical passion—one last time. "Kiss me more."

"I will, love," Cormac said earnestly. "I will. I'll kiss you again and again." He swept her up and carried her to the bed where he laid her gently down. "But first tell me you love me. Tell me you'll marry me."

Her flesh had awoken, and she writhed against him, trying to pull his body over hers. *One last time.* Her throat ached with the knowledge it'd be their last time together. "Kiss me. I want you to be inside me."

"Not until you say the words," he said, his voice husky. "Not until you say you'll be my wife."

"I won't say those words." She pulled away from him as all her hurt and shame erupted to the surface. She couldn't do it, couldn't lie to him, and making love would be a lie. She couldn't pretend she could experience passion without emotion. "You broke your promise to me, and instead of giving me a reason, you think to distract me with a marriage proposal. You toy with my heart as though I'm still a girl of ten. No, Cormac," she said, cursing the crack in her voice. "You're just as they say. You *are* the devil."

He sat up, and the look he gave her was bleak. "Then you should've known better than to trust my black soul."

They both startled at the banging on her door.

"What?" She bounded off the bed. Anything to get away from him.

Fiona spoke urgently from the other side of the door. "Sorry, mum. So sorry. But the—"

Marjorie flung it open.

"So sorry." Fiona stared, wide-eyed, looking from Marjorie to Cormac and back again. "But I wanted to warn you. You told me to keep my ears open for talk of the bailie. But he's *here*. Now. In the drawing room with your uncle."

"The bailie is here?" Panic flared in her chest. If only Cormac would help her deal with the situation. And now it had appeared on her own doorstep. She prayed she wasn't the one who'd led the bailie to her uncle's. "What ever could he be doing *here*?"

"He is a respectable man in society, Ree."

Her focus shot to Cormac, seated at the edge of the bed, chin in hand. She glared at him, not particularly eager for his opinion at the moment.

Even though she knew he was right. It could be a matter of a simple explanation. "Did you hear him say why he was here?" she asked her maid.

"No mum, he just bustled in, him and that wife of his—"

"His wife?" Marjorie shuddered at the memory of rumbullion and hideous women in feather-plumed hats. "Adele is here, too?"

"Aye, and a nasty piece she is," Fiona muttered, and then her jaw dropped, appearing shocked she'd spoken aloud.

She ignored Fiona's comment. Her maid's peculiar muttering was to be expected, and Marjorie had only one concern at the moment. "Did they ask for me, or are they here only for Humphrey? Tell me, Fiona, are the children safe?"

"Aye." Fiona straightened proudly. "Archie came and took them all."

"What?" Marjorie gasped, stumbling backward into the wall. She propped herself against it, her fingers feeling cold and drained of blood.

"He came to pay a visit. He told me he wanted to help, and took the lads with him back to Saint Machar." She fiddled nervously with her apron. "I didn't do wrong, did I?"

Cormac flew from the bed, strode by them to the door.

"Where are you going?" she demanded. A clammy chill prickled her skin all over. *Archie had the boys, Archie took Davie.* She forced herself to stand upright. She went to grab her wrap from where she'd tossed it on a chair. "I'm going with you."

"You canna!" Fiona gasped. "It's almost full dark outside."

"Aye," Cormac said, his voice steely. "Listen to the maid. You can't leave. Lock yourself in. Open for none but me or Fiona."

Their eyes caught, and time held still. The gravest of looks crossed his face, as though he'd come to a great decision.

"I'm going to make this right," Cormac said, and he stormed from the room.

But Marjorie knew she wouldn't be there when he returned.

Chapter 33

She'd told him no. Marjorie had refused his proposal, and he'd seen the surety in her eyes.

Cormac upped his pace, thinking of Gregor's fine chestnut gelding, stabled at the Broad Street mews. He'd make it to the docks faster on horseback. But it was the horse of a wealthy man, and galloping through the darkness, he'd summon every eye in Aberdeen.

Wealth. He'd told Marjorie she deserved a wealthy lord. Was that why she'd balked at marriage? Was the prospect of life with a fisherman not so appealing after all? He frowned. He'd not give the notion a moment's credit.

She'd been so angry when he'd told her he couldn't destroy the *Oliphant*. Surely it was simple anger that drove her refusal.

Because surely Marjorie loved him. She'd told him before that she loved him. God help his cursed soul if she didn't.

He cursed his soul, wondering why he hadn't said the

words to her sooner. He loved Marjorie more than life, so why hadn't he told her when he'd first had the chance?

But even as he speculated, he knew why. He was a coward. Losing his brother and then his mother had almost destroyed him, and he'd been afraid he'd get hurt again. So he hadn't told her of his love—as though, by not saying the words, it might not exist.

Furious with himself, he ran harder through the streets. He might be a fool, but he'd be a coward no more.

He'd convince Marjorie of his love. Sacrificing his blackened soul, if need be—his *devil's* soul—to do her bidding. He'd failed those he loved before. He'd not fail now. He would find Aidan. He'd make his brother stop whatever mischief he might be about. For Ree.

And then he'd stop Archie and Jack and whomever in hell else he had to stop to make her happy.

He stood, panting, at the head of the quay, ready to confront a brother stolen from him thirteen years ago.

The moon was bright, and the modest sloop bobbed in a shaft of white light. The *Journeyman*. Cormac imagined he felt his brother's presence close by.

"Cormac," someone said from the shadows along the edge of the pier.

He tensed. The voice was new to him, but something in its timbre struck a chord in his heart. It was Aidan's voice.

Cormac turned, wondering how it was he hadn't noticed the figure seated along the dock, feet dangling over the water. Aidan had always been the only one able to sneak past him.

"Is it truly you?" Cormac's chest tightened with emotion.

Aidan stood, stepping into the moonlight. Even in the dark of night, Cormac could see that his brother's skin had grown weathered, his tone duskier, with lines about his eyes and mouth. The years had hardened him.

Cormac went to embrace him but stopped. Gone was the playful scamp of their youth. Instead, the man who stood before him had a body scored with the muscle of hard labor, his rigid stance speaking to rage barely contained beneath the surface. "Aidan . . ."

"There's a name I've not heard in some time." He gave Cormac a hard smile.

It was a type of vertigo, meeting this brother, whom he'd loved above all, as though they were strangers. "What are you called, then?"

"For years, I was simply *Boy*." He tilted his head, examining Cormac through slitted eyes. "I thought I'd seen you, you know. Earlier on the dock. But then you were gone, and I thought mayhap you were just a ghost. I live among many ghosts."

Cormac didn't know what gulf his twin needed to cross, but he did know that he wanted Aidan back among them, and he'd help him across this final stretch. "I felt like I died when they took you."

"Funny that," Aidan said, his tone brittle. "I just about died in truth."

Cormac swallowed. What had his brother endured, who had he become? He appealed to a different tack. "How long have you been back in Scotland? Why didn't you try to find us? Why did you not come home?"

"Home? I've no home. Scotland is *your* home."

Deep inside Cormac, a ten-year-old boy fumed, and he fought the urge to cuff his brother. "Are you angry with *me*?"

Aidan shrugged. "You're right, of course. I have much anger. None of it for you, Cormac." He stretched out his hand. "Come, let's meet as brothers."

As they clasped hands, Aidan attempted a smile, but Cormac could see the uneasy strain of it. His brother cut a quick glance at the *Oliphant*, and Cormac wondered what he might be hiding.

"Let's walk from here. We can walk, and you can tell me news of our esteemed family," he said sardonically. "I imagine Mother didn't take the whole kidnap nonsense very well."

Cormac bristled. "Mother died within the year."

Aidan blinked slowly. It was a simple movement, but a brother *knew*, and in it Cormac saw a lifetime of pain, of hopes dashed.

"I'm sorry," Cormac told him. "She loved you too much. We all did. We all do."

Aidan looked away, casting his face in shadow. "And the rest of them?"

"Father died, too. At the Battle of Dunbar."

"You'll have to forgive me, brother mine," he said with a bitter laugh. "My knowledge of Scottish history isn't what it should be."

"Of course. It was 1650 when Da died. A few years after you'd been taken. The others are alive. Anya is wed, and is with her husband in the west. The rest live in Dunnottar."

"Dunnottar?" Aidan stopped for a moment in astonishment.

"Aye, in the castle there."

"You jest. Who exactly did Anya wed to win the family such a prize?"

Cormac allowed a grudging smile. "No, 'tis not like that. There's a jest to be found, but it's the castle itself. It was nearly destroyed in the wars and tumbles about our ears. I keep waiting for the villagers to kick us out, but nobody seems to have the heart."

"Dunnottar," Aidan mumbled again, and then there was a protracted silence.

Cormac was growing impatient with their act. It was too much to make sense of, too overwhelming. But there was one thing he could wrap his mind around, and it was Marjorie, and his sole desire to help her. Thoughts of his goal focused him.

"What are you doing here?" Cormac nodded back to the *Oliphant*. "Please tell me you have naught to do with *those* men."

"I do and I don't," Aidan said, a snide grin cocking the corner of his mouth. He stopped walking. "And now I'm afraid I'll need to cut this reunion short. I've got business, and my . . . associates would not take kindly to me having such an extensive parley with a stranger."

"Wait, Aidan. I need you to stop whatever this *business* is. For Marjorie."

Hearing her name, a strange look flashed in Aidan's eyes. It wasn't pleasure. "So you finally married that brat, is it?"

"It's not like that."

"Then how's it like?" Aidan enunciated each word with disdain.

"We're not married. Ree's grown into a good woman."

Aidan rolled his eyes. "I'll bet she has."

Cormac stepped close. "You'll mind your tone where Marjorie is concerned."

Aidan exploded into laughter. "Some things never change. Last I saw you, you were in my face about Marjorie. And here you are now, thirteen years later, in my face."

Cormac panicked. He'd fantasized for years how their reunion might be, and it was not this. He didn't understand why it was going so awry. "Please, Aid. Let's just start this over. Marjorie works with the poor now. With young boys. She felt your kidnap quite keenly. And now she's come unhinged at the thought that more will be stolen from our shores. That Jack you deal with . . . he's a smuggler of children."

Cormac waited, hoping for an outraged reaction at that last revelation.

"Aye," Aidan replied instead. "I know it."

Cormac scowled. He didn't know the extent of what his brother had endured these past years. He thought of all that'd transpired in his own life, knowing he was not one to pass judgment. He could only try to make Aidan understand. And if he refused to understand, Cormac would make certain his brother didn't stand in his way. "Marjorie wants these men stopped. I plan on being the one to stop them. And I'd ask that you're far from the *Oliphant* when that comes to pass."

"Still saving Marjie, eh?" Aidan sneered. "I've my own objectives to attend, Cormac. My own ghosts to chase. And they don't have to do with you, or your *Ree*, or any of your callow concerns."

Conflicting emotions roiled within Cormac. Reuniting with his brother should've been a joyful event. And yet he couldn't help but feel he wasn't entirely happy to see Aidan, particularly under these circumstances.

Aidan turned, hunched from the cold and with hands in pockets. Cormac watched as his twin walked away from him and back into the night.

Chapter 34

Can't leave the room, he'd said. Marjorie rifled through her wardrobe, digging for her warmest wrapper. She'd leave indeed, and get to the bottom of this affair with Archie. She had saved those boys once; she'd save them again. And no man would stop her—not Cormac, not Archie, not even Jack the poor excuse for a pirate.

She felt Fiona rustling around at her back, setting the room to rights, and it made her angrier. Even her accursed *maid* had insisted she stay inside.

Locked in. No man told *her* to lock herself away. She'd been independent for years. She'd be independent long after she exorcised Cormac from her system. And that's precisely what she'd do. Exorcise him like the demon he was.

She tugged the long woolen shawl out with a feline growl, embracing her anger as armor against her heartbreak. *Angry.* She'd be angry, not hurt. Later she'd let herself feel the hurt. But first she'd do what needed to be done.

"Your Cormac wilna be pleased," Fiona said under her breath.

"Would you *stop* that infernal muttering. The Lord preserve me, girl. Say your piece, or shut your mouth." Marjorie slammed the door to her wardrobe. "And he's not *my* Cormac."

Fiona gaped at her.

Marjorie haphazardly wrapped herself in the shawl, regretting for a moment that she'd snapped so at her poor maid. But then a thought followed fast on its heels. That *poor maid* had endured more hardship at the hands of a bully father than Marjorie would know in a lifetime. Crossing her arms at her chest, she considered Fiona anew. "Well," she said firmly, "you *could* come with me."

And the speed with which Fiona had them whisked down a back staircase and out the door was startling.

Saint Machar glowed yellow in the bright moonlight. Skeletons of trees destroyed in the wars still hovered about the church, casting eerie shadows on the facade.

"Crivvens." Fiona clung to her arm. "It looks a frightful place at night."

"Nonsense." Marjorie tugged her maid along. "It's a place of the Lord, whatever time of day."

"That doesn't mean it don't make my skin crawl. Like a goose over my grave, mum."

"I am not your *mum*," she spat, pulling her arm free. "Would you please call me Marjorie?"

Fiona gave her a weak smile. "All right then, Marjie."

"*Marjorie.*" Remembering her anger, she pressed on, striding down Chanonry Road toward Westhall. "The boys will be asleep, up there," Marjorie said, nodding to the triangular upper story. "But Archie"—she grimaced—"stays for a time before the fire, in the library. It's where he sees his patients during the day."

"May I ask you a question, mum . . . Marj . . . Marjorie?"

"It seems you just did," she retorted, and then shook her head at her own cheek. She couldn't let impatience get the better of her. The truth was, the night had unsettled her, and she was happy to have her maid's company. "My apologies, Fiona. Please, what is your question?"

"Why are you so angry with Archie? He seems a good man. A caring man."

"They all do, don't they?" Cormac had also seemed a good and caring man. Flustered, she scrambled for an explanation, then said simply, "It remains to be seen what our Archie is about." She gave Fiona a sharp look. "I have a question for *you*, though. What was Archie doing visiting you at your home?"

Fiona inhaled sharply, and Marjorie would swear that, if it were daylight, she'd see a blush on her maid's cheeks.

"He helped me once," she began tentatively. She raised her left hand, holding her index finger to catch the moon's light. "He'd come to your uncle's to pay you a visit. I'd cut myself in the kitchens, badly. Archie saw me just after it happened. He told me if I didn't let him dress the wound, I'd lose my finger."

The maid shrugged, looking nervous. "He said you wouldn't mind if he came to the vennel to check on it. He needed to put on a clean bandage. He said it wasn't wrong of me to let him come." She cast her eyes down. "But still, I never told you, and I'm sorry for that."

"Goodness, Fiona." Marjorie grabbed the girl's hand to study it. Sure enough, a thin scar wound around the top of her finger, white as a cobweb in the moonlight. "What do you think of me? Imagining I might begrudge you a *finger*, for goodness' sake." She dropped Fiona's hand. "Of course it's fine that he came to see you. It's just . . . I wonder that . . . why did he visit again?"

"We talk. Sometimes. When he comes to see you or your uncle." Fiona looked away, her cheeks decidedly flushed, visible even in the moonlight. "He said he'd heard about some trouble down by the docks. Said he was . . . concerned."

"Mm-hm." Marjorie eyed her maid thoughtfully. She was a pretty thing, if a mite peculiar, with a wide and open face, full bosom, and blushes that betrayed her every whim. Pretty enough to explain Archie's visit? She wondered.

The housekeeper let the women in and showed them to the library. They found Archie where Marjorie had predicted, sitting on an armchair before the fire, reading.

He nearly jumped from his seat, startled. "How did you get in? You didn't bring that MacAlpin fellow, did you?" He spotted Fiona behind her, and face softening, he sprang to meet them. "Is aught the matter?"

"What indeed," Marjorie snapped. "The question is, what have you done with the boys you took?"

Fiona gravitated toward him, giving him a warm smile. "I told her they were safe in your care, Arch."

Marjorie shot her a look, raising a sharp brow at the nickname. Suddenly it wasn't just the boys' safety that concerned her.

"The boys?" His gaze was locked on Fiona, and there was something charged in his eyes. Stepping closer, he began to reach out, but then hesitated, and quickly clasped his hands behind his back instead. "They're all tucked upstairs."

She felt the tension between Archie and her maid and bit the inside of her cheek to remind herself of discretion. What a strange and unexpected mystery within a mystery. "I'd like to see them, if I may."

"Who?" Archie finally looked at her. "The boys?"

"Who else?" Impatient, she simply hiked her skirts and headed to the stairs.

"They're upstairs, where they always are," he said to her back. The sounds of Archie's and Fiona's hushed murmuring ushered her out of the room.

The makeshift dormitory was a windowless room with a low, gabled ceiling. She stood at the doorway, letting her eyes adjust to the utter blackness. And though it took her a moment to make sense of the sleeping forms, the heavy breathing of over a dozen boys greeted her, even and peaceful.

It was just as Archie had said: they were all asleep.

She tiptoed in until she found Davie, a smaller figure in the corner. His cheek was crushed against his pillow, mouth open, his face serene. She stroked a finger along his forehead, sweeping the hair from his brow. *Safe.* Something that'd been clenched in her chest loosened, and she breathed a relieved sigh.

She stood, staring into the blackness. There were a couple of problems that remained. If Archie wasn't the kidnapper, who was? And why was Archie receiving money from the bailie?

Careful not to wake the boys, Marjorie went back downstairs, worrying the questions in her mind. Fiona and Archie stood together before the library fire, and she had to clear her throat to get their attention. They sprang apart at the sight of her.

Archie fiddled nervously with his cuffs. "Did you see them?"

If she didn't have more pressing matters on her mind, she'd have asked the two of them what was going on. But instead she said, "Safely tucked in for the night, as you said."

"I was telling Fiona. I implore you. It's not safe here." Archie hesitated, looking from Marjorie to Fiona, unsure which woman he should address. "You must return home."

Annoyed with the whole situation, Marjorie turned her back on him and dropped unceremoniously into a chair. "First I have something to discuss with you, Archibald."

"But it's not safe. The bailie . . ."

She meticulously folded her woolen wrapper. "Oh, I know about you and the bailie."

"His is a dishonorable household," Archie said fervently. "You both must hurry back to your uncle's. The lads are safe with me."

He gave Fiona a tender look, and for Marjorie, that mawkish expression was the last straw.

"I've seen what safe means for you," she said brusquely. She'd grown tired of roundabout men who told her what to do, with no explanation for it. She'd state the situation plainly, if nobody else would. "I saw you receive money, when I was at the bailie's home. Is taking money in exchange for children what you'd call *safe*?"

Archie's eyes flew to her. "Losh, no, Marj! I'd never do such a thing."

"Then how do you explain the fact that I saw you skulking about the bailie's back rooms, taking payment from his manservant, not long after Davie's disappearance?"

He sputtered for words, and just when Marjorie thought she'd trapped him, he surprised her with an entirely different excuse. "The money . . . that wasn't from the bailie. It was payment from his wife. I made Adele a tonic. Against pregnancy."

His gaze swept to Fiona, as though the maid's recognition of his innocence were paramount. "I've long suspected the bailie of nefarious doings," he insisted. "Their lifestyle exceeds what would be expected of an officer of Aberdeen. I slowly ingratiated myself to him, watching and waiting all the while." He pulled his shoulders back. "When Davie was taken, the time had come to act, and act boldly."

Fiona puffed with pride.

"*You* had suspicions, too?" Marjorie sat forward on her chair. "But why didn't you simply tell me?"

"I tried. That day at Humphrey's. But your Cormac was—"

"Once and for all," Marjorie snapped, "he's not *my* Cormac."

Archie's eyes widened. "Be that as it may, Cormac

struck me as . . . how shall I put it . . . arrogant about the matter. I assumed you were safe in his care."

"I'm in no man's care."

Fiona grunted as though she knew better, sharing a little eye roll with Archie.

Marjorie popped up from the chair. She had to turn her back from the sight of them cutting doe eyes at each other. "So how do we stop the bailie?"

"I must stay here all night," Archie said with great bravado. "I've heard the *Oliphant* leaves at dawn. I'll guard the boys until then."

Though Marjorie knew his gesture was brave and true, his earnestness nettled her. Cormac flashed into her mind, and she scowled. She'd seen bravery, and it didn't sit perched on a leather armchair, behind a locked door, bearing a snifter of brandy.

"I'll stay with you." Fiona couldn't say the words quickly enough.

"Then you and I shall keep watch," he said grandly.

Marjorie looked from Archie to Fiona. The attraction was plain between them, but she wondered about their difference in class. Though Archie didn't come from great wealth, he *was* studying to be a physician, and some would find his choice of a maid shocking. If they were discreet, Marjorie supposed Fiona's looks were enough to elevate her above her station. Indeed, her maid was ripe and lovely, and clearly there was something about her that made Archie feel like the man he struggled to be.

Marjorie looked down at her feet. She recognized love when she saw it. It made her feel empty and alone.

"Will you be safe?" Fiona asked her.

"I'll rush back to Humphrey's straightaway. I'll lock myself in as I'd promised and wait for Cormac." Marjorie managed a smile. "You've the right of it, Arch. Cormac will help me."

The lies spilled easily enough from her mouth. She

knew what she had to do, and it wasn't cowering in her bedroom. She may not have the skills to sink the *Oliphant*. But there were men imprisoned on board, men who'd set sail at dawn, to spend the rest of their days toiling on a plantation far from home. She'd get on that boat, somehow. *She'd* free them.

―――――

Humphrey's house was pitch-black when Cormac returned. He took the back stairs two at a time—he couldn't see her soon enough.

It'd been wrong not to tell her the truth. He'd tell her about Aidan. He vowed it was the last secret he'd ever keep from her.

Together they'd find a solution. Together they'd convince Aidan, and then Cormac would save the men. There was no other way; he saw that now. They belonged as a pair. Everything felt wrong when they were apart.

He burst through her door, but the bedroom was empty. Baffled, he ran his hands over the sheets as though he might somehow find her hiding there.

He heard a scuffling behind him, and spun. But instead of Marjorie standing there, it was the wee scullion girl. His heart fell.

"Where is she?" he asked, and his voice came out as an accusation.

"She went with Fiona." The girl spoke quietly, and Cormac had to tilt his head to hear. "They raced off."

"Where?" He forced his voice to evenness. It'd do no good to terrify his only source of information.

"I heard . . . mayhap there was talk of a man, and a ship," she said, not taking her eyes from her feet.

Cormac's heart stuck in his throat. Could Marjorie have gone to the ship without him?

She could, and she would. She'd been furious with him and apparently feeling more betrayed than he'd ever have imagined.

How had he let it come to this? He needed to find her,

tell her the truth, and make her his. If she didn't believe he loved her, he'd show her.

Cormac raced back into the night. He'd destroy that ship, even if it destroyed him in the process.

Chapter 35

Marjorie couldn't just sit by and watch as a dozen or more of her countrymen were snatched from their families and displaced to a foreign shore where they'd spend the rest of their lives toiling for some plantation owner.

Granted, she wasn't quite sure how, precisely, she'd go about saving them, but she told herself she'd figure it out as she went. And sure enough, though she'd wondered how she was to magically alight on the deck of the *Oliphant*, the rope ladder was down and waiting when she arrived. "Well, thank you, Jack," she said under her breath.

It meant someone had arrived before her. The bailie perhaps? She stood completely still, struggling to listen, but the only sound from above was the natural creak and groan of the ship's timber. Whoever the visitor was, they'd gone below.

But surely *somebody* was on deck. She scanned the railing, knowing there must be at least one sailor on watch. It took a few minutes' wait, but finally she saw him, a tallish figure sauntering toward the rear of the ship. She opened her ears, waiting for the sound of distant chatter, but there was only silence. She'd just have to hope he was the only man on deck.

Though the ladder swayed in the darkness, Marjorie managed to clamber on, and more easily this time. She'd learned the hard way it was best to focus only on the cut of the raw rope in her palms, rather than dwelling on the water that slapped and churned below, now an eerie gunmetal gray in the moonlight.

Hoisting herself over the railing was another matter entirely, though, and she was grateful none saw her shimmying and kicking over. She made it, and sat on deck for a moment with her skirts in a tangle at her knees. Scooting her back against the railing, she ducked into the shadows to scan for sailors while she caught her breath.

The man she'd spied was now leaning over the aft rail. Even if she squinted, all she could make out were the white stripes of his shirt in the night. She assured herself that, if she remained quiet, he wouldn't spot her either.

She looked to her right and clapped a hand over her mouth in shock. The little Moorish boy from before stood there, silent as a wraith. She drew in several unsteady breaths, waiting for her heart to stop thudding in her chest. "You frightened me," she said in a barely audible whisper.

Before he could open his mouth to speak, Marjorie put a finger to her lips, begging him with her eyes to keep silent. She pulled a bit of hard-boiled butterscotch from her pocket, and sent up a silent thanks to the boys of Saint Machar—because of them, she never left the house without a sweet tucked away in her skirts. She mimicked eating, and he took it hesitantly, sticking the very tip of his tongue out to test it. A sudden smile split his face, white teeth glowing against dark skin. She fought the urge to hug him to her.

The boy nodded to the bow, and she wondered what he thought her purpose there was. She peered into the darkness. Why would he send her to the front of the ship? It was where the younger boys had been held, in the forecastle.

But the men had been imprisoned aft.

She stood. She needed to find them, free them, and somehow trundle them all down the rope ladder and to safety. She fingered the hairpins studded throughout her low bun. It'd been years since she'd picked a lock—thirteen to be precise, when last she'd seen the MacAlpin boys, and they'd all played a trick on the maid—but she'd simply have to try her best.

Cormac. Her heart fell. She truly did need his help, needed *him.* His glaring absence made her feel lonely and uncertain.

The guard's cough broke the silence and shattered her reverie.

She shook out her skirts. She may not have Cormac, but she did have herself, and she needed to pick a direction and move quickly. The watchman leaned on the rail smoking a cheroot, and she imagined she had but a minute or two to find her way to the prisoners.

Marjorie began to tiptoe aft, praying the men were still shackled there. But the boy grunted and grabbed her arm. Again he nodded to the bow. Had Jack moved the prisoners?

Shrugging, she headed where he directed, thinking it just as well. Though she hated placing the guard at her back, it was probably best to put some distance between them.

Strange, hulking shapes loomed on deck, and she slunk along in their shadows, grateful for the general creaking of timber that concealed her approach. Finally, the sound of voices came to her from below. She slowed her step.

She recognized Jack's voice and scowled. He'd apparently survived whatever damage Cormac had done to him.

And then she heard it. A word cut through the night, so peculiar and out of place, it stood out from the conversation. And yet it was absolutely familiar to her ears. *Botanicals*.

She swayed, catching herself before she collapsed. It was her uncle Humphrey speaking. Her heart began to kick again, her chest sore from the fitful pounding. Terrified, she edged closer.

More words filtered up to her, odd words. *Soil . . . propagate . . . the cane . . .*

They'd captured her uncle. The bailie had been at his house earlier. Had he taken him captive? But why? Surely not for his knowledge of *gardening*? She crept closer, keeping to the darkest areas in the center of the deck.

Jack's voice rang out again, posing sharp questions to the old man. Anger erupted in her like hot lava, searing all impulse away and then solidifying, leaving Marjorie's will hardened and nerves stilled. Humphrey was the only family member left to her—she wouldn't stand idly by as somebody harmed him. Hands fisted in her skirts, she strode to the forecastle.

But she halted abruptly. She'd be a fool to go any farther empty-handed. Her eyes skittered along the deck, making sense of details in the darkness. There were pulleys and poles, and a variety of wooden trunks—but nothing that would serve as a weapon. She eyed mysterious metal prongs and cleats, but they were all bolted down. There were also ropes, so many ropes, skeins of it all around. It draped overhead, lay coiled on deck, and dangled from the railing in heavy loops.

She remembered an intricate ship's model Humphrey had once constructed. *Humphrey.* Her heart clenched, and she willed herself to be brave for him. Her eyes went to the railing, and the wooden pins around which the rope was looped. *Belaying pins*, her uncle had told her. They rested like pegs in holes along the rail. Holding her breath, she grabbed one, jiggled, and pulled it free.

It was smooth and solid, the length of her forearm, like a rolling pin from the kitchen. Although she'd likely prove worthless at wielding the thing, it was sound enough for a weapon, and the heft of it gave her confidence.

Mindful of her step, she tiptoed to the forecastle entry, which was no more than a dark archway near the bow. She ducked in, stopping on a shallow landing, where a ladder led down a narrow shaft to the deck below.

Men's voices echoed up to her, and she could clearly discern distinct words and speakers now. "Cormac MacAlpin," a strange man growled. "Or is it *Lord Brodie*? Why are you here?"

She drew in a sharp breath. *Cormac?*

Was he below? Why would he be with the smugglers? Was he a party to their misdeeds? But surely not—it was *Cormac*. She had to believe that, no matter what had come to pass, she knew him. She *knew* Cormac's goodness.

"The question is, why are *you* here?" Cormac retorted, his voice hostile and ragged.

Cormac. He *was* there. There was a tingling rush through her chest, like the blood returning to her veins. She'd never heard a sweeter sound than the angry words he'd just spoken.

She wasn't alone. Even now, he was there and trying to save Humphrey. Cormac had told her he wouldn't help her, yet there he was, doing his all for her and her family.

He'd lied to her when he said he wouldn't help. The blasted man had simply been trying to protect her.

Well, blast the blasted man, *she'd* help *him*. Tucking the wooden pin in her skirts, she squatted down, gingerly venturing onto the top rung of the ladder. She wasn't such a fool to think she could drop into a meeting of smugglers and kidnappers and save the day, so breathing as shallowly as she could, she carefully stepped down a few rungs and then waited, utterly still, listening to the drama unfold below. When the time was right, she'd offer Cormac whatever assistance she could.

"'Tis best not to ask why. The MacAlpin is an unexpected boon, but a welcome one." Jack was laughing, and from the sound of it, he stood just by the base of the ladder. Marjorie wanted to spit down at him. "Yet another strapping man to add to the cargo."

A sharp ache cut like glass in her throat. They were discussing the prisoners, and it seemed Cormac was now one of them.

The ship lurched. "Heaven help us," she breathed, gripping the rungs.

Footsteps pounded like erratic drumbeats overhead. She stepped down another couple of rungs, hunched so as not to be seen from above or below.

Someone shouted an order, and it was shouted again, repeated over and over, in a cascade down the deck, until it diminished from hearing. There was another lurch, and the sound of clanging and snapping.

They were leaving the dock. She clenched the ladder so tightly the blood left her fingers.

She was in it now. But she was in it with *Cormac*. Her breathing grew gradually more measured. She had faith that somehow, together, they'd set all to rights.

"What's the meaning of this?" Humphrey shouted.

"Easy, old man," Jack said. "I told the men if I dallied here too long, to get us under way. Looks as though you'll have a chance to demonstrate your vast expertise in situ—isn't that what you'd called it, you pompous blowhard? What say you, Aidan?" The familiar name added to the frantic alarm already trilling in the back of Marjorie's mind. "You spent years in the Indies. Shall we give these louts a taste of plantation life?"

"And what a fine flavor it is," Aidan replied. "A bit like rum and chimney soot."

The word *chimney* amped her internal alarm to a fever pitch. *Aidan?* Surely there was more than one Aidan in the world. There'd been something familiar in his voice, though, and it niggled. But surely *Aidan MacAlpin* hadn't returned, after so many years.

She had to know. Marjorie descended another rung. Gathering her skirts high, she squatted for a quick peek at the cabin below. It was dim, lit only by a few lanterns hung on the walls.

Though she saw only two men—Cormac and a man holding him at gunpoint—she knew others were there. She heard Humphrey's heavy-chested breathing, sensed Jack standing just by the base of the ladder. Terrified, she bit her lip not to make a sound.

Cormac's eyes flicked to her, and he mouthed a curse. His captor looked up, too, and her heart stopped in her chest.

She shouldn't have looked. She should've popped back up when she saw the gun pressed at Cormac's temple.

His captor cocked a brow, and his cool nonchalance was eerily familiar. Cold sweat prickled her back. He held a gun to Cormac's head, so why did he not sound an alarm at the sight of her?

She peered at the man, holding her breath. He stared back at her, and she felt naked in his gaze. Was *this* the Aidan who'd spoken?

Could it be *the* Aidan?

Her breathing sped as her mind processed the impossible. She scrutinized him, straining through the darkness. Her pounding heart ticked away the seconds, knowing each moment she was exposed was one too many. She compared the two of them, and though the MacAlpin twins hadn't been identical, there was an echo between these two men, in their dark hair, their height.

But it was impossible.

His captor whispered in Cormac's ear, and Cormac nudged him with his shoulder. The man shouldered him back, and disbelief hit her like vertigo. She blinked hard to stop her head from reeling. It was something she'd seen a thousand times—the MacAlpin boys jostling, taunting, shoving.

Aidan.

She was elated, relieved, puzzled, anxious—mostly, she couldn't fathom it. Was Aidan also held captive by the smugglers? But why would he aim his gun at his own brother? Could he be a smuggler himself?

Scampering back up the ladder, she closed her eyes, letting the revelation wash over her. Cormac would've seen him the night he left her to investigate. *That* was why he hadn't wanted to sink the ship. He'd seen Aidan and hadn't wanted to do anything to endanger his long-lost twin.

Her eyes flew open. She'd *known* something had come to pass. He'd kept silent, but she'd sensed it. She shouldn't have doubted him. Cormac hadn't turned his back on her—on the contrary, he'd secretly returned to save the prisoners. To save Humphrey.

He loves me. She felt it to her soul, knew it in her bones. She wanted to laugh and cry at the same time. He loved her, and it explained so much.

And yet one mystery remained. What would the smugglers want with her uncle? She hunched low on the ladder, straining to hear more.

"Calm yourself, man. We have need of you on the plantation. But you'll get paid. In fact, we'll settle our accounts with profits from the sale of *this* fool." It was Jack's voice, and he was obviously talking about selling Cormac. The thought sickened and terrified her both. But pay whom? Who else was involved?

"These Highlanders fetch an especially high bounty," a woman said, and though her voice was muffled, Marjorie picked out a few words. "They've a scarcity of lands yet a surplus of mettle. Ideal laborers."

There was a round of laughter, and something about the throaty feminine chuckle struck a chord. *The bailie's wife.* Marjorie's stomach churned.

"Aye, precious," Jack said. "Selling the MacAlpin will get us more than enough to pay off Lord Keith."

The rare sound of her uncle's laughter rumbled up to her.

The blood drained from Marjorie's head. Without

thought, her hand flew to her temple, her palm clammy and numb.

Pay off Lord Keith. Humphrey Keith. Her uncle.

The ship pitched again, and this time Marjorie slipped and tumbled from the ladder, plummeting to the deck below.

Chapter 36

She lay there unmoving, feeling like a broken doll strewn along the wooden planks. Marjorie gave herself a moment to figure out if she'd done any permanent damage.

"Ree!" Cormac tried to jerk away from his brother, but Aidan's fingers dug into him. Cormac had always been able to take his twin in a fight, but the gun barrel jammed at his temple held him back. "Are you all right? Speak to me, love."

Pushing to a seated position, she gave him a nod, and it sent pain thrumming up her body. She shifted and gave a roll to her shoulders, realizing her left side had absorbed most of the damage.

"Good." His relief flipped into anger. "Then tell me, what in hell are you doing here?"

Fingers curled hard into her upper arms as Jack snatched her from the floor. He wrenched her close, and she couldn't help yelping with the painful shock of it.

"Get off her." Cormac bucked against Aidan. "I swear to God, I'll cut off your stones and feed them to the fish. If you harm her, I'll flay you, and then I'll—"

The click of Aidan pulling his pistol to half cock stilled him.

There was a gun at Cormac's temple, and it made her feel outraged and helpless. How could Humphrey be involved in something like this? "What's happening?" she demanded of her uncle. "Why are you here?"

"Och, Ree," Cormac whispered. The look of pity on his face would've warmed her if it hadn't also confirmed her suspicions. "I'm so sorry."

She watched Cormac, saw the machinations on his face. He'd be thinking about simply turning and attacking his brother, despite the gun. "Don't," she whispered. Her pride and well-being meant nothing if he got himself killed.

"So touching," a woman's voice purred.

Marjorie's eyes flew to the corner of the cabin, knowing already whom she'd find. The bailie's wife stood in the shadows, looking like a Turk in what she imagined was Adele's lush interpretation of female sailors' clothing. The sight of the woman's smirk made Marjorie ill. "Why are *you* here? Would someone tell me what's going on?"

"Let Marjorie go," Cormac said, his voice low with fury. "She has naught to do with this. Let her go, and you can have me."

"I already *have* you, MacAlpin." Grinning, Jack gave Marjorie a shake. "And now I have your wench as well."

She flailed in the smuggler's grip. The sensation of utter powerlessness infuriated her.

Humphrey's sagging cheeks went red. "That wasn't part of the deal. Let the girl go. You *will* give me what I'm owed, put us in that . . . that dilapidated craft you keep on deck, and you'll not see either of us again."

"*Craft?* You mean my captain's gig? Ach, but that's the boat *I* use to get to shore." Jack paused, feigning consideration. "No, I think not."

Marjorie tried to stomp on the smuggler's foot, but he sidestepped her with an amused laugh. She made an exasperated growl, feeling like a trapped animal. "Humphrey! Why are you even with these people?"

"Shut her up," Aidan growled to Cormac.

"*You* shut up." Marjorie raised her chin high, as though they were ten again.

"You were to stay out of this, girl." Humphrey's jowls quivered with exasperation. "Whatever I do, I do for *you*. So you won't die a destitute spinster. But like a fox in the henhouse, you insist on hunting for mischief. *Always* it's been so."

It was a side of her uncle she'd never seen, and she flushed red, feeling like a child put in her place. Tears stung her eyes, hurt more by his words than from any of Jack's pawing.

"You'll not speak to her that way," Cormac said, his voice like frost.

"You?" Humphrey pushed his chair back and stood, moving as slowly as a barge out of harbor. "You tell *me* how to speak to my niece? *You're* a dead man." Even in his anger, he looked befuddled. "I never did trust you MacAlpins . . ."

"Gentlemen, please." The bailie's wife sauntered into the fray, going to Jack's side. Marjorie coughed from the thick scent of her perfume, a cloying mix of sandalwood and cloves. Adele distractedly petted at the smuggler, giving a quick twirl to his hair. "You overestimate your value, Humphrey. Unlike your niece here." She tweaked Marjorie's ear. "I imagine she'll fetch a fair price, even though I'd wager she's no longer a virgin."

Marjorie sputtered in outrage, flinching away from the other woman's clutch. "You . . . you wench! You're a . . . a . . . a nasty, spiteful, hateful *virago*."

"Am I indeed?" Chuckling, Adele leaned closer, taunting her. "Such fury, *Lady Brodie*. Perhaps a honeymoon sail to Barbados with your 'husband' will cool your anger."

Cormac wrestled against his brother, but Aidan pressed the pistol even harder into his temple. The sight of it put ice in her veins.

"What about *your* husband, *Lady Forbes*?" Marjorie asked, her voice level and cool. "Is he involved in this, too?" She shifted her glare to Jack. "I hear three's the charm."

Jack nuzzled Marjorie's neck, inhaling deeply. "Don't tempt me, luvvie."

She recoiled with an outraged gasp. "You disgust me."

"I warned you," Cormac snarled through gritted teeth. "Get off her."

Tittering with laughter, Adele traced her fingers along the smuggler's collar. "When it comes to the finer things, my husband *the bailie*"—she smirked with contempt— "is a dilettante. But Jack, here, has more of a sense for women . . . for wealth . . ."

An unearthly groan shuddered the ship's timber underfoot. Marjorie's heartbeat kicked up a notch.

"We're wasting time." Cormac began to wrestle free, but his twin kept the barrel dug into his skin. "Go to the devil, Aidan," he sneered at his brother.

"I hear it's you who's the devil." Adele turned a languid gaze Cormac's way, giving him a sultry wink.

Marjorie jerked against Jack's grip. His hold on her was the only reason she hadn't already clawed the witch's eyes out. "You're naught but a . . . a . . . *harridan*, who's lured my uncle into a web of deceit and disrepute."

Her uncle huffed with indignation. "Relax, girl. There's nothing disreputable about it. I'm an investor."

"Investor?" she asked, perplexed.

"In their plantations." Humphrey looked away, directing his words to the smuggler. "An investor who's about to grow very angry indeed, unless I am escorted from this tub posthaste."

"Investor?" Jack mused, echoing Marjorie. "You're a so-called botanicals expert, who'd best start proving more obliging. The cane crops are failing. I'm beginning to doubt your competence, old man."

"The gall of you!" Marjorie exclaimed. Hurt and confused she might be, but nobody insulted her family.

"You're a saucy chit." Jack tried to nip at her ear. She smelled him coming, and she ducked her head away.

"Saucy?" Marjorie wriggled an arm free and jammed her hand in her skirts. "I'll show you sauce."

Cormac stiffened, his single-minded focus on her, and it felt to Ree as though they were in a pot set to boil over. She decided she'd be the one to raise the heat.

She jabbed the belaying pin hard at Jack's groin. She missed, but it caught his hip, and he grunted. But then the smuggler only laughed, snatching her weapon from her as easily as a toy from a child.

"A little she-wolf, is it?" Jack flung the pin down and scrubbed his hand up her bodice, groping her. "I enjoy a lass with backbone. Now let's see how far it can bend."

Marjorie thrashed like a wild thing, horrified by the unmistakable hunger on his face.

"Leave her be," Cormac said, rage seething in his voice. "Aidan, let me go, or I swear to you, one of us dies right here, right now."

The bailie's wife pulled a tiny lady's pistol from her stocking and aimed it at Marjorie. "I've had enough."

"A woman's envy," Aidan mused. His unconcerned tone infuriated Marjorie more than Adele's pistol. "Isn't that one of the deadly sins?"

Adele cocked her weapon. She stood stiffly, arms outstretched in front of her. "Step away, Jack. We'll take a loss on this one."

Tension stilled the room. Even Aidan seemed to hold his breath at Cormac's back.

Marjorie felt the smuggler hesitate, and Adele gestured with the barrel of her pistol. "I said move away. Now."

Marjorie stared at the bailie's wife in disbelief. "You won't shoot me."

"But I will, chit."

"You cannot. You will not." Humphrey stepped in. Disbelief made her uncle's tone manic. "Jack, control your woman. Think of it. Think of what you lose if the girl gets shot."

The girl. Marjorie was *the girl*, and she was about to

get a bullet in her chest. The blood drained from her head. It couldn't be happening.

"Jack can remove the loss from my take." Adele edged away from Humphrey, getting a clearer line on Marjorie. "Let go of her, Jack. I'm doing this."

The smuggler flung Marjorie away. As she spun to the ground, her perception of every sight, every sound, grew heightened. There was a deafening crack. Marjorie shut her eyes tight, bracing for it. She sensed Cormac tearing from his brother, leaping toward her.

She hit the ground, and her head whipped forward, hard. Warm wetness splattered on her. She waited for pain to bloom, the pistol shot reverberating in her ears with each pound of her heart. Hesitantly, she took a deep breath in, expecting the sharp stab of a bullet wound.

But nothing happened.

Footsteps stuttered before her. She looked up just as her Uncle Humphrey fell to the ground. His body hit the timber with a disturbing sound, like a rattling exhalation.

She shrieked. The wetness was Humphrey's blood, she realized. Acid rose to her throat, and she choked it back.

Thick gray-black smoke choked the cabin. She coughed, and smoke and bile burned her throat. "Humphrey?" Marjorie scampered to him. She patted at his body, knowing in her head that he was dead but still somehow unable to believe it. She pulled her hands back, and they were warm and sticky with his blood. A high keening sound filled the cabin, and she realized it was her.

Adele was shouting now, as was Jack. Marjorie thought she discerned Cormac's voice, too, but it was hollow, as though he called to her from a distance. "Ree!"

She made out his form just as the smoke began to clear, and then quickly looked back at Humphrey. She curled closer to her uncle. She needed to be right there in case he woke up, in case a decision was made and what had just happened might magically un-happen.

Cormac reached for her. "He's dead, Ree."

She looked back down, and her senses aligned, slamming back into place with shattering clarity. A puddle of blood, looking more black than red, surrounded Humphrey's body. *Dead*. Her uncle was truly and irrevocably dead.

"No," Aidan bellowed, and Marjorie gasped at the violent cry cutting through the chaos. Aidan grabbed his twin, snatching Cormac away from her. "I've got this one, Jack. You mind the women."

Caught. Humphrey was dead. Aidan held Cormac at gunpoint. *Captured*.

Jack had won.

In that moment she knew perfect hatred.

Chapter 37

Marjorie sprang from the body of her uncle, her dress grisly with blood, shrieking like a phoenix rising. The sound pierced Cormac's soul.

She flew at Adele, hitting and scratching, and Jack crowed with pleasure at the sight of the two women grappling like mad cats.

Thankful for all their childhood wrestling matches, Cormac prayed Ree could hold on while he scrambled for a plan. The ship groaned underfoot, followed by the pattering of footfalls and a number of shouts overhead. He wondered if they were coming to a stop. Whatever was happening, he needed it to play out quickly.

Cursing his traitor twin, Cormac nudged his head hard against the pistol barrel. "Go ahead, then, *brother*. Shoot me if you will."

"I warn you, Cormac. Don't test me." Aidan let up on the pressure. He leaned close to Cormac's ear and growled, "I'm as angry as a Campbell."

Cormac's eyes widened. A cascade of memories came to him in an instant. Playing Campbell and the Ogilvy fire, playing Campbell and Montrose. *As angry as a Campbell.* It was a hint.

"A Campbell, eh?" Jack laughed. He was distracted, staring at the women, licking his chops like a hungry wolf. "Well, lad, you'll be rich as one when we're through."

"When *you're* through," Aidan whispered in a voice only his brother could hear.

Cormac ducked. Aidan swung his gun and fired, landing a killing wound to Jack's chest. Both brothers coughed the acrid clutch of gunpowder from their chests.

The women froze as the smuggler's body reeled backward, hitting the wall of the cabin. Adele stared in shock for a prolonged moment, then, as understanding dawned, she began howling madly, cursing a frenetic stream of French.

Marjorie dropped, scrambling away on all fours. The ship pitched, and Cormac saw that she was after the belaying pin, rolling erratically along the floor.

Adele turned on him and his brother, her hands extended like claws, with murder in her eyes. *"Fils de salope!"*

"Ta gueule," Aidan spat back at once, in a strangely rich accent. Though Cormac had no idea what he'd just said, the contempt on his brother's face said it all.

Marjorie leapt atop the pin and then sprang from the floor, coming at the bailie's wife, swinging wildly. The wood struck Adele's skull with a hollow knock, and the woman fell like a sack of grain, curling into a ball, her head clutched in both hands.

"You killed him!" She flew at the bailie's wife. "You murdered my uncle!"

Cormac caught Marjorie, restraining her. "It's all right, love. We've got her." He spoke gently, trying to calm her, and gradually she stopped her flailing. "It's almost over."

"Cormac . . . my uncle . . ." Marjorie's breath jerked and hitched, and he pulled her closer, stroking and kissing her hair, his voice a steady stream of reassurances.

Aidan watched them with an unreadable and not necessarily warm look in his eye.

"Ahoy!" A voice hailed from above.

Cormac helped Marjorie to stand, his arm wrapped protectively around her.

"Oy," Aidan called back, loading his pistol.

"What's the racket, then?" someone shouted down the ladder.

The three of them looked at each other. Finally, Cormac called out in reply, "There's been shooting."

"I'll say," Aidan mumbled.

The ladder creaked with someone's weight. "Is it safe?"

They stood frozen, staring up to see who was descending. All but the bailie's wife, who continued to writhe in pain, keening a single, high note. Aidan gave her a disgusted glance. "*Ist*, woman."

"Ahoy there!" Black-booted feet emerged into view. "I say, is it safe?"

Adele, Marjorie, and Cormac spoke in unison, just as the bailie reached the floor of the forecastle. "Malcolm?" *"The bailie?"* "Forbes?"

"Aye," he said, scanning the room with narrowed eyes. "I went to Saint Machar to pay Archie a visit, and he alerted me there might be some trouble down by the docks."

Marjorie looked baffled. "But I thought the ship was under way?"

Though she'd directed her question to Cormac, it was Forbes who answered. "Aye, and so you were. But it's a slow-going vessel, and I could get myself rowed to Ireland with enough coin." He stared disdainfully at his wife. "But it seems all the coin at my disposal was never enough for you, was it, Adele? Fortune was within my grasp, but you couldn't wait."

"You don't seem surprised to find her here," Marjorie marveled, taking in the disaster around them. "Your *wife*, among pirates and kidnappers."

Adele moaned. "Jack was no pirate."

"Pirate, smuggler, what's the difference?" The bailie walked to his wife and squatted by her. "When Archie mentioned how he'd treated you for your *pregnancy*, I knew. Seeing as pregnancy with me is impossible. Isn't that right, precious?" He brushed the hair from her brow in a mockery of tenderness. "I followed you to the docks once, saw this fine schooner. I'd thought perhaps you'd found yourself a plantation owner. But a common brigand?" He shook his head. "Well, dear heart, you'll have plenty of time in which to acquaint yourself with thieves, seeing as I'll be arresting you for murder."

Adele flinched away from his touch, keening more loudly.

Marjorie looked uneasily to Aidan. Cormac knew she wanted to trust his twin as badly as he did. "But I still don't understand why *you're* here," she said.

Aidan flashed them a cold smile. "That happy to see me?"

"Don't be preposterous." Marjorie reached her hand out, touching his arm tentatively. "Of course . . . I'm beyond happy. You must understand it's a shock—"

Aidan flinched away. "Spare me your treacle. I'm here to find the man who took me thirteen years ago. I've worked, and I've watched, and I've waited." He pinned his brother with a flat stare, declaring, "Many years, I've waited. And *nothing*—not you, not our family—will stop me. I *will* find him. I'm close now. He profits from the sales of *this* ship."

"Not for much longer," Cormac said, just as there was a long, shuddering groan.

Marjorie reached for Cormac. "Are we moving again?"

"Perhaps," he said, furrowing his brow thoughtfully.

"Perhaps?" The bailie pulled his wife up to standing. "What say you, *perhaps*? I'm taking her ashore," he said, with a disdainful nod to Adele.

"Aye, I think we'd all best get to dry land." Cormac turned to Marjorie. "You wanted the ship destroyed. And so I decided on a wee bit of . . . insurance."

Bristling, Aidan holstered his pistol at his back. "Insurance?"

There was a sharp creak and then an unearthly moan as the ship pitched sharply, canting the deck to an uneven slope. A lantern on the wall guttered out, sinking them in near darkness.

Cormac gave them a broad smile. "She's sinking."

Chapter 38

"How?" Aidan was smiling widely, and in it Marjorie spied the first flicker of warmth she'd seen since their reunion.

"I punched out the rudder pins," Cormac said proudly.

"You sabotaged the rudder." Aidan nodded appreciatively. "The moment we left port, she'd have begun taking on water from the stern." He thought for a second, then asked, "But why aren't the pumps working?"

"I fixed those, too. Pumps don't work without their handles." He winked at Marjorie.

"You dove under the ship?" Marjorie's eyes grazed him, and they widened, noting his trews, the color darker with damp.

"Brilliant," Aidan whispered.

"Not so far under," Cormac replied with a crooked smile. "Come, now." He took her arm, ushering her to the ladder. "Time for you to get off the ship."

Though she felt her legs moving, she was having a hard time connecting thoughts with movements. Cormac had been in the water. Water that would soon be up around their ears if they didn't get off now.

"Can the girl make it?" Aidan's tone was condescending.

His scrutiny focused Marjorie. She was not weak. She would not be weak.

"I'm fine," she said, gripping her skirts. But her fingers were ice cold.

The ship lurched again, and Marjorie's stomach with it. They were on a sinking ship far from port. The entire situation was unthinkable madness.

"The water will be coming fast now." Cormac turned to the bailie. "Take the women ashore. Now."

There was a low groan, and water trickled in from the seam between floor and wall.

"The prisoners!" Marjorie's shout sounded hollow in her own ears. She remembered the prisoners. They were on a lower deck. They'd drown.

There was a sharp crack, and the trickle of water turned into a gush. Water seeped higher, swirling around their ankles. It lapped at the bodies strewn on the floor, casting the hem of her dress a ghastly shade of rust.

"Get me out!" Adele shrieked, shaking her husband's arm. Alarm thickened her accent. "You . . . you . . . *sale con*! You will get me off this ship!"

Marjorie watched the bailie, his face colorless as parchment, as he scampered up the ladder with his wife. But she could only stand paralyzed, unable to wrap her mind around what was happening. One of her feet was poised on the bottom rung, but freezing water churned around the other. She knew she should get out of there, but all she could think about was what would become of the body of her uncle.

"Ree, love," Cormac said gently. Cupping her cheeks in his hands, he gave her a slow, chaste kiss. It felt like good-bye, and her throat ached with anguish. "You must go. Now, Ree. The lower deck will be flooding fast now."

"Wait." Tears finally sprang to her eyes, spilling in a hot torrent down her chilled face. "What about you?"

"I'll bide a wee longer," Cormac said. The corners of his eyes crinkled with a rueful smile. "I've a hold full of slaves to rescue."

"As do I." Aidan stepped up behind his brother, and Marjorie made a choked sound, somewhere between a laugh and a sob.

She stared at Cormac one last time, memorizing his eyes, the color of a stormy sky, and the furrow in his brow, visible beneath a dark swatch of still-damp hair. She would see him again in no time, she assured herself.

With a mute nod, she forced herself to move.

Next she knew, she was floating in a five-person dory, her body numb, wondering how, exactly, she'd made it up and off the ship. She spent the next agonizing minutes trapped in some dreadful hallucination, watching as the moonlit masts of the *Oliphant*—and Cormac—slowly sank beneath the waves.

———

Mayhem ruled on deck. There were two launch boats— the captain's gig and a whaleboat—each intended to carry only ten. Crewmen struggled to unhitch them in the darkness, lowering them into the churning waves. Some sailors clambered down the rope ladder, fighting to be first on board, while others simply dove from the railing in terror, attempting to swim ashore. It was rumored that the force of a sinking ship was enough to suck a man down to the bottom of the sea.

Cormac looked landward. Aberdeen harbor was an inky black swatch in the distance, standing apart from the glimmering, starlit sea. They weren't so far from land—a strong swimmer with his wits about him would make it.

"Slaves are held aft," Aidan said simply, shouldering by his brother.

Cormac nodded and followed close behind. "We need to get them before they drown. She'll sink fast now."

He attuned his ears, picking out cries from the prisoners trapped on the lower deck. Gauging by how low the ship rode in the water, the men would be chest-high in seawater.

They stood at the top of the companionway ladder, peering to the hold below. Water sloshed, shimmering in the moonlight like a black mirror.

"No time like the present." Cormac nudged past his brother, descending the ladder. His legs were soon immersed, but he kept going, ignoring the sharp bite of frigid water stealing across the tiny bones in his feet all the way up to his thighs. "She's locked tight," he said, jiggling the submerged latch. He slammed his shoulder against the door for good measure, but the deep water prevented any momentum.

The prisoners heard the commotion, and began howling and pleading with renewed intensity.

Aidan was right beside him, the calm on his face at odds with the water lapping against their torsos. "Quiet," he bellowed, slamming his hand high on the door. Head tilted low in concentration, he held both hands underwater, blindly assessing the lock. He glanced up at Cormac, and said, "Your dirk."

"My dirk?"

"Aye . . . No," Aidan said suddenly, "not the dirk, the scabbard. Give me the scabbard." Raising a brow, he stuck his hand out. "Unless you'd care to bide here a wee longer?"

Scowling, Cormac retrieved both the weapon and its scabbard from his belt. Water lapped at their armpits now, and his fingers fumbled in the icy water.

Taking the scabbard, Aidan slid open an outer pocket, pulling out the tiny knife and fork kept for eating. He replaced the knife, handing it all back to Cormac except for the fork, which he levered against the door, splaying the two tines wide. "For the lock," he grunted.

"Impressive, Aid." By the time his brother was through, Cormac had clumsily reattached the weapon at his waist. He put his hand out for the fork. "I can do it."

"No." Aidan shouldered his brother aside. "I've some experience with locks and shackles."

Aidan's expression was strained, and in it Cormac glimpsed the ghosts of his brother's past, saw how they haunted him. "By all means," Cormac told him quietly, stepping back to give him the most of what meager moonlight seeped down the hatch.

Aidan ducked under water, and Cormac found himself holding his breath in sympathy. The ship moaned incessantly now, complaining about the watery grave that was subsuming them all.

His brother popped up for a breath of air, then went back down again, until finally the door cracked open. They shoved hard, the thick wood moving sluggishly against the water. The rank stench of penned men swirled out to them.

"Easy," Aidan growled, as the first of the prisoners began to push his way out. They were panicked, like trapped animals, clawing over each other for freedom.

"Easy, lads." Cormac pushed past his brother, deciding he'd be the one to usher the men free. The haunted look on Aidan's face spoke to memories too tortured to bear. "One at a time . . . that's the way."

There were just fourteen men in all, and he and Aidan quickly got them on deck and off the ship, where they jammed into the boats going ashore. A few of the sailors spared contemptuous glances for their former captives, but most seemed occupied with saving their own hides.

Relief swelled through Cormac. The first boat—the captain's gig—was already overloaded and bobbing its way back to harbor. The whaleboat was ready and waiting.

They'd saved the men. It was what Ree had wanted. What *he'd* wanted, too, if he were being honest.

It was a foolish impulse, but even though he knew Marjorie was safe, Cormac wanted to see where she was, to imagine he savored the moment with her. There was one boat smaller than the others, a dory, its clean white paint glowing gray in the black water. Eyes adjusting, he made out the figures on board—a few men, and two smaller silhouettes, the women.

He smiled. Forbes had been desperate to return to shore, but she'd made the bailie stay to watch. His smile grew broader still, imagining what *that* scene might've looked like.

"When you're done goggling like an ape, we should get ourselves off this tub."

Cormac shot his brother a look, expecting to find a glare to match the spiteful words. But instead, Aidan had a playful expression on his face, and in it Cormac saw the ghost of a ten-year-old scamp. He cuffed Aidan on the shoulder. "You first, if you're so skittish."

Cormac turned back for one more glance of Marjorie, and his heart jumped in his chest. The crazed lass was standing now, and the dory bobbed wildly as she struggled for balance. One of the men was trying to pull her back down before she capsized them, but she was staring stubbornly, gesturing wildly.

Dread snaked through his chest like a chill fog. He looked up, frightened by what he might see. Cormac heard it now, in the way that sight aids hearing. The little Moorish boy was tangled in the ratlines, crying quietly. Though the child appeared stoic, Cormac saw terror in the tension of his small body, in his rigid grip on the lines.

"You go," he told Aidan. "I've one more to save."

His brother squinted at the masts, and Cormac pointed. "There, by the topsail."

"God's bones," Aidan exclaimed. "You *always* get to play the hero. Not this time." He strode to the mizzenmast. "We're in this together."

Cormac had to chuckle, despite the danger. He tossed the rope down to the whaleboat, shouting, "You're under way, lads."

There was a sharp crack, and the brothers staggered, grabbing onto the base of the mizzenmast as the *Oliphant* tilted wildly. White spume swirled on deck. Cormac and his brother shared a grave look. "She's going fast now."

Aidan leapt up, scrabbling like a spider up the web of lines. "I'm ready to get out of this water anyhow."

Cormac climbed beside him, until they reached the boy, perching on either side of him. "Hold him."

Weaving his legs in the ratlines for stability, Aidan grabbed the boy around the waist. Though the child had a clawlike grip on the lines and was tangled besides, they couldn't risk him falling to the deck below. "Got him. Cut the lines."

The mast shuddered, and they caught themselves on the lines, the boy yelping in terror. There was a deafening and unearthly groan as the deck sank beneath the waves.

Cormac unsheathed his dirk and began sawing away. "Can you swim, lad?"

The boy gave a frantic and wide-eyed shake to his head.

Aidan caught the boy's weight as Cormac sheared the last of the lines free. "No matter. We've got you."

The mast tilted at a sharp angle over the water. It seemed the water was rushing up to meet them. There wasn't enough time to climb back down. "I'll jump in," Cormac said. "You toss him down to me."

Steadying himself against the wooden yard, Cormac edged along the footrope to the very end of the yardarm. He gave his twin a last glance. He'd half-expected some jest about heroics, but Aidan only nodded gravely. Cormac nodded back. And then he leapt.

He slammed into the freezing water, and it felt almost warm on his chilled skin. A few rapid breaths brought his senses back to him. Chafing the water from his eyes, he called up to Aidan. "Now!"

Aidan wound the buntline around his left fist to anchor himself. He clutched the child in his right arm, shifting him to his hip. Cormac watched as his brother whispered something in the boy's ear, and the two clasped hands. Then, swooping as far as he could over the water, Aidan swung the boy free, and let go.

The boy screamed, tumbling through the air in a slow-motion dive, his arms spinning like pinwheels. Cormac treaded water, trying to be close enough to snatch him from the waves, but not so close that the boy would land on him, injuring them both.

He hit the water with a hard splash, and Cormac dove under at once, hands splayed apart and waving before him, searching. He found a tiny wrist and seized it, swimming back up and wrenching the child above the surface of the water.

He swam for Marjorie's dory, hauling the boy at his side. Seawater stung his nose and slapped in his eyes, but he headed toward the sound of her voice. The child gasped for air, but it was only panic, for Cormac made sure to hold his head above water.

He heard her yelling, over and over, "Row! Get closer! Row, damn you!" The sound was like a clarion call, guiding him up from hell.

Finally, his hand slapped the hull of her boat, and Marjorie leaned over the side, reaching out to them. "Give him to me," she urged, hauling the child up to her. She wrapped an arm around the boy, stretching the other to Cormac. "Thank God. Thank heavens."

Their gazes locked. She looked beleaguered and bedraggled and scared, and she was the dearest creature he could ever imagine.

Cupping Cormac's cheek in her palm, she gave Cormac a gentle smile. Her hand was warm against his frigid skin. He knew then he'd do it all over again just to see the tenderness in her eyes.

"I love you, Ree. You believe me now, don't you?"

"Aye," she said, and she was laughing, despite the tears she scrubbed from her face. "As I love you, Cormac. As I always have."

He sighed heavily, relieved. She was his, as it always had been, as it always would be.

But then it struck him. He looked around in confusion. "Where's Aidan?" Swimming alone, his brother should've beat him there, or at least been right behind.

The sun was beginning to lighten the sky to slate. He shielded his eyes, not from the light, but to make sense of the monotony of gray horizon smothering gray sea.

But all he saw was the tip of the mainmast submerged into water the color of steel.

Chapter 39

His arms sliced rhythmically through the water, and Cormac imagined himself a fish, streaking back to the schooner, now completely submerged.

They weren't so far from shore, the water not so very deep. The *Oliphant* had struck the bottom and was canting toward him, slowly tilting onto its side. He shifted, stroking through the water with an eye trained on the empty space marking the ship's grave.

There.

A head bobbed up, then back down again. Aidan was clawing at the water as though trying to climb an invisible ladder with one hand.

Cormac dove back under, launching toward him. Close now, he saw the web of ratlines floating like kelp just beneath the surface of the water. Aidan was snagged among them, like a trapped fly.

The schooner continued to tip, a languorous movement, like Poseidon reclining upon the seabed for a rest. Aidan gasped for air, then disappeared for good.

Cormac surged forward until the muscles in his arms

strained with the effort. The *Oliphant* was easing onto its side, dragging Aidan to the bottom. He would not lose his brother a second time.

A final, hard scissor kick brought Cormac's fingertips to the fringe of lines. He gripped tight, fighting the panicked, helpless sensation of being tugged down. Hand over hand, he climbed along the ratlines toward Aidan.

Cormac could just make out his brother beneath the surface. Aidan was on top of the lines, his legs braced against the mast, struggling to untangle his arm from a thick snarl of ropes, his movements a dreamy slow motion.

Cormac reached for the dirk at his back and cursed the empty scabbard. His knife was long gone.

Sucking in a huge breath, Cormac dipped his head below the waves. Inch by inch, he felt his way along the knots toward Aidan. Panic clawed at his mind like a hungry rat. He shut his eyes, forcing his muscles to ease. Alarm would only steal the last of his breath.

Imagining a slowed heartbeat, he ran his fingers along the lines. He was a fisherman. He'd untied hundreds of knots, blinded by as many storms. This was no different.

Aidan's struggles slowed. Stopped. His body drifted beside Cormac like a wraith.

He forced it from his mind. He had to trust the cold to keep his brother.

He probed the nest of lines, ignoring the increasingly shrill pleas of his body. Holding his breath took all the force of his will. His lungs were emptied of air, but rather than collapsing inward, the sensation was that his chest might burst. He compelled himself to stay submerged, feeling as though he bore the weight of the sea itself on his chest.

The knot.

He found it. A single knot trapped Aidan's forearm. Cormac traced his fingers over the long oval of it. *A sheepshank.* Sailors tied it in the middle of a line to shore up damaged rope. But there was a trick. Simply remove the tension, and the knot will slip loose.

Cormac worked frantically now. Though he fought the spasmodic urge to inhale water, still it found a way to seep in, tearing at his throat. Folk said drowning was a peaceful thing, but it wasn't. Drowning was a violent thing. The sea was savage, trying to seep into him, ravenous, relentless.

He hauled Aidan's limp body close to him, and with a twist to ease the tension, the knot fell apart, and his brother slid free.

They flopped Aidan over the side of Marjorie's boat, and the sudden pressure on his belly sent water spewing from his mouth. Cormac climbed in behind him, guiding his brother's head, leaning him over the side. Cormac slapped hard at Aidan's back while he worked to catch his own breath. Both of them were racked with tremors. Aidan hacked fiercely as the last of the seawater erupted from his lungs.

Marjorie was at Cormac's side, and her warm body pressed against him felt like a furnace. At the mere suggestion of heat, unstoppable shivering seized him.

"Thank God," she cooed at him, laying frantic kisses along his cheek and chafing heat into his arms and back. "Thank God you're alive."

With a grunt, Aidan spat one last time over the edge of the boat and shifted away from them.

Cormac coughed sharply into his hand, taking a moment to catch his breath once more. "We saved Davie. Saved the men."

"I know." She combed eager fingers through his hair, pulling a wet shock of it from his brow. "I know you did. I'm so sorry if I ever doubted you."

"I sank the boat," he said.

She looked to where the *Oliphant* once was and gave a little half laugh. "Clearly."

"I did what I promised, Ree." Cormac's body finally relaxed, and his breathing grew even. "You know what this means, right?"

She looked back to him. The morning sun was low in

the sky, and it made her vibrant eyes glimmer like lapis. "What?"

His heart swelled at the sight of her. Glorious, brave, impetuous Ree. *His* Ree. "You'll marry me."

Marjorie tucked her hand in his, and it was all the anchor he needed on this earth. She leaned in for a tender kiss. Touching her forehead to his, she whispered, "Without question."

Epilogue

Only in her wildest dreams had Marjorie imagined this.

Her, at Dunnottar, by Cormac's side. The grass was green and lush from the spring rains. Red light streaked the late afternoon sky, casting bands of orange and crimson across the gently rolling waves far below. The two of them lingered beneath a makeshift trellis, pine boughs laced with flowers arching overhead. The scent of bluebells and sea lightened her soul.

"What is it, Ree?"

She glanced up, and her breath hitched, seeing her wildest dream of all: *Cormac*. Her husband. They'd married, facing Cormac's sea.

He raised a brow, silently pressing his question.

Joy overcame her, and she felt it as a physical thing radiating from deep inside. "It's just that I love you."

"And I, you." He cupped her chin for a lingering kiss. Reluctantly, he pulled away. When he spoke, his voice was husky with emotion. "Always, I've loved you."

Marjorie beamed. She took in the scene around them. Folk milled about Dunnottar's grounds, and as the moon began to challenge the sun in the sky, a small bonfire appeared, drawing smiling faces and cups of whiskey like moths to flame. "I still can't believe it."

"Believe it." Cormac's gaze tracked hers, looking at his siblings gathering around the fire. "I'm sorry your uncle isn't here to share this," he added somberly.

She nodded, her voice too tight with emotion to speak.

He took her hand and squeezed it. "*I'm* your family now."

It was a simple notion, but it filled her all the same. She gave him a loving smile. "And them?" She nodded to the MacAlpins: Bridget, Gregor, Declan. And though Anya was far away, Aidan's presence eased the sting of her absence. Their faces were at once familiar, and yet they were still strangers, too, in many ways. "I suppose they're my family, too, now."

"Them especially. You know they've always loved you." He laughed low. "Perhaps a bit too much. That day you appeared on the beach, I thought I might have to strangle Gregor. And then there's Bridget. I think my distance from you vexed *her* most of all." He sighed, stroking her hand. "I only wish our mothers were here to see it."

"I think we were still babes when they first wished for this wedding." She twined her fingers with his. "They were always so close. It's funny to realize how young they were. I remember overhearing them jesting about me and one of the MacAlpin boys."

As though on cue, Aidan rose. Thinking nobody watched him, he strolled from the crowd.

A pang of sadness pierced her joy. She wondered if *that* MacAlpin boy would ever find peace. Aidan had vowed to find the man who'd stolen him, but Marjorie couldn't help but wish he'd let go of the past and move on. "I wish he'd give up this quest of his."

Cormac squeezed her hand. "My brother will never give up."

"What a shock to see him again." She knew Cormac had always battled guilt, and she looked for it now on his face. Getting his brother back was cause to rejoice, but she knew, for Cormac, seeing proof of Aidan's misery would mean his guilt redoubled.

Davie scrambled past suddenly, and they both laughed, torn from their reverie. The boy ran straight for Fiona, tangling himself in her skirts.

"Now *there's* the real shock." Cormac eyed Fiona. "Wedding the *young physician surgeon.* Your maid is an enterprising one indeed."

She nudged him with her shoulder. "She's a married woman and no longer my maid."

"Ah, but such a hasty betrothal." He nudged her back.

"Mock not, Cormac MacAlpin. I think it's lovely how Fiona and Arch took Davie into their care." She giggled. "Though the whole thing was a wee bit on the hurried side." She *had* raised a brow at that, but having abandoned her maidenhead in an Aberdeen Inn, she wasn't one to throw stones. "They're simply getting a fast start on their family," she reasoned.

They watched Fiona squat down to straighten Davie's shirt. "Will you miss her?"

"Fiona?" Marjorie smiled, thinking she *would* miss her. But she'd quickly grown fond of the wee scullion girl who'd been promoted as her replacement—not to mention how touched and amused she was by the soft spot Cormac had already shown the younger girl. "Actually, I'm happy for her."

Her eyes went back to Cormac's twin, standing on the periphery. "I wish I were happier for *him*, though."

The growing shadows emphasized the darkness on Aidan's face. No longer was he the happy-go-lucky scamp of their youth. Something dark lurked deep inside him. She wished he'd abandon this insane wish for retribution. She'd convince him, she decided.

She'd help Aidan, her and Cormac both.

Her *husband.* The thought made her swoon. Grinning broadly, she snuck her hand around and gave a surreptitious tweak to his backside.

"You're a saucy one." He laughed. "What was that for?"

She put her hands on her hips, mimicking outrage. "Isn't it about time for the wedding night?"

"Indeed, and not a moment too soon." He looked around. Gregor was standing up, calling attention to himself. "We just need to get all of *them* to leave," Cormac added in a low voice.

Cormac's older brother was shouting for a toast, and Marjorie led her husband closer to the fire to listen.

"There are those of us who never thought we'd see this day. This MacAlpin devil wed." Gregor was as confident and dashing as ever. The sun was at his back, and it picked golden strands in his light brown hair. Turning to Cormac and Marjorie, he raised his cup. "To my little brother. And to Marjorie, the angel who came between the devil and the deep blue sea."

Cormac lifted her chin and pressed the sweetest kiss to her, a kiss holding the promise of forever. Joyful tears stung her eyes as she realized that even the *wildest* of dreams could come true.

Author's Note

Years ago, I stumbled across a mention of chimney sweeps and learned of the dreadful fates suffered by many of these "climbing boys." Children who'd grown too big would often die, trapped in the narrow passages. Others were simply stolen, transported to faraway lands where they became forced laborers. Some people argued that working in the fresh air and fields was healthier for them anyhow.

This stuck in my craw for years and was the kernel from which this latest series grew. I wondered what would become of a child stolen from his homeland. Who would he be as a man? What of his family? Interestingly, it was the brother, Cormac, who was the first character in my mind. The rest barreled quickly on his heels.

For those of you familiar with my first books, this latest series is a departure for me. Though I will always be as careful as possible with history and fact, here I deal in broader strokes: I don't re-create specific events, and my characters are not based on real figures.

Even the clan I chose can be read as more emblematic

than literal. By the fourteenth century, Clan MacAlpin had become a "broken clan." Even so, they are iconic. Once the kings of Scotland, MacAlpin is an ancient clan, seen today as more a meta-clan, rife with legend. Inextricably linked to Scotland and to nature, the name MacAlpin shares a root with *Alba*, the old word for Scotland, and also with the word *alpine*.

That the MacAlpins are both utterly Scottish and yet not associated with events of my chosen era gave me the freedom to explore a story more purely about family in a small corner of Scotland—here, a story of lovers and brothers.

And how about that castle? If you've traveled to Aberdeen, you're likely familiar with Dunnottar, a spectacular sight on the northeastern coast. Interestingly, it was, in fact, linked to the ancient MacAlpin kings. But from there, it's pure fiction, folks.

Although some of my claims were true—Dunnottar was largely destroyed in sieges in the early 1650s—it was still used as a prison and fortress throughout the seventeenth century and didn't fall into ruin until the early eighteenth, well after my story takes place.

I will surely outrage a lot of purists out there, and considered changing Dunnottar's name, but I wanted you to envision with me just the sort of spectacular Scottish ruin I'd pictured for my family. Dodie Smith's *I Capture the Castle* has always stayed with me, and you're seeing its faint echoes here with my MacAlpins. They are my version of a family of personalities who've installed themselves in a tumbledown fortress.

And I hope you enjoyed the beginning of their story, because there sure are a lot more MacAlpins waiting in the wings. Visit me at www.VeronicaWolff.com to see what's to come.

Turn the page for a special preview of
the next novel in Veronica Wolff's
Clan MacAlpin series

Devil's Own

On sale March 2011
from Berkley Sensation!

Stonehaven, Aberdeenshire, 1660

She wasn't chilled. Her back didn't ache. She wasn't in a barn, nor was she seated upon a three-legged stool. She wasn't in the milking room, and her cheek was most certainly not nestled deep in the thick, musty wool of a sheep's haunch.

No, Elspeth Josephina Farquharson was at a country dance.

Well, not really. But she shut her eyes, dreaming what one might be like. There would be laughter, girls with broad smiles walking arm in arm, big jugs of ale. The pipes would set into a lively reel. She swayed in time.

The door creaked open. The room stilled. Footsteps sounded. The heavy step was confident, masculine.

It was him. He approached from across the room, his eyes only for her. He swept her into his arms.

The reel began again, and he pulled her, steady as the tides, into the middle of the dance floor. His breacan feile wrapped about her legs as he swung her. She gazed up, easy laughter on her lips, staring into his . . .

Elspeth's hands froze on the sheep's teat.

Brown? Emerald green? Gray as a storm-choked sky? Nay, blue.

She sighed, smiling.

She gazed up, laughter on her lips, at his blue eyes. He had a smile just for her. It was naughty.

"Elspeth, I say. Are you deaf, girl? That sheep's wrung dry."

She sighed again, heavily this time. Her eyes fluttered open. It was her father who stood there, not the dream man.

"Now come up to the house," he said. "It's accounting time, and you know you're the one with the head for books."

Elspeth scooted back from the sheep, clapping her hands clean. "Aye, Father."

Even though the family farm was small, she the only child, and her mother long dead, her father needed her. And when he needed her, she always went. How he'd managed before her was a marvel.

"You know I don't have a mind for reckoning." He gave a loving poke to her temple. "Not like my wee Elspeth."

She smiled weakly. The day was coming when she'd need to sit her father down and have a serious talk. He'd sold five head of perfectly good cattle to start a woolen business. Without consulting her. And now she was the one left to milk the sheep *and* mind the accounting. But the books told a grim story, and it grew grimmer by the day.

She worried that they may not even have enough left to buy back their cattle, if it came to that.

They returned to their two-room croft house, and Elspeth pulled her chair close to the fire. Candles were dear, and the hearth was the only spot bright enough for reading.

"How would I survive without you?"

She looked up to find his warm smile, and tenderness seized her heart. Her parents had been long married before they'd been blessed with their only child. When her mother died in childbirth, she'd left her newborn babe with a man old enough to be a grandfather.

Her father waited expectantly for a reply. His frizz of gray hair erupted up from his head like a halo, or a misshapen bird's nest.

No, he couldn't survive without her. Nor would she want him to.

"Good thing it shan't come to that." The words pricked her, and she forced a smile. She'd spoken the truth: living without her would never be in question. Any dowry there'd been in linens and woolen goods had been sold off long ago. And what coin there'd been for making Elspeth's plain features more attractive to a prospective husband had gone to the beasts instead.

"Here's your things, then." He pulled her wee worktable by the fire. It bore a sheaf of papers and her precious quill, and the sight of it automatically switched her mind to the business at hand.

"Thank you," she said, already engrossed in her papers. She fished out that month's tally, squinting to focus.

With a *tsk*, he rose to stoke the fire higher. "Stubborn lass. I wish you'd allow yourself a reading glass. I've heard talk of a man in Aberdeen who fashions spectacles. They even have a wee ribbon to hold them to the head."

She tilted her chin to bring the numbers into focus, skimming her eyes over the lines. They'd had this argument before. "You know we haven't the money."

"But we've spent less this month. Or it should read so in that book of yours." He came and hovered over her, and she shifted so as not to lose the light.

"Less? How is that possible?" She scanned the rows, and one number caught her eye. Growing stern, she put her finger to mark her place. "Da, how is it this month's expenses are lower, and yet our earnings haven't changed?"

She craned her neck to stare a challenge at him. He'd

sold personal items off before, and Elspeth wouldn't put it past him to do something foolish like sell off her mother's wedding band. She frowned, for it wasn't as though she'd ever have call to wear anyone's wedding band.

"I've begun to trade. With *Angus*." He paused, letting the farmer's name hang.

"Angus." Shaking her head, she looked back down. Her father dreamed of marrying her off to the man. "Not that again."

Though Angus Gunn was kind enough, and his neighboring farm profitable, he didn't make her swoon like all the great heroines swooned. And if Elspeth couldn't have a great love like those she read about in her novels, then she'd rather skip the whole enterprise entirely.

Besides, she knew of another woman who'd stolen Angus's heart long ago.

Elspeth shut her eyes, pinching the bridge of her nose. "What, pray, have we to trade with Angus?"

"Our sheep's milk for his oats."

Her eyes flew open. "Raw oats? However will we mill them?"

"They're to feed the sheep."

She bit her lips not to speak the first words that came to her tongue. She'd simply have to talk to Angus herself. Perhaps arrange to trade for *milled* oats so they could fill *their* bellies instead of just the sheep's. "Very well, Father."

There was a knock at the door, and he bolted up, a wide grin on his face. "Speak of the devil."

Elspeth rolled her eyes. When would her father get it through his thick skull that she neither wanted Angus, nor he her?

The farmer stood in the doorway and gave her father a stoic nod. He was so tall and so broad, he had to hunch to fit. "I put the oats by the barn."

He shooed Angus in. "Come in, come in. Say hello to Elspeth." He swept an arm in her direction. "Doesn't she look lovely by the firelight?"

"Oh, Da," she muttered under her breath. Her father

thought her the bonniest in all Scotland. Little did he know that what men likely saw was a shy spinster, with plain features adorning a too-thin frame.

Spotting Elspeth, Angus slipped his bonnet from his head, crumpling it in his hands. "Good day, Miss Elspeth."

She put her papers down and gave him a warm smile. She didn't have feelings for the farmer—he was in love with her best friend, after all. But that didn't mean she didn't think him a kind and dependable soul. "Good day, Angus."

An awkward silence filled the room.

"Very good, very good," her father said, looking from one to the other.

"If that's all, then." Angus turned as if to leave.

Her Da shot her a meaningful, wide-eyed look, nodding encouragement.

Elspeth shrugged. She'd never been good at idle chatter. "Do bide a wee, Angus. We . . . we've just stoked the fire, and I'm afraid I've had enough of numbers this day."

"Very well." Angus went to the corner to retrieve another stool.

"What's the word from town?" her father asked jovially. "I hear the oldest MacAlpin girl has returned a widow. Lost her husband to a war wound, or some such." He looked to Elspeth. "You two were mates. What was the lassie's name?"

"Anya?" Her heart soared. Was it possible her dearest friend had returned? Though sadness for Anya's loss pierced her, Elspeth couldn't help but beam. "Anya MacAlpin is back?"

She cut her eyes to Angus, feeling instantly guilty. He'd not weather the news so well. Long ago, Anya's sudden marriage had struck him hard.

Sure enough, he still faced the corner, standing frozen. She was certain Anya was the reason Angus had never married.

Her smile faded. Would that a man felt half for Elspeth

what that farmer held in his heart for the oldest MacAlpin sister.

Anya hadn't wanted the marriage either, but it'd been forced upon her by her father. Seeing her heartbreak was what had hardened Elspeth's resolve so many years ago. The day she watched Anya carted away in tears, Elspeth decided either she'd marry for love, or not at all. And now to think her friend was already a widow, while Elspeth seemed destined to remain forever a maiden.

Her father seemed baffled by the tense silence, and filled it with mindless chatter. "Quite a year for that family. Cormac—and what a strange, dour fellow he is, aye?—he up and marries the prettiest girl. From Aberdeen proper, she is." He shook his head, marveling. "And now there's a rumor the brother's back, too. The twin. You remember the lad who was stolen? Aidan?"

"None would soon forget that name," Angus replied, his features once again a stoic mask. He pulled his stool before the fire.

Elspeth put her hand to her heart. "Young Aidan lives?"

She hadn't known the MacAlpins when the lad was taken. But like every other villager on the outskirts of Aberdeen, she'd heard about the kidnap. Folk said he'd been mistaken for a poor climbing boy. Everyone had presumed him dead or worse, indentured to a faraway plantation.

Angus shook his head. "Not so young anymore."

The mysterious Aidan popped into her head, a shadowy, featureless silhouette. What came of a man after such an ordeal? And what would he look like? If he'd turned out half as handsome as his twin Cormac, he'd be handsome indeed.

"Aye, he's returned. But the family is keeping a tight lip about it." Her father leaned in. "He was a slave in the tropics, I heard. They say he was branded."

"Branded," she gasped. Owned like a common slave. And yet he'd escaped. And with secrets, no doubt.

She shivered, letting her mind wander. How on earth

had he made his way back to Scotland, sailing all the way from Jamaica, or Barbados, or Hispaniola? Battling pirates, almost certainly.

Aidan MacAlpin would be dangerous, swaggering. Just like one of the heroes in her books. Would he speak a foreign tongue? Months on the open seas, his skin would be as smooth and brown as a cowry shell.

The sun beat down overhead. The timber planks were hot beneath her bare feet. She stood, gazing across the endless sea. The afternoon was sultry. It loosened her muscles. She felt heavy with the heat. Wanton.

She sensed him, and turned. He was climbing up the ladder, his virile form rising from the cabin below. His sun-kissed skin glowed with the fine sheen of exertion, accentuating his rippling muscles. He called to his sailors, his voice commanding.

But then he saw her. Their eyes met, and the rest of the ship fell away. He stalked to her, his very being intent on one thing and one thing alone. Her.

Elspeth's breath caught. She put her hands in her lap, wringing her skirts. She hoped the men blamed the flush in her cheeks on the heat of the fire.

She pretended to listen to her father, all the while enjoying the wicked pattering of her heart, as she let herself imagine.

Enter the rich world of historical romance with Berkley Books.

Lynn Kurland

Patricia Potter

Betina Krahn

Jodi Thomas

Anne Gracie

Love is timeless.

penguin.com